DOSE OF AGONY

SHADOW HILLS ACADEMY: RELENTLESS
BOOK THREE

STACEY TROMBLEY

A DOSE OF AGONY

SHADOW HILLS ACADEMY: RELENTLESS
3

STACEY TROMBLEY

I

ALONE IN DARKNESS

Cool silk sliding across my calves is one of the most incredible sensations I've ever felt, but it's ruined by the thudding of my panicked heart. The unnerving sound of scraping against the stone flooring, followed by the rattling of an ancient predator's growl, drags me from a deep sleep.

The sound immediately halts the moment my eyes fly open. The room is pitch black and utterly still now that the sound has stopped. Unease rushes through my veins. My limbs and lungs freeze in place.

I don't dare move as my mind works through rational thought.

I'm alone—or at least, I should be—in Jarron's room.

He hasn't been back to the academy in the weeks since the war began in his home world, but I've been sleeping in his bed, surrounded by his smell and these decadent silk sheets, every night because it's "safer" here.

This isn't the first time I've heard or felt the presence of something else in the darkness, though, and it instantly makes me regret my choice not to go back to my itchy blankets and tiny bed in Minor Hall.

Slowly, the hair on my arms rises.

I stare, horrified, yet uncertain what it means.

The darkness around me is thick. Charged with alien power that most certainly is not coming from me.

Is some powerful magical being watching me? And if so, who?

The air remains still. Is it in my head?

My heart aches with several emotions. Sadness because I miss Jarron. Hope because part of me prays I'm right and he is here watching over me, waiting to see if I'll wake so he can pull me into his arms.

Fear because there's a high likelihood that if someone is here, it's not my demon boyfriend watching me from the foot of my bed.

My lungs burn, but I refuse to give in. I wait. And so does the darkness, still and quiet.

I press my eyes closed. Nothing changes. The charge in the air dissipates.

And I allow my lungs to suck in those desperately needed breaths as quietly as I can manage.

I can clearly imagine that scraping sound was from massive leathery wings sliding against the stone floor. The rumble so much like what I'd heard from both Jarron's and Mr. Vandozer's monster-like forms while in their most instinct-driven states.

But the longer the silence stretches, the more my heart settles. There's no more scraping. No claws carving the stone. No rumbling growls. Only the gentle whisper of the wind outside the large glass windows feet away.

The weight of loneliness and longing retake their place in my heart. Reality settles in my mind that I must have been dreaming. Or at the very least, if someone was here, they are gone now.

While that means I'm probably not in immediate danger, it doesn't mean there isn't cause for concern. Maybe it was only a dream that felt incredibly realistic.

Or maybe I'll wake to find a message.

Just a few weeks ago, I'd been getting strange, cryptic notes regularly, signed "The Jinn."

Will I find another pinned to one of the bedposts? Nailed to the door?

Now that I know the true identity of the jinn, it should alleviate some of my fears, but it's a hell of a lot more complicated than that.

I came to Shadow Hills Academy at the beginning of the school year intent on finding my sister's killer and getting revenge. Instead, I uncovered a secret organization that's forcing children to fight to the death for entertainment.

My sister was one of their contestants, that much is true. But she didn't die.

She fought in the games and lived. She won.

She became the jinn.

So, in theory, a note from the jinn is a message from my beloved sister, but it's also a message from an enemy.

While I adore my sister, and I know she still loves me, she's also trapped in a magical contract that renders her a slave to Mr. Vandozer and the rest of the Cosmic Council. A message from her is also a message from *them*.

My chest is tight as I lie alone in the dark room. I stare up at the dark coffered ceiling, wondering if I received a message, what my sister might have to say to me, even knowing the words may not be her true thoughts and feelings.

My sister, who was once a normal human like me but is now a powerful magical being.

She has immense magic in her blood. She has power over me that I cannot even fathom.

3

She's everything I've always feared.

I am just a human in a magical world.

I'm vulnerable. I'm prey to these creatures.

And now, my sister is one of them.

But I've long since learned that magic and brute strength are not the only forms of power. I refuse to be weak. I refuse to continue running.

I refuse to hide.

Magic or not, I swear I will find and destroy the man who did this to her.

The sky is just beginning to lighten, which is my cue that I'm not *completely* insane for waking at this point. There isn't much to do at six a.m., but with the way my mind is spinning, it's not like I'm going back to sleep, so I may as well make the most of it.

I flick on all the lights and open the blinds to expose the sun just beginning to peek over the horizon, and I decide to begin my search for evidence of my intruder to prove it wasn't all in my head.

I'm not sure which option I'd rather be true—my nightmares feeling so real I can't tell what's reality or that someone really has been slipping into my room while I sleep.

On second thought, never mind.

When I put it like that, it's clear I'd much rather have a warped sense of reality than literally being stalked.

I slip out from between the smooth sheets. My feet hit the cold tile, sending a shiver down my body.

Jarron's room is massive, with sleek, dark walls and furniture. There's a set of crushed silver handcuffs sitting on the table by the bed but otherwise very little decor anywhere except the one cabinet in the corner.

The doors to the closet and bathrooms remain closed.

Everything is in pristine condition.

I walk out onto the balcony, welcoming the chilly breeze on

my hot skin. There's a light frost on the grassy field below, and the mountains in the distance are snowcapped, but I know spring is near. Most afternoons have brought lovely weather, not that I've had the chance to enjoy much of it.

I take two deep breaths of the fresh air and then turn back to search the room once more, losing hope with each step.

I even resort to digging through a few of the closed drawers by Jarron's bed.

There are papers in haphazard piles mixed between books. These are mostly Jarron's notes on his random research topics. There are also several art sketches. Buildings and animals. A school uniform skirt. A close-up sketch of an eye.

These are all the things he once had in a massive pile in the middle of his room, now tucked away out of sight.

Jarron's sketches are skillful but fairly abstract. Not enough to get a full sense of his perspective, just small flashes.

There is one watercolor painting of a bedroom much like Jarron's here at school, except the world beyond the balcony is not the mountains of Idaho; it's the red sky and twin moons of Oriziah. I drop the painting back into the pile.

Jarron once told me he had nothing to hide from me and he didn't mind me looking through his personal belongings. Even so, it feels a little invasive, so I don't go far.

It's not like the jinn or the council would hide a message under piles of research notes and sketches.

Just as I'm about to shut the drawer and give up, something shiny grabs my attention.

In the corner of the bottom drawer is one single brass key.

Here in the magical world, keys are rare. There's no reason to lock things when magic can do a much better job at securing what you want hidden. Maybe it's a magical key with a spell interwoven into the metal. Or maybe it's simply a symbol.

I leave the key where I found it and give up my search, admitting that there's no note from my enslaved sister or my nemesis. No claw marks or streaks of blood. Nothing out of the ordinary.

Part of me is relieved. Part of me is disappointed.

I want to talk to Liz so badly it hurts, even if it's through the carefully controlled, veiled threats of the council. Instead, I'm stuck with no way of contacting her or helping her at all.

There's no worse feeling in the world than helplessness.

My chest tightens.

I've never been the wait-and-see kind of person, but right now there's little I can do. I shake my head and curl my hands into fists. The only way I can keep anxiety from suffocating me is to *do* something.

My sister needs help, and I'm going to give it to her one way or another.

Even if it means breaking all the rules.

If those creatures still see me as prey, all the better, because they won't see it coming when I destroy them.

2

ESCAPE PLANS

Backpack in hand, I slip out of Jarron's room and quietly sneak down the hall.

There's only one place in the school that makes me feel empowered while he is absent. It's far from these halls and not technically the safest option for me given the circumstances.

When Jarron left for his home world, he set up several things to ensure my safety, including ensuring I do not leave Elite Hall until he returns.

I agreed to the plan willingly because he's right; it's not safe. I'm a target for an extremely powerful group of supernaturals.

The new headmaster, Ms. Bhatt, has also agreed to excuse me from classes until the conflicts on Oriziah are settled.

But that was weeks ago, and I'm beginning to feel trapped. Sometimes, the risks are worth the reward.

I *need* my potions.

And this early in the morning, there are very few students up and about. Classes don't start for almost three hours. Which means my risk of danger is low, and my risk of any of my body-guards catching me.

The red eyes of a vampire flash at me from down the hall but slip away quickly.

Two wolf shifter girls pass by, chatting idly, and pay me no mind. It's quiet this time of the day.

I slip down the only path I'm not suppose to enter, toward the main areas of the school.

My heart pounds like I'm breaking out of prison. Excitement just to be out of these same few rooms and halls. Fear that I'll be found out and made to turn back to safety.

I quickly pass under the massive archway, and a thrill jolts through me. I'm out of Elite Hall for the first time in weeks!

My lips curl into a triumphant grin, and I pick up my pace—only to be halted by the flash of sharp canines.

I skid to a stop with an embarrassing gasp.

Reddish skin. Black horns. Sharp, predator fangs.

Their lips spread wide into an annoying grin. "Good morning, Candice. Are you gong somewhere?" Laithe asks smoothly.

I groan.

"Did you take a wrong turn?" They look over their shoulder.

"It's six in the morning," I grumble, crossing my arms like a stubborn child.

"You act as if I woke you." Laithe's reddish skin is brighter than usual, their horns shiny.

I shrug. "Why are you up? You should be sleeping like normal people."

"You are currently my most important responsibility, and you are awake."

"I was just going to check on my potions and be back before you even realized."

Laithe snorts. "You agreed to these rules, remember?"

I wrinkle my nose. "Yes, but that was like a month ago." Three weeks and three days to be exact. "I can't stay in here forever. My potions are probably ruined by now."

"As I've told you, we have a competent ally looking over them."

"Thompson is not exactly a potions master."

"Are potions really more important than your safety?"

"Potions very well may *be* my safety! They may be what stands between me and the Cosmic Council."

Laithe tilts their head. "You don't believe in our ability to protect you?"

One of Jarron's security measures was to assemble a few allies to watch over me. Thompson, Manuela, Laithe and Stassi. Mostly, it's Laithe, though. I think because they have a magical link, so Jarron can get moment-by-moment updates on my protection.

"For now? Sure. But one day, I'm going to face them again, and I need a means of defense." *I need a means of attack,* but I don't say that part out loud.

"Well, *for now*, you need to stay back there." Laithe points behind me, back to Elite Hall. They're right. I know it. I'm supposed to stay here because it's safe. But I'm also right that potions are important. I need to have access to my only form of magic and protection.

"What happens if I just... run past you?"

I recall the time I tried to enter through the Minor Hall wards to approach the makers of the Akrasia Games—the Cosmic Council. Jarron slammed me against the wall and growled, "*Don't you fucking dare.*"

At the time, it was frustrating, but thinking about it now does strange things to my body. Laithe wouldn't dare do that to me.

"I wouldn't so much as touch you, but I'd alert Jarron."

My stomach sinks. "Is he—"

"He is well. Stressed but in no danger. However, he fears his absence from the palace will put his family and people at increased risk. He will come here if needed, though." Laithe lifts a brow, making the "threat" clear.

Jarron will return if I'm not following our agreement. And him coming back here is bad for the tension on his planet.

I sigh. I want Jarron to be here desperately, but I also don't want him to increase his risk or make it easier for those assholes to take his throne just because I'm throwing a hissy fit about not being able to brew potions for a month.

My shoulders deflate. I take one last longing glance down the hall and then turn on my heel and march my butt right back into Elite Hall, accepting temporary defeat.

Laithe matches my pace with smooth steps and no comment.

The smile remains on Laithe's lips, their steps light.

"You're in a good mood," I comment. Is it because they won our battle of wills? Or something else?

They've been surprisingly calm these last few days, considering the prince they're bonded to is off fighting a war and they've been left behind. I expected frustration and nervousness.

"You are *not* in a good mood," Laithe counters.

I wrinkle my nose. "I know I'm only human, but if I don't get some coffee stat, I'll be the most dangerous creature in the school."

"More bad dreams?"

I shrug. Are they dreams? I suppose maybe they are. Tricks of my imagination seem more likely, but I guess tomato-tomahto.

"It's hard to sleep in there without him."

Laithe nods slow and deep. Their movements are smoother today, I realize. I glance over their nails—black, sharp, and shiny—and up to their eyes—brighter red than usual.

"You've fed?" I guess.

Laithe's lips twitch.

I take that as a yes and file the new information away.

As we continue walking, my stomach tightens. It's almost

tempting just to turn and run back out of Elite Hall. I'd get a taste of freedom and Jarron back for a little while.

If only it wouldn't require a gamble of his safety.

I don't like that he is not around. He's off in another universe, dealing with a potentially violent conflict. I get updates from Laithe, but they're vague enough it usually requires multiple pointed questions to draw more understanding.

According to Laithe, no major action has taken place during this "war" yet—no fighting, no attacks, and no *direct* threats— but there are groups of rebels in camps surrounding the capital that are growing in size. More and more people are traveling from the outskirts of the world to the capital island. More and more rebels buying into the idea that Jarron shouldn't be the next king.

When we make it back to the sunroom, I find a few more familiar faces.

Did they wake because I left the hall too?

"*Hey*, princess. How's the ivory tower feeling these days?" Stassi grins at me from one of the armchairs beneath the glass panels. Neither he nor Manuela, who sits across from him with her girlfriend, Lucille, appear annoyed at me, so maybe it's just chance that they woke this early.

"I haven't grown my hair long enough to escape just yet." I cross my arms and lean against Stassi's chair.

He frowns like he has no idea what I mean.

"You've got a long way to go," Lucille remarks. I absently run my fingers through my shoulder-length brown hair.

Manuela snorts. "You don't need the long hair, Candice. No man can keep you locked away if you want out bad enough. That's the takeaway from Rapunzel."

"Is it?" Laithe asks with a rise of their brow.

"It is for me."

11

I smile. "Just feeling a little stuck. I need to *do* something, and this one won't let me work on my potions."

"You're studying. That's good for now, isn't it?" Lucille says. Her eyes tell me she's sympathetic but agrees that I should remain where it's safe. She's a petite red-headed shifter that's possibly the most beautiful woman I've ever seen. I don't know her all that well, as she keeps mostly to herself.

"Her boyfriend is at war. Would you feel content studying?" Manuela challenges, squeezing Lucille's thigh gently.

Lucille's eyes soften. "I suppose not."

Manuela leans forward and whispers, "If you need help skirting Jarron's rules, let me know. I'm always in for a bit of rebellion."

"I heard that," Laithe complains.

Manuela winks at them.

"Jarron isn't actually forcing me to stay," I say. "I'm just being a good girl for now." I shrug, clearly disappointed.

Manuela nods. "Well, maybe you need a strategy session. Is it Jarron's war that you want to help? Or all that other stuff." She wiggles her fingers, sharp nails glinting in the rising sunlight.

My lips part. It's fairly common knowledge now that the Akrasia Games are actively running, and rumors that my sister is involved have begun to surface, but even if not, Manuela is in the know for most of it.

All those rumors about the games and my sister are another reason I shouldn't leave Elite Hall. Jarron's threat and our allies are enough to keep most of the Elite in line but not the entire school.

The Akrasia Games are a tense topic.

"Definitely other stuff," I answer. "I mean, it's all interconnected anyway, but my sister is a priority."

"And how do you help her?"

I sigh and plop down in one of the empty chairs. Everyone scoots in a bit closer.

My revenge mission here has quickly become a rescue mission. A rescue mission I am woefully underprepared for. "The only way I know to free her"—I lean in and say it quietly because as much as I'm not the bad guy, this might sound less than ideal to people I don't trust—"is for a new set of games to take place."

Lucille's brow pinches in concern"You mean, you want to help run the Akrasia Games?"

"No," I say quickly. "Certainly not. I don't want any other innocent people to die. It's just the only way I currently know that will free Liz from their control. Once the next set of games are completed, the winner becomes the jinn, which will free Liz." She'll have some kind of magical gag that stops her from sharing information about the games, but she'll be able to seperate herself from the council and that's the important part.

By winning, my sister has gained power, but not freedom. Not yet. There must always be a jinn to continue the games. So, she's bound to the council until a new jinn takes her place.

"And the information on the games is guarded so well," I continue, "it's really hard to learn more about the magic surrounding it."

"Killing Mr. Vandozer won't help?" Manuela asks.

I tilt my head. "I mean, it can't hurt."

Laithe chuckles.

"But, no. He's not the only one she's bound to. It's the whole council, and who knows if death would sever that bond? Maybe it would automatically pass to someone else? I don't know."

"Okay." Manuela scoots in. "Here's an idea. You have a new set of games, except instead of low-level beings, you trick the most corrupt dickwads in existence into signing the contract and watch as they kill each other." Her savage grin exposes sharp canines.

Sick joy spreads across my chest. "Sounds great but complicated."

Obviously, it's a better solution than letting a bunch of innocent kids enter, but there are complications.

"I don't exactly relish the idea of choosing who will die. If I could get the council to fall into that trap, that would be wonderful. I just don't think they'd do it."

Manuela chuckles. "True and true." She leans back in her chair, arms slung over the armrests, studying me like I'm a puzzle she's working on. "What you really need is information. You need an inside source."

"Do you have a suggestion?" Laithe asks calmly. So calm, I get the feeling there's more to those words.

A threat.

I swallow. Does Laithe think Manuela knows something she shouldn't?

Manuela's grin turns vicious, and my stomach clenches.

I look over her comfortable posture. She's a powerful witch with dryad blood. If it weren't for Jarron, she'd be the exact kind of person I'd steer clear of. I only trust her now because Jarron does.

If Manuela does have insider information, why didn't she come out with it before when Jarron was seeking out Mr. Vandozer as a suspect?

"Or you could just let the bad guys do their thing." Manuela tilts her head slightly. "Let the real games happen and your sister will eventually be free."

"Manuela," Lucille reprimands.

"What? What they do is not her responsibility."

I twist my lips. I'm also not a big fan of that suggestion. She wants me to sit back and do nothing. Hope my sister is freed by natural progression. But how long will that take?

"Saving your sister comes first, right?"

I pull in a long breath through my nose. "I suppose it's an option," I concede, even as my stomach aches. "How would I find them after that?"

"Why would you need to?" Lucille asks.

"Because I intend to hunt down the entire council and slaughter them once Liz is free."

Manuela goes entirely still, piercing eyes narrowed in on me.

She didn't like that answer.

Heart pounding, I straighten. "Thanks for the brainstorming. I need some coffee now." I smile and wave, even as my chest remains tight as I escape the tense conversation.

That conversation was illuminating but bordering on perilous.

Manuela knows something. She might even want something she's not ready to reveal yet.

Laithe follows me silently down the hall, ever my steadfast protector.

I consider asking Laithe their take on Manuela but of all my protectors Laithe is the most aloof so I doubt I'll get very far.

Instead, I file away my concerns and curiosities for another day when I'm more prepared, and brew a cup of my coffee in the speakeasy and settle in to begin the only thing I can do while stuck in this place.

Gain information.

3

BEHIND ALIEN EYES

The Rejected Prince

A High Orizian's mate becomes his very reason for existing.

A passion so deep those lucky enough to find themselves the subject of this adoration describe it as heavenly.

It's widely known that Orizians rarely pair with natives of their own world, yet these pairings are as passionate and solid as any fated mates. Little else is objectively known about the nature of Orizian mates, however.

During my travels, I've had the opportunity to speak with a few females bonded to High Orizians and I've learned that unlike fated mates, the pull is one-sided until the bonding is complete. Meaning, only the High Orizian is aware of the link.

Though the beings mated to Orizians express sincere happiness now, they explained that it wasn't always that way.

Loving a being as dangerous as an Orizian has its challenges, particularly before they are bound, when they're uncertain of the creature's motives.

To be pursued romantically by a natural predator is unnerving, to say the least.

And yet, this pursuit is significant to the High Orizian experience, so much so, one of the most frequently told legends is that of Elixian, The Rejected Prince.

Elixian was a young prince, heir to the High Orizian throne, who lived more than a thousand years ago, and yet his story is still told as a warning. This oral tradition still strikes fear in young Orizians.

As the tale goes, Elixian imprinted on a human, who was unaware of worlds outside her own. He fell in love with her, indisputably. No other could ever compare to her.

He began his pursuit, but she feared him, even despite his efforts to be a place of safety for her.

One day, he followed her on a journey through the forest, where she was in peril, but instead of a protector, she saw him as threat. She panicked and fled to the nearest town. She sought safety in a tavern, where she was subsequently attacked by a group of human men.

Elixian eventually hunted down her attackers, but this only added to her trauma.

To Elixian, this event was proof that humans were even more dangerous than his kind. He passionately argued that she should trust him. Unfortunately, that wasn't how his chosen saw it. She continued to run. He continued to pursue.

Elixian's chosen, name unknown, always associated the prince with danger. She called him a monster.

She called him a demon.

And eventually, she formally rejected him.

He only wanted to protect her, but because he didn't understand her customs or her fears, his pursuit caused a rift that even the deepest devotion could never overcome.

Elixian is known now as the Rejected Prince. Though other Orizians have since failed to earn a mate, Elixian is the most remem-

bered because this failure had a significant effect on the politics of Oriziah.

He is the one and only first born Orizian heir to be refused the throne, because he could not successfully earn his mate's trust. If his mate could not trust him, the people of Oriziah could not trust him either.

He was labeled as unworthy.

Instead, the line of succession changed to his sister and continued with her children from then forward.

Orizians can only earn the throne once they have earned their mate.

Worse than losing the throne, the Rejected Prince, Elixian, lost his sense of self and, eventually, his world.

It is said that the rejection of his chosen mate crushed his soul, leaving him to live only half a life.

This prince turned violent in the years after his rejection. He lost control of his magic to a destructive degree. He became the very beast his chosen believed him to be. He became unrecognizable, even to his friends and family. His depression led to violent outbursts and cruelty. His crimes led to his banishment from the planet.

Though there could be many explanations for his change in behavior, this rejection remains, to this day, one of the largest fears of Orizian males.

Orizian culture states that to be rejected by your mate is to lose your very soul.

4

THE GIRLFRIEND TO BONDED-MATE PIPELINE

"I wish you wouldn't read that." Laithe's nose wrinkles.

My attention shifts to the demon sitting across from me in the speakeasy. Laithe watches me close but gives away no more emotion.

I sip my coffee.

I've been scouring this book in particular for weeks because it's the one Liz guided me toward before I knew she was still alive.

Behind Alien Eyes.

When I first found this book, I didn't think it had much information about chosen mates, but as I read through it, I realized there was a fair bit of information scattered through it, like the chapter about The Rejected Prince.

I've only found a few books that can help me understand more of what's happening with the conflicts on Oriziah. They tend to be secretive about their traditions and how their politics work. I've begun studying the different species on the planet and their role in society, but it still feels incredibly vague.

For example, Laithe is from the same planet as Jarron, but is a different species altogether. From what I've read, Laithe's species is one of the weakest on Oriziah and bound to the magic of the soil they were born to. The only reason Laithe is free to roam other worlds is because of his magical link with Jarron.

What I'd never have learned about Laithe from the textbook is that they are genderless. Neither male nor female. Laithe has never seemed to care much about gendered pronouns but once I learned this I decided it didn't make sense to call them he/him. It's a challenge to change how I perceive someone, and remember to alter my langue correctly, but it's felt like the right thing to do.

Though Laithe doesn't express much emotion, I don't miss the subtle hints they're more at ease when I use the neutral langue with them.

I'm not perfect, but I'm trying.

My brows pinch. "Why?"

"A book about a sacred Orizian culture written by an outsider is less than ideal."

"Well, there aren't books on the topic written by Orizians," I remark stubbornly.

"For good reason."

I twist my lips. I look down at the book. It's certainly not the greatest source of information. Even as I read through it, I've found moments it's clear the author only has partial information and is piecing things together.

I'd like to honor Laithe's wishes, but it's difficult to let go of my only source of information.

Plus, Liz sent it to me. Maybe there were more reasons than just the note she scribbled in the back of it.

Still, I concede and shut the book. I've read it cover to cover once already anyway.

I busy myself by grabbing a second coffee with hazelnut flavoring.

"You know, you could have anything you desire delivered straight to the room," Laithe says as they lean against the table. "Or if you'd prefer to make beverages yourself, you could have a machine installed."

"I like coming here," I say, finishing the perfect balance. I take a sip and allow the caffeine to soothe my agitated soul. Then, I take my seat back at one of the high-top tables.

"We could also redesign the room to look exactly like this. Or give you your own room if you'd prefer." Laithe sits across from me, looking comfortable, despite refusing to drink anything I offer.

"I have my own room, in Minor Hall," I bite back, feigning more annoyance than I actually feel. I don't mind staying in Jarron's room. What I mind is not having control over where I go, even if it's for good reason.

"A tiny thing that may as well be considered a broom closet."

I roll my eyes.

"And has been proven to be inadequate at achieving its main purpose—keeping you safe."

I've come to realize that though Laithe is generally quiet, they are rather stubborn. Since we have that in common, our conversations tend to be circular.

Minor Hall has protection spells designed to keep any powerful beings out, but more than once, Mr. Vandozer and the jinn proved those protections do not apply to them, rendering that aspect of the hall worthless.

I'm consistently tempted to argue that Elite Hall isn't any better at keeping the jinn out, but I always bite my tongue because I know that's not really the point.

Here, I am surrounded by powerful allies who will protect me. In Minor Hall, most of my protectors would be incapable of reaching me without causing themselves harm.

I sip on my coffee and narrow my eyes at Laithe. "So, how long will I be trapped in Elite Hall?"

"For the foreseeable future."

I sigh.

I know Laithe would greatly prefer to be in their home world, assisting Jarron during the conflict. Instead, they're on babysitting duty. It's annoying for both of us. I should be more appreciative.

"Although, I do have a surprise for you this morning," Laithe says after another few moments of silence. "One that will allow you to *temporarily* leave Elite Hall."

"Oh?"

"You woke too early, so you'll have to wait now." They quirk a brow, and I nearly groan at the smug expression.

"Why tell me, then?"

Laithe shrugs, smiling. They like taunting me, don't they?

My heart does a little skip when I consider that the surprise could be a visit from Jarron. It sinks quickly, though, because based on our conversation today, it's clear that's not in his best interest.

I absently rub the spot on my neck where his faded bite marks just barely linger.

Laithe's eyes darken. "He won't like that."

"What?"

"His marks have nearly faded."

I bite the inside of my lip. I almost blurt out that he could come back to renew them any time he wants, but my cheeks heat at the thought of suggesting it.

Technically, a simple bite isn't all that meaningful. There's no magic in what Jarron did a few weeks ago. It's just proof of an interaction—an *erotic* interaction. Which is the part I get bashful about.

But based on the way everyone changed their behavior

toward me the moment those two little marks appeared on my neck, proof that my relationship with Jarron was progressing, it clearly means something.

Regular bite marks fade quickly though, and don't create any magical links between the two creatures. A claiming mark is similar on the surface, but entirely different at its core.

A bite is a casual hookup. A claiming mark is a commitment. *Take my mark.*

I shiver at the thought of those words. I've run that moment through my mind so many times I've lost count. I told him no, and though he didn't take it too badly, part of me still feels guilty.

But a mark is the supernatural equivalent to a proposal. It's not a full bonding, but it's the first step. So it's normal for me to be nervous about that, right?

Even so, even a mark like that isn't permanent. I could walk away if I wanted. I could still change my mind.

I'm still not certain what it will mean to let him mark me. I'm not sure if it will reveal truths I'd rather ignore.

I know, without any doubt at all, that Jarron cares for me. Wants me. Maybe even loves me.

But that love developed when we both believed Liz was dead and he hasn't exactly been around since we found out she was still alive.

He has plenty of reason for that absence, obviously, and before he left I was pretty well convinced the Council's belief that my sister is his mate was incorrect but three weeks of absence has allowed old doubts and fears to brew. *What if* he chose my sister when we were young, and he developed feelings for me in her absence? *What if* his true mate is Liz but he still wants me?

Is he hoping to have both of us? Is there a way for him to change his mind?

The thing is, I can't get these answers without a mark. Because Orizians can't talk about their chosen mate until she's accepted him. The mark is a way around that, where we'll be magically connected enough to feel that truth.

He could mark me, in an attempt to win me over, despite his true mate being someone else. Would he do that? Probably not, but I won't know for sure until I take the risk.

So I'm stuck in this place where I don't know for sure that my heart won't be shattered when I take that mark.

I should have just accepted the offer weeks ago when I'd had the chance. But no, I'm a stubborn little girl terrified of hypotheticals.

Less than a year ago, I'd been so against all things supernatural. It's wild how much that's changed.

Not long ago, I feared him. Now I fear a life without him.

Maybe there are more twists coming. Maybe I don't even understand the full extent of what it means for a demon to choose someone.

Those fears are a big part of why I keep reading this book, written by some random woman with dubious sources.

I choose to sit in this weird limbo, with tons of evidence that I am indeed Jarron's chosen but still some against it, confused and afraid.

Instead of following the compulsion to continue seeking answers where I shouldn't, I move *Behind Alien Eyes* into my bag and pry open the other book I brought with me titled *The Meaning of Marks*, which is all about the different kinds of marks and bonds supernatural beings can leave on others. Laithe lifts that brow again. I ignore the minor pang of embarrassment.

The whole bite vs. mark bond thing is complicated, and it's different for every species of supernatural, so I'm still working on wrapping my mind around it.

I let Jarron bite me because a wolf had tried to force a mark on me, leaving rough puncture wounds and enough magic to make it so the scars wouldn't fade for a long while. Jarron's much more pleasant bite covered that and removed any leftover magic.

The next step in the girlfriend-to-bonded-mate pipeline would be a mark. The first one usually happens on the wrist. That mark would open up a small magical link between us that would allow him to know where I am and what I'm feeling.

Laithe wants me to take the mark because it would free him from babysitting duty. If Jarron could track me and know when I was okay all the time, I wouldn't need the middleman.

But since I'm stubborn to a fault, I need all the information I can get about what I may be getting myself into before I make my choice.

Before I came to this school, I promised myself I'd remain independent of the supernatural world. I wanted to be powerful on my own, not with anyone's help. So, to accept a claiming mark from Jarron, in some ways, feels like a betrayal to my past self.

Even if I've come to the conclusion that my past self was a moron.

So many of those beliefs came from the fear of what Jarron was. We had a bad moment once four years ago—when he turned into his demon form and stalked my sister.

My stomach sinks.

It's hard for me to even think about that night now. Because what if it's the true evidence that Jarron chose Liz that night, not me? Why else would he have stalked *her*?

I shake the thought from my mind.

Information. That's something—one of the only things—I can control right now. I will arm myself with as much knowledge as I can get. Beginning with what exactly it means to allow a magical being to mark me.

5

A NEW INNER CIRCLE

"Are you ready?" Laithe's smooth voice pulls me out of my focus. I look up from my scattered notes to the clock to find it's already almost 8:30 a.m. I'd spent over an hour reading, jotting notes to try to help it all settle in my mind.

Most of it is information I already know, but writing it down helps me conceptualize it better.

Bite: non-magical, surface level only. Heals just as any wound would. Some supernaturals bite out of pleasure or desire to inflict pain, others as a source of sustenance, like vampires and some species of demon.

Claiming mark: A bite that creates a magical link between the two beings. Will last for several months, depending on the magical strength of the being who gave it. These can be erased if replaced by a stronger magical being. This magical link can create a limited psychic and/or emotional link, where the two beings can feel as the other feels, see what the other sees and speak through the magic. The strength of this link depends on magic level of the being, and the strength of the emotional connection. Marks are not limited to one, and with each new mark the link grows in strength.

*A **Bond:** A permanent link that will never erase or diminish, regardless of separation or time. It magically connects the two souls forever. To achieve a bond with a High Orzian, it requires a series of marks. One on each wrist and each ankle. A bond with a fae requires a spell and ceremony. Wolves, a community ceremony during a blood moon.*

I stand and stretch my cramped muscles then follow Laithe from the speakeasy and out into the hall. "So, are you going to tell me where we're going yet?"

"The main entrance of the academy."

"Oh." I have no idea what kind of surprise will be at the main entrance. Although, I'm excited just by the prospect of being able to leave Elite Hall.

I haven't even been allowed to attend my classes. Other than a few meetings with Mrs. Bhatt and the occasional private lessons from Professor Zyair, I may as well have dropped out of school.

I bite my lip as I finally pass through the entrance from Elite Hall into the main hallway.

It doesn't take long before I hear loud chattering up ahead and I realize there is an enormous crowd at our destination. I don't think I've ever approached the main entrance hall from this direction before because staring down at the front doors from the second story is bizarre. There are hundreds of people gathered, looking up at me like I'm royalty or something.

My heart hammers faster.

The memory of my first moment in this school rushes back to me. I walked through those massive doors and found myself suffocated by the packed bodies staring up at the demon royalty.

I swallow, realizing that I am now that royalty, at least to those looking up at me. Maybe it's temporary. Maybe it's fleeting. But for the moment, that's who I am.

"What is going on?" I whisper to Laithe.

They just smile.

We walk down one side of the marble stairs to find Mrs. Bhatt waiting for us with a big smile. She's always been rather stiff to me, but she hasn't ever done anything against my best interest, so I try to like her.

The crowd parts to allow me passage onto the platform between the two sets of stairs. That's when I see Lola and Janet, and my panic is broken.

Lola flutters up and hovers in front of my nose, her purple wings beating so fast they're a blur. Then, she spins around and lands on my shoulder. "You okay? You look pale." Her voice is quiet.

"Barely managing not to freak out."

Janet smiles sweetly. Though I'm the only truly human of my friend group, Janet is close. She's part troll, and her skin has a slight green hue, but you wouldn't know it unless you were looking for it. She curls her arm in mine.

"Do you know what this is about?" I ask them.

"I've heard rumors, but they're kinda hard to believe."

I frown, but before I'm able to ask anything more, Mrs. Bhatt begins speaking, her voice magnified over the whole room. "Welcome, students. Today, we have a special announcement."

The chattering settles, but whispering continues as an undercurrent.

"It has been several months since we've done an update to the typical inner circle lists. As you know, the school allows the two top students to select three people to be an official part of their inner circle. Those students will have all of the same opportunities as the top students. They will have access to every corner of the school, including Elite Hall and the highest clearance sections of the library. But things are very different now than they were at the beginning of the year when the lists were last established. Trevor Blackthorn has disenrolled from the academy, leaving us with not only an open space but an open list. The student council and the staff have deliberated about how to handle this change. We debated several different replacements, but one concern we had was that we did not want to alienate the Orizian's loyalty that were in controlling power previously. The obvious choice would have been one of the last remaining royals—Auren and her brother from the Frost Court. Auren herself was the one to pitch a new idea. Instead of splitting the lists and choosing a separate culture to share the honor, we decided to allow the second list to be an extension of the first. The second list will be created by the name at the top of Prince Jarron's."

I blink, my palms slick.

"Jarron's list remains firm, as we've verified several times over the last months, and even with his infrequent attendance due to conflict in his home world, he is still very much committed to the school—and those he's established as his inner circle. Which means, our second inner circle list will belong to his first rank. Candice Montgomery."

My stomach twists, and my vision peppers with black for a moment. Janet squeezes my arm tighter.

"What?" I breathe. And a chorus repeating the sentiment drifts through the crowd. The disbelief and shock are obvious. But there is also a scattering of annoyance and bitter laughter.

"But she's from Minor Hall," someone calls out, followed by grunts of agreement and whoops of pride.

I take in a deep breath.

"Now, this is a new established rule, and Candice has not yet had a chance to think over her choices. I have a suggested order, but of course she can make any changes she prefers. Candice, please come forward."

Still dizzy and confused, I'm surprised when my feet move. She holds out a parchment for only me to see.

Janet

Lola

Thompson

"This is our estimation, but if you would like a day to decide, we absolutely could justify that."

I swallow but shake my head. "No, that's perfect."

Of course, choosing which would get the first spot out of Janet and Lola would be near impossible, so I kind of like that Mrs. Bhatt chose the order. Or else, I could say it was just alphabetical order.

"You're certain?"

"Yes."

She smiles big and wide. "Wonderful! Let's make the official announcement then. Corolla, would you please do us the honor?"

A red pixie soars up over head.

"Wait!" I call out before I fully thought it through. The pixie pauses, as does Mrs. Bhatt.

I lean in to ask Lola.

"You're both on the list. I didn't pay much attention to the order, but I just had a thought. Do you want to write the names, Lola? Is that like a good thing or demeaning, given the situation?"

Lola blinks. "Oh, um..." Her wings shiver.

"Let Corolla do it," Janet answers for her in a tight whisper. "Some people see pixies as lesser than others. They're workers. Let Lola be more than that."

My lips curl up. "That sound good to you, Lola?"

She swallows, her eyes darker than usual. She nods firmly.

This is such a strange situation for all of us.

"Never mind," I call to Mrs. Bhatt. "Proceed."

Mrs. Bhatt gives me one look that betrays her minor annoyance, but she nods to Corolla, the red pixie who continues her flight through the air. I notice a herd of pixies huddled together in the corner, high above the other beings heads.

The red pixie grabs a pen and delicately scrolls out my name on a framed parchment. Followed by Janet's name. The crowd whispers frantically.

Then, Lola's name. A crowd of pixies begins to buzz. I'm not certain what that means.

Finally, Thompson's name is scrawled on the parchment, and a deep, short-lived howl rings out, followed by several growls of annoyance. A handsome Black shifter pushes forward through the crowd until he reaches us.

He gives me a fist bump, his grin wide. "Thanks, buddy."

I smile.

The rest of the strange ceremony wraps up quickly and is more of a blur than anything. Several people walk up and talk to me and my friends, offering congratulations.

"So, will you two be joining Elite Hall?" Stassi asks with a wiggle of his brows and a charming smile.

"No," they both answer simultaneously.

"No?" he asks. "You could be the first pixie to ever be in Elite Hall!"

"I know." Lola shrugs. "But I'd rather make a point. I've been treated badly by my own clan for not performing well enough on exams and that's unfair. People in Minor Hall can be badass too."

"Yeah, we can!" I hold up my fist.

Stassi's expression of shock turns slowly to me. "You aren't in Minor Hall anymore."

My lips part, but I pause. I mean... I'm living there now, but I haven't technically changed halls. I suppose that line is a little blurry.

"No, but we are," Janet answers. "And we're going to prove our worth without Elite Hall."

We make our way back, my new inner circle around me as well as Jarron's and several other Elite supernaturals I vaguely recognize. I almost feel like we have groupies all of a sudden.

I'm certain it will calm down shortly, but as of right now, people want to be seen with us. Three Minor Hall no ones.

Except, we're not no ones anymore.

Lola, Janet, and I spend the whole rest of the day together in Elite Hall, with my guardian demon watching from the other side of the room.

We chat about everything that could change now. We exclaim about how insane it is. We also talk about the possible downsides, like that all of their future accomplishments could be attributed to just "knowing the right people."

I have the same concern. What if I'm only ever remembered as the girlfriend of the demon prince? And not for the things I have done myself.

"Listen," I tell them eventually, "if you ever don't want to be on the list, just let me know."

Janet purses her lips.

"No, we want to be on the list," Lola says. "It's badass."

"Yeah," Janet agrees. "We have some concerns, but the benefits are worth it, at least for now."

"So long as you're here, we should at least have access to the hall, right? We need to be able to hang out with you. This way we won't need a specific invitation every time."

I bite the inside of my lip. That's fair.

"Do you think..." I start after a long pause of silence.

"What?" Janet asks.

"Do you think it's fair concern that... well, what if the attention is overestimating my connection to Jarron? They're acting like I'm a princess. Like I'm for sure the future bride of the crown prince. What if—what if it all changes?"

Janet's eyes are sympathetic. "You're still doubting if —"

"No," I say quickly. "Yes." I frown. "I don't know."

Lola snuggles in closer to my neck, offering comfort.

"I trust in Jarron. I just can't help but wonder..."

Janet's eyes soften. "It's definitely a fair concern..." she says slowly. "But only emotionally."

"What does that mean?"

"I mean, it's scary for sure, and it'll hurt if it all ends and things change, but you're not losing anything logically. What happens if it all goes away? You're back to the badass potions prodigy you were before. You don't need the attention. You don't need the extra surface-level allies. You don't need the leg up it all gives you. You will have a great future with or without—" she waves vaguely "—all this."

I swallow and look down at my hands.

"Janet's right," Lola says. "It would be heartbreaking, but it isn't worth fearing the loss. All three of us have a great future ahead, with or without Jarron Blackthorn being part of it."

"I love you guys," I whisper. "Have I ever told you that? I feel like I don't give you enough appreciation. You've always been amazing to me."

Janet pulls us both into a hug. "You just added us to an Elite inner circle list, and you think you don't appreciate us enough?"

I roll my eyes but laugh along with them.

Things are already so different. What will change next?

6

DEAR DIARY

Liz is alive.

Liz is alive.

Liz is alive.

Liz is alive.

It's still hard for me to wrap my mind around that. After months of searching for vengeance against my sister's killer, I found out there is no killer. She isn't dead. She's alive.

It's incredible.

But it doesn't mean she's safe. I could still lose her after all of this.

My little sister, who was my best friend, is now a powerful magical being that I somehow have to save.

How do I save her? How do I manage all of this?

Me.

No one. Inconsequential.

I know that's not true. I am not no one. No matter how all of this shakes out, I am not no one.

Still, those thoughts filter in more often than I'd care to admit. I need to prove them all wrong.

But how?

Can I justify killing nine innocent people to save one?

Does it make me a bad person to even consider it?

Allowing my sister to remain enslaved is even more inconceivable than the terrible thing I must do to save her.

Does it make me a terrible person that I would?

I would kill to save her. I would destroy my own soul for her if that's what I had to do.

But there has to be another way. Right?

7

POWER AT MY FINGERTIPS

In the last two days since I received my own inner circle list, more and more, I'm feeling suffocated here, doing nothing.

I'm researching, sure. I'm studying High Orizian. I'm learning what I can about that culture. I'm studying potions theories. I read through *Art of War*.

Those things are not getting me any closer to uncovering a way to save my sister without a terrible immoral act. I can't keep doing nothing.

I've considered my conversation with Manuela several times.

Part of me is hoping to use her offer of help to get me some freedom without putting Jarron at risk, but then again, there was something off about that conversation.

Some undercurrent I couldn't grasp.

Manuela may have an inside link to the Cosmic Council? And if so, that means I can't trust her, right?

I stare absently at the flickering flames of the fire in the speakeasy hearth when someone sits beside me on the velvet cushions.

"I have something to lift your spirits," Thompson says, voice uncharacteristically soft. He's been off too for the last few weeks.

Can he tell I'm in my feels today? That I'm contemplating drastic action to get out of this rut I've agreed to enter.

"Oh?" I ask.

"Want to see it now?" he asks. "Or did you want to be alone a while longer?"

I press my lips together as I consider. As much as it's difficult to muster the energy to stand, let alone pretend to be excited about whatever new "surprise" he has for me, I should do something. Anything other than this. Something to kick me out of this fog I've fallen into this morning.

I force myself to stand.

"It'll be worth it. Promise." He grins.

"If you say so."

"Best news you've had since Jarron left."

My heart lifts, and he must notice the spark of hope in my eyes because his shoulders sink a little. "Not quite as good as Jarron coming back, but second best, I'm sure of it."

My lips twist. "All right. Let me be the judge of that." I nudge him with my elbow.

I follow him out of the speakeasy. Several sets of eyes stop to watch as we pass by. I get less of the weird attention here in Elite Hall than I did in the main halls of the school before, but it's still there. It's been a bit worse since my inner circle reveal.

Apparently, people have a lot of opinions on whether or not I deserve my own inner circle. Not that I can blame them, I'm not sure I deserve it either. But I'll take it because even though it's such a weird and aristocratic tradition, I want my friends to have access to my prison. If I need to deal with a little bit of negative attention for that, I'll take it.

People will get used to it eventually.

We cross through the sunroom, where Stassi now sits

surrounded by a group of shifters whose sharp gazes stick to Thompson like glue. Stassi, however, gives me a friendly wave.

I'm surprised, though, when we enter the hall toward my—well, Jarron's—bedroom. There's nothing else down here. This hall was exclusively for the Orizian royalty, of which there are none left. Except me, to some people.

"Where are we going?" Is the surprise somehow in my own room? And if so, won't it look weird to enter my bedroom alone with an attractive shifter while my boyfriend is away? It wouldn't be the first time people started rumors about Thompson and me, but it would be worse now because Jarron and I are publicly *together*.

"You'll see."

"Is it in Jarron's room?"

"What?" He jerks his attention to me and then pauses. "No. No, it's not. Sorry, I can see why this would seem weird. It is somewhere different, back in this hall."

He continues walking, and to prove his point, we pass the door to Jarron's room and continue forward. Are they giving me my own room?

We passed the side hall to Trevor's and Bea's old rooms already. What else is down here?

"I have a confession, though; this isn't my surprise."

"No?" My heart picks up speed. I don't know why I'm nervous, but I honestly have no idea what this could be at this point. Except, maybe my own room. Which, I guess could be cool, but do I want to give up sleeping in Jarron's bed? No. No, I definitely do not. Maybe it's for the best, but I certainly don't want it.

"No, this is Jarron's surprise," he tells me. "I helped with it a little —although, maybe not to your satisfaction. I did try, though. Before he left for Oriziah, he had a meeting with Mrs. Bhatt and made a few demands, as you know. Well, one of them was this room. Since it was important for you to stay in Elite Hall during his absence, he knew you'd need a few things to keep you truly comfortable here. I think this will make a big difference for you. It's not going to solve any of the big issues or anything, but it's still a huge step."

"Okay..."

The hall ends in a fork. One leads to a long hall. I can see two mahogany doors, but it continues on around a bend. The other leads to a large circular room with several bronze doors. Those are what grab my attention the most.

"What is all this?" I ask, spinning around. I've never been all the way down here. I know Laithe must have a room in the area. Are these more bedrooms?

"There are a few additional rooms for the inner circle down that hall," he tells me. "Manuela technically has a room here; she just doesn't use it favor of sticking around her girlfriend. And Stassi prefers to be close to his pack."

"Do you have a room here now?"

"There are some available. I wasn't sure how you'd feel about it, though, so I haven't selected any. Lola and Janet could take them too if they wanted. And you. If you cared to move out of Jarron's room and have a little independence. They often go unused, but they're reserved, regardless of if the inner circle uses them or not."

"Hmm." This is all very interesting. "So, I have the option of selecting my own bedroom. Is that my surprise?"

"No. If you wanted a room, you'd be directly next to Jarron." He points to the bronze doors. "These are different."

I swallow. "Okay."

"I can't show you all of them. Some are private. One belongs to Bea and Trevor, apparently. Not sure how long it will remain for them, but for now, it's private. Another is Jarron's—only he has access to it, so that would be for him to share if he chooses. One of them is yours."

I purse my lips. "This is all very cryptic."

"I suppose it sounds that way. But once you see what yours is, it'll make a little more sense. Honestly, I suspect Bea's and Trevor's is some kind of sex cave with chains and whips and things."

I grimace. "Stop saying the quiet part out loud!" I laugh. The image is a bit much for me to handle.

He shrugs. "Just calling it like I see it."

"So, they're just recreational rooms of whatever the inner circle wants?"

"Something like that."

"So, what's Jarron's?"

"I wouldn't tell you if I knew." He nudges me with an elbow, and I glare in return.

"All right, well, what's mine, then?" I cross my arms.

He walks up to the fourth door from the left. "Laithe is already inside; don't let him scare you. Ready?"

"Of course I'm ready, dummy. Just open it."

He smirks and then swings the door open, and smoke billows out into the hall.

I suck in a breath. The smoke dissipates quickly, revealing a massive room with wooded rafters crisscrossing below a cathedral ceiling. There's an iron chandelier holding at least a hundred candles with real flickering flames. The walls are all tan brick covered in shelves of jars filled with so many different liquids and solids I can't even keep track. And in the middle, six rows of counters with three cauldrons on each.

It's bright but cozy and absolutely beautiful.

"He was concerned it wouldn't be big enough." Thompson snorts.

"You don't think that's a valid concern?" Laithe asks. I blink, noticing them for the first time in a set of leather armchairs beside a flickering fireplace on the far left of the massive room. It's so cold my breath comes out puffy.

"I didn't say that."

My mind spins. It's my own personal potions workshop. My lips curl into a smile of awe, even as tears prick my eyes.

I stare up at the ceiling and the elaborate, exposed supports. The vintage-looking chandelier decorated in black metals and brass accents.

"Jarron's gonna be pissed he missed this," Thompson murmurs, watching me.

"It's incredible," I breathe. "I don't even know what to say."

"If you want a distraction from all the feels," Thompson says more confidently, leaning against one of the counters, "you can take a look at my shabby brewing attempts." He nods to the three cauldrons smoking behind him.

I tilt my head. "What did you do?"

"They're yours from Under Hall. I tried to keep them alive, but I'm not nearly as good as you. The stunning spell should be fine; I'm fairly proficient in those. Although, yours was a little different than what we use in our pack. The nullifier might be okay. The death potion, I didn't even keep. It was so far off by the time I got caught up on what it needed that there was no salvaging it."

I look over the three potions, starting with the nullifier. It's a bit thick, and the color is off a little. I think I can adjust it enough for it to be usable, though. "I'll have to test it out on someone," I say and then grin. "Who wants to volunteer?"

"I'm sure Jarron will when he comes around," Laithe purrs.

I spin to face them. "Is he coming soon?"

"He will try. Our days are faster in Oriziah, and there's no easy pattern to follow, timing-wise. He might be free at three a.m. your time and not again for two weeks. He tried to make it this week, but it didn't work out. He does want to come around soon."

"Things are still—"

"Things haven't changed much on the war front. He's afraid if he leaves for long, though, it will prompt the rebels to make a move."

I hold back a sigh. No one enjoys being part of a war. I should be thankful nothing terrible has happened yet.

"How is it so cold here, but there's a fire over there?" I blurt out, again struck by the strange dynamic.

"Oh! That's the coolest part," Thompson says. "Come on, check it out." He grabs my arm and pulls me across the room. Once we pass the third row of cauldrons, the air suddenly shifts. Warmth seeps into my bones.

"*What?*" I say stupidly. I look up and around. There's no physical evidence of the change.

"There's a magical barrier," Laithe says. "It keeps this side a comfortable temperature."

"Actually," Thompson says, putting a finger in the air to grab attention, "they were going to have it only be the seating area of the room that's warm and the rest changeable temperatures, but it was my idea to put the barrier smack in the middle of the room so you can brew both cold and warm potions at the same time!" His eyes and smile are massive.

I chuckle at his excitement. "That was a good idea," I admit.

"Yeah, it was!" He pumps a fist.

I roll my eyes, despite my grin.

"The barrier to start with was Jarron's idea, and I gotta thank him when I get the chance. I mean, I guess I shouldn't have to babysit you as much in here as I used to, but still, at least I won't have to freeze my ass off when I do."

I walk over to the sitting area. There is a taupe leather

loveseat and two matching swivel armchairs. And against the wall is a familiar machine.

"*No,*" I draw in disbelief.

"It makes chai," Laithe says before I can even ask. "And coffee if you'd prefer. Although, it's really not healthy to ingest so much caffeine at your age."

I side-eye him.

"What?"

"If she bonds with Jarron, that sort of thing will not matter in the slightest," Thompson remarks.

Laithe shrugs.

My stomach twists, but I ignore the feeling. I already know where Thompson stands on the whole chosen thing. He put his money on me a long time ago. I would take Laithe's reaction more to heart, but they give nothing away as usual.

There's an open space near the front of the room. Just brick walls and wooden flooring. "Something supposed to go back there?"

"A little extra space in case you had something in mind," Laithe says. "One thing we considered was workshop space for Lola's and Janet's projects. If you wanted an excuse to have them nearby more often."

"Ooh, I like that idea." I wouldn't mind any excuse to spend more time in the room anyway. It's the most beautiful thing I've ever seen. Like a mix between a middle ages tavern and the speakeasy. Sleek in some ways, rough in others. It's cozy and chaotic and incredible. "I'll ask them what they think."

I look around again, still unable to get enough of it. My heart is full.

"Why do I love it so much?" I whisper.

There's a pause while Laithe and Thompson allow me to sit with the thought. Or maybe they just don't know how to answer.

"What's not to love?" Thompson eventually says. "The room is badass."

"Yeah, but..." I turn to face him while I work through the feelings swirling through me. "It's not just the room. It's great. It's beautiful. A private getaway. And potions give me something to do. But I don't know. I was never in love with potions this much before I came to Shadow Hills. I guess I'm just having an existential crisis." I huff out an awkward laugh.

Silence stretches again. But this time, it's Laithe who breaks it. "It's something you can control."

I blink.

"You expressed feeling trapped, not because you aren't comfortable here but just on principle. You've expressed you feel like you need to be doing more. Potions work isn't the answer to it all, but it gives you something that you can control now, in the between time."

I bite the inside of my lip.

"Damn, dude," Thompson says. "You a mind reader or what?"

I laugh again.

"Only Jarron's," Laithe says matter-of-factly. "But Jarron understands her quite well, so that gives me an advantage."

"Right," I mumble. "Wait, that's kinda weird. You like know everything about me, then?"

Laithe smiles. "Certainly not."

I cross my arms. "Way more than I've ever told you."

"If it helps, you will have just as much access to my inner workings if you ever bond with Jarron."

I flinch. Deep inside, I'm still scared of that. It shouldn't be that scary. Connecting with someone I adore and trust. It's not the permanence; it's the... control.

Shit, Laithe is totally right.

"Well, that's enough psycho analysis for me today. I'm gonna get to brewing."

Laithe bows their head, amusement still lingering in their eyes. Then, they stand and walk from the room slowly.

"Do you want me to leave too? Or do you mind if I stay?" Thompson asks.

"You're welcome to stay," I answer absently.

I check out the other two potions Thompson attempted to keep alive for me. The stunning potion looks great to my eye. The expeller was also lost in the shuffle, apparently—Elliot, another wolf shifter I'd befriended during truth or dare a while back, dropped the cauldron while transferring them over yesterday.

Luckily, it's pretty easy to replace and will only take a week or two. I jot that down as an important first one. I'll also start another nullifier and another death potion. I found a recipe for a very strong paralysis potion that I like the idea of as well.

After that, I'll have to continue more research on potions I can use against my enemies.

Once we establish I'm not at all upset with him for his work on my potions, Thompson settles in beside me while I work on preparing my first few projects. An hour flies by before I notice how quiet he is.

The expeller is bubbling already. The nullifier only has a few ingredients, and I still have to prepare several more of them. But I stop my work and look him over.

Thompson is staring blankly at his hands.

"Something wrong?"

He looks up suddenly. "Oh, sorry. I zoned out."

I set the jar of unicorn bone meal on the counter. "Tell me," I say. I haven't spent much time with him over the last few weeks since the caves. We haven't talked about what he admitted to me. We haven't talked about much at all.

"There was another advancement on my pack last week," he

45

admits. "Nothing new or groundbreaking. It just makes me anxious being so far from them and now..."

I frown. "Now?"

"Now, I'm wondering if my time here is going to be fruitful after all."

I take a seat on one of the wooden stools. "What does that mean?"

He sighs. "I didn't mean to burden you with this."

"Thompson, you've proven to be a real friend. Let me be a friend back."

"Have I? Have I been a real friend?" he asks. His brow is pinched, his whole body tense.

"You've helped me more than—"

"But do you trust me?" he blurts out. "I mean—" He runs his hands over his face.

I frown. This has been weighing on him for a while, I realize. Did I just not notice?

"I mean, you said you didn't know if you could trust me before we entered the caves, and you haven't spoken about any of it since. So, I didn't know if that was still true."

"Oh," I mumble. "Well, I suppose it colors our friendship a little bit, knowing you only came here and befriended me in hopes that we'd become your allies. It—well, I've thought a lot about it, and the truth is, I understand. You needed help. What else were you supposed to do? I believe everything you did was sincere as well. You didn't lie or fake things, that I know of. The thing that scared me was the idea that if you were my ally for what you could gain, what would happen if someone gave you a better offer? What would have happened if Mr. Vandozer came up to you and said that if you betrayed me, he'd make sure your pack was safe? Would you have done it?"

My stomach sinks. He just said he doesn't know if this will be worth his time. Could that still happen now?

"I sought out a specific route that was the most moral I could find," he said. "The one that won't bite me or my pack in the ass later. I refuse to hurt anyone else to help ourselves."

My stomach clenches. *Is that what I will have to do to save Liz?* "Right," I whisper.

He doesn't seem to notice my change in demeanor. "It's just that, Jarron was my hope. He has all the power and influence I could hope for. He could save us. And I think he would. I think I achieved what I set out to do." He stares down at his hands again. "And then, I lost again because now Jarron is gone. He's trying to save his own people, his own land. How is he supposed to help me too? He doesn't have the time to even think about my problems, let alone the resources. He needs them all for the war. I'm back to the drawing board. And no, I will not betray you to save myself. I won't do it. I swear to you. Make me swear a magical vow if you want. I don't care. I will not hurt you."

I swallow. "Okay," I whisper. "I believe you."

He sighs. "I just think... I might have to find a new way. And that may require leaving the school."

"Oh no." My stomach sinks again. "I get it, though, if you need to. I trust you, okay? We'll be friends even if you leave."

He nods.

"Is there no one else at the school who could help you? At least, in the meantime?"

"There's really only two others that might have some ability to help, and neither of them seem to be big fans of mine. Besides, I don't have anything to offer them."

I absently rub my lips. "Maybe I can help."

His eyes light up. "You think?"

"I don't know. People are always looking to get on Jarron's good side, so maybe I could have some pull? It's worth a shot." I'm assuming the two in question are Auren and Manuela. Auren is questionable. But Manuela is at least on team-Jarron, and it'll give me a chance to feel her out a little bit.

"Okay." Thompson nods eagerly. He's more desperate than he's trying to let on.

And suddenly, my purpose shifts. I still have a lot I need to do. Potions are important, and my sister is even more important, but this is something pressing that I can do now.

And I'm going to do everything in my power to help Thompson.

8

I WILL BREW POWER

I stand in front of the seven bronze doors at the end of the hall, arms crossed and eyes narrowed like the mystery behind them is some kind of adversary.

I stayed up for hours, thinking about what kinds of things could be behind the doors. Does it matter? Nope, not really. But door number three is Jarron's.

He has a secret room here he never mentioned.

Jarron doesn't hide a lot from me. Except, you know, the big things he's technically not allowed to share.

Like who his chosen is.

I bite the inside of my lip. I don't like not knowing, and something about wondering what's behind this door gnaws at me.

It's the kind of uneasiness I shouldn't dwell on. So, I force myself away from the annoying questions and force myself to enter the chamber made just for me.

In here, I have access to power. I'm able to create, with my own hands, weapons I can use to destroy my enemies.

Today is dedicated to potion making. I've been away from my work for far too long, and I have a lot to make up for. So, while everyone else is in classes that I'm no longer allowed to attend, I will brew myself some power.

None of bodyguards have shown up to badger me, so I'm largely left alone.

Another perk of my new workshop.

It doesn't take me long to make adjustments to my current potions and begin three more. Potion making involves a lot of waiting time, so after an hour, I've run out of pressing tasks.

I pick up a book about potions studies to browse in hopes of finding a few others to begin.

An interesting dry potion piques my interest. It will require extra research to ensure it will perform well on demons, but otherwise it's a winner. I also throw in a more typical paralysis potion.

I also found a strength reducer I like. It's not the most powerful potion, but it's easy to reduce down to less than a milliliter, meaning a drop anywhere on the skin will lessen a powerful supernatural's strength.

I've used nullifiers on supernatural beings before, which drains their magic, but it only helped so much. Sure, it saved us against Mr. Vandozer back in the fall, but I still nearly died because it didn't drain any of his natural strength. He was still a massive creature with claws and fangs.

A weakening potion would help with that issue.

Soon my neck starts aching and my stomach growls. I shut the book and heave a dramatic sigh. It's already smack in the middle of lunch period, and I haven't ingested anything other than a few sips of water.

I could order food to be delivered here—more perks of Elite life—but I prefer to have a change of scenery, so I order food ahead of time and then grab a book to eat lunch in the speakeasy.

There aren't many students in the halls this time of day, but it is in the middle of lunch hour, so there are a few.

The most powerful and influential always head to the lunch-room to commingle, but there are several lower-level Elites who spend every spare hour studying and practicing to keep their rank and others who hide from the hierarchies, maybe just so they don't expose their position within them.

Given these traditions, I'm surprised to find Auren sitting in the sunroom alone.

"Hey," I mumble awkwardly when she looks up and stills.

"Hi," she says. "I'm surprised to see you without a bodyguard."

"Laithe is probably hiding around here somewhere." I chuckle awkwardly. It occurs to me when Auren's lips curve into a tense smile that perhaps I should be nervous being alone with her.

She's one of the more powerful beings in this school, but she doesn't strike me as a particularly dangerous supernatural anymore. One crack of my nullifier—strapped conveniently to my upper thigh next to my obsidian dagger—and she'd be more than possible to defeat, but she has actively tried to harm me in the past. I shift from foot to foot, fleeting anxiety shooting through me.

"I wouldn't hurt you, you know."

"I know." Determination swells in my chest. "I wouldn't let you."

When her lips curl this time, it seems much more sincere.

"It's just hard to know who to trust these days."

"Right. Yeah, I get that. And I don't exactly have the best track record."

"True." I smile. "I did want to thank you, though, officially. I don't know what your motives were, but thank you for pushing to give me the list."

"Oh. Yeah, I'm pretty sure the school would have rioted if I'd taken that list. And I figured you had more need of it."

I narrow my eyes briefly. Was that a dig?

"I mean your friends. Lola and Janet should have access to Elite Hall. They gain the most by being on the list. If I were to choose people, it would have just been my brother and Mia, and they're already in Elite Hall with all kinds of stupid benefits we don't need or use. So, it made a lot of sense. Mrs. Bhatt was super into the idea, for whatever reason."

I frown. "Mrs. Bhatt is weird."

"Is she?"

"She hated me when she first came here. Now, it's like I'm the teacher's pet." I absently rub the spot on my neck where Jarron's bite barely lingers.

"Funny how fast things can change in the supernatural world. She's probably trying to make it up to you if she didn't treat you well before. If not, Jarron would make her regret that choice."

I shrug. "She never did anything bad. She just seemed annoyed that I existed, like she thought I was the reason for all the demon heirs absences."

Auren snorts. "And mine. One little human came in and took out all of the most powerful supernaturals in the school in a single semester. Epic."

I shrug. "It wasn't my fault."

"No, but it was because of you all the same."

My brow pinches. "All I did was exist." And investigate the most powerful students in school, but that didn't lead to much.

"You're Jarron's weakness. He was so unshakable before you. If Mrs. Bhatt had seen the change in him, she'd have known better than to treat you as anything less than royalty."

I cough. "I'm not royalty," I say quickly. "It's bizarre that people think of me that way."

"It's how our world works. You are Orizian royalty until proven otherwise. No one wants to make the mistake Mrs. Bhatt potentially made—and me, if I'm honest. If you do end up as the future queen of Oriziah, every supernatural wants to be able to say they treated you well all along. And with the way Jarron prioritizes you over everything else, no one has a choice but to follow suit. Like it or not, princess, you are a princess."

I twist my lips. "For now."

She lifts a brow. "You're doubting your future with Jarron?"

I shake my head.

A good portion of my doubts disappeared that night in the cave when Jarron didn't kill me in his mindless demon form, then proceeded to call the Cosmic Council fools. He destroyed that cave system, reaching me before I was harmed.

He chose me in that moment.

And though it's not a definitive answer, it felt like it then.

But even so, it's all so mindblowing. I'm still working to convince myself that this could be *real*.

Much like those doubts that haunt me about my weakness as a human in a supernatural world, there are still doubts that maybe I misread the situation.

"I'd love to believe Jarron is my end game, but there is still a lot between now and happily ever after."

Her eyes soften.

"And for now, I'm not used to it. The attention. The influence. The pandering. It feels both empowering and invalidating. Like I'm a child everyone must protect. I'd rather they all just get out of my way so I can prove myself."

She studies me.

"Luxury accommodations, no classes, and literally anything you could possibly want at your fingertips? What's not to enjoy?" She flicks a brow.

"Not *anything* I want," I mumble. The memory of leathery wings sliding against stone sends a thrill through me. I don't even know what I'm feeling anymore. I blink and refocus. "Anyway, I'm off to some of the perks of being trapped here—sushi for lunch. See you around."

"Yeah, see ya."

I finally pass through the sunroom and find a light-brown-skinned brunette wearing a pantsuit leaning against the wall of the hall, watching me approach.

"So, I *do* have a bodyguard on duty," I say to Manuela.

"You thought we'd leave you as easy pickings?"

Apparently, my conversation with Auren boosted my confidence a bit. "Only idiots consider me easy pickings."

She grins. "Love the confidence, princess, but it does tempt me to challenge that assurance. Could you stand up against me with those potions hooked on your thigh?"

My heart skips a beat. "Suppose you could find out."

Her grin widens. "I'd enjoy every moment of it, win or lose. But I'm not in the market of pissing off demon princes."

"You've never been afraid of him before."

"Making an enemy of Jarron is not in my best interest. That doesn't mean I am afraid. I simply stay on his good side for a reason."

Hmm. Interesting comment. "I was just headed to grab some lunch in the speakeasy."

She nods. "I'll leave you to it, then. But yes, I'll be around if you happen to need me."

Manuela has never been much for socialization, so this isn't at all surprising, but as I begin to move past her, I pause. "Actually, would you mind joining me? I had something I wanted to talk to you about, and now's as good a time as any."

"Propositioned by the princess. You do like to surprise your allies and enemies alike, don't you, little human?"

I raise a brow at that last bit. Jarron once threatened the whole Elite table never to call me "little human." She's already pushing the envelope without him here. I wonder if I'd be safer spending time with the fae princess who nearly killed me when she cheated during a hand-to-hand combat spar, sending ice magic into my heart.

I'm certainly less wary of the ice princess than Manuela.

"Sure do," I say with a grin. I don't want her to know her words had their intended effect.

Maybe this is a bad idea.

9

A PROPOSITION

The unnerving feeling remains as I enter the speakeasy alongside the powerful dryad witch. There are two wolves at a table who stop talking the moment we enter and slip out behind us like we're mobsters about to rob the place.

Manuela doesn't seem bothered by that.

Only a moment later, a vampire comes out from a side door near the fireplace and delivers a plate of sushi to the table we select. I mutter a thank you, but the vamp is already gone.

"So," Manuela purrs. "What did you want to proposition me with?" Her eyes slide down the side of my arm. Suggestive but somehow respectful at the same time.

Is she only doing this to get under my skin?

I'm reminded of the last time I had a one-on-one conversation with a powerful and unnerving female supernatural. Bea tried very hard to get under my skin back when I was fake-dating Jarron, and while it worked, I was more than able to keep up with her.

I have to remember that I'm not a weakling human like they

all think. Magic has no bearing on my ability to kick supernatural ass if I need to.

Manuela included.

I hope.

"What does the little human princess want from the tree witch?" she asks, voice still low and sultry.

I consider pointing out her repeated use of the term "little human." She's very clearly trying to push my buttons. Should I push back or ignore it?

"It's not for me, per se."

She leans back in her chair and flicks a brow.

I eye my plate of sushi, then after a beat, grab the chopsticks and take a bite. If I'm going with the ignore option, it means I have to show it doesn't bother me.

"Not for you, huh? So, you're running around as a lacky for someone else? Or is it for one of your little Minor Hall friends?"

"Not a lacky, just trying to help someone I care about. And no, it's not for Lola or Janet."

She eyes me while I take a second bite of sushi.

"This person doesn't even know I was planning to talk to you, actually." I mean, not technically.

She remains quiet for a while, just sizing me up with those golden eyes.

"Get to the point, princess," she finally says with a wave of her hand.

I set down my chopsticks and swallow my current bite before I begin. "I'm not exactly well versed in how the supernatural world does this sort of thing, so tell me if this is a laughable request. Or if I'm going about it all wrong."

"There aren't many faux pas here. Just say what you need."

"I was hoping you might be able to help Thompson."

This time, both eyebrows shoot up. Silence stretches long enough for me to shift in my chair, uncomfortable.

"I don't know exactly what we can give you in exchange, but—"

"You underestimate your own power, little human." She crosses her arms. "I'm simply considering the implications of helping the wolf who is, by most perspectives, Jarron's greatest threat to winning your devotion."

I roll my eyes. "Thompson is not a threat to Jarron."

"That remains to be seen."

I shake my head. "Anyway, I was under the impression that these kinds of favors were in exchange for another favor."

"Not necessarily. And when you begin a proposition saying you don't know how you can repay it, that puts you in a vulnerable position."

"I thought you said there weren't any faux pas?"

"There aren't. You are simply doing yourself a disservice."

"Okay. So, what exactly did I do wrong, then?"

"You are implying you need my help more than I need you. Instead, begin strong. Imply your target should want to help you. In most cases, that will be true, so long as you don't let that wolf of yours drive a wedge between you and your prince. Most supernaturals will bend over backward to do you a favor just for the chance at getting close to demon royalty."

"Why, though? Without a specific benefit to them, what does that prove?"

"Just being seen around you could lift someone's reputation quite powerfully."

"Not yours, though. Not in this case. You're already quite close with Jarron."

"True, but lead strong, and if the other party requires more, they will begin the bargaining."

I sigh. "All right. I need you to do something for me."

"Better." She runs her fingers along the armrest of the chair. "Best if you compliment me in some way. And perhaps imply there are many people who could serve this purpose. If you can get them to feel like they must compete for the opportunity, you'll have all the control you need. Try, 'I have need of a favor from someone magically gifted in spells. You're one of the top students in that area, correct? Would you be interested in being part of my endeavor?' You'd have them eating out of the palm of your hand." She grins, exposing elongated canines.

"Would I have you eating out of the palm of my hand?" I ask.

Her lashes flutter, and for the first time, I get the feeling I have the upper hand in the conversation. She's obviously trying to help me, though, hence the supernatural negotiation lesson, but it still feels good to have a slight advantage.

"Perhaps you would, little human."

"Well, do you want the chance to help me or not? We keep beating around the bush."

Her lips tip up just slightly. "Very well. Go on. How can I help you help Thompson?" She wrinkles her nose when she speaks his name. She's not a fan of the wolf shifter, apparently.

"He's having some trouble back home. More specifically, his pack needs help."

"Unsurprising. He's from a tiny pack with no allies that routinely pisses off the large packs surrounding them."

"I would like you to help them defend his land."

Manuela jerks back as if I'd slapped her. "You want—you ignorant, foolish girl."

My stomach sinks. My eyes widen.

"Do you have any idea—" She stands and turns her back to me. "Thompson is a squirmy manipulative ass. Did he tell you to come to me? You said he didn't know you were coming, but did he imply it? Otherwise, why would you ask *me* in particular?"

Suddenly, I feel very small, and very guilty for some offense I have no idea about. "He needs help from a stronger supernatural." Should I not mention that he was hoping for help from

Jarron? I suppose it'll be fairly obvious, but I'll just skip over that bit for now. "We were discussing if anyone in the school could help because otherwise he's going to have to leave. Jarron is preoccupied, obviously. Auren hates me. You are one of the strongest left."

"Auren doesn't seem to hate you as much as you think." Her shoulders relax a bit. "He didn't mention my people's history with the land his pack resides over?"

My eyes flare. "No. He didn't mention that."

She takes in a long breath then retakes her seat. The lines of tension never quite leave her face, though.

"Well, one of the original dryad clans inhabited those lands for centuries, and many of our ancestors' spirits remain in those roots. We have no access to them any longer thanks to the wolves who took over."

I swallow. I'd never— "I didn't know about any of this."

"No one ever seems to. I'm certain your friend is aware, though. The spirits are active in the sacred lands, a portion of their territory."

I consider this new information. Could I possibly be in the wrong for trying to help Thompson? Is his cause less moral than he let on? Or are these territory wars simply not new and will be ever waging through time?

"Can you tell me more about it? What happened to your people that they lost access to those lands?"

She waves her hand. Her expression is hardened but not emotional. Is that a mask? "Wolves breed like mice, and they constantly need more land. Humans are bad enough, but even in the rural parts of the continent, where we have been able to haunt humans successfully enough to keep cities from building or negotiated protected parks, the wolves have taken more and more of those places from us."

"Dryads are quite powerful, aren't they? Couldn't they have just—"

"Couldn't they have fought back harder? Once the wolves assimilated into human territories and took political control of which lands were erased and which weren't? And when we weren't allowed to use magic in human spaces or we'd be hunted down by the magical control agencies?"

"Wow, so, this was... intense."

"Look, we haven't had it as bad as some other species or types of people, but for a wolf to ask me to defend land for them? Land they occupy now after they drove us away from it themselves? That's insidious on a whole different level."

I nod absently. "Okay, yeah, I get that. I'm sorry I didn't know."

I don't want to prod her on sensitive things, but it does sound like she's not necessarily angry at all wolves, just on the concept of defending this land that used to be her people's. Obviously pretty legit feelings there.

Maybe there's some possible negotiating, but regardless, this conversation has gone as far as it should for now.

"I'm sorry for bringing up a touchy subject, but thank you for explaining. At least now I know a bit more of what I'm getting myself into."

She nods, expression still much more guarded than before.

"Be careful with that wolf, girl. He'll manipulate you in any way he can, especially driving you away from Jarron."

IO

FRIENDSHIP PROBATION

Lola and Janet freeze the moment Thompson enters the potion room that evening. I'd told them a brief explanation about what happened with Manuela, and it's seemed to affect them more than it did me.

Now, I've got to talk with the final part of my inner circle about it. The one who will have the most perspective and the most at stake.

Thompson's shoulders tense when he notices Lola's and Janet's reaction.

"What?" he asks. When no one answers, he drops his bag on the counter and strolls around the bubbling potions to the flickering fire, where we've been chatting for the last half hour.

"I told them about helping you," I begin.

He takes a seat, shoulders relaxing slightly.

"And about how I approached someone this afternoon."

His eyes light up, but he examines me closely. His face falls slack as he realizes it's not good news.

"It didn't go well. I'm curious if you know why."

Thompson swallows. "I'm not particularly liked by a lot of this school." He says it more like a question than a statement.

"It was Manuela who I spoke to," I explain.

His lips part, and his eyes darken. "Shit."

"So, you do know why that topic in particular would have bothered her?"

His jaw clenches. "Yeah, I can imagine. But—" He shakes his head. "I'm sorry. I should have warned you. She didn't—you're okay, right?"

"I'm fine. But why didn't you tell me she's got a connection to your land? She's the second most powerful supernatural, outside of Jarron. Who else do you think I'd have approached to try to help you?"

"I don't know." His lashes flutter. "What did she say, though?"

I take in a deep breath. "She called me ignorant and called you a manipulator. Said I should be careful around you."

"I'm starting to think she's right about that," Lola says, buzzing over and hovering between us.

Thompson looks down at his feet. "I know I haven't always been upfront about my motives. But I swear I've never intended to make anything worse for anyone else. That stuff with the dryads is old news. For us, at least. It's not something we talk about a whole lot. And while I knew she didn't like me, I didn't really think it all through. Or maybe—" He presses his lips together.

"Maybe what?"

He sighs. "It's going to sound bad."

"If it's truth, it's truth. We'll deal with it," I bite the words out, already preparing my heart for whatever damning thing he's going to tell me now.

"Maybe part of me wanted you to ask her."

63

The room falls silent in the moments after that statement. I don't know how to take it.

"What does that mean?" Janet asks, more softly than I would have.

"I mean, she has a good relationship with Jarron. I know she's not going to harm you, so if anyone could approach her about this, you could. I never anticipated needing help from the dryads, but it makes so much sense. It could really, really, make a big difference."

I lift a brow, not exactly thrilled with that answer. But perhaps not as angry as he expected me to be.

"So, you sent her off to talk to possibly the most dangerous student at this school for your gain without even knowing what she was getting into?" Lola says, darting forward and buzzing in front of his nose.

He sinks into the seat and holds up his hand in surrender. "I didn't know she was going to talk to her. If I did, I would have told her."

"You knew," Janet says. "If you allowed yourself to think it through, you'd have known."

"I knew it was a possibility."

"Plausible deniability," I say, then heave a deep breath. I tap my knee as I try to think it through even more.

"She wasn't too mad, was she? I mean, she gave me a real good glare on my way in here, but she's not like ready to attack us, is she?"

"Us?" Lola asks. "Do you mean *us*?" She points to me. "Or do you mean your pack?"

He frowns. "I mean, me and Candice."

Awkward silence stretches between us. Thompson runs his fingers through his hair.

"I'm sorry," he huffs finally. "It was a cruel thing to do. I should have mentioned the history. It's probably not as bad as she made it sound either."

I lean back in the chair. "I think she was mostly pissed on principle. A wolf asking a dryad to help keep land they once stole from the dryad people..."

"We didn't steal anything. I mean, we took advantage, maybe, but..." He stares off past my shoulder. "All this happened several generations ago, long before I was born. But the story goes that there was this big battle—the last one between wolves and dryads, I think. It was over this massive section of land that held some sacred places among their people. The dryads were defeated and driven away for thousands of miles. My ancestors were not part of the battle, but they were some of the first to arrive in the aftermath and claimed the land."

"Your pack may not be responsible for driving them out," I say, "but I'm not sure it would have made much of a difference. Any wolf asking a dryad for help keeping what wolves stole..."

He sighs. "I know we're still wolves, but my pack is also witches. We even have some dryad blood. It's weak, but of all the packs, we're the least close to their enemies. I wish they'd see it that way, but I guess they wouldn't."

Janet leans forward. "How do you have dryad blood?"

"When my ancestors first claimed the land, they took a small pocket near the dryad's place of worship, near where the largest battle took place. Many wolves were superstitious about those parts out of fear, so even though it was a desirable plot of land, any other packs were driven out by signs of dryad spirits. My pack was stubborn and remained, despite the hauntings. Turns out, though, there was actually one young dryad who was orphaned during the battle hiding there, leaping between trees for many years, raised by the spirits left behind. Our people found her but left her be. They allowed her to stay, even though technically, she was a risk to the pack. When other wolves came through, they protected her and kept her secret. She was an innocent, and they had no reason to harm her. Well, many years later, she fell in love with one of the pack members. They had children together. She was my great-great grandmother. After many generations, hints of her magic still remain in our blood."

"That's an incredible story, actually." I find myself wondering if Manuela knows it. It would probably make no difference in her perspective. The wolves are still the oppressors. One exception doesn't absolve them of the guilt. But perhaps it does give them a bit more even ground than she realized. I don't know.

"We haven't even heard much about dryads in our day and age. We feel and see the spirits in the forest, but they don't affect us much, except a few nights a year. It hasn't exactly been a central part of our experience."

"But that war eternally affected the dryads."

"Yeah, I know," he says. "It was a stupid hope. I'm sorry I put you at risk for some lofty dream."

I sigh but then nod. "Apology accepted." I point at him. "But you're on probation."

One side of his mouth tilts up.

"Listen," he says in a soft tone, "you don't have to do anything else to try to help me. If Jarron is ever able, I'd appreciate his assistance, but otherwise, it's my responsibility to protect my pack. I'll—I'll take care of it."

"Yeah, you will," Lola says, arms crossed and chest puffed out.

"Okay," I concede. "The only other option I had was Auren. I suppose you could handle approaching her?"

"Yeah," he says, but the light has left his eyes.

II
A DREAM OR A NIGHTMARE

Heavy wings scrape along stone tiles.

The rumble of a powerful monster crackles through the air.

The smell of magic is so palpable it sends a shiver through my whole body.

My eyes fly wide open, heart already pounding.

This time, though, the darkness of Jarron's bedroom is not still.

The rumbling does not stop.

I grip the cool silk sheets of Jarron's bed tightly against my chest.

The shadow of the monster falls over me, and I can't breathe. Can't think.

I wait, wondering if this will be it. Mr. Vandozer has found me and will carve me into pieces to spite Jarron.

The sounds halt.

My whole body clenches. Heart skips a beat. Eyes press closed.

Moments pass, but nothing happens.

Finally, the pressure of the magic washes away. I suck in panicked breaths, and they come out in puffy clouds.

I sit up, heart still hammering. The room is pitch black but entirely still.

I could feel it so clearly—that dark magic pressing down on the whole room—that it's very clear the threat is gone.

What in the world?

That was not a dream, right?

I hop out of bed and rush to flick on the overhead lights. My heart shudders when I find parchment pinned to one of the posts of the bed. The note is scribbled harshly in black ink.

Holy. Shit.

One day soon, you will be mine.

So, obviously, it's not just in my head.

But what does it mean? Could it have been Jarron? Why would he leave me such a cryptic note if so?

I rip the page from the bedpost quickly and read the words three times before I settle back into a sitting position on the bed.

If it was Jarron, then why? He's been forced to stay away from me for weeks because of the conflict in his world, but would he come in the middle of the night to deliver a cryptic note and then leave?

My stomach twists.

I read the note a fourth time and try to console myself.

I miss him, and I really wish he was here.

Or maybe I wish I could be there with him, fighting or helping in some way.

As much as I want this message to have been from him, it doesn't make enough sense.

One day soon, you will be mine.

God, I'd love for those words to mean Jarron wishes to claim me. As much as the thought makes me nervous, it also excites me.

The meaning is entirely the opposite if it came from Vincent Vandozer. I really, really don't want it to be a threat from an evil monster, but the more I read through the words, the more I can't help but admit the dread in my bones is there for a reason.

12

I am so close I can taste it. So close to achieving everything I've worked for.

My victory is at hand.

Do you taste it, like I do? Do you quake because you know I am near?

I am watching. I am waiting.

One day soon, you will be mine.

13
PERFECT PUNISHMENT

The fact that Vincent Vandozer is still living is a thorn stabbing me in the gut, and it's so much worse that he has active control over my sister.

He can make her do anything he wants.

Nothing about that is okay. And I cannot allow it to happen.

I am watching. I am waiting.

So, it's his face I imagine as I brew my death potion. I remember his scream of rage when I used the nullifier on him and how powerless I was against a demon, even after my potion sucked the magic from him temporarily.

If only it could have been permanent.

I pause, ladle mid-stir as a thought crosses my mind. My lips part. Excitement swirls in my chest.

What if the potion wasn't temporary?

It's likely not even possible to make a potion that would alter a being's magic in that way. But what if it were? I continue my slow stir of the potion, considering the possibilities.

That kind of potion would be incredibly powerful. Incredibly dangerous. It could be used against Jarron. Or any royal line. It could change everything. Not just in one world but in all of them.

The ripples would continue on and on.

Is that why it's never been created? Or because it's impossible? Or because the only person who would want such a potion is a human who has no power herself?

If a supernatural wants to destroy someone, they'd kill them, not take away their magic. But damn, that feels like some serious kismet.

If anyone deserves to feel powerless, it's the man who used other beings' desperation to gain power against them. He lured them in with the bait of magic.

Now, I'd take it away from him.

A warm, fuzzy feeling fills up my chest at just the thought of that. Making him live a whole, long life as a human.

"What are you smiling about over there?" a small voice asks.

I jerk my attention to the door, where Lola hovers above Janet's head. They're both grinning at me.

"Oh, nothing new. Just plotting revenge and world domination."

"Oh! Do tell," Lola says as she darts to me. She flies over the cauldron but begins to cough and drops heavily onto my shoulder.

"Careful, Lola! You can't just fly into potion smoke like that." The smoke shouldn't have a ton of effect, but she's so tiny that even the vapor could be a proper dose to harm her.

She continues heaving up a lung, so I grab her by the waist and hold her in my open palm.

"Are you okay?"

"What was that potion?" Janet asks, rushing up to check on her.

"Luckily, it was just the nullifier. Whatever you do, *never* fly through that one." I point to the corner cauldron.

"What's that?" Janet asks, leaning toward the cauldron in question.

"Instant death."

They both grow quiet, Lola's coughing suddenly finished. "Define instant death."

"If brewed right—which no promises, honestly—one drop will kill instantly and leave no trace."

They remain quiet. Lola blinks three times.

"Is that... legal?" Janet finally asks slowly.

They've never really hung out in my potions labs before. It was always my private project that only Jarron or Thompson would join, usually because they were playing bodyguard.

But now, this place can be all of our projects' space. Janet set up her massive canvas—almost the length of her body—in the corner. She's working on a spelled painting that will hypnotize anyone who stares at it for longer than a few seconds. Now, she can work on it here while I'm brewing.

And bonus, this means she gets to come hang out with me during her art class for basically the rest of the year. Inner circle privileges for the win.

Honestly, I'm super excited just to see her process. I'm going to have to talk to Laithe about creating a separate spell barrier for sound so Lola can work on her spell-weaving violin. One of her final projects for this year is a song that will put someone to sleep.

Not something she can reasonably practice in here where we can hear it.

As of right now, Lola seems happy to have an excuse not to work while hanging out in my new workshop. But eventually, she'll need to study too.

"No," I say finally. "No, it's very much not legal. Apparently, another benefit of Elite Hall—literally no one cares." I don't mention the fact that I was brewing this potion in Under Hall with the masses. I've kept that little bit of information quiet. Thankfully, Thompson figured out that truth before working on my potions while I was locked out. That might have been a bit unsafe. Now, so long as I'm not stupid about what I talk about or where I use it, no one will look at it twice.

So, I grin at my friends, uncaring about my illegal, violent activities.

"You're a little scary, you know that?" Lola says, still on my shoulder.

My grin widens.

"Is that what you were smiling about?" Janet asks.

"No," I admit. "I was thinking about my nullifier, but it was fantasy more than reality. I had an idea for a revenge plan that was just so poetic..." I stare wistfully into the distance. "But I'm pretty sure it's not physically possible."

"Pretty sure?" Lola asks. "You're pretty sure or sure?"

I side-eye her. "Pretty. I'm not trying not to get my hopes up."

"Well—" she hops up and hovers a few feet away, careful not to touch my potion steam, "—that's all well and good, as long as you still try to make it happen."

"I thought y'all were scared of me. Now, you're encouraging my violent fantasies?"

"I didn't say it was a bad thing." Lola's wings pulse with a soft glow.

Janet sighs. "I mean, it is a little scary. But I also fully understand your perspective. You're working against the kind of people who lure in magicless children to fight to the death. It's real hard to do worse than that. Anything is justified at that point."

I open my mouth to respond, but she cuts me off with wide eyes.

"Well, not anything," she adds quickly. "I don't mean anything."

"I know," I say. "I know there are always ways to take things too far. I think you guys would like this scheme of mine, though. It's actually less cruel? For the most part."

"You're fantasizing about ways to get revenge that are less cruel?" Lola asks, sounding almost disappointed.

I blink, realizing she's showing us a darker side of herself here today. I like it. "Only technically. I'm pretty sure he'd prefer death. But if I could achieve this, it would be so beautiful. It's maybe dangerous, though? It's probably better just to kill him."

"Okay, well, now we have to know what it is."

I hop up to sit on the counter beside the nullifier. There's so much space in this room I can get comfortable almost anywhere. Janet leans back against the next counter, where the cauldrons are harmlessly empty. Lola continues hovering.

"I was thinking, what if there was a way to make a nullifier that's not temporary?"

Janet tilts her head. "What do you mean?"

"I mean, draining a supernatural being of all their magic. Forever."

Her eyes widen.

"Like I said, I'm pretty sure it's impossible. But it just seems so poetic. He preys on low-magic beings. What if I could make him become one and live that way?"

God, it sounds so beautiful.

"Ooh, I see what you mean," Lola says. "I'd still rather he die, though."

"There would be some serious repercussions to that kind of potion, you know," Janet says, forever the more prudent of our group. "I bet that's one that even Elite Hall wouldn't protect you from. If anyone outside of your circle found out you were attempting that kind of thing..."

75

My stomach sinks, but I nod quickly. She's totally right.

In the supernatural world, everything is about power. The strongest supernaturals want to be my friend because I could help them gain more influence, through my relationship with Jarron. They want more power.

How much would that change if they found out I might have the ability to take away their magic altogether?

I'd be the most dangerous person in this school.

I bow my head as a thrilling rush washes over me. Shit. I like that feeling way too much.

If I had the power to take away magic— "You're right. Just the idea of stealing magic is indescribably dangerous. It was just a thought."

"A thought you should be very, very wary of." She nods sharply.

A loud pounding on the door makes me jump. I give a look to both Lola and Janet, who seem equally unnerved by the timing.

"Expecting someone?" Janet asks.

I shake my head and then resettle my potions to answer the door.

I pull open the heavy door, and my eyes widen when I find Manuela leaning against the doorway casually, that sharp look in her eyes.

"We need to talk."

14

1 ENJOY TESTING YOU

I swallow in response to the dryad-witch hybrid demanding a conversation. Our last didn't go as terribly as it could have, but it also didn't go well. Power pulses from her, making me even more wary of the situation.

I try hard not to show how it affects me. "Okay," I say as calmly as I can manage.

"Let's go for a walk," she says, swinging the door wide for me.

"You're very demanding," I comment, aiming for casual, but I obey and exit the room, leaving my shocked friends behind.

"And you like it." Her smile eases the tension in my chest.

I blink. "Only a little," I say, voice quieter than it should be. "I prefer to be in control, personally."

"Ahh, a girl after my own heart. Does Jarron enjoy being controlled?" she purrs.

My cheeks heat, and I decide not to comment.

She stops in the middle of the circular room with all the bronze doors. So much for a "walk." We only took a few steps.

My gaze darts to Jarron's door and then back.

Her smile remains steady. "Do you know what these are?"

"Private spaces for the demon heirs. I don't know what specifically, though."

She quirks a brow. "Some of them are private personal spaces, but I happen to know at least one of them holds a portal."

My eyes widen. "A portal to…"

She grins wide. "Scared, princess?"

I cross my arms. "I've never been a big fan of portals."

"Prey instinct." She nods absently. "You're a fierce one but not entirely immune to that fear running through your veins. You know the kind of creatures that could come from a portal. You know what they could do to you."

I grimace. "What's your point?"

She turns and leans against the third bronze door, arms crossed. "With that tangent? Just more advice, I suppose. That fear is your intuition; it can be helpful. It can also send you into a spiral, turning you into true prey. Use that instinct, but always remain in control of it. What's my point in asking for a conversation? I have a new deal to offer."

My lips part. She waits for me to respond, and I let the silence linger for a few moments. "Oh?"

She nods. "I am not at all interested in helping the wolf. I am, however, interested in furthering an alliance with you, and I think there is a way we can help each other."

Okay, so this isn't about Thompson. That's slightly disappointing since I would still like to figure out a way to help him, but it's also very intriguing.

"And your plan has something to do with portals to Oriziah?" I try not to look utterly freaked out.

She chuckles. "Not exactly. But also, not entirely incorrect."

"I'm not just walking through a portal to hell because you

ask me to." *No matter how scary you are.* I don't say that part aloud, but she grins like she heard it anyway.

"You do know you'll have to go there eventually, right? Future Princess of Oriziah—is afraid of Oriziah. It's so ironic."

I roll my eyes and ignore the squeeze in my belly. "You just got done telling me that I have reason to fear and that it could save my life or something."

"Ahh, yes. I'm just testing your resolve." She pushes back from the door. "Come with me."

I follow her down the shadowed, narrow hallway toward Jarron's room and the main areas of Elite Hall.

"When are you going to share this plan of yours?"

"Now."

"You enjoy beating around the bush."

"I enjoy testing you."

"Have I passed your tests?"

"Most of them," she says. "You have much to learn, though, little princess. That's all right; you have time. You are young and new to the magical world. Your potential, though, is delicious. That is what I care about."

I am certainly learning a lot more about the dryad witch lately.

Manuela leads me all the way back out into the sunroom. She gives one look to a wolf couple sucking face in the largest velvet chair, and they scamper away like she stepped on their tails.

"You scare everyone, don't you?"

"They have reason to fear me. And to be honest, though I can smell your fear." She turns to face me with those bright eyes. "You show it least of all." She waves to the velvet chair, prompting me to sit. "Which is one of the reasons I like you."

I sit in her suggested seat and watch as she runs her sharp nails over the walls surrounding us. A shimmer falls over the room.

"So, this is serious business, then?" I ask, resisting a shiver.

"Indeed, it is. We will be discussing a few things I'd rather not be overheard talking about with you of all people."

"Me?"

She takes a seat beside me and sinks into the chair, slumped casually. "Yes, you. The current resident princess. The one everyone wants to protect, just for the chance to be noticed by Jarron."

Which implies she intends to put me in danger. My heart begins pounding rapidly.

"It is in my best interest to keep you safe as well, girl. I am simply less inclined to treat you like a china doll."

"Well, you call me 'little human,' 'princess,' and 'girl' enough for me to not entirely believe that."

Her grin widens. "Do you not like it, princess?"

"I'd prefer you refrain from calling me anything little. And human just sounds derogatory, like it's somehow a bad thing. I don't see it that way, so I'd like it if others didn't either."

She tilts her head. "So, princess is still on the table, then?"

"If you want." I shrug one shoulder. "Now, what's this proposition of yours?"

"I, too, have a friend in need of aid."

My brows lower. "Aid I can give?"

"Don't discount your own abilities, princess."

I roll my eyes. "Just being realistic. Will a potion aid them?" And if so, why not go to a potions master, like my family? Can she not pay? Is she not in a position to trust just anyone?

"No, a potion will not. You, however, are in a unique position to help them. I can't give you much more details than that until we've established some ground rules. What I will add is that this person has information you require. Helping them, will help you. I am certain of that."

I intertwine my fingers and lean forward. "What sort of information?"

She waves her index finger. "Not yet."

"Does it have something to do with the Akrasia Games?" And if so, does that automatically disqualify her as someone I could trust?

Or maybe she knows of another contestant. A former winner, perhaps?

She raises a brow. "You don't listen very well, do you?"

I lean back, arms crossed. "Fine. What are your rules?"

"Jarron cannot know."

I sit up. "Excuse me?"

"The reasons for this will become clear once you meet with my contact, but you cannot tell Jarron you are planning to meet someone. You cannot tell Jarron once you have. He cannot know about this deal, at all, ever."

My mind spins through this new information.

"You want me to lie to him?"

"I want you to withhold information. That is not the same as lying. Trust me, princess, there will come many times that you will have to lie or deceive in your future."

I sigh. "I am no stranger to lying or hiding or faking. What I don't like is having to lie to someone I care about. And someone who I trust to keep me safe more than anyone else on this planet. I am concerned this favor is not in my best interest if I have to lie to Jarron about it."

"Jarron is stubborn. He will think there is no way to trust my contact, but I will personally ensure your safety. My friend will *not* hurt you. She needs you, in fact. Her life is over if not for your help. She will likely die. If she survives, she will live a half-life—something none of us want. But Jarron would rather eliminate the perceived threat rather than help her."

I take in a long breath. "I need more."

"More what?"

"Specifics. I need to know what exactly I'm gaining by helping this person. I need to know what I'm risking. Otherwise, it's a no-go."

She frowns. "Very well. My friend knows a way to end the Akrasia Games for good."

15

DESPERATELY NEEDED INFORMATION

She knows a way to end the Akrasia Games for good.

My heart rate picks up speed again, but this time for an entirely different reason than fear. "You're certain?"

She nods.

"If you know that she knows, and she's your friend, why can't you just tell me?"

"That's not how favors work," she tsks.

"Well, you're supposed to be on our side. That information is incredibly important."

"You can save your sister without this information. But if I give you this information without the bargain, it will result in the death of my friend. I would be betraying her to help you. In that case, I'd rather aid you in saving your sister another way. If someone must die, let it be strangers, not friends."

I frown. I don't like that solution either. "Okay, so this person can tell me how to end the games for good, but I have to help her, without telling Jarron?"

"Correct."

"I have a few more questions."

She holds out her hand, as if waiting impatiently.

"Will helping her hurt anyone else?"

She narrows her eyes. "No one innocent."

I purse my lips. Interesting answer.

"How you choose to help her is up to you, but you must promise not to harm her in the process of this war and fight against the Akrasia Games."

"Are you going to make me swear?"

She jerks her head back. "Heavens no. Could you imagine what Jarron would do to me? No, this is a promise between allies. If for some reason, you cannot own up to your side of the bargain and my friend is harmed by your actions, I will be extremely displeased. But in truth, I care more about your well-being than hers. If you are harmed, Jarron will kill me. If you are harmed, I will lose the influence I've worked hard to gain. So, no, a vow would be counterproductive, as it would increase your risk. This deal will be a gentlewomen's agreement and nothing more."

Okay, I like that answer.

I examine her for a few beats, excitement building slowly. My body knows my answer before I do.

"All right, I'm in."

Manuela's grin turns feline, smooth and pleased. "I will set up the meeting for my next scheduled shift as your protector. That's three days from now. We will do it during classes, so you won't be noticed missing."

"Wait, where am I meeting her?"

She holds out her hand, her smile remaining firm, but she gives no indication of answering that question. My stomach sinks. She's going to make me walk through a portal, isn't she?

I let that fear press on my chest for a few moments before I make my choice. *Use my fear, but don't let it control me.*

I shake her hand.

"I'm very pleased to be doing business with you, princess."

16

ORIZIAN STUDIES

"Nimsete, Candice."

My gaze rises from my textbook to find a red-skinned demon with black horns bowed to me, standing in the entryway to the speakeasy.

"Nimsete, Professor Zyair." I smile. This is only the second time I've met with him since my seclusion began.

"How are your independent studies going?"

"Oh, well, you know, not as well as they would be if I had the structure of daily classes."

He lifts a brow. "That's not because you're incapable of learning an immense amount on your own. In fact, I suspect you could exceed expectations by studying at your own pace. If you are not doing as much as you would, that is due to your own motivation. Tell me, are you not motivated to learn about Orizian culture?"

Oh, great, more guilt.

"I am interested. Greatly interested, actually. It's mostly that some other topics are more pressing."

"Like?"

I sigh. "Like... brewing potions to protect myself. Like learning about the Akrasia Games, so I can figure out how to save my sister."

Though my involvement in the Akrasia Games hasn't been a secret for months, and my sister's involvement is now pretty common knowledge as well, most people in the supernatural world don't react well to the casual mention of the games. I'm tired of beating around the bush, though, and for whatever reason, I trust this professor.

To his credit, he doesn't so much as blink at my divulgence.

"How about following the war, that—if I may be so bold—centers around your family."

My stomach twists. "I would love to understand more about what's going on with the war, but Laithe isn't very forthcoming. And it's not like there are any books I can study about events happening now."

"No, there are not. But have you considered the possibility that you might be thrust into that conflict soon? Wouldn't it be of utmost importance—behind your physical protection, of course—to understand as much about the culture and language of the world you are so entangled in?"

Apprehension curls in my gut. "Yes."

He smiles. "Wonderful. Now that's settled, let's see if we can get you caught up."

My private lesson with Professor Zyair lasts for a full ninety minutes and consists of monotonous repetition of strange words I've been trying my best to memorize.

"Good work today, Candice. I feel I have adequately motivated you to being serious about your Orizian studies, and so I'm confident you will make great strides this week. I'd also like you to write an essay. It can be on any topic regarding the culture. I'm sure your friend Laithe would be more than helpful on the matter. It won't require much studying. It's the translation that will be the most work. I would like it written in Orizian."

My eyes flare. "I don't know that many words—"

"You can write the essay in Earth English and translate each phrase. Use the English alphabet for now. Perhaps next week, I'll assign you to translate the English words into High Orizian symbols. That's also an important skill, but for now verbal understanding is priority."

I wrinkle my nose. That is not going to be fun. "All right. How long does it have to be?"

"Two pages."

I nod. "I have a few questions if you wouldn't mind diverting the topic for a few minutes."

"Of course not."

"This might be an odd question, so I hope it's okay. But are you nonbinary? Or what are you pronouns?"

His brow flicks up, but it's followed by an amused smile. "My species is genderless if that is what you mean."

"Yes. So, do you prefer to be referred to as they/them in English?"

He tilts his head.

"I ask because I've begun using those pronouns for Laithe, and I thought maybe you'd like the same?"

"Gender is meaningless to my people. You can refer to me in any way you like."

Same response Laithe first gave. "But saying 'he came to Elite Hall to instruct me' is incorrect, isn't it?"

"I suppose so."

"So, I will use genderless pronouns."

His smile deepens. "If you'd like."

Close enough. "Also, could you tell me more about the hierarchy of Oriziah? I understand that the High Orizians are accepted rulers but that hold is tentative at times. I don't know much about the other races."

"Certainly. I wouldn't call them races, but rather, they are entirely different types of beings. Species is more correct, though it doesn't always translate well based on Earth's understanding where there is only one high-order species. In Oriziah, there are dozens of sentient species with complex reasoning capabilities. Species with their own cultures and languages, capable of creating meaningful change to the overall society of Oriziah. I'd prefer using the term clans, for these subgroups, though it is slightly more complicated than that. Though these species do have a tentative hierarchy, you should be careful assuming any one group to be lesser than another."

I nod and begin taking notes.

Orizian clans.

"A majority of these clans willfully hold on to their more animalistic natures, but again, remember, they are not animals in the way humans tend to think of animals. They have the ability to create change within the world as a whole. These clans are predators who hunt prey, sometimes consisting of their own kind. To them, only the strongest thrive and are able to procreate. That is the essence of what drives them, and they have no desire for anything different. Some studies refer to that subsection of Orizians as the beastly class. I'm not a fan of such language, but you'll see it written on occasion."

Beastly. Scary but not beasts.

"This subsection tends to be the most supportive of the High Orizians."

My attention darts back up to them. "Oh," I mumble. "I hadn't expected that."

"If the only benefit of the High Orizians was their intelligence, they would not accept them as rulers. But the High Orizians also have powerful magic. These groups have no problem with a powerful race ruling the world. That being said, they also have no problem challenging them. If a rebellion begins, they join quickly just to see if the current structure will crumble under opposition. If the ruler's strength holds up, they back down and fall in line.

"On the opposite end of the spectrum, we have the Nahar. They are the spiritual leaders of the planet. Each of the three enlightened clans contributes a judge to create the Nahar Muhakham, which translates roughly to Bright Tribunal. That council is trusted even beyond the royal family."

Bright Tribunal. Spiritual judges.

"They make rulings like judges on Earth?" I ask.

"Only on spiritual matters. Have you done any studies on the Amelisian War?"

My brow pinches. "It sounds familiar. Is that the war that was resolved quietly and the rest of the interdimensional community doesn't fully understand how?"

I read about that war vaguely when I first started at Shadow Hills. The war and its resolution are shrouded in mystery.

"It is indeed. That is simply because the Bright Tribunal made a ruling based on the spirit of the people. Once the council made a firm ruling, the rebellion was dismantled."

"So," I say slowly. "What was the ruling? Or am I not meant to know?"

Their expression doesn't change. They're calm and cool, hands clasped together. "I will tell you only what is common knowledge, and perhaps you can fill in the missing pieces yourself. The core of the conflict was the belief that the royal bloodline was too diluted to be considered truly Orizian any longer and therefore they had no right to rule the planet. Can you wager a guess at what convinced the Bright Tribunal they were still true Orizians?"

My lips part. I look down at my notes, but there's nothing

there that would even hint at an answer to this question. Nothing I can figure out from this conversation at all. They still seem to assume I have the required pieces to solve the puzzle, though, so maybe it's beyond this session. I think through many of the things I've learned about Oriziah.

The spirit of the beast inside. Bea called it her "demon" side once.

She is also the one that explained, *to earn the love of your chosen is to earn your right to rule.* There's so much to unpack in that conversation and that topic, but even so, it all comes back to that one particular thing, doesn't it?

"V'rta," I mumble.

Professor Zyair doesn't respond, but their eyes turn bright and their lips spread into a wide grin.

That word, I learned when I was actively taking Orizian as a class, which simply means "chosen." But I'd learned previously that word is significant to Orizians. It's what they call their mates.

"The Bright Tribunal are only called upon in times of great trouble. When the very structure of society is called into question."

"Has the Bright Tribunal been called for the current conflict?"

"No." Their eyes remain steady on mine. "Not yet."

17
ANOTHER TEST

Manuela's wink that morning is my only hint that her plan is still on.

In the last three days, I've continued working on potions as usual, as well as doubling my Orizian studies after that loaded conversation with my professor, meanwhile trying very, very hard not to show how anxious I am.

Today, I will meet with Manuela's "contact" who supposedly knows how to end the games for good. Today, I will put my own safety at risk for information.

I'm thrilled and terrified.

My deal with Manuela involves keeping information from Jarron, but she never said anything about Lola and Janet, so they're fully aware of my plans for the day and will be waiting for my return before dinner. If I don't show, they'll run straight to Laithe for help.

That, at least, makes me feel a little bit better about trusting Manuela.

I might still fall into a trap, but at least someone will know what happened. Cheery thoughts, I know.

So far today, I've drunk a bit too much coffee and forced some eggs and bacon down my throat to balance it out. I've been parked in an armchair in the sunroom, pretending to read a book on Orizian clans that I very much should actually be reading.

Only Stassi has stopped for chitchat, and that was before he was distracted by a lanky redhead who smiled in his direction.

I've been sitting alone for the last hour, and it's starting to drive me insane. We didn't ever make any specific plans. Am I supposed to do something? Go somewhere? When exactly will the meeting take place?

No idea.

I'm just sitting here, waiting to learn how I'll meet with some possible ally and find out if the risk is worth the reward.

So, I'm on edge, leg bouncing eagerly for hours.

Finally, at a quarter till noon, maybe a half hour after my nerves have calmed enough to actually focus on my High Orizian book, Manuela strolls by again. She grins and places a normal-looking key on the chair next to me.

She glances at her watch. "Meeting begins in thirty minutes. I'm curious if you can figure it out on your own." She winks, and then walks away.

"What?" I exclaim, but she's already halfway down the hall.

"I'll be in the library if you need a hint."

More tests. What is it with this one that I need to prove myself all the time? I huff out my annoyance, but then I grab the key and leap to my first assumption—the bronze doors.

Or maybe I'm only hoping it's the bronze doors because I'm still secretly desperate to know what's behind them. At least one holds a portal, which I'm not enthusiastic about, but it would also make a lot of sense for the situation. The others, I have no idea.

So, I rush to the very end of the hall, past Jarron's room, and stop in the middle of the hall with seven bronze doors.

One is my workshop. The rest are a mystery I'm eager to solve. I first take a long look at the key. It's got a sort of bronze sheen to it but otherwise looks just like a regular door key. The kind not often used in magical places.

With no hints, I have no choice but to guess.

I start on the left because I have no clue which will be the correct door, and I plan to go one by one until a lock clicks open.

Except, the key doesn't fit into the slot.

I try all seven doors— not even a close fit.

There aren't any extra doors in Jarron's room, so that's a no-go. I could try Manuela's room, but the thought of entering it while she's not there is enough to give me the stress sweats. No thanks. That'll be a last resort.

Where else could she be sending me?

And why would she test me? There has to be some kind of hint somewhere, maybe in our previous conversations. She mentioned portals. She mentioned there was a portal behind one of the bronze doors. But if it's not those, what else could it be?

I narrow my eyes. Maybe the clue isn't the door but the person I'll be meeting. Though she gave very little information, there is one person that crossed my mind during that conversation.

How could I help someone with my specific influence? Who would be in danger if Jarron knew where they were?

Mr. Vandozer is a possibility, but unless she's leading me into a legitimate trap, he could not be my contact. I'd betray my promise to Manuela in a second if that's who she wants me to protect.

But there's a much more reasonable answer to that riddle.

I look down at the key. There's really nothing behind this except a hunch, but I may as well try it out.

I walk back toward Jarron's room, but I turn down a secondary hall and stop at a room that's been abandoned for months. I waste no time sliding the key into the hole and turning it smoothly. The door to Princess Beatrice's old room clicks open.

~

I hold my breath as the door to Bea's room swings open, but I release it when I find it's completely empty. And not just empty but dusty. No one has been in here for months, it seems.

I narrow my eyes. I solved the puzzle, but I don't seem to be any closer to the answers I need. What now?

It's unnervingly silent. The air completely still.

Until I reach the center of the room, where I feel a buzzing warmth.

I frown and spin around, searching for a sign of something magical. The room is the same as I remember it, besides the layer of dust. The far wall is covered in massive windows looking out over the mountains in the distance. The room itself is similar to Jarron's but slightly smaller.

The tiny magical charge is the only hint I can find.

So, I follow the feeling, like a stupid game of hot-cold.

I move toward the couches by the bright open windows—the air gets colder. I step back and try toward the dresser against the wall—warmer. I step again. And again. Until the buzzing increases. Just a subtle vibration of magic coming from the full-length mirror.

I swallow. Do I really have to walk through a portal disguised as a mirror?

And if so, was this always a portal? I shiver at the thought. I'd once spent over an hour in this room, trying on formal gowns and having my hair done by the demon princess for the banquet where I was presented as Jarron's girlfriend.

I stare at my reflection in the mirror—faded dark marks decorate my throat. They used to be bright red.

I looked past my reflection's shoulders only to notice that, though it's light and distant, it is most definitely not Bea's bedroom. I turn to peer over my shoulder in the real world, checking to be sure I haven't already transported somehow, but no, I'm still in her room, dusty but brightly lit. Mirror-me is somewhere else, though, and the longer I stare, the more obvious it becomes.

I take another step toward the mirror and reach out. The glass ripples like water when my fingertips come into contact with it. Dammit, I really do have to step through a mirror, don't I?

I study the environment behind mirror-me. There's a balcony overlooking black cliffs, with shifting waters below. The sky is dark but reddish and scattered with stars and twin moons.

My chest tightens, but so does my resolve as I come to grips with the fact that I will be stepping into Oriziah for the first time.

This is reckless, but there is no chance I'm turning around now.

I'm not afraid of Bea. Even though she led me to the Akrasia Games the last time around, which is proof enough I shouldn't trust her, but Manuela was right.

Not only could she have the information I desperately need, but she also needs me in return. I have leverage here.

If Bea kills me or sets up a trap that delivers me to the Cosmic Council, she will never, *ever* be free in her world while Jarron lives. She'd have to put all of her eggs in the rebellion. A rebellion I don't suspect her betrothed agrees with, considering he's currently working with Jarron to stop it.

With me as an ally, Bea has a chance to earn forgiveness for her crimes. The bad blood could be washed away. She could be free again. An honored and beloved princess, instead of a fugitive.

My confidence rises. I can do this.

I just need to make sure she always believes she has a chance. No matter what she says, what her plan is, I have to at least pretend to be on board until I get back to the school.

I need to learn how to end the games once and for all. There has to be a way to finish this and free my sister without being part of the corrupt system and sacrificing innocent people for my own gain.

I take in one final deep breath.

Then, I step through the mirror into an entirely new world.

18
WELCOME TO HELL

The air is heavy and thick, causing my lungs to seize in the first moments on the black sands of Oriziah. There is a beach with crashing waves in the distance and the rattling of strange creatures somewhere in the background. Above, the dark-red sky is covered with beautiful stars and two orange moons. It's icy cold, despite there being no wind at all.

My lungs catch up to the change in pressure, but my limbs are shivering uncontrollably.

I don't get the chance to examine more of this world, though, because the shadows a few yards away begin slithering.

The portal didn't place me on the balcony as expected. Instead, I'm out in the open, on the ground between two large rocky mountains. Vulnerable. Alone. And I have no idea where to go.

The hair on my arms rise slowly. I swallow, fear pulses through my limbs, and that's before all sound halts.

I can no longer hear the strange buzzing or crashing waves.

Air rushes over my skin, and I spin to see what caused it just to have a nightmare come to life before my eyes. The darkness is

STACEY TROMBLEY

thick, and all-consuming and yet somewhere I can see it slithering. Coiling, ready to strike.

Black magic swirls and hisses, pooling together until it gathers into the form of a massive beast towering over me.

I stumble back a step, limbs now quaking for an entirely different reason.

Red eyes blink in the center of the shadow's head. The monster doesn't immediately attack, and I wish that were good news but instead, it turns its head to watch as two more shadow monsters form behind him. He was just waiting for backup.

I can't breathe. I don't know where to go.

My mind clouds with panic. I try to remember my defenses. I have my obsidian blade and a few potions—but I have no idea if they would work on these things.

Without missing another beat, I whip out the blade and hold it out. I hope these things don't notice how much it trembles in my grip, but I get the feeling they're not concerned with my attempt at defense, regardless of my terror.

They glide toward me, spreading out so they're surrounding me. Cornering me.

They click and hiss to each other, and I press my eyes closed tightly. My life doesn't flash before them; I'm too terrified for that. I just brace for the pain.

The hissing rises to a crescendo, closer and closer.

Until a deafening roar pierces the air around me. My legs buckle, and I fall to my knees in the sand so coarse it's painful, tiny particles scratching at my skin like glass. A new beast rises behind me.

I can feel it.

The rumbling of ancient magic. The crunch of powerful steps, shaking the ground.

A blast of magic blows my hair forward, and I almost fall face first into the uncomfortable sand. I peek up to find the shadow beasts shrinking back, almost as if—cowering.

They hiss and grumble, hunched over near me.

The new beast steps even closer, sand crunching beneath their taloned feet.

Tears stream down my cheeks.

My muscles clench in anticipation as the monster reaches me. But instead of carving into my flesh, the talon-tipped hands gently grab me by the waist.

I gasp as my body is jerked up and leaves the ground. Leathery wings flap three times, and then I am dropped onto a stone platform only feet above the shadow beasts.

Still panicked beyond all reason, heart pounding so hard it hurts, I look up to find myself on the balcony I'd first assumed I would arrive on.

And a High Orizian, with pale leathery wings, paces in front of me.

19
THE TEA IS PIPING HOT

The winged beast paces back and forth in front of me while I attempt not to die of a heart attack. There is a cave-like room beyond the balcony that's too dark to make out from here.

"Come," the monster growls then stalks into the shadows. There is a feline grace to its movements. Though its coloring is reminiscent of Mr. Vandozer's, it's much smaller. Possibly feminine? I've never seen a female Orizian in demon form, though, so it's more or less a guess.

If this is Bea, is that good news? Minutes ago, I was prepared to meet with her. Now, I'm ready to sob myself into a puddle.

Another moment of sucking in panicked breaths, and then I finally gather enough courage to follow the demon into the darkness, where I find a cozy room lit only by a few candles with blue flame.

There is a basin of water, a shelf filled with liquids—potions, I assume—a stone table with two stone chairs, and a velvet couch. The latter feels a bit out of place, to be honest.

"Sit," the demon growls at me with that echoey voice.

I obey, dropping like lead into the stone chair, limbs shivering uncontrollably.

The demon growls in frustration, her wings contracting and flaring several times.

Then, her head falls back, and her spine arches. She cries out as magic shimmers over her body.

Only a moment later, the beautiful, Gothic Snow White stands behind me, panting.

Her lips are painted red, and her pointed eyes are rimmed in dark liner with shimmering white accents. Perfect makeup even in this situation.

"What the hell, Candice?" Bea pants. "Why did you show up like that? Do you know what almost happened?"

I swallow. One look at me should make it quite obvious that I know exactly what almost happened to me. I'm still trembling fiercely from the encounter. "Yeah," I breathe. "I know."

She sighs, running her fingers through her hair nervously. It's then I notice that her hands are shaking too.

"Manuela sent me," I force out. "She—she didn't. She said you knew I was coming."

"Yes, well, you're early." She huffs. "Early enough that my sentries nearly devoured you before I even knew you were on your way."

She looks me up and down, and I try my best not to appear like a weak little human in fetal position. I need to be strong. I just don't know how.

"You've been bitten," she comments mutely.

For a moment, I think she means by the shadow beasts, but her eyes linger on my neck. My hand rises to Jarron's bite marks.

"That's the only reason the sentries paused long enough for me to arrive."

I don't respond, mind still spinning.

"We have a lot to discuss, clearly. Let me get you a tonic before you sully my rug with piss."

I cough, but somehow manage enough energy to be annoyed. "If I haven't peed myself yet, I doubt I will now."

She chuckles but doesn't respond otherwise. She combines a few liquids into a ceramic mug that are steaming in an instant and then sets it in front of me. "Drink. It will calm your nerves."

I wrinkle my nose both at the bitter scent and the idea that I need help not being a trembling fool.

"Most *demons* would have pissed themselves if faced by those nightmares," she says as if she knows exactly what I'm thinking. "Let alone humans. Give yourself credit—you were less fearful than expected."

"Sure, yeah, that makes me feel better." Still, I sip the bitter liquid.

"It has been a long time," she comments, taking a quick sip of her own steaming mug.

I blink, trying to reorient myself. I'm meeting with a possible ally. A girl who has betrayed me in the past.

"It has," I agree.

"I wasn't sure I believed that you would come. I always knew you were fierce and brave, but I suppose I should stop underestimating you."

I resist the urge to roll my eyes again. "I'm not sure I can trust the sincerity of that compliment."

Her red lips curve up. "I can understand that. But it is sincere. For the record, I'm sorry for my role in your harm. Your sister's too."

I frown. "What exactly was your role in that?"

My sister was targeted by an older demon, who believed her to be the crown prince's chosen mate. He manipulated her into the Akrasia Games, where she could have died. So far as I know,

Bea had no role in that. What she did do, was get me an invitation into the Akrasia Games when I was seeking information on them.

Bea huffs and sits in the chair across from me. "Getting to the point quickly, I see." Her eyes drift to the stone table, distant and somber. "My role in your harm was simply that I invited you to the game initiation."

"Which is exactly what I was hoping for at the time."

"But it nearly resulted in your and Jarron's death."

Nothing new there, except the apology. "So how about your role in my sister's harm?" Anticipation coils in my stomach.

She presses her lips together and looks down at her lap. "I—" She closes her mouth and takes in a long breath. "I intended to confess this information to you during this meeting, but it's harder than I expected to get the words out. This is my most shameful act. The crime that haunts me."

My stomach sinks, but finally, my mind is sharp and in the moment. The only thing I'm concerned with is the demoness in front of me and whatever damning information she's about to spill.

"I am the one who told Vincent... about Jarron choosing a mate."

My blood runs cold at that admission. My mind spins, trying to put all the pieces together. Someone told Vincent Vandozer that Liz was Jarron's mate, which is why he targeted her, but we never knew who began the rumors.

The identity of a High Orizian's chosen mate is supposed to be a sacred secret until the mateship is accepted.

Which means, if Bea is the one that passed along this information then she's the one responsible for *all of this*. That's what she's telling me.

My lungs squeeze, making it hard to breathe.

"Drink," she whispers.

I wince. I've already taken a sip and felt the brief relief, but I can't help but wonder if it's safe.

"I will not harm you, I swear it. I understand you questioning my motives and my morality, but I also believe you know that I need your help."

I force the hot mug up to my lips and gulp down the tonic. The liquid burns my throat, but the moment it warms my chest, my tension eases.

I breathe deeply, trying to help the soothing feeling take root.

"Why should I trust you? Or help you, for that matter, if you're the one that caused all of this?" I try to remind myself that I need to keep her on my good side, or there would be literally no reason for her not to kill me. She needs to think I can be an ally, not an enemy.

She winces. "My information made it possible, yes. And I'm sincerely sorry about that. It was a mistake. A terrible mistake. But I did not know what Vincent would do with the information. I didn't know about the games or his schemes for an uprising. I had no idea he would go after your sister. I didn't even know that's what happened until far too late."

I take another long pull of the tonic, allowing the calming nature to relax my body and mind so I can think clearly. "Why then?" I ask. "Why did you tell him?"

She sighs. "Because I was a foolish child. Both cocky that I knew something he didn't and bitter because you got the better prince."

My eyes widen. "The better prince?"

She shrugs. "I was naive. Selfish. Stupid. I loved Trevor, but this was before I'd let him mark me. Before I felt his devotion and the rightness of our bond. I'd been raised to believe I deserved to be a princess. Jarron could give me the right to rule; Trevor could not. I was jealous."

"And so, you enacted a plan to become queen anyway."

"No," she stammers. "No, I never had that intention. As much as I was an egotistical idiot, I'd never have wanted to harm Jarron. Ever."

"You understand why that's hard to believe?"

"I do. And it's a doubt you would not be alone in. In fact, Vincent made that assumption from the beginning. He assumed that I'd be on board with his plans because it would give me access to that one massive step up in power. The one I'd missed out on when I was chosen by the second prince instead of the heir. Trevor is absolutely wonderful. I adore him. And I no longer believe I am entitled to any of it. I don't know that I even want it, at this point. I don't deserve it. I've hurt so many people, and for what?" She runs her fingers through her hair, her expression clearly showing pain.

My heart aches for her. A strange feeling for someone I should hate.

I believe her, I realize.

At least a little bit. She's seeing the error she made and how it's affected her. She'll do what she can to fix it and reverse the damage. Does that mean she wouldn't do it again? I don't know.

"I told Vincent about what happened at Myre Island," she says, eyes still cast down. "I told him with certainty that Jarron had imprinted that night. I didn't think it would mean anything. It never crossed my mind that he would pursue Jarron's chosen. The idea is disgusting, truthfully. But Vincent has been off for years. Some of his family believe—well, something happened to him to cause this shift. His soul is damaged."

She shakes her head.

"I don't know for certain," she says. "But I didn't realize the darkness of his nature at first. He was a mentor. A teacher. I trusted him. And I sincerely had no idea what he would do with the information. He prodded me for more over the next year, and

I didn't realize at the time that he was trying to pinpoint who Jarron had imprinted on. None of us knew for certain who his chosen was, but it was obvious it was one of the two Montgomery sisters. That information was easy to reveal. After that, it was just speculation. But it got to a point that he began to scare me. He must have been doing research on you two for years. He was making plans, learning what he could about you. I know this because I didn't give him a name until the end of the school year, a couple of weeks before your sister died."

I frown. "So, you gave him Liz's name?"

She nods. "He was pressuring me and began threatening to tell Jarron what I'd told him. He knew Jarron would hate me for it. It would change everything. But Vincent was so determined I knew which one it was. He clearly had an idea in his head as well. He hinted he thought it had to be Liz. I think he wanted it to be true. She was an easier target. She was more pliable and desired power in a way you never showed interest in. So, I blurted out her name.

"She was apparently planning to enroll at Shadow Hills, did you hear about that? Turns out Vincent believed the moment she entered the school, Jarron would scoop her up and he'd miss his chance, so he pounced the summer before. I wish I'd known that at the time, what he planned. But even after the games happened and Liz was announced as dead, I knew I couldn't say anything. Vincent could ruin me anytime he chose, and he reminded me of that repeatedly. I was wrong, but I didn't know how to fix it by then. Even if Liz was the wrong sister, it would be close enough to the truth that Jarron would know where the information came from, and I'd lose everything. That ended up happening anyway, and to be honest, I deserve it." She takes in a long breath and holds it for three full seconds before releasing it. "Again, I'm sorry. I'm very sorry for my ignorance and pride and how my actions have hurt you and your family so deeply."

My head pounds. Should I hate her for this?

Should I include her in my list of names to destroy in retribution? Is it worth betraying Manuela for that?

Princess Beatrice still has information I need. She has access to ending the games. Something good can come from this, even if the bad can never be erased.

"You have information," I blurt out. "Manuela said you can help me to end the games. Is that true?"

She nods slowly. "I have information that can help you. I have to be honest with you, though. I'd truly love to see the end of the Akrasia Games, but I am also in a difficult situation. Just talking to you puts me at risk. I want what you want, but I have to negotiate something in return."

"Okay." I frown. "What do you need in return?" I quietly pray that all she needs is for me to convince Jarron not to harm her. I can do that. Maybe it won't be easy, but I can and will convince him that Bea can be an ally. If she needs *more* than that—

"I need you to promise not to hurt me."

I flinch. "Why would I?"

"It's difficult to explain, without revealing—" She shakes her head. Her jaw clenches before she meets my eye. "This is the secret to ending the games. The magic that binds it all together will be erased for good... if you kill every single member of the Cosmic Council before they can replenish."

My brows pinch. "Replenish?"

"So long as one member remains, new members can be sworn in. For example, Jarron killed three in the caves a few weeks ago, but they've already been replaced."

That's the secret? She revealed it just like that? "So, all ten need to be killed at once?"

"They need to be killed before any realize what's happening and flee." She nods.

I swallow, already thinking through possible plans for how to make that work.

"And I need you to make me that promise." She places her palm over her lips, like she's afraid to utter these next words. Then, she finally whispers, "Because I'm one of them. I'm part of the Cosmic Council."

20

THAT FINE LINE GOES BOTH WAYS

I stare wide eyed at Bea. Her admission hangs thicker between us than the Orizian air surrounding me.

"You..."

She closes her eyes. "I told you he had a grip over my whole life. He could have ruined me at any point, especially once I told him Liz was Jarron's chosen. Everyone would believe I'd betrayed Jarron and I would be banished. I had no choice but to join the Cosmic Council. At least, I thought. In truth, if I'd known the full scope of his plans, I would have just come clean and hoped for the best. I'd have helped Jarron and Trevor protect you two from Vincent. But instead, I did the cowardly thing and accepted his invitation. I knew it was bad. Knew it was corrupt. But I didn't understand what the Akrasia Games truly were until I watched it play out. They haunt me to this day. Maybe I should be content with just dying alongside the others for being part of it, but I'm a coward. And I am not ready to die." Her voice breaks on those words.

There's compassion in my heart, even as rage burns in my veins.

"I'm a villain, I know, but I don't want to be." She sniffs.

I've admitted to myself, more than once, that she and I are similar. I once thought I might have ended up like her if I'd been born with power.

Would I have done what Bea did?

I don't think so, but how can I know for sure?

Do I believe her exclamation that she is "so sorry" for what she's done? Or is that a ploy to get me on her side? She could just go all in with the rebellion and become the queen if she can kill Jarron. Then again, Trevor is against the rebellion. He's sided with Jarron. Maybe that's why she's coming to me now.

This is hard. Harder than I'd expected.

I can't trust her, can I?

So, then, why do I want to?

I wish I could talk to Liz, get her perspective on what happened and why. I wish I could see the things Bea said to the council and to Liz. I wish I knew more.

"Do you think you were right?" I whisper, my own selfish insecurities coming out.

"Right?"

"About Liz. Do you think you chose correctly."

Her eyebrows rise. "Do you remember in the school when I told you I was betting on you?"

I nod.

"I didn't mean in the games."

"You—" I shake my head, trying to regain my focus. Is she saying she was betting that I am Jarron's chosen? And what exactly does that mean?

"No one can figure it out for you, Candice. As much as Vincent is delusionally convinced Liz is the right one, we may never know for certain. Only Jarron and his mate will have that assurance."

My shoulders slump. "It's such a strange tradition to hold your culture on."

Her lips curl. "It is, but there is no force more powerful in our world."

I run my fingers through my hair. "Wait." My mind spins back to the previous topic. "You told me the answer I came for, without any assurance I'll make you that promise."

She nods. "I didn't see any other way. You weren't going to agree until you heard what I had to give."

"But it's impossible. If you're one of them, how do I kill all of the council members, without killing you?"

She's set me up for failure. Does she expect me not to notice that?

"Or... do you plan to give up your spot before our plan is enacted?" And if so, to who? And why hasn't she done it already? Whoever she chooses would have an automatic death sentence.

She sighs. "It's a challenge, but not impossible. I cannot give up my place in the council yet, or else I'd have no way to know where they will be or how to contact them. I will give you that information once you agree not to harm me. That's why I feel content in telling you the answer because you still need me. I can tell you there's a meeting in three week's time, that's how long we'll have to prepare. You and I can work together to end the games."

Three weeks. I could save my sister in three weeks. "Without Jarron knowing."

"Correct," she says. "He wouldn't trust me. And I wouldn't trust him, not with this. He'd just kill me alongside the others."

I could still do that too. Does she really trust me enough not to betray her?

She winces. "This only works while you're not linked with him."

Those words echo in my mind. *This only works while you're not linked to him.*

I don't fully understand the relevance, but it sits on my chest heavily. "You're telling me, I have to stay unbonded?"

She pauses, then sighs. "Not just unbonded, but unlinked. A bond is irreversible, a mark isn't. Even Trevor and I aren't bonded yet. But a temporary link, like a claiming mark, would give him access to your emotions and your whereabouts. He'll figure it out. It's another thing that will piss him off when he finds out. If he learns of this plot of ours, he'll assume I'm just trying to keep you from him. That would also be strongly frowned upon in our culture."

I press my lips together tightly. She's certainly being very forthcoming with me, but the Bea I know is manipulative. Is she living out enough consequences that she's growing as a person?

Or is this all part of the game?

It does sound suspicious that she's actively trying to keep me from accepting a mark from Jarron.

"You just said I need to figure out about who his true chosen is on my own. Isn't a mark the way to do that?" I tilt my head.

"It is. And it would be wrong of me to tell you not to do it, but please understand that my life relies on you waiting. If you want to take this information back to Jarron, you can tell me now. I swear I will not harm you. You know a way to end the games; maybe that's enough for you. I can find a replacement for my spot on the council and a new hiding place. If that's what you want to do, that's fine. Just please tell me so I can protect myself."

I tap my knee, considering. "No," I say finally. "No, that's not what I want."

I'm uncertain if I can trust Bea. But I never got the feeling she was out to harm me. Even when she gave me the Akrasia Games invite, she was hesitant, and I had gone to *her* asking about them. She has done some terrible things, though, and she enjoys having the upper hand.

It's possible the last few months have humbled her greatly, but that's not something I can rely on.

"I need some time to think about this. But I will promise not to tell Jarron until I tell you one way or another."

She lets out a breath. "Fair enough."

She guides me back out to balcony, to the portal mirror, facing the pit below where I was almost eaten.

"Don't ever drop in unannounced," she warns, shifting the mirror so it's facing the safe flat stone of the overhang.

As I step through the portal, the last thing I see is Bea grinning wide. My stomach sinks.

I better not be getting played.

21

DEBRIEFING

I enter my workshop directly after returning to the school via portal, mind buzzing and eyes stuck to the ground, but I'm shocked into reality when I see Janet pacing back and forth, with Lola soaring in anxious circles over her head.

"Candice!" they exclaim in unison. Lola reaches me first, slamming into my chest, and Janet throws her arms around my shoulders, squishing us all together.

"Whoa," I mutter. "I wasn't gone that long!"

"It's almost sundown," Janet practically screeches in my ear. Lola mumbles something unintelligible between us. "We were about to go to Laithe."

"How..." I look around, but there are no windows in the workshop, so I can't double check. It's a moot point anyway. Who is more likely to mistake the time? The person who was just in another world, obviously.

"Time moves different there." Janet sighs. "We couldn't really estimate how long it would take. How long was it for you?"

"An hour, maybe two. I was almost munched by some shadow nightmare creatures." I shiver. "But Bea saved me, and we had a good, long talk." I shake my head, still feeling over-whelmed, almost numb really.

Janet now notices my shell-shocked state, guides me over to the armchairs, and turns on the fire with a flick of her wrist. "Do you need anything? A tonic? Tea? Soda?"

"I haven't eaten anything in a while."

"Food!" Lola chirps. "I'm on it." She darts toward the door but comes back only seconds later. It's easy to order food here in Elite Hall.

"How did it go?" Janet sits in the chair across from me and leans forward.

"Interesting. I—well, I guess I got what I went for, but it's not like it was an automatic solution. It's going to be tough. And complicated."

They console me for a moment before the food arrives, and we talk casually about the situation while we chomp on the BBQ chicken pizza Lola ordered.

I give them a quick rundown of what Bea told me, and I'm already feeling much better now that I have food in my system.

"So, you just have to kill ten anonymous, powerful beings all at once. Sounds easy." Janet rolls her eyes. Sarcasm isn't common for her.

"But don't forget that you have to kill them all but can't kill them all because you need to agree not to kill the one who gave you the information," Lola says, with her chin up.

I chuckle at their reaction. "That's exactly what I learned, yeah. But Bea will give me access to the powerful beings and insider information on who they are and what their powers are. So long as I promise not to kill her."

"I mean, sure. But you also have to do it without Jarron's help completely. How are you planning to do that?"

I sigh. "Potions?"

"It's possible but won't be easy; you're right. I really, really don't like that you have to keep all of this from Jarron." Janet shifts in her seat. "Are you sure you can't just tell him the truth and convince him we need Bea's help? He'd do anything for you."

I grimace. "Maybe. Maybe I could convince him, but I don't think he'll trust her enough to work with her. So, we'll be back to killing ten anonymous powerful beings, without any access to knowing who they are or where they'll be. That's an impossible mission. And I can't just let them keep control of my sister."

"So..." Lola says softly. "You're planning to go along with her plan?"

"I don't know." Do I have a choice?

We sit in silence for another few minutes.

"Well, let's talk it through, then," Janet says.

"Yeah," Lola agrees, darting up and flying around us each before settling onto a perch on the coffee table.

Janet leans forward, a serious expression on her face. "If you tell Jarron, you are pretty convinced he won't allow you to work with Bea."

"Based on the things she told me today, I think he'll kill her."

They gasp together. I tell them about her confession, of being the one to have told Vincent about Jarron imprinting.

"She's the one responsible for all of this?" Lola whispers, expression one of sincere distress.

"Not responsible," I say, realizing I'm taking Bea's words sincerely to heart and using them to defend her. "She was the catalyst, yes, and obviously that holds weight, but if I believe her full story—" I tilt my head, considering. "And I think I do."

I blink several times, letting that new truth settle in.

"If I believe her story, then she didn't think anything bad was going to happen from spilling the secret. She was being bratty and prideful and stupid, but it wasn't malicious."

"But that doesn't make it okay."

"No, but it makes her redeemable, doesn't it?"

"If you say so." Janet crosses her arms.

Lola flies in a circle then hovers between me and Janet. "Okay, so if you don't tell Jarron and you wager everything on Bea, what happens? You have to hide the truth from Jarron, but can we make sure you stay as safe as possible?"

I nod slowly. "It means I can't let him mark me, not until this is over."

They both still.

"If I were to accept a mark, he'd know when I go to meet her. He'd know I'd been to see her already. I wouldn't be able to keep it a secret." I don't actually know how much he'd be able to read through just a single mark, but I am certain he'd at least know when I left the planet and when I was in any danger, which obviously is a good thing on many levels, but in this case—

Lola sits cross-legged on her perch on the coffee table. "How long?" she asks. "How long would you have to keep pushing him away?"

I wince at that comment. That's not what I'm doing, is it?

"Three weeks," I answer. "She intends to enact the plan in three weeks."

"That's not too long," Lola says happily.

"Yeah, I mean, it could be worse. He's not even around anyway." Janet presses her forefingers against her lips as she thinks. "We can tell Jarron right before it all happens." Her eyes light up at that idea.

My brow furrows. I'm not so sure I agree.

"What?" she asks. "You make all the plans; it'd be all set. He'd have no choice but to go with it to protect you and make sure everything works out. Right?"

"Yeah, maybe."

"You don't want him to?" Lola guesses.

"No! No, I want him to be there for sure. I just think we'll run into the same problem. Bea will be a part of this. He'll just kill her along with the rest."

Janet's lips part, but then she shuts them.

"What?"

"Is that... the worst thing in the world?"

My stomach sinks, then shock sets in. Janet thinks we should kill Bea?

"I mean, look, I don't want anyone to die who doesn't have to, but she's just as much a part of this as the rest of them. She deserves punishment as much as anyone. So, if we're all on board for killing off the bad guys here, it certainly shouldn't be a deal-breaker that she's included in that."

Logically, that makes sense. "I see your point," I say slowly, working it out in my own mind and heart. "Part of me doesn't want to do that, though. I mean if she has to die, then, yeah, for sure. I'll choose my sister over Bea any day, but there's some-thing deep down that makes me really not want to betray her."

"Intuition?" Lola asks.

I frown, looking down at my hands.

"Do you think she'll know it if you plan to betray her at the last second? Do you think it'll turn out worse for you?"

"I don't know," I whisper. I guess it could be that. I do have a strong intuition, but I've never used it for anything other than potions work before. I don't really consider it as an actual form of magic, but that doesn't mean it can't be helpful. "I don't know what it is. Just, something is telling me that it's a bad idea."

"How about this, then," Janet says. "We go along with Bea's plan, but if she makes you swear something, you make sure it's vague. Make sure it gives you some leniency to tell Jarron if worse comes to worst. Don't promise you will never let harm come to her or something, you know? You have to be able to tell Jarron to protect yourself, or it's not worth it at all."

I nod absently.

"And our secret bond remains." She holds out her arm where the tiny mark sits on her tan skin. The three of us swore a secret bond a few weeks ago. It'd hurt us, if we ever spoke the secret aloud. "If you ever get into trouble, you use it."

My eyes widen. "Use it?"

"You start saying the secret out loud. It's gonna hurt like hell, but it will notify Lola and me that something is very wrong, and we'll come and find you. We will tell Jarron, instead of you. That's how you stay safe in all of this."

I look to Lola, eyes still wide. She looks equally as impressed as I am.

"You're fucking genius," I tell Janet. And I mean it.

Hope wells in my chest. This plan is going to work. I can feel it.

22

BEHIND ALIEN EYES

The act of wooing a chosen mate is a delicate process for High Orizians. It requires more than the flaunting of beautiful feathers like a peacock. It is deeper.

These demons play the long game.

They will court their mate slowly to avoid scaring them.

Inside the alien being, everything is focused on the object of his adoration, but he cannot expose those powerful emotions until the right time.

He must work to become everything she wants because it is ultimately she who chooses. She has the power in the relationship.

These commanding emotions can be difficult for High Orizians to cope with when they are in this phase of life. Waiting is the hardest part when one's very soul is on the line.

This is where the cultural tradition of V'charin began.

The High Orizian will throw their passion and excess energy into the building of a house specifically for his chosen. They fill it with everything their future mate loves. Her style, her smell, her favorite colors, her hobbies.

It is a soothing act to allow the demon to visualize his future life— if he is lucky enough to earn a mate's love. While he waits, he can surround himself with her essence.

Eventually, his hunt will begin, and it will not end until the day she accepts the bond or formally rejects him.

Until that day, he will remain in a state of constant planning and worrying. The burden is his alone to carry. For failure is his worst fear.

The acceptance of his mate is his very reason for being. Everything else is secondary.

23

THE DEMON BY MY BED

My eyes fly open from the dead of sleep. The room is pitch black, and a chill washes over my whole body.

I am flooded by paralyzing fear.

Growling reverberates through the whole room.

What if it's not Jarron? What if it's someone else? Someone that's been stalking me. Taunting me. Someone who most definitely does not want something good.

What if these are my last moments alive?

My heart races. My mind spins with fear.

Don't let fear control you.

"Jarron," I force out, "is that you?"

The growling softens. "My bright one awakens for me?"

I gasp at the sound of his rumbling voice. "I'm awake," I say breathlessly.

The weight of his powerful magic settles over me and sends a shiver down my spine. The silhouette of a massive black body appears beside me, looming over me.

A sharp talon glistens in the moonlight as it nears me. My breath sticks in my lungs, and I cannot move.

The claw catches on the fabric of the sheet over my body and tugs. The silky blanket slides against the bare skin of my thighs, all the way to my feet, until I'm exposed to the monster beside my bed.

"So beautiful," he purrs.

I shiver again.

"Do I scare you, bright one?" His soft tone is so foreign from a demon filled with terror-inducing power. "I do not wish to scare you. Do you want me to leave—"

"No!" I say quickly, jerking up only to realize that puts me inches from his fangs. "Don't go." I'm hypnotized by those all-black eyes.

Immense fear rushes through my body, but the feeling is not entirely bad. In fact, I want more of it.

"Do you want me to change forms?" he purrs. "It is hard for me currently, but I can if you are too afraid."

"No," I answer, still not backing away. "You don't have to change." I lie back against the silk sheets, the demon leaning over me, closer and closer.

His clawed hand rises. His breaths are labored. "Do you fear me?" he whispers.

"Yes," I say breathlessly.

He winces and pulls back.

"But don't stop."

I squirm beneath the weight of his magic. He hasn't physically touched me yet, and to be honest, it's possible the touch would be painful, but this feeling pulsing through every inch of my body is building such incredible anticipation.

I don't know what I'm doing here. I can't believe the delicious desire flooding me at the literal monster hovering over me. Why do I like this?

I close my eyes and tilt my head back, arching toward him.

There is something very wrong with me, but the responding purr tells me he very much likes this kinky part of me.

His claw taps gently against my chest. I flinch at the sharp contact. He slowly, gently, slides his claw down my skin toward the hem of my tank. I whimper, helpless, knowing I should not be enjoying how close I am to being carved wide open.

Death teases me, but it's so riveting that I greet him with open arms.

A ripping sound sends my eyes flying open again, and I suck in a breath as cool air hits my bare torso. His talon easily slices through the fabric.

He purrs again, pleased with his work.

"You like this?" he asks.

"Yes," I pant. I think I'm certifiably insane here, but damn if it doesn't feel good. Should it? Probably not.

"The desire building in your body is so beautiful, bright one. I never imagined such a beautiful sight would be mine to behold, and yet I know there is so much more to come."

He licks his lips, tongue black as the night clinging to him.

My desire is building but so is the reality that I do not know where this will lead if I allow it.

"Can you—can you turn back now?" I ask, caving to those legitimate concerns.

The demon pauses, looking me over one final time. Then, he closes his eyes and remains frozen for several moments.

I wait, still panting, still so close to being exposed to him.

This terrifying demon who cares deeply for me, who I trust so fully I'd not only allow myself to be vulnerable to him, but to enjoy every second of the terror.

Finally, magic shimmers over his body, and then he is Jarron. Sharp cheekbones, tan skin, and dark brooding eyes. He lets out one breath in this form, before I fist the lapel of his shirt and tug him to me. He gives no resistance and falls against me.

His lips meet mine fiercely and somehow softly all at once. I wrap my free arm around back of his neck and pull him in tighter, seeking more and more of him. His lips explore mine. Our tongues collide, and I groan low in my chest.

I'm such a damn simp for this boy.

His hands grip my waist as he settles in on top of me.

"Jarron," I pant. "How are you here?"

The logic finally makes its way back to my mind. I want to keep doing this. I certainly don't want him to stop touching me. But the curiosity is too much. He's here. He's back. But for how long?

"I cannot stay away from you for long, sunshine." He murmurs the words against my neck while his lips seek out the spot where his marks just barely remain.

He doesn't comment on the bite marks, though. He just nuzzles the soft skin.

"You have given me the greatest gift tonight," he says. "I was willing to be content with a glimpse of you, but instead, I got a taste." He pulls away enough to look me in the eye.

"You know, it's creepy to spy on a girl while she's sleeping."

He chuckles. "I'm sorry. My culture is so different from yours, and my demon's instincts are very difficult to control."

I swallow. "Is it he who pulls you here at night?"

"Yes," he says. "My demon's need to protect you gets stronger at night when we know you are alone. There may also be some less wholesome desires in there as well, but I'm not sure how much you're interested in hearing those confessions just yet."

Oh, I'm very interested. Just still a bit wary.

"Maybe another time." My body is still buzzing from the terrifying touch of talons on my skin and the heavy make out. My resolve might snap if he were to give me those *confessions*.

He takes that as his cue to roll to the side so we're lying beside each other.

"My world's time runs different than yours, and the dimensional leaps make it hard to estimate. So far, I keep getting here at night, probably because it's when my demon's urges feel strongest—when you're alone and vulnerable."

"But how do you know it's night here if time doesn't line up the same?"

"Context clues from Laithe mostly. We know when he is sleeping, and he is our strongest assurance that you are protected. It soothes the demon slightly that you are staying in my bed, but not quite enough to ease the tension."

I sit up suddenly. "So, it was you who left the note?"

Jarron's expression falls. At first, I think it's sadness because it wasn't him, but then I read the guilt in his eyes.

"Yes, I'm sorry. My instinct takes control sometimes still. It's not ideal, but I didn't have full control over him that night."

I blink. I guess that's why the note was so cryptic and weird. I resettle into his chest. "Next time, tell him to sign the note or call me 'bright one' or something so I know it's from him."

Jarron chuckles. "I'll try."

"It scared me," I tell him.

"I'm sorry," he whispers.

"Well, I'm glad you're here. Why did you say it's hard for you to shift?"

"It always takes a little bit of time to readjust to Earth when I come back, and because of the tension in our world, I am fueled by danger and anxiety. It's harder to let go of that tension in order to shift."

"Is it really dangerous? Back home? Laithe keeps saying nothing is really happening."

"Yes, at times it is. I don't leave the palace very often, but the few times I've met with the rebels, I am at risk. And we have increasingly found spies among our servants, so things are heating up slowly."

I bite the inside of my lip. "Is there anything I can do to help?"

Jarron pauses, looking me over. "No," he says finally, but I get the feeling that's only a partial answer. "Not directly. My biggest concern is that you remain safe and out of the reach of the council and Vincent Vandozer. If there are spies in my ranks, there could be in the school as well. Please, please be careful. Don't leave the hall without Laithe ever. Do you understand?"

I ignore the pit in my stomach. "Yes, but how could there be spies at Shadow Hills? If someone new were to show up, they'd automatically be a suspect."

"Mrs. Bhatt has cut off midyear transfers to eliminate that risk. But it does not have to be new students. Some of my enemies have the ability to shapeshift."

"Wait." I twist to look up at him. "They can shift to look like someone else?"

"I know of none that are strong enough to impersonate a specific person, no. That would require an immense amount of magic and skill. But they could appear as a wolf or a falcon and go under the sensors then shift into a random humanoid student dressed in uniform. It's also possible for our enemies to manipulate one of the existing students. Most are afraid to turn on me, but if they were properly motivated or even brainwashed into believing the opposition... We just don't know what could happen."

"Would they really send spies after me?"

He stares at me with those deep brown eyes for a long while before answering. "You are my weakness, Candice. They may not know it yet, but I would do anything to keep you protected. They could have my world under their thumb in an instant if they used you against me."

Is that proof that I'm his chosen? They are using Liz against him, and he's not bowing to their demands. But would he if they had me?

A warm, fuzzy feeling fills my belly, but around the edges, there's an ache of tension.

I feel like I'm so close. So close to having something incredible. Something that would paint the rest of my life in more extraordinary ways than I could have ever imagined. And I want it.

That's the scary part.

Months ago, I didn't want it at all.

Now, I'm desperate for it. And terrified at the thought of losing it.

"Can I ask you something?"

"Anything," he says. His fingers drift over my arm. His eyes flit to the place the fabric of my ripped tank falls limp, just shy of exposing my breasts. I don't move to adjust it. I like the tortured expression on his face.

"Why did you stalk her? Liz, I mean. That night you changed on Myre Island."

Jarron swallows and looks me in the eye. "I'm not proud of that, you know.'

"Yeah, I get that."

He sighs. "I was getting closer and closer to my manifestation. The signs were beginning to show, but I begged my parents to stay through the end of the summer. Looking back, that was a mistake, but even knowing it, I would have had a hard time leaving."

"How does that work, though," I ask. "You are born in your other form, right?"

"Our race is a transitional one—we shapeshift between two different forms even from the time we are born. But we are tied to the world we are in until we come of age when the shifting becomes controlled. As adolescents, on Earth we are human and on Oriziah we are demon. We cannot control our form until this manifestation. The process of learning to control this change can be difficult. We usually begin the process of training on Oriziah because it's safer for those around us. My demon was instigated, though, and it brought him out faster than expected. I wasn't ready. He was powerful, and I hadn't been fully trained on how to control him. I wish... I wish that night had gone very differently."

"What instigated you, though?"

He pauses and doesn't respond for long enough my heart picks up its pace.

"Jarron?" I whisper.

"I think that might be an answer for another time." His voice is hoarse. He doesn't like it any more than I do.

"Does it have to do with not telling me outright who your chosen is?"

He nods. "You are trying to logically understand something that is supposed to be based on faith. Trust."

He wants me to know the truth, but he wants me to trust him enough to allow him to claim me first. His demon wants me. Jarron wants me.

That should be enough.

It should be. I should open myself to the possibility.

But of course, there's the deal with Bea. I cannot keep her secret if I let Jarron mark me.

Maybe it's an excuse, but I use it for now. I sigh and curl into him. His arms slide around me, cocooning me in his warmth and his scent.

This is the place I never want to leave.

24

WE CAN'T WIN ALL BATTLES

I wake to an empty bed. The sun steams brightly through the windows at the balcony.

I manage to force myself up but allow a moment to reminisce about last night. It almost doesn't feel real.

Jarron was here. He came to see me at night.

Those nightmares were actually him, I realize.

Creeper. I roll my eyes but laugh at the same time.

I don't really feel too weird about his stalker behavior since I'm technically in his bed. So, he's just entering his personal room. And I'm not beyond excusing every red flag for more of this bliss.

I just hope he doesn't shatter my heart.

With renewed excitement, I rush off to my workshop to begin three new potions. I've done research trying to choose several new ones, and I'm ready to get them started.

I grab my safety gloves and goggles. I'm not always the most careful potion maker, but this feels prudent given the circumstances.

Very carefully, I funnel my low-dosage stunning potion into

one side of a double vial. One vial at a time. I know what a low-quality stunning potion feels like from a few months ago, and I'd really like to not repeat the experience, especially with one of these.

This potion will pack a much harder punch than my last batch, and those took down a wolf shifter. I fill up one side of ten double vials with my new stunning potion and have enough left over for three regular vials.

Then, I set to work—extremely carefully—filling the second half of the double vials with Thompson's suggestion. An expeller.

In these small, separated containers, each potion is safe and simple. But with one click and a quick shake, they'll combine and create a tiny stunning bomb.

Anyone within range will be shocked harder than a police-level stun gun.

My lips spread into a pleased grin as I imagine Mr. Vandozer's body convulsing under the power of my new concoction.

Once those are complete, I begin the three new potions.

A set of nullifiers, with modifications from the previous batches. A paralysis potion that, after careful consideration, I've established will absolutely work quite well on High Orizians. And a weakening potion. This one isn't as strong as I'd like it to be, but there's no harm in getting a version started while I continue my research. I have a couple of ingredient replacements in mind to try as an experiment. There's little risk for this one in particular, so I'm eager to just give it a shot and see how it goes.

As I'm stirring my paralysis potion, I drink up the imagined panic on Mr. Vandozer's face when he realizes he cannot move. The vision is so beautiful it makes my soul ache with longing.

I want him to feel my wrath. I want him to know that even the powerless can destroy him. I want him to beg for mercy.

And it's this feeling that strikes me with a clear answer to my dilemma.

If I pass up this opportunity, if I say no to Bea, I'm back to being trapped. I'm back to having no clear avenue to reach my enemies. No clear route to save my sister.

If I tell her no, I will remove myself from the driver's seat. I'll have no control over what happens next. I'll be a victim. A child along for the ride of the more powerful beings.

That's not an option for me. It's never been an option. I just didn't know how to get out of the situation.

Now, I do.

Is it perfect? No. Is it even the right thing to do? Also, probably not.

But am I going to do it anyway?

My lips spread into a vicious grin.

Fuck yeah, I am.

"You look pleased as a kitten."

My gaze darts up to find a brown-skinned wolf shifter watching me from the doorway. "Hey," I say then continue my smooth stirs of the paralysis potion.

"Don't let me stop you from enjoying your revenge fantasies." Thompson approaches and leans casually against the counter across from the actively bubbling cauldron.

I glance up at the clock. It's one o'clock, just at the end of lunch period. "Don't you have a class to get to?"

"Actually, no. I don't."

I frown. "No?"

He shakes his head and puts his hands in his pockets. "I talked with Mrs. Bhatt an hour ago, and I've already said my goodbyes to the rest of the group during lunch hour."

My hand freezes, mid-stir. "What?"

He smiles, but there's a sadness to it. My stomach twists.

"No," I whisper. "You're not leaving."

He sighs. "I am. I have to."

I drop the ladle and rush around the counter to face him. "There has to be a way to help you."

He stands up straight and puts both hands on my upper arms. "You've tried. I've tried. Unfortunately, that's not always enough. I need to do what's right by my pack."

"You asked Auren?"

He releases my arms and nods. He shuffles his feet. "She wasn't mean about it or anything, but there isn't anything I can offer. She's not into being the alpha female of a tiny pack like mine, apparently." He chuckles, but there's bitterness to it.

"Her loss," I mutter.

When he smiles this time, there's a small light in his eyes. "My pack needs me home. If things change in the Orizian war, please feel free to send a few troops my way. But until then, we've just got to survive a while longer."

"I really don't want you to go," I say, crossing my arms. Thompson has become a true friend, at least to my naïve human mentality.

"We'll see each other again; I know it. And if you ever really need help, I'll be here. I can't leave the pack for long, but I can take a few trips once in a while, especially if there are portals involved."

I sigh. I wish I'd been able to convince Manuela to help him. But it's not my place to tell her how to feel about that sort of thing. It's way beyond my understanding.

"It makes me feel helpless," I whisper. "I don't like that."

He smiles, but it doesn't reach his eyes. Then, he pulls me into his arms. "I know. Me neither."

"I'll find a way to help you," I murmur into his chest, but even I don't know if I can trust my words. I want to. I really, really want to help him. But some wars just aren't yours to fight.

Some battles have to be put on the back burner, no matter how much you hope for a good outcome.

"We're both going to come out on top, princess. You'll see."

I cling to those words. For days, or weeks, or months, however long it takes, I'll cling to that hope.

We'll find a way. We'll both make it out on top.

25

I'M IN

A few hours after Thompson left Shadow Hills Academy for good, my heart is still aching, but my determination remains strong. I enter the sunroom before sunset and find exactly who I'm looking for.

I slide into the chair beside Manuela, who's sitting across from Stassi.

Manuela's eyes swing to me and then back to the wolf shifter chattering on and on about some beautiful witch he saw earlier today. "She's almost as beautiful as Candice over here!" he says with a wide grin.

I return his smile, and he continues on about the perfect shade of black her hair was, with golden highlights.

Though he's been known to flash interested looks to Lola on occasion, their little fling seems not to have progressed past minor flirting. I feel so out of the loop on Lola's and Janet's life now that I can't go to classes or lunch with them. I try my best to ask lots of questions, but neither are very forthcoming. They blush and shrug and mumble that everything is fine or unchanged. Janet hasn't mentioned Marcus in a while, leaving me to wonder if she's no longer in a relationship with the Major Hall mage. And Lola's been single as long as I've known her, beside her weekend-long fling with Stassi.

"Do you have an answer?" Manuela murmurs.

Stassi pauses, his expression one of minor horror at the interruption. "What?"

"Nothing," Manuela answers smoothly. "Tell me about the gold in her locks," she prompts.

"Right!" he continues on. "Last week, she wore it straight, but today it was wavy and—"

"Yes. I'm in," I say under my breath.

"Wonderful. I'll pass it along."

Stassi pauses mid-sentence with a frown.

"I thought you preferred redheads?" Manuela asks him.

His eyes light up. "Oh, I love them all."

I snort. Of course he does.

"But there is something about this one. The way her hair was both light and dark. It hit the light just perfectly and—"

I stand to leave, and Manuela lifts a brow. "Thursday," she tells me.

I nod and then wave goodbye to them both.

"Why do I feel like I missed an entire conversation?" Stassi says. I stifle a chuckle and head off to bed, both hoping for and fearing that a certain demon prince might show up while I sleep.

26
NEW ALLIES

I spend the next two days fervently working on potions and my demon studies.

My second lesson with Professor Zyair went exceptionally well. Learning another world's language is remarkably challenging, but I'm starting to catch on to the basics.

I look like such a studious good girl, following the rules and studying hard. No one would guess I'm secretly meeting with a demon fugitive to enact a plan to assassinate ten magical beings in a matter of minutes.

Manuela gives me strict instructions this time.

"Enter the looking-glass at exactly eleven fifty-nine. Make your step small and carry this at all times."

She gives me a small vial of black liquid. Apparently, a smell that will temporarily scare off any of those shadow creatures.

I'm tempted to ask Manuela if Bea reprimanded her for her willy-nilly process of sending me into the portal the last time. She told me I solved her riddle quicker than she'd planned, but I decided not to add on to her guilt for almost getting me killed.

"Trust me," she tells me just minutes before I head into the demon princess's bedroom. "You'll be safe this time."

I almost roll my eyes.

There's no such thing as safe when conspiring against the Cosmic Council with a fugitive demoness.

Does this make me a vigilante? I think it does. I need to make myself a sticker or something if I survive this.

Bea's arms are crossed in her human form, her lips in a sly grin as I step through the looking-glass like an absolute pro, feet solidly on the stone platform looking down over the pit filled with shadow creatures.

"Well, there you are." She smiles sweetly, but there's a bead of sweat on her brow.

"I wasn't almost eaten this time," I say, hiding how proud I am at my lack of fear. My lungs are still tight, though, and I force long, even breaths.

"Great job." She rolls her eyes and then grabs my hand, pulling me into the shadowed cave ahead. My knees wobble, but my steps somehow remain steady.

"Where are we, by the way?"

"If I told you, I'd have to kill you." She winks, waving to the same seat I took the last time around. "Just kidding. Jarron would be able to find me if you told him about the portal in my old room, so I'm dead the moment you decide I'm not worth your time. We're in the Karinch mountains, a good thousand miles from the capital." She smiles.

I plop into the stone seat, hands in my lap awkwardly. "Why are you doing this, then?" I ask. "You've never struck me as the kind of person who would put their life at risk to help someone else."

"Because my choice now is to live a half-life as a betrayer who harmed not only innocent people but ruined her family name and possibly our world—or do everything in my power to undo the damage and gain it all back. I'd rather die trying to fix it than accept who I've become."

She creates another tonic draft for me. Even though I didn't have that same nightmare run-in, my body is tense from entering this alien world. The tonic helps relieve the tightness in my lungs, and I gulp down the Orizian air much easier after a few sips.

"You know, I always liked you," she says, "but I never got the impression the feeling was mutual."

"Really?" I blurt out. "On Myre Island, you avoided me and Liz. You didn't even talk directly to us."

She sighs. "Yeah, well, back then, I was a bitch."

I snort. "But you're not now?"

Her glare is lethal, but then she shakes her head and loosens her expression into one of subtle amusement. "I supposed that depends on your perspective. I understand a lot more. And when I said always... well, I suppose I don't mean *always*. I was threatened by you two back then."

"Threatened by two magicless humans?"

"Two beautiful, capable humans who had the attention of Jarron. I was afraid you'd take Trevor's attention too." She shrugs.

"So, you were an insecure bitch." I nod slowly.

She barks out a laugh. "I suppose so."

I take a long sip of the tonic.

She settles into the seat across of me and sips on her own steaming beverage. "So, you've decided to take my deal?"

I nod. "I think we can help each other. I'd like that to be true, at least."

"If things go well, we could be sisters one day." Her beautiful brown eyes dart to the table and remain on her hands clinging to the mug.

"I'd like that," I say in an attempt to ease the tension. "But mostly, I'd like to get my real sister out of the hands of those assholes."

"And I'd like to see them all suffer." She flicks a brow. "I'm so ready to end this."

I swallow but keep my chin high. "How are we going to do it?"

She stands and grabs a rolled parchment from a shelf against the wall. "In three weeks, we have a tentative meeting set between all the members of the council. These kinds of meetings are rare, so it's important we're prepared. It might be months before we get another chance like this." She opens the parchment to reveal beautiful calligraphy handwriting that I can't even pretend to read. Not only is it in High Orizian, but it's in the native lettering. I'm not nearly fluent enough for this.

She points to a specific line. "I know the time and place. And most importantly, I'll know if anything changes. We'll work together to kill them all before that meeting is finished."

This could be a soup recipe for all I know. Still, I keep my gaze focused on the gibberish below, pretending I know exactly what I'm looking at.

"Do you have a plan for that?" I ask, finally pulling my gaze away from the parchment.

"Not particularly, but considering you're a potions prodigy, I assume you can come up with something along that line."

"Poison?"

"Unfortunately, it won't be quite that simple."

My brows lift. I didn't think poisoning ten people at once would have been considered simple, but okay.

"There are ten members of the council at any given time, and they are significantly powerful beings of many different worlds and species. No one type of poison would work on all of them, at least not quickly. The council also has some tactics to protect us against poison, so we'll have to work around that."

I narrow my eyes and wonder about my death potion. Everything I read claimed it was universal. Should I mention that?

I decide to let her keep talking and figure out my side of things later.

"There is also the issue of some of their abilities. One of the members is a mind reader. She requires very close proximity, and some beings are able to block her—like me—but she can indeed read thoughts. Another is a transporter, so if anything appears wrong in the slightest, he'll leap out of there in a second, and you won't get the clear swipe we'll need."

I take in a long breath. I didn't expect this to be easy, but it's feeling overwhelming right now.

"The good news is that part of the meeting involves swearing silence, a spell that involves ingesting a liquid which we will all drink together, so poison is a possibility, but I have some concerns."

"We just need to be very deliberate on how we do it." I need details. I pray she's willing to give me all of them.

"I will write down every name, and their species, so you can do the research to figure this out. We'll plan it together, and I'll execute."

"You'll execute?" I don't like the idea that I'll need to trust her to achieve this. Why can't I be there?

Other than the whole mind-reading thing.

"If you enter the room within hours of the meeting they'll smell it. Remember, extremely powerful beings. So, you can help me plan it, and we'll have Manuela set up the looking-glass so you can watch things unfold from my room at Shadow Hills. We'll make it work. But before I give you the full list, I need a specific promise."

My heart clenches, palms sweating already.

"You're nervous," she says, watching me closely. Her eyes narrow.

My heart pounds faster. "I'm worried about making too firm of a promise not to tell Jarron," I admit. "I don't have any intentions of hurting you, I swear, but I worry about my own well-being too."

She leans back in her chair, arms crossed, and just watches me for what feels like several minutes. "I want this to work," she says softly, "so badly. I'm desperate for things to go back. I don't want to side with the council. I don't want to side with the rebellion. But if I can't make this deal with you, that's my only choice."

I wince.

"I want you to swear that you will not do anything that will cause me harm, including telling Jarron about our deal or my portal into the school, until I give you permission."

I think through this wording. It's possible my plan with Janet and Lola will work, but there's risk.

"What happens if you're incapacitated or you betray me? I don't see how a promise like that is fair for me."

She narrows her eyes. "Did you have something else in mind?"

"Personally? I want you to trust me without magic."

Her expression falls. I've never seen her look so unarmed. It's not fear, exactly. More like a mix of vulnerability and surprise. It's raw and real.

Tension slips from her shoulders. Almost like she's given up.

"I'm scared," she admits.

"Me too," I say. "No matter what, this agreement puts us both at risk. We have to trust each other. We could make magical agreements and vows up and down all day, but it will not give us complete protection. Nothing will."

Tears well in Bea's eyes, and for the first time, I feel like I'm really seeing her. Demon or not, she is a young girl who's scared.

142

"I'm willing to trust you without any magical reassurance," I tell her softly.

She presses her palm over her lips, eyes unfocused. I let her sit with this new energy between us. I allow her the time she needs for my words to settle.

"I've never had a real girl friend," she whispers. Her hands drop to her lap. Her eyes remain distant.

I blink. That wasn't the response I expected.

"Trevor has really been my only friend for as long as I can remember. I have allies. Subjects. Worshippers. But never someone I truly trusted, except him."

The crease between her brow deepens.

"He hates me now." Her voice is both hoarse and soft. "Since he found out what I did. He knew that I'd slipped and mentioned Jarron choosing a mate at Myre Island, but he didn't know specifics until after you became involved. He's protected me from harm since then, probably only because his demon instinct won't let him do anything else, but he doesn't trust me anymore."

My heart aches for her, but we both know she did it to herself.

Tears trickle down her rosy cheeks as she finally meets my stare. "Maybe it's stupid. Maybe it'll result in my death, but I will trust you too." She holds out her hand to me, red nails chipped and scraped.

I stand, ignoring her hand.

Her eyes grow big, looking up at me. This time, the fear is clear. She gasps when I wrap my arms around her in a tight hug.

Her body shakes slightly against me before she eases into the embrace. When I pull back, she wipes her eyes.

"I'll do what I can to keep you safe," I promise. "And so long as you hold up your side of the bargain, I'll defend you. I'll try my best to convince Jarron to forgive you."

She swallows and nods, sniffling slightly. Then, she stands and crosses the dark room to a rickety wooden dresser, where she pulls out another sheet of paper and returns it to me.

I take the paper between two fingers, eyes wide, staring at the names of the men and women I will personally kill. Before I can dwell long on that thought, Bea clears her throat.

"What have you been doing?" I ask, looking around the room, aiming for casual conversation. We're officially in business now but without a contract. "Have you been hiding here for months?"

"Here and there." She shrugs like it's no big deal. "I have more than one hideout. And no, I don't do much. I hide like a sniveling coward, feed my monsters guarding the place, keep watch, get updates from Vincent on the war, and occasionally sneak out to get my own perspective on the current atmosphere. Jarron hasn't sent any hunters for my head, so it's not too terrible. He's preoccupied with bigger fish. But if I'm found, he'll kill me without a doubt."

"Couldn't you just hide in the human world or something?"

She sighs. "I'd love to travel to the fae world, but since those portals were all mysteriously closed off, that's a no-go. I'm sure I could hide in the human world, but I couldn't just go to another magical school and pretend everything is normal. Since Jarron spends so much time there, he'd find out and come find me. Either way, his demon has made it very clear that he considers me a traitor and a threat to his mate. That isn't going to go away easily."

Another scary question rises up on my tongue. "Your plan to earn his forgiveness, does it only work if I'm his chosen? What happens to you if we're wrong?"

"It works best if it's you. But if we can save Liz due to my actions, it would help either way. At least my crimes wouldn't have cost Jarron his mate. I would just have to re-grovel to the other sister at a later date and hope she forgives me." Again with the casual one-shoulder shrug. There is no brightness in her expression, though. Very little hope.

She's tired; I can see that much, and I don't blame her. I can't imagine what it would feel like to live in hiding, fearing for her life and being separated from her mate.

"Could you—could you tell me more about the V'rta tradition?" I ask. "Everyone is so closemouthed about the chosen mate thing. You're the only one who ever told me like it is." And yes, those truth bombs were usually intended to hurt me or manipulate me in some way, but truth is truth.

"There's a reason for that, you know," she says. "Take me as your warning. Drop the wrong bit of information to the wrong person, and it puts everything at risk."

I bite the inside of my lip. "I don't need specific information about Jarron or Liz or anyone else really. I just want to know if there's more to the tradition than people are telling me. I mostly just want to understand how you knew. How did you know Jarron made his choice? I keep hearing 'there are signs' and 'it was obvious,' but what? How?"

"There are some things that only Orizians should know," she says. "Our chosen are sacred. They're our legitimate weakness. If these things become common knowledge among the outside worlds, it puts us at more and more risk."

"Was it because he turned?" I press. Was him stalking Liz that night proof?

"That is part of it. It's not definitive, but it's highly unlikely a demon would turn in that situation without a powerful reason. Since we know his loved ones were not attacked, and he was not harmed or threatened, it makes sense to assume something else pushed that change."

I swallow. Something else. "Why would his chosen cause him to change?"

145

"Mates are High Orizians' vulnerability. We are much more volatile around them. Smaller slights or minor threats feel bigger when your mate is involved, particularly if they are a physically weaker species."

My stomach clenches. That really doesn't tell me much, though. "Is it true they build a house?" I blurt. It's such a stupid part to pick out of a stupid book I shouldn't put so much stock into. It's just physical proof. Something I can find. Something I can see with my eyes and touch with my hands. "Or what about purring? Is that something that's related?"

"Candice," she whispers, leaning forward, her soft eyes capturing mine, "you're seeking something you're not meant to find. You can't line up every box and understand it all in logical ways before you make your choice."

I slump deeper into my chair.

"You're afraid. I understand. But everyone, no matter what the culture, takes risks when they fall in love. You either trust them with your heart or you don't."

I do trust Jarron, but I feel so out of my depth with all of this. I hate not knowing.

"You are not supposed to find proof. There's danger in that, not just from outside forces. Has anyone ever told you what happens to a demon when they're rejected?"

My eyes flash up to hers.

"Their souls are torn apart. The demon spirit splinters from their essence, and it becomes a war between two separate and powerful beings. It changes them completely."

Several images pop into my mind. Darkness permeating the school halls.

Jarron in human form, talking to me with that demon voice.

Thompson telling us about the rumors that Jarron's demon is taking control.

My demon and I are not on the same page about some things.

Shit.

Then, I remember the excerpt from that book about the Rejected Prince. He changed. Turned violent.

Is that—could that be happening to Jarron?

I felt like things were better with him, but then again, I have barely seen him in weeks. He's been in Oriziah so much it's difficult to say. And the one time he did come to see me, he was in his demon form. He said it was "hard" for him to change back.

Ice floods my veins. More evidence of something I do not want to be true.

I'm supposed to trust. Have faith.

"Rejection doesn't always have to be formal," she says softly, as if reading my thoughts. "Just choosing not to be with them once you've learned the truth is a form of rejection."

The kind of rejection Liz is doing right now? Maybe against her will, but it's still happening. Is Jarron struggling through the phases of V'rta rejection? Am I a Band-Aid for that? And if so, can I even blame him?

"Has anyone been keeping you updated on what's going on here with the war?" she says suddenly.

I whip my attention back to her. Is she trying to change the subject? "A little, but Laithe doesn't like to share much. I only hear bits and pieces."

"That's what I expected. The truth is, you don't have to know, but I feel it's only fair that if you want to, you have access to the truth."

"Truth?"

"It's not going well."

My stomach sinks. "What do you mean? Laithe said things are fine, that no fighting has started, and Jarron is safe."

"Just because no blood has been shed yet doesn't mean it's going well."

My heart picks up speed.

STACEY TROMBLEY

Then again, can I trust Bea's words?

"I'm not saying this to scare you." She raises her hands in surrender. "It's not like it's a lost cause or anything. If I thought that, I honestly would not be here talking to you now. But there's little the crown can do to stop the uprising at the moment. The people of Oriziah, as a whole, have always been more powerful than the royals. If they united behind one cause, it wouldn't take much to topple the whole system, and that's happening now."

"But... not all Orizians agree."

"True, but they are not so convinced that they're willing to passionately defend the prince either. So, if the opposition is growing, neutrality on the other side is not helpful. It is still the High Orizians against an increasingly growing population of rebels. Once the fighting begins, it will end quickly, particularly because one death will quell the masses. Jarron's own loyalists will turn on him quickly to save themselves if it means ending the rebellion. As much as the prince is adored and followed so closely, there are too many that would turn on him and make Trevor the new ruler in a second if it meant saving themselves or their family. It's a small sacrifice to too many of them."

"Is that what you want?" I whisper. "For Trevor..." I know she said she didn't want to be the queen anymore, but if inaction would give it to her, how is that bad?

"No," she says quickly. "Not only is that not what I wish for anymore, but I'm afraid. Vincent's plans don't stop at Jarron. I don't know what they are, but I don't believe that a successful rebellion will put me and Trevor on the throne and be the end of it."

Some groups desire anarchy. Is that what Mr. Vandozer is after?

I take in a deep breath. That's not altogether surprising, I suppose. It didn't make much sense to think he just wanted the second prince to be king for no particular reason.

"Why are you telling me all of this?" I whisper. My heart and head hurt simultaneously.

"Because I suspect no one else has, and you are not a child who needs to be left in the dark. You deserve to understand the risks. And also because it adds to the necessity of our plan. Killing the council and freeing your sister won't end the rebellion, but it will cut off the main source of fuel. And with both of you free, Jarron will be able to claim his mate publicly. That is when this will all end for good."

Claim his mate publicly. My cheeks heat. "He has to do it in public?"

"He will have to make a public declaration at some point, yes, but it's not like the first claiming has to be done in public."

Claiming his chosen will end the war. That's the part I'm stuck on now.

My stomach clenches. Have I just been a selfish bitch who's stretching out this war due to her own fears and selfishness? Or is it not that simple?

My heart clenches at the question brewing on my tongue. I'm terrified to say this out loud, but I feel I have to. "So, claiming his mate will end the war?"

She takes in a long breath. "Yes, but..." Her eyes narrow as she very clearly measures her next words. "It will only end the war if Liz and Vincent stop their campaign as well. At this point, Jarron will need the Bright Tribunal to side with him, which is easier said than done. Especially with things as they are now. Vincent has the ear of the clans. With Liz herself declaring that she is the prince's chosen mate and that she's rejected him, it's possible the council would rule Jarron's claim false, if he came forward with you. If the clans believed he was willing to lie, it would make the rebellion worse. That would do irreversible damage to his reputation."

I run my hands through my hair. "Why would Liz do that?" I whisper. Why would she claim to be his chosen?

"Because the Cosmic Council has firm control of her. They can make her say anything they want. And they don't intend to give it up. Ever."

My brow pinches. "Ever?" I whisper. "I thought she'd be free eventually."

"Well, traditionally, a new set of games would take place to free the current jinn. Liz would then be freed but magically gagged. Except, she's pissed off the council. She's lucky they haven't killed her already if I'm honest."

I cough. "What?"

Why hadn't I considered this?

"The council is able to control her, but only so long as they keep giving direct commands. During that last little stunt of hers, she actively worked against their best interests by sending you secret messages. She's become very good at following the letter of their commands but completing her own agenda at the same time, and that's exactly why she's a liability. They cannot risk setting her free.

"This whole campaign against Jarron wasn't supposed to happen like this. Vincent intended to truly bond with Liz, but now, she's refused him, and he's not at all happy about that. Now, he's using her magical bond to the games to force her to play along with his rebellion. He's kissed her in front of massive packs of demons, declaring her to be Jarron's mate. He's made her agree with him, swearing she is Jarron's chosen but she doesn't want him. Not only is she very useful right now as a slave, but she's also a liability if she's ever freed."

I drop my butt to the stone chair, limbs limp. "Shit," I mutter.

She's a pawn to them. I knew that, but the realization that no amount of waiting will help her is a heavy one. Even if a new set of games were to take place, they wouldn't allow Liz to go free. I'd held on too heavily to that hope. It's hard to let it go.

"How does their control work?" I ask. Information. I need to continue gathering information. "There are ten members of the council. Do they all have the ability to make commands?"

"Yes, each one has some level of control, but there's a hierarchy. If two different council members give conflicting commands, the one with the most magic wins. That is the command the jinn will be forced to obey."

And yet, Mr. Vandozer seems to be the one in control. He isn't the most powerful in magic, is he? "Then, couldn't you override his commands?"

She has more power, not just by blood but also because of her link with Trevor.

"If it were only me and Vincent, yes. But the others are on his side. If they agree, he wins that internal battle. They've all given him right to leadership, so long as he continues promising them the fall of Oriziah."

If Bea is right, then to win the war, we have to defeat the Cosmic Council first.

"Liz is the key to all of this," she whispers. "Regardless of whether she's his chosen or not, that question, that doubt, is enough to continue the war. Once Liz is free, Jarron's choice will no longer be questioned, and the war can end. It's the only way to win without making major sacrifices."

So, I need to agree to deceive Jarron, complete a full assassination of ten massively powerful beings *at once* without his help, or else either Jarron or my sister will die.

27

The Cosmic Council

Emily: Sphinx
    Asad: High fae, Crackling Court
    Gabbai: Dragon
    Dara: Griffin
    Daamodor: Ancient witch
    Aceline: Serpent shifter
    Gaffney: Kappa
    Halvard: Cyclops
    Beatrice: High Orizian
    Vincent: High Orizian

28

I MUST KILL NINE MASSIVELY POWERFUL SUPERNATURALS. NO BIG DEAL.

I stare down at the list of names.

Names of people I am going to kill.

I still don't know how I feel about that.

Part of me is terrified that I'll fail. Scared that I will have to kill people and what that means about me as a person.

But another part of me, deep down, is thrilled.

I feel powerful, knowing that I can and will do this.

I will free my sister from the Cosmic Council and ensure they never harm another low-magic being ever again.

The first name is, surprisingly, Emily.

What a basic name. I had a frenemy named Emily a few years ago. She thought stealing my boyfriend made her somehow more valuable than me. I proved her wrong by training for a month in her position on the field hockey team. She went to second string and—shocker—the boy, whose name I can't even remember now, dumped her for someone else in the same week.

My favorite tactic in the human world was showing how much their power moves didn't affect me. I didn't kill them with kindness. I didn't get even. I just built up my strength in ways they didn't see coming.

Emily, my new enemy, is from a long-hidden line of sphinxes. She has psychic powers, as well as strong spell magic.

I know exactly how I want to destroy Vincent Vandozer. For the rest, I'll have to do specific research to make sure my planned spells and potions will work as intended on them, and that they won't see it coming with stupid abilities like mind reading.

Before the sun sets, I have a book on each of these species. I also have a list of my current potions. I'll have to double-check their affected species.

This is a lot more complicated now that I have multiple creatures to fight and they're not simple witches or wolf shifters. These are some of the most powerful beings in the known universe.

I barely sleep the next three days, studying more and more about these creatures. And the thing that sucks the most is that, if anything goes wrong at all, I'll have to start over. They can just be replaced with a new powerful supernatural.

Even when I'm not researching potions or these beings I intend to kill, I'm daydreaming about that moment. Each one, I picture gagging and foaming at the mouth, begging for my mercy.

I know it won't happen like that, but the sadistic terrible part of my soul comes alive at the image regardless.

Bea gave me a quick rundown of how the ceremony generally goes. They have a taste tester before they serve the wine. They then take their vow one at a time, which is when they will sip from their glasses.

I imagine the meeting, step by step, measuring each possibility. There are so many variables to consider, but my one bit of good news is that I do indeed have a potion that will affect each and every one of these creatures.

The problem is, I can't use it as is.

What happens when one person drinks first and falls dead in an instant? The rest will panic. One will transport out, and it will all be a failure.

I shake my mind from the daydream and grab my notebook to scribble a bit in bold.

Instant death is no good.

—DELAYED DEATH POTION.

I underline it three times.

Then, I rush off to the Elite Hall library for more research.

"Candice?" Janet says softly.

I look up quickly from my notebook, eyes frantic.

"Have you been sleeping?" she asks.

I blink three times. "A little," I admit.

"Babe," Lola says, buzzing close to me, "you need some rest." She sniffs twice. "And a shower."

I jerk away from her. "It's not that bad."

Janet tilts her head.

My shoulders deflate. "Do I really smell?" I look down at my wrinkled top.

"Only a little," Lola says sweetly, her purple wings twinkling.

I can't help but chuckle. Okay, maybe I'm obsessing a little. "I only have two and half more weeks to get ready. This is *everything*."

"Yeah, maybe," Lola says. "But you're more likely to make mistakes if you're not taking care of your mental health too."

Mental health? What mental health? My sister's life, and the future of an entire world, is relying on a human girl being able to kill a demon, a fae, a dragon—shit, I don't even remember the rest of them right now.

My point is, I am incredibly stressed, and sleep just isn't even an option for me right now. "Even when I lie down, my mind won't turn off."

Janet walks over to my chai cart. There are several shelves of potions I never touch on the shelves behind it. She grabs three small vials from the shelf and a plastic card with brief instructions, then brings them over to me. "Easy sleeping tonic. Use it. The more sleep you have, the easier it will be for your brain to keep up. Health matters, and all-nighters will be detrimental eventually."

I sigh, accepting the liquids. "Fine, fine. I'll sleep a full eight hours tonight."

"Make it nine," Lola mutters. "And a shower."

I shoot her a glare but also acknowledge that they're just worried about me. "How are your guys' projects coming along?" For the last two weeks, they've each worked on their big projects in here while I worked on mine.

"Great!" Lola chirps. "I'm more or less enjoying the song-writing part because the spell is stupid."

I smile. Lola has easy access to pixie dust that can put someone to sleep, so a sleeping spell seems pointless for her personally.

Janet leans against the table. "I'm having a hard time with mine. I feel like the magic isn't strong enough."

"The painting is amazing," I tell her. Every time I glance at it, I'm careful not to look too long, but I don't want to look away, honestly. It's this beautiful cavern, with shades of amber and purple and black so dark I'm surprised it's real. There are twinkling lights inside and so many layers of stone it feels like a maze.

Every day, I feel like it can't get better, but she keeps adding more layers of shadows and highlights.

"I didn't mean for it to turn out like that, actually. But I kept thinking about that song—you know, from the Akrasia Games?

It was a creepy circus song, kinda like I'd planned to use, so I think the whole painting sorta turned into that memory."

"Oh!" I say. "I didn't realize." Suddenly, the imagery is a lot darker to me. Instead of pretty, it's horrifying.

"Even dark and scary things can be lovely," Lola adds.

I nod. Definitely true.

"I'm not necessarily worried about pretty. Interesting is just as good."

"Well, it's definitely interesting. I always wanted to keep looking at it to find out what's inside those shadows, but now that I know what it is—" I shiver. "I might avoid it."

Janet chuckles.

"Have you come up with anything new for your big plot?" Lola asks me, looking over my scribbled notes.

"I found a new death potion. It's not as strong as I need it to be to work on all of them, but I'm trying to see how I can maybe alter it to make it stronger. Oh! And I did throw in a few antidotes in my last batch of potions. Just in case."

That was Janet's idea. She mentioned how much of a difference it could have made the last time, when Jarron was magicless. She's totally right. I probably should have thought of that before. I can't imagine a circumstance in which Jarron ever accidentally gets nullified, but even so, we may as well learn from our previous mistakes.

It's not like I don't have the cauldron space.

I'll be sure to make an antidote to the death potion as well, once I decide on one. Which honestly has to be extremely soon, or I'll risk not being able to finish it in time.

"And the nullifier?" Lola asks.

"No real progress there." I shrug.

Lola looks disappointed, but she darts around the room, taking a careful look at each of my current works in progress. "You'll figure something out."

I don't have the heart to tell her that right now, making a permanent nullifier is not very high up on my priorities list.

"And if you don't," Janet says. "You could always just bluff." She winks.

My brows rise, almost impressed with her suggestion. She's the one that was nervous about the idea of a permanent magic eraser, now she's suggesting I lie even if I don't achieve it.

I kinda love it.

Right now, the first thing on my mind is getting my sister away from the creatures who intend to kill her the moment she's not of use anymore.

29

IF YOU LIKE IT THEN YOU SHOULDA PUT A CLAIM ON IT

"Where's your boyfriend, *little human?*" a low voice calls when I cross through the sunroom. I ignore the comment as I always do, but from the corner of my eye I note the three males huddled by the windows watching me. One of them I recognize as fae, but the others... I'm not sure.

I don't like not knowing.

The situation is the same whether they're wolves, vampires, fae, or whatever these beings are. They want to make me feel uncomfortable; they want to see how far they can push me to get a reaction.

The longer Jarron is away, the worse the backlash has gotten. It's going on almost six weeks now, if we don't include his visit the other night. Part of me wonders if I'll even see him for my birthday next week.

"Everyone is so convinced you're the one," the boy with shining green eyes says.

I pause but don't turn.

Apparently my reaction is enough to encourage him though,

because he pushes away from the wall and takes a step toward me. "And yet he keeps leaving you all alone."

There's a jolt of fear in my limbs, but my mind is sharp. My prey instinct safely tucks to the side and I take quick inventory of my defenses.

The obsidian blade is strapped into my boot instead of my thigh, since I haven't been wearing skirts as often—why wear the uniform when I'm not going to classes anyway? In my pocket, I have three potions. I could toss the stunning bomb to see how that works. That would shut them up quickly, but I'd certainly hit a few innocent bystanders.

I also have a nullifier, which would not help much in this circumstance. It's the third potion, one of my new concoctions, that is itching to be used.

"Don't you remember what happened the last time he left you all alone?"

I turn toward the three boys.

One is short and stalky, with pale skin—a vampire, maybe? Another is tall, with broad shoulders, shaggy dark hair and bright-green eyes, but he doesn't have the look of a fae. There's something—different about him. An essence both wild and brutal.

The last has pointed ears tall enough you couldn't mistake him for anything other than fae. It's his words though, that fill my body with anger.

"Care to remind me?" I say, unable to keep the irritation out of my tone. I flex my fingers.

The last time Jarron left me alone this long, a set of wolves attacked me. I could remind them of what happened after Jarron found out about it—he almost destroyed the school and sent the whole pack into hiding. Or I could remind him of the fact that I killed the wolf that bit me.

But I'd rather he find out the hard way.

The green-eyed boy in the middle looks bored.

The vampire licks his lips. "I'd love to remind you."

I openly gag.

Someone watching from afar chuckles. No one seems intent on stepping up to protect me, though. Do I have no babysitters today? No one wants to protect the "princess" today. Maybe they all just want to see what I'm made of.

That's fine. I have a lot of pent-up energy. I could use a workout and an experiment rolled into one.

I put my hand in my pocket, slyly slipping off the cap of the vial I want so badly to use—just in case.

Maybe they're all beginning to doubt my place with Jarron. The remnants of the bite have almost faded.

"Try me," I say and crook my finger like an invite.

The vampire jerks, eager to come at me but the green-eyed boy growls. "Careful, Jacks. Don't be dumb," he warns. His voice is so low it's similar to Jarron's in his demon form. *What is he?*

The substance pools into my palm.

"Yeah, Jacks," I croon. "Better be careful. Are you sure you're even *strong enough* to claim me?"

Three things happen at once. The vampire charges. Several of the witnesses jerk forward as if they've finally decided to step in. And I remove my hand from my pocket and blow.

The vampire is lightening quick, across the room in a second. The powder from my palm puffs up into a little cloud of dark smoke right in his face, now inches from mine.

The vampire freezes in place, eyes wide.

His fangs are out, hands curled, ready to grab me but he won't be grabbing anything any time soon. His limbs are frozen still. Only his eyes move, comically darting around in panic.

I've been experimenting with a few new things, like a dry spell concoction. This one is simple and only works when breathed in. It also wears off within minutes, but that should be all I need to make my point this time.

The crowd pauses short of reaching me. Some people chuckle, others whisper in surprise.

"Idiot," the brutal green-eyed boy says, before approaching slowly and stopping between me and the frozen vampire. I step back.

"Your turn?" I ask, heart pounding harder than before as I'm faced with this new threat. I still don't know what his species is. How powerful is he? I'm not certain the powder would even have worked on him, but that won't matter now because I only had one.

My fear is building. Something tells me this one wouldn't be so easy to beat.

I was assuming one use of potion and my point would be settled—they'd stop messing with me.

He nods to the vampire, and the fae boy grabs his frozen form by the waist and drags him away.

The strange guy holds up his hands in surrender. "I'm not as dumb as he is," he says with a smirk. "I won't be baited, nor would I take you against your will. But I will make one quick offer."

I swallow.

"Your prince hasn't been around in a while. So if you happen to be feeling lonely, I'm willing to help." His smirk is somehow both handsome and slightly unhinged. "I've heard demons don't mind sharing—"

The voice cuts off with a roar and a crash as two forms slam into the wall by me. I flinch, and stumble another step back.

My heart lifts at the sight of a very sexy demon prince with hair falling into his eyes, hand around the taunting boy's throat.

"Let me be very clear," Jarron growls. "I. Do. Not. Share."

Uhh, the things that voice and those words do to me right

now are not PG 13. My chest rises and falls. The other two boys have already scattered, but the one against the wall has a fierce scowl. "It was just an offer," he forces out.

"That you will never make again," Jarron says. "You might think yourself big and important, but this is my domain, and she is *mine*."

I barely hold back a whimper. God, I'm such a fangirl.

"Where's that vampire," Jarron growls.

The boy bares is teeth. "It's not Jacks fault you haven't claimed her yet. Maybe you should get on that if she means that much to you."

Jarron releases the boy's neck and straightens. "Get out of my sight. And if that vampire ever so much as looks in her direction again I'll rip his throat out with my bare hands."

The green-eyed boy looks like he wants to say more. His eyes dart to me, but then he nods, and smoothly turns and walks in the opposite direction.

A direct threat from Jarron and yet he's generally unnerved.

I shake my head, amazed that he doesn't even seem to fear Jarron. Who is he?

Jarron's dark gaze sweeps over me and instantly my heart warms, everything else forgotten.

My mind spins through so many different memories.

The boy I cared for years ago.

The boy who terrified me. The boy I ran from.

The boy I hated and plotted to destroy for assumed crimes, but who slowly and carefully proved me wrong, day by day.

The boy I fell for, despite conflicting feelings.

The boy I still fear, for so many reasons, including that I want him too badly.

"Sunshine," he says in that smooth baritone voice that sends a shiver down my spine.

I fall into his arms without another thought.

His warmth envelops me. His power unnerves me in the best possible way, and I am completely lost in him.

I push those thoughts away and look up at him with a bright smile. Something in his chest rattles. That little purr he does on occasion that I've come to adore.

"What are you doing here?" I ask.

He pulls back. "Do you want me to lea—"

"No!" I say, despite the smile playing at his lips. It widens at my plea. I curl tighter into his arms.

"I've missed you more than you could possibly know," Jarron murmurs against my hair.

"I've missed you too," I admit.

He hums happily.

There's a crowd gathered to watch our warm reunion. It's only been a week since I saw him last, technically, but that night felt like a fever dream.

A dream I'd very much like to reenact if I'm honest.

Jarron finally looks up and acknowledges the crowd surrounding us. "Where were you headed?" he asks me.

"The speakeasy."

He takes my hand with limber fingers, and we walk down the hall toward the speakeasy. The crowd parts for us, whispering and gawking boldly, but we both ignore them. Just as I ignore the butterflies in my belly.

Should I tell him about the very inappropriate things that ran through my mind at his verbal claiming of me?

"Chai?" he asks.

"Caramel latte, but I can—"

He gently brushes me to the side. "I'd greatly prefer to make it if that's all right."

I grunt but allow him to craft my desired beverage. I wonder if he's ever made one of these before.

"You don't like the machine in your workshop?"

"No! It's amazing," I blurt out. "But I don't like being stuck in only two or three rooms. I still like the sunroom and speakeasy to change it up sometimes. It makes me feel a little less... trapped."

His brow furrows, halting his work with the steaming machine, and he steps closer to me. I look up, mesmerized by this closeness. Our chests are a breath apart.

He brushes the hair from my eyes, the pad of his thumb gently sliding down my cheek to my nose before he swipes the soft spot beneath my eyes. "Have you not been sleeping?"

Thank fuck I showered last night, is all I can think. I'll have to thank Lola and Janet for their little intervention yesterday.

"Actually, I slept a full nine hours last night." I grin.

I grab my finished drink, skipping the fancy toppings I sometimes like to add, and pull him with me to a velvet bench.

"And how many hours did you get in the week before that?" he asks casually.

"Less," I admit. "I've been a little obsessive about my potion-making—" I cut myself off. I'm not sure what I was even going to say, but the realization that I can't tell him why I've been obsessive hits me hard and causes my stomach to clench. Is it wrong to lie to him about this? I really don't like doing it. But...

"Oh?" he asks smoothly. He examines me as I take a sip of my sweet drink. Instead of pushing for details, he asks, "You said you're feeling trapped?"

"It's tough being stuck inside the same area for weeks at a time, even if those areas are wonderful."

His face falls slightly. "I'm sorry—"

"I don't blame you," I tell him quickly. "I understand it."

He frowns.

"And you being here now helps." I scoot a little closer.

He leans in, pressing his lips to my hair.

"How long will you be here? An hour?" I ask.

"No, actually—" he straightens, face still tense "—I intend to stay for a full week."

I sit up. "Really?"

"Which means we can go to classes if you want. Well, you can go to classes. I will not be leaving your side the entire time."

My heart drops. Shit. That sounds absolutely amazing, except it means I won't have the chance to work on my very, very important work with Bea. I'm going to have to pass a message on to Manuela. Or will she already know?

And I can keep working on my potions, but the research on specific species will be suspicious.

Crap, I need to hide those notes.

My stomach clenches, already regretting agreeing to keep this from him. How can I go behind his back like this?

But how can I not?

I remember Bea's tears. Her desperate desire for us to be friends. Could I turn on her? Can I relinquish the power it gives me to actively be a part of the battle against my enemies?

Jarron has been willing to allow me to fight before, but this time it's different. This time, it requires trust in a person he considers a traitor, someone who betrayed him.

"How are things back at home?" I ask, forcing my thoughts back to the present.

"Well enough," he says.

I resist a frown. Is that the truth? "Well enough you can take a break from the politics? Or well enough you had to leave for your own safety?"

Jarron whips his attention to me. "Why would you think that?"

I shrug. "Because I get no information. I just want to make sure you're okay. You can tell me if something is wrong."

He nods absently. "Things are complicated. It's hard to explain it all because there's a lot and so much of it is cultural."

"But it's good for me to begin learning, isn't it?"

Unless he doesn't intend for you to be involved, a little voice says.

My stomach sinks again. At this rate, I'm going to have an ulcer soon.

"Of course," he says, with a forced smile.

Shit, this is going to be harder than I thought. "So, tell me about it."

He sighs. "What do you want to know?"

"Maybe tell me about the Bright Tribunal."

His eyes widen. "How do you—"

"Professor Zyair," I say quickly, "has been giving me private lessons here. We figured keeping my Orizian studies going is for the best."

Jarron stands, shoulders tense. "Laithe can give you instruction—"

"Laithe is not a teacher. And they rarely give me any information. I have to ask ten questions to get a simple answer. I don't understand why this bothers you."

"Your education is extremely valuable, especially in Orizian," he says slowly, "but I trust no one."

I frown, still sitting, and not fully understanding his reaction.

"Anyone could be working against us, Candice. Anyone at all. Even Professor Zyair." He breathes deeply. "I'm going to come with you to classes all week, so that'll be fine. But once I go back—"

"Jarron," I reprimand before he can tell me I have to stop my private lessons.

"You can keep meeting with him, but I want Laithe to be there every time. No one else. Only Laithe."

"Why?" He knows what Laithe knows, at least some of it. So, does he want to keep track of what I'm learning? "You want them there as a spy?"

He frowns down at me. "Sort of, I guess," he admits. "but not how you're thinking. I trust you, Candice. I don't trust other people with you. The information he gives you and the information you give back could all affect this war. I just need to make sure I'm on top of all of it."

I swallow. Does he really think Professor Zyair could be part of the rebellion? Or passing along information?

They could also read into my uncertainty and how little I'm kept up with current events. That I'm left alone here a lot.

Okay, I guess some of that could be bad in the wrong hands.

"Okay," I whisper.

He presses two fingers beneath my chin and lifts so I meet his intense stare. "I care for you more than anything else. I know it doesn't always seem that way, but it's true. This is all really over-whelming for me. It's scary. I'm scared," he admits.

Those words disarm me in an instant. I stand and wrap my arms around him. "What are you scared of?"

He huffs out a bitter laugh. "Everything."

I lean my chin against his chest, peering up at him, waiting for a more specific answer.

"I'm afraid of losing control. I'm afraid of something happening to you. I'm afraid of being a failure." He closes his eyes. "I already feel like a failure."

I suck in a breath. I want to tell him that's not true, but his world is imploding. What would my words even mean in the face of all of that?

I nod against his chest. "I know it's overwhelming, but I'm— I sometimes feel like I'm not actually a part of it. I'm a pawn, at best. You care about me, I know that, but I don't always feel important. How could I be if I'm kept in the dark?"

He winces at the words, staring at me like I've kicked his favorite puppy. Finally, he whispers, "Okay. I'll try to keep you informed however I can. But there's—" He stops and looks up to the ceiling. He takes a few long breaths.

"What?"

"There are some things I can't say aloud. Things—" He shakes his head, but his thumb absently brushes over the veins in my wrist.

The spot where he would mark me if I let him.

"Things that will take time to understand."

30

REJECTED PRINCE

The spot on my wrist seems to tingle the rest of the day, and my brain is burning.

I want to focus on the amazing news that Jarron is here with me now, and he will be here for the rest of the week. He's not going to miss my eighteenth birthday!

Best news of all, I get to leave Elite Hall. I can take walks on the grounds. I can go to classes and sit in the lunch hall with my friends.

But the lies sit like an elephant on my chest. I hadn't decided whether I was going to let Jarron mark me before my deal with Bea, but now the idea that I can't is suffocating me.

Now, I'm trapped in that way too. I don't have the choice to get those answers, not without major sacrifice.

Two more weeks.

In two weeks, maybe—*maybe*—the council will be dead. My sister will be free. And I'll be able to let Jarron mark me.

If he still wants to.

It feels like too much to hope for.

Just the reminder that the lying and hiding is temporary helps me breathe a little easier.

Part of me wants to be annoyed with Jarron for how he continues pushing information about the war away from me. Like he doesn't want me to know.

And if he's keeping truths from me, then does that justify my hidden truths?

Or does it just make me a hypocrite for being mad?

I lie in Jarron's arms, again barely able to sleep. The silky-smooth sheets feel sticky tonight.

"What's wrong?" Jarron mutters eventually.

"Everything," I whisper against his bare chest. His arms feel so good, but that's more reason for my anxiety.

"Tell me."

I swallow. "I'm worried... I'm worried that I'm going to lose you." In more than one way.

"What do you—"

"I'm worried you're more at risk than you're letting on. That you're in danger when you leave. I'm worried you don't want me to be part of your world. I'm worried that the council is right and I'm just a replacement."

Jarron growls at those words, but he doesn't refute them.

I know he can't, but that doesn't stop it from being immensely frustrating.

Tell me I'm yours, I internally beg. *Tell me they're wrong and it was me all along.*

I wish I hadn't been such a stubborn fool six weeks ago when he'd asked me to let him claim me. I wish I could give in now and just rip the bandage off.

He wraps his fingers around my wrist and tugs it to his lips. He's gentle as he kisses the pulsing veins. "I'm not above begging, Candice."

I shiver and then blink away the tears. That wonderful

feeling chases away those doubts, but it also makes way for more.

"Let me mark you," he whispers. "Let me claim you. Let me give you the information you're asking for. Please, Candice."

The breath lodges in my throat, and I pull my wrist back from him.

He freezes for an instant, shocked at my refusal.

Do I want that? His mark?

I let the question linger in my mind, but the answer is clear.

I'm scared. I'm terrified, of what I'll learn once I have access to his emotions, but I want him anyway.

Yes, I want it.

But doing that will chase away my only chance at working with Bea.

If I'd let go back before the war started, I wouldn't have had weeks to brew on it, to let the doubts grow like weeds in my mind and I'd know.

Now, I put myself in a situation where I can't even have that much.

"Tell me what you need, Candice." His voice turns hoarse, that slight echo shifting into the tone. I know if I were to open my eyes, I'd see pitch-black eyes on his handsome face staring back at me.

"Time," I answer honestly. I just need time to work this out.

"Okay." He gaze is so soft. "That's fair. Anything else?"

"Distract me," I say.

His muscles tense, hands tightening on my waist. Sharp claws press into my skin, immediately causing my heart to race.

"You're going to have to be more specific than that," he says in a low growl that does things to my body. "Because I don't know if you want what I have in mind."

I laugh nervously. I think I very much want what he has in mind, but that doesn't make it a good idea.

"Maybe I should get the handcuffs out?" he offers more softly.

A flood of power and relief rushes through me. I'm not so sure I want to get out of bed and do something quite so active, but the idea is delicious anyway.

He knows—just as Laithe did—I crave control. It's my weakness.

My deal with Bea gave me some control. Gave me a way to do something, but it also trapped me in a new way. It tore me away from Jarron's team for a little while. And now that he's here, I'm faced with that reality.

I don't like it at all.

"No," I whisper. But I spin and pull myself over his chest, straddling his waist.

His eyes flare. There, that power is what I need.

"But you're onto something," I whisper, leaning down to kiss him. He meets my kiss, opening deeply. His taste envelops me when his soft tongue meets mine.

I rock against him—dangerous, dangerous territory.

I would like to do so much more with him. I know he wants that too.

I run my hands down his biceps to his forearms and his wrists, pulling them up and squeezing them together. I continue exploring his lips and tongue with mine. He writhes beneath me, moaning deep in his throat.

I like that a lot.

I bite his lip hard, and he hisses, "Fuck, Candice."

I grin. "Not tonight," I whisper.

He growls softly. I pull back enough to admire the sight of this powerful, sexy-as-sin man beneath me, willingly at my mercy, willing to give me anything I want. His stomach muscles are tight, his pecs stretched, and his dark eyes pierce me with their intensity.

"Tell me what you're thinking," I demand, voice low.

"I'm thinking about all the things I'm desperate to do to you."

My eyes flare. "Tell me," I say breathlessly.

His eyebrows rise. "Candice," he says. "My thoughts are—"

"Tell me," I demand.

His jaw clenches. "I'm thinking about flipping you off of me and changing forms just to see that look on your face again."

I flush. "What look?"

He smirks. "When I crouched over you and your body writhed beneath me—terrified but so turned on."

Fuck, I was not ready for that. My body clenches.

"That's the one," he murmurs smoothly. "You like it, don't you? Being afraid of me. You want more of it. You want me to devour you, as a beast and as a man."

I whimper at those words, at the imagery.

"Tell me," he says, voice gravelly. I'm still gripping his hands above his head, but somehow, I'm at *his* mercy. I can barely breathe.

"Yes," I pant.

His chest rumbles with that deep purr.

My eyes fly open at a new thought. Sex with him, right now, with so much uncertainty is unwise, but maybe there's something else that can scratch that itch for now.

I press my chest back down to his, lips going to his neck. My teeth are nothing like his, flat and weak, but I press them into his skin hard. He groans, and I smile. "Bite me, Jarron."

He flips me over so his weight is on top of me.

His lips seize the soft skin of my throat. I gasp, throwing my head back, ready for the pain and pleasure to take control of my mind and body, but his lips graze the skin, followed by his tongue. I shiver.

I'm panting, desperate for this one connection with him that

I'm allowed. The one way I can give myself to him entirely. A bite is pleasure, with no magic. Not a commitment, not a link.

My whole body jerks at the sharp press of fangs against my delicate skin, but he stops at just the gentle teasing press. He's taunting me, teasing and I could throttle him for it. But the feeling is nearly as wonderful as it is irritating.

His jaw tightens, just enough for me to arch into him and utter that one single plea. "Please," I gasp, almost involuntarily.

Jarron obeys.

His jaw clenches, powerful and demanding, and his fangs sink into my flesh. My vision flickers black, with the flare of pain.

I grit my teeth, but the discomfort is brief and an instant later it's like it never happened, allowing me to stay more aware than last time.

He sucks the blood from my body into his. Warm and soothing. He moans, his muscles clenching my arms so tight it borders on painful.

That inferno of pleasure takes its time to flare to life this time, but somehow that only makes it all the more intense. A blistering sensation spreads slowly like venom through my bloodstream, savoring it's possession of my body.

Jarron hungrily takes, and takes. Devouring. All-consuming. I want him to take more. I want to be dismantled to my very essence by this man.

When he pushes his body against mine, I feel his desire and it sends a new sensation through my body. My head lolls back and I moan in earnest.

He pauses, jaw still clenched on my vulnerable throat, but his body stills, as if surprised by the sound. He sucks harder against my sensitive skin, and I writhe beneath his hold. I whimper in his grasp.

He groans and bites harder. That's when my back arches, head dropping back, and my vision blurs.

That sweet, sweet bliss takes control, and I'm lost to this feeling. I'm falling, falling, falling, lost in his sensation so overwhelming and yet beautiful. I could live here, forever, in his trance where there is no pain or fear; there is only me and him and this feeling.

All at once, the pleasure ends and it's like I'm dropped in a bucket of cold water. I'm gasping, gripping his back in clenched fingers.

"No," I whisper, but already my mind is resettling in my body and I remember that he must stop. Shit. I'm reeling, spinning out of control. Trying to find my feet. My cheeks are burning hot. My body pulsing.

He drops his face into the crook of my neck, breathing me in as I pant. "You are fucking glorious."

I grin at that comment and soak in this feeling.

31
HE WASN'T SUPPOSED TO HEAR THAT

After the bite, I sleep like a rock, but since we're being studious and going to classes this morning, I still need to wake before I'm ready. Part of me wants to remain in his bed for the full week, giving in to the pleasure we're both desperately seeking. But obviously, that's very dangerous territory. So, instead, I force my heavy limbs up before Jarron gets out of bed and head into the bathroom.

He's still sleeping when I turn on the shower. The burning hot water eases my stiff limbs into relaxation. My fingers drift over the fresh marks on my neck.

Is that what a true claiming mark would feel like?

The wolf had tried to claim me, but I never felt the full effects because I killed him before he finished the process. I'd never felt his emotions or heard his thoughts, like apparently a claiming mark would allow.

With Jarron, that would be—intense, to say the least.

I know a bite is known to be erotic for demons, but I still can't get over how intense the feeling is. How all-consuming it is. It's truly out of body.

My body tenses, thinking about his desperate hunger, the way he devours me like I'm the sustenance he needs to stay alive. How it's brutal and beautiful at the same time.

Would it be the same if he took me in that way in his demon form?

My cheeks heat at the thought. I'd admitted last night how much I like that fear. He saw it. He knows the effect it has.

I quite like his demon form, in ways I would have never thought possible.

That fear is an exhilaration I've never felt, and I can't control what it does to my body, even if I don't understand it.

The hot shower was supposed to relax me, prepare me for a long day with a lot of attention, but instead, my body is winding up again. My blood is pumping fast. My limbs are pulsing.

And I suppose that's going to keep happening while Jarron is this close to me, sleeping in the same bed. So, maybe it's best if I alleviate some of that tension now.

I make sure the door to the bathroom is locked, and then I think about that demon who has such power over me while I *take care of things.*

Finally, my body and mind are relaxed by the time I'm washed and dressed. My hair is still damp, but I'm running out of time to get breakfast before classes, so I brush it out, throw on some quick mascara, dress, and leave the bathroom ready to face today.

But instead, I find myself facing a very intense demon prince.

I stop in my tracks, fingers paused in my wet, stringy hair. He's leaning against the closest armchair, hands in his pockets in a posture that oozes ease. But his eyes are fiercer than I've ever seen them, and though his bottom half is leaning back, his shoulders and neck are tense, slanted forward and giving the impression that he's an instant away from pouncing.

I swallow.

His eyes are fully black, not a drop of white to be seen.

"Mark my words, bright one," he says in a gravelly, ancient voice, "one day it will be me giving you that release."

I suck in a breath, face blood red in a second. I... thought I was quiet.

"I will earn the right to watch you come apart in pleasure."

32

FORGET HOMEWORK, I NEED TO CATCH UP ON THE DRAMA

I'm fairly certain my cheeks remain red the entire day.

The fresh bite marks are an easy excuse, though.

"Nothing to be bashful about, little human. Biting is a normal part of this world," Manuela says, passing me in the main hall.

She winks, and Jarron glowers at her.

"It's a term of endearment," she tells him when his chest begins to vibrate.

"It's fine," I tell him. "We're good. She's just teasing."

His shoulders relax slightly, allowing her to continue past without more conflict. "You've interacted more while I was gone?"

I nod. I can't tell him the full extent for obvious reasons. "She's one of my regular babysitters."

"My impression was that she tended to avoid social situations, even when... *babysitting*." He says the final word like it leaves a bad taste in his mouth. It's true that even when Manuela was around before she was fairly aloof. She's not exactly the warm and fuzzy type and nearly everyone is afraid of her.

"Yeah, that's true sometimes. Not always. I asked her for help with something, and she was—well, a challenge but willing to entertain me."

Jarron's lips twitch. "Am I allowed to ask what you needed help with?"

My chest tightens but I force a smile. "Oh! Yeah. Though, I don't want you to feel guilty or obligated. You've got enough on your plate."

He stops in the middle of the hall. "Candice, if you need something, there's nothing I would prioritize over you."

I look at my feet bashfully. "It's not technically for me. It was for Thompson." I rush the rest out. "He has some pack issues going on. We would have asked you to help, but you've been busy. Anyway, it didn't particularly go well. Manuela isn't a fan of Thompson, or wolf shifters in general. But she and I left things on a good note."

"Hmm," he says.

"What?" I ask sheepishly. He obviously has thoughts about this.

"Nothing. It's just interesting. Is that why Thompson left the school? His pack issues?"

I nod.

"I can still put out word that I am aligned with the heir to the pack; it might help a little bit. Everyone in the supernatural community will know full well I'm not going to be very active in supporting the pack, right now, but the fear might slow the progression some."

I nod.

"But Manuela is a hard person to befriend. She doesn't take easily to anyone. I wonder if I should be threatened by her interest in you." He eyes me subtly.

My cheeks are still flushed from earlier, so I doubt he notices if they get even more warm. "No, you don't have to worry about that." Manuela is... interesting, but I have zero intentions of anything more than friendship with anyone other than Jarron. "You have all my attention."

He squeezes my hand a little tighter as we enter my first class —High Orizian.

Jarron is tense for the first ten minutes or so—like is he even blinking?— while Professor Zyair is as cool and calm as ever.

The rest of the day continues much the same.

My teachers are even more accommodating than they have been since I was bitten. They started giving me preferential treatment the moment those marks appeared on my neck without any bidding at all, and now it's worse with the demon prince glued to my hip.

Only Professor Zyair seamed at ease having Jarron in class.

In potions, my teacher pulled me aside and asked me about my independent studies. I told her what I was working on, and she tried not to look shocked at the amount I've been brewing. I took the opportunity to ask if a permanent potion was possible.

"Oh, a permanent potion is indeed possible—depending on the type, of course—but quite difficult. And I don't say that to undervalue your talent. It's a very different thing to make a potion that will have a deep enough effect to change a being permanently. The most common form is something that alters DNA. A virus, perhaps, is possible but extremely dangerous to work on for obvious reasons."

Jarron fidgets in his seat, clearly uncomfortable with this idea.

"That's not something I'm ready to get into right now. I appreciate your input, though." And I mean that. I'm not going to be working with live viruses any time soon. I can certainly look into DNA-altering magic, but I have a feeling it's not something I'll be able to achieve in three weeks' time.

"However, elongating the usage of a potion is always possible. It will get more and more challenging the longer you extend the use, but I can give you some book suggestions to get you started. They can be found in the Elite Library. And given your passion and abilities, I am confident you'll be able to teach yourself these high-level skills in no time." She grins at me before her eyes flash to Jarron.

"Thank you," I tell her. And then, for funsies, I complete one of the year's potions projects perfectly in the hour before class ends. This earns me annoyed glares from the other students, but not one of them has ever truly tried to befriend me, so who cares if I'm showing off or not?

When we finally reach lunchtime Jarron nudges me as we walk down the hall. "Is it everything you hoped it would be? Being back in class?"

I snort. "I feel like I've missed nothing the last several weeks."

His lips twitch. Although, to be honest, as we enter the domed lunchroom filled with massive packs of supernaturals, I recognize that this is what I've mostly been missing.

I get to spend time with Janet and Lola in Elite Hall, but it's different when they're so out of their element.

The lunchroom is the school's natural habitat.

I spy Marcus on the other side of the cafeteria, ducking his head away from eye contact. That's a bad sign. I'd begun to suspect their relationship had fizzled out, but this nearly confirms it.

The biggest shock for me, though, are the pixies.

Since the beginning of the year, the pixies would dart around in their little swarms, hanging out with several different groups and tables but never ours.

Lola was never included.

So, imagine my surprise when that same swarm of pixies is

now hovering over the table with Lola and Janet. Stassi sits there too, which is news to me.

Laithe and Manuela are at their usual Elite table. Elliot, the shifter who sat with us a few times last semester, is back to his wolf pack.

Janet squeals when she sees me approaching with Jarron, even though I saw them twice in the halls this morning.

"I'm so excited you're back!" Janet says. "Both of you." She grins at Jarron.

"Thrilled to be here." He winks.

"I'm sure you missed your girl, didn't you?" Lola chirps, circling her perch another three times before settling down.

Jarron squeezes my hand. "Very much. It's really good to be back. It's amazing how normal it can all be, even when other things are... not."

"How is everything in Oriziah?" Janet asks, munching on a roll from her tray.

"Tense," he answers slowly. "But it's fine. Nothing major has happened yet."

That yet lingers over the table. We all feel it. What big thing will happen? An attack on the palace? An assassination attempt? A death?

I swallow and try not to think too deeply about it.

The group of at least a hundred pixies vibrate a few feet above the far side of our table, drifting closer to us.

"This is different," I mutter, eyeing the swarm of pixies.

Janet's eyes flare, but she says nothing.

I didn't know a whole lot about pixie behavior or societal structure before coming to Shadow Hills, but I've learned a lot since. Lola is essentially a pariah to her people simply because she failed to test out of Minor Hall fast enough.

She had to put a troll to sleep using her pixie dust but has performance anxiety, so she failed, and it cost her whole family and community. The story of her saving my and Janet's life against a minotaur by using her pixie dust has gone around the whole school, so the group started warming up to her a little after that. This, though... this is different.

Now, the pixies seem to be following her around.

Lola has expressed determination to stay in Minor Hall to prove a point, even though her worth is now being acknowledged. Being in Minor Hall doesn't mean she's lesser than the rest. She's strong and smart and capable, regardless of what her failure in one test claimed.

And the way she was treated for this perceived failure is unacceptable.

I can tell Lola feels a little torn about the attention.

"Yeah, ever since the list, it's been like this," Janet says.

"Well, it's a little bit more intense today with you here, but they've definitely been around more."

And this is exactly why it's bothered me not being out here with the rest of the school. I've asked Janet and Lola both what's been new, and they never mentioned the pixie palooza.

"So, you're accepted back into the community now?"

"They act like the last eight months never even happened," Lola says. Her arms are crossed. There's a slight purple glow to her wings and cheeks that make it clear that even if she's a bit bitter, she's thriving on the change in attitude. A little good karma finally came her way.

"It was their loss to start with," I say louder. Who cares if they hear?

A male pixie with red wings and dark-brown skin in a full tux lands on the table in front of me. My eyebrows rise. "I quite agree," he says with a surprisingly low voice. He has a short afro and broad shoulders—relative to the rest of his seven-inch-tall body, at least.

Another red pixie swoops down from the hovering hoard

above and drops to her feet beside him, followed by a yellow one. Both female. "Yeah, obviously," the red female says. "But there were reasons for it, you know." She crosses her arms and puffs out her chest.

"Shut up, Olivia," the male says.

"What kind of reasons?" I ask, not hiding my indignation in the slightest.

"It's motivation," a voice buzzes over my head. I jerk away from the sudden sound by my right ear. Then, a third female appears in front of my nose, purple wings vibrating. "When you don't live up to expectations there have to be consequences. It clearly worked for Lola; she got stronger because she had to."

I curl a lip in disgust. Lola's grimace matches mine. "Tell me this isn't your sister," I say.

Lola snorts, a smile teasing her lips. "Anita, meet Candice."

Anita flutters around and lands next to the little group of pixies on the table. The rest still buzz above, watching the events from afar.

"You're really trying to take credit for her accomplishments based on your cruelty? Ew."

Anita flinches. "She got stronger, didn't she?"

My mouth opens to respond, but Janet beats me to it. "Lola got stronger because she had unconditional love and support from her friends. Stop justifying your meanness. It's gross."

"Yes!" I say in solid agreement.

"If Lola wasn't such a sniveling weakli—"

"Get out," I say, not even recognizing the anger in my chest. "Leave now. You're not welcome here."

Anita gasps. But then, a shadow swipes over the table, pushing every pixie except Lola up and away from our portion of the table, creating a barrier between us.

Lola's jaw is ajar.

"Thanks," I mutter to Jarron.

He nods but says nothing.

"Lola, if you want them allowed back in, just say the word," I tell her. "They're your family, so I can deal if you want them here."

She puffs out her chest. "They can come back tomorrow. For today, we'll let them squirm."

I grin and watch as the pixies scatter, splitting into several smaller groups and then reconvening on the other side of the lunchroom.

"They haven't apologized or anything?" I ask eventually.

"Most of them, no. My sister acts like I should be *so grateful* I'm allowed back in the group, even though I'm in Minor Hall." She rolls her eyes.

"But Tyrane has been very kind." Janet wiggles her eyebrows.

"Tyrane?" I ask, eyes darting to Lola to gauge her reaction. Her wings glow a little, but she holds her chin high, trying hard not to show any emotion.

"A very handsome red pixie, who has given her a lot of attention lately," Janet says.

"Ooh, the male that showed up a few minutes ago?"

Janet nods eagerly, clearly excited about the development. I'm reminded of the time a wolf shifter rudely asked Lola why she didn't have a mate. Is this Tyrane her mate?

"And how does Lola feel about that?" I ask.

Lola doesn't respond, so Janet leans in.

"She lights up every time he looks at her," Janet says. "But she claims it doesn't mean much."

"I don't forgive easy," Lola says. "Although, he has been very sweet." She bites her lower lip.

I resist a smile. "Make him fight for it," I encourage her. "You know your worth."

At this, she lights up again, her eyes open and chest out.

33
A WIN IS A WIN

I feel more relaxed after lunch period, and I find I'm very excited for combat class.

For once, I might actually have a sparring partner!

I haven't had a proper partner in weeks, even before being trapped in Elite Hall. Jarron is not pleased with the idea, but I finally convince him to face me in the ring. He accepts the magic blocking cuffs and takes a defensive stance on the opposite side of the mat.

The rest of the class gathers to watch.

It's quickly clear though that Jarron has zero intention of making the first move, which is a challenge for me because I'm not used to being the aggressor. I size him up, trying to think about his potential weaknesses. His magic is very powerful, so he likely over-relies on it, but even so, he'll still be strong and fast.

I take a few careful steps toward him and prompt him to do the same. He obeys.

Finally, we're within striking range of each other, which would be a dangerous position to be in if I thought he was going to make an aggressive move. I'm certain he's not.

So, I take my first strike, just a test to see how he'll react. Quick as lightening, he jerks out of the way and resets across the circle. I face him, eyes narrowed.

Wash, rinse, repeat.

Jarron hasn't seen many of my tricks, so I can probably get a surprise hit on him, but I keep wondering if a hit will even do anything. Even without magic, he's large and thick with muscle. My little human hands won't do much.

And it's not like I want to go for vulnerable areas, like his eyes or nose. I don't actually want to hurt him. I'd save those scrappy tactics for life-and-death situations.

For this fight, I'd like to take him to the ground. That would be my ideal goal.

Is it possible?

We dance again, his eyes turning sharper as he waits for my next strike.

He knows I'm serious. This isn't a game, and I'm trying to learn how to do this right. My life might honestly depend on it in the future.

But it's really hard to take down someone stronger than me when they're not making any active moves. I need to use his weight against him.

I begin a smooth pattern of swings, which he avoids easily each time. I speed up, keeping the same pattern. Left, left, right. Left, left, right. Left, left, right. Every fourth swing, I turn lower, aiming for his thigh.

One the third try, he lets me land a hit to his leg.

I grin like I'm pleased, yet I'm anything but.

I don't let up my advancements. I swing, he shifts. I swing, he shifts.

Then, once his eyes flicker away from hands and to my waist, I change it up.

I twist, breaking the pattern and slam the back of my elbow

into his chest. He grunts, but the hit itself wouldn't have done anything. It's his shift away from the second swing that does him in because I've placed my foot right behind him.

His eyes flare as he loses balance. I give a small push to his chest, and over he goes.

Jarron's back slams to the ground. He lays there, staring in shock up at the domed ceiling of the arena.

I pant, kneeling next to him, one hand still on his chest. I don't intend to embarrass myself trying to wrestle him now that he's down. But it does feel good to know I was able to get in one good hit. If it were a real fight, with a being I wouldn't mind fatally harming, I'd have had an admittedly short opportunity to grab my dagger and shove it into his heart.

Of course, it took me six tries just to get into this position, with a demon not actively trying to hurt me but still. A win is a win.

In the next blink, though, I'm on my back, a very heavy male body pressed on top of me. His eyes are pitch black, full horns growing through his hair.

The class gasps, followed by panicked shouts.

"My bright one is impressive," he purrs down at me.

I swallow, suddenly very aware of my vulnerability in this situation. And every place his body touches mine.

"Jarron," a tense voice calls. "It's time to let her up now."

Coach is watching from the edge of the map, fear in her eyes.

Jarron wrinkles his nose. "I would not harm her," he says, voice echoey and filled with power. Even without magic, somehow it pulses through him, a low hum that doesn't disappear with the magic blockers. Maybe they aren't strong enough to fully block his power. "This was a fun dance," he tells me. And then rises to his feet and holds out his hand to help me up too.

I work to catch my breath while Jarron raises his palms to coach, his body slowly losing its demon-y flare.

"I think that's enough for today," she tells us, her breath short.

I chuckle but accept that one spar is enough. I spend the rest of the period stretching and doing a few punching exercises with Jarron while we absently watch the other students fight.

"You're good at this," he tells me after a while. "I didn't know this was another talent of yours."

I roll my eyes. "My parents had us in combat classes at an early age. I might be decent by human standards, but there's a lot to make up for against magical beings."

"I suppose I understand how you won that fight against multiple Elite wolves now. Potions *and* a talent in combat."

"I wouldn't call it talent."

"Well, I would."

I leave combat class feeling drained and hyped at the same time, hand in hand with Jarron. It felt really good to get some of my excess energy out, and that one small beat on Jarron helped raise my confidence.

The cool, fresh Idaho air feels fantastic on my lungs, and I suck it in greedily. I've spent so much of the last few weeks indoors. I have access to the balcony, where I can breathe in the open air, but I rarely use it without Jarron around.

He was right; it's amazing how normal things can feel even while the rest of my life is on the brink of imploding.

34
DEFINE ENEMY

After classes are through for the day, Jarron comes to my workshop with me. He stares up at the ceiling for a few moments then strides to the end of the room, fingers sliding over the countertops. Then, he continues his march around to the other side of the room.

He turns on the fire and watches it light and flicker for a few seconds.

"What?" I ask him finally, watching his methodical examination of the room.

"Just checking it out," he says.

I put my hands on my hips. "And?"

"It's... fine," he says.

"Fine?" I nearly shriek. "It's amazing. What are you talking about?"

Jarron shrugs and comes back to meet me at my active cauldrons. "I have high expectations for this place. It has to make up for—" He pauses, reconsidering his words.

I frown, eyes narrowed. I hadn't really considered that this would be the first time he's seen the workshop since it was his doing.

"But it's not impressive to you?"

"What you're doing with it is impressive," he says, nodding to my seven active cauldrons and the table with several books and notebooks open. I follow his gaze, and my stomach drops.

Delayed Death Potion

I can clearly see my scribbled notes about which potions I intend to use in my assassination attempt. And one of the loose pages between books? The list of names.

I slyly shift over to my notes and slip that list beneath a book, shut my journal, and stack a few books, pretending to tidy up.

"I don't mind the mess," he says. "I'm happy to see you've been hard at work."

I smile sheepishly.

Yep, hard at work planning an assassination heist behind your back. No biggie.

"How is the espresso machine?" He nods to the corner.

"Fantastic," I say and prove it by making us both perfect chai lattes.

He accepts his but only takes one sip before abandoning it.

"Are there any beverages I could create that you'd actually enjoy?" I ask.

"I enjoy everything you make."

I roll my eyes. "No need to lie."

He smirks. "I suppose there are some, but I wouldn't expect you to make them. Humans generally consider them... unsavory."

"Bloody pig-guts or something?"

Jarron chuckles but doesn't give a real answer.

I begin my methodical check of all my potions and even begin the delayed death potion I'd finally landed on, using my teacher's suggestions on how to strengthen the dosage and speed up the brewing time. I only have two weeks, and that'll include the process of boiling the concentration down as low as physically possible.

For my plan to work, I really, really need it to be a minuscule dose.

Within thirty minutes, I have my main weapon bubbling. Good timing because just a few moments later, Lola and Janet arrive.

They greet Jarron again like it's the first time they've seen him in months and then begin showing him around the workshop he had built like it belongs to them.

I can't stop grinning the whole time, and based on the light in Jarron's eyes, he's enjoying it just as much.

We spend a full ten minutes talking about Janet's spelled painting, which really seems to interest Jarron. He asks her questions about which types of spells she's used so far and if she's put any potions in the paint.

Her eyes widen. "No," she breathes. "Oh my God, I should have used potions in my paint!" She twists to look at me, brow furrowed.

"Is that even possible?" Lola asks.

I shrug. We all turn our attention to Jarron, who smiles, amused at us all. "Yes, it's possible. No, I don't know how."

Janet turns big eyes to me. I don't want to admit that it might be too late for her to use this tactic now—the painting is nearly finished. I don't think there's any big way to alter it now. But maybe... "When it's finished, maybe you can add an embossed top layer."

Her brows rise. "What would that do?"

"Add some texture and depth. But we could make an embossed paint imbued with an interest puller." I walk to the shelf and grab a book in which I know I've seen something about the interest potion. "The tricky part is altering the ingredients to make sure there aren't any negative reactions. You'll need to find some embossing paint and bring it in so we can study the ingredients. There might be alcohol in it, which is nearly impossible to work with in potions."

"So, find an alcohol-free embossing paint. Got it." Janet nods firmly. "I'll look tomorrow."

We spend another hour or so chatting about Janet's painting and Lola's music while I baby my new potion. Lola wiggles while she talks about her song. "I wish I could show you, but well, you wouldn't hear much of it."

"You could put us to sleep tonight," I say. "When it's time for bed!"

"But that would take away some of your *private time*." Lola winks.

I blush.

Jarron chuckles. "Sleeping with her is never a waste of our time."

"Well, not today," Lola says. "I don't think I'm ready yet. But I'll take you up on that when I'm closer to being finished."

"Deal," I tell her.

We have a steak dinner all together in my workshop, which is stupid delicious, and I feel so full. So good. Even though I'm keeping secrets from Jarron, and there's this undercurrent of anxiety about that, it feels amazing just to be with him.

"So," Lola says, once she's finished with her tiny steak, "I'm stuffed. Hey Jarron, have you heard from Bea at all?"

I cough on my bite. "Lola," I say through my food, eyes wide.

"What? I'm just curious. Trevor is working with your family, right? He hasn't sided with the rebels?"

"Trevor is on my side, yes. Bea is not."

We all still, letting his words settle.

His shoulders tense. "My brother is... not happy about any of it. But he has chosen his family."

We're quiet for a bit.

"She's his chosen," I say softly after a while. "Wouldn't he do anything to protect her?"

"Yes, he would," Jarron says. "Which is why I will never expect him to reveal her whereabouts or plans. There's a great amount of tension between us, even though I know he's making large sacrifices to help me. I constantly wonder if he's hiding something. If one day, he'll change his mind and put a dagger through my back for her."

Jarron's own loyalists will turn on him quickly to save themselves.

Was that a warning?

I swallow, heart clenched. Even though I know Bea has different intentions, that thought is terrifying.

"He can never harm her or do anything to put her at risk, but that does not mean they must always be on the same side. Mates can turn into enemies. It's not easy and almost always results in tragedy, but love does not mean you always agree on major things."

"So," Janet says softly, "you still intend to—"

"My brother knows full well," his voice is so firm, filled with violence, "if I ever see her again, I'll kill her."

An hour later, we're packing up to leave the workshop and I get the chance to pull Lola to the side. "What the hell was that?" I whisper-yell at her. "Bringing up Bea?"

She squeaks but leans in close. "We needed to know for sure. What if he was willing to forgive her?"

I sigh. "Well, he's obviously not."

"Right. But at least we know definitively."

"Everything all right?" Jarron asks from the door.

I force a big smile. "Yep! Almost ready." I rush to grab a book and my bag from the counter and then walk through the door Jarron is holding open for us.

Janet gives me wide eyes before passing us both and continuing toward Minor Hall.

"What was that about?" Jarron asks as we stop in front of his bedroom.

"Nothing. They just—" I pause, trying to come up with some kind of explanation. How much did he hear? All of it? None of it?

"They were asking about Bea's role in the games the other day and wondering how the secret got out... about your chosen."

Jarron winces. He pushes open the door and follows me in. "I hate that it's a topic of conversation at all."

My lips part, blood running cold in guilt.

"It's not your fault," he clarifies. "It just shouldn't have ever happened. And yes, I am firmly convinced that Bea is responsible. She did this." His jaw clenches.

I cross my arms, feeling dizzy. I take in a few deep breaths. Jarron walks up behind me and wraps his strong arms over mine. His chin rests on my shoulder.

"I swear I'll make her pay for this one day. She will get what's coming to her. And anyone who aids her will feel my full wrath."

A shiver shudders through my whole body.

Does that include me?

35
I NEED YOU TO TRUST ME

My anxiety only continues building through the week. I swear, Jarron has been watching my every move incredibly closely. I've seen him reading over my shoulder more than once.

I can't tell if it's honest paranoia or if he's suspicious of something. He hasn't said anything. He hasn't commented on my potion choices or the subjects of the books stacked by the armchairs—books about some very specific species of supernaturals.

And more and more, I find myself desperate for the week to end so I can get back to my preparations. I'm only able to get bits and pieces done here and there while Jarron is watching my every move and while my heart is racing every time it even crosses my mind.

The nervous butterflies don't leave my body for days. I can't stop thinking about Jarron's words. His promise that he'll punish Bea and anyone who would help her.

I know he cares about me, regardless of who his chosen mate is, but if he sees my role with Bea as a betrayal—

I shake my head to clear it from those thoughts. I just have to succeed.

Succeed, free Liz with Bea's help, and no matter who ends up on the throne beside Jarron, we'll be okay. We'll find a way to be okay.

My sister will be free. The war can end.

I'll survive the blistering pain of heartbreak if need be.

We just have to succeed.

"Happy birthday, sunshine."

Jarron pulls me into his arms, still wrapped up in the smooth silk sheets together. My heart lifts, twists, and falls back down. I hate how much fear is ruining these wonderful moments.

"Thanks," I whisper into his chest.

"Everything okay?" He studies me closely, a small frown on his lips.

"Yep."

He doesn't look convinced.

"Bad dream," I add on.

"Want to talk about it?"

I shake my head. "Just going to enjoy the day."

I sit up and stretch out, working to shed the anxious thoughts from my mind.

I inhale sharply. My chest fills with joy.

On the coffee table by the fireplace, is a massive bouquet of red, green, and blue calla lilies. Even the colored ones are so dark that at the right angle they look black.

I hop up immediately and pick up one of the dark flowers. "Thank you," I murmur, smelling it and trying to savor the wonderful scent.

Then, I rush back to my bag beside the bed and pull out my journal. I carefully wedge the calla lily between the pages and press it closed.

"What are you doing?" he asks, utterly appalled at my action.

"Saving it."

"By crushing it?"

I chuckle. "Yes. As wonderful as fresh flowers are, they only last a couple of weeks, like this. The last time you sent me flowers—which I loved, by the way, even if I didn't want to admit it—I didn't save any of them, and I regretted it when we were apart. And actually..."

I flip toward the end of my journal and carefully pull out a flattened, dried lily, holding it out to him. Pieces of the dark red pedal flake off the moment his fingers touch it. He looks horrified.

"I received another bouquet—from the jinn, I assume—during that time. I kept one, even knowing it wasn't really from you because I refused to let some bully taint a good memory. I wanted to have a piece of that time to remember. Now, I have a real one to save instead."

My heart clenches at the thought that I might need that one day, but I shake off the feeling and allow myself to enjoy the now.

"Why would she send you flowers?"

My chest tightens. I suppose I didn't explain the gift that had come with that note back when we were tracking them. "They were the same kind of flowers you had given me before, so for a moment, I thought... but the note inside of them read, 'He's not yours. He was never yours.'" I keep my gaze steady on the closed book.

Jarron is quiet for several beats. There's no sign he's angry or annoyed. He just lets me feel the emotions. Or maybe he's dealing with his own. I don't know.

I don't think I want to know.

"Was she like that?" he murmurs. "It's been a really long time since I knew Liz. Before the games, was that the kind of person she was?"

"No," I say quickly, finally meeting his stare. There's little to read on his expression, though. He's tense, but that's all. "No, Liz was kind. Mostly. I mean, she liked attention and sometimes was mean to people who threatened that, but no, she never taunted people. She wasn't a bully. She cared about me most of all. She wouldn't want to hurt me like that."

He scoots off the bed to sit on the ground beside me. "So, why do you think she would do something like that, then?"

I twist my lips. "I don't know," I whisper. I honestly hadn't really thought that through. "We don't know how much the council is controlling her or watching her. Maybe it wasn't her idea. Or maybe it was a hint at the council's motives, without being obvious she was trying to help. Like she had to make it seem harsh so they wouldn't catch on that she was getting around their rules?"

Jarron's brow pinches. "What rules?"

My face falls. I forgot some of that information came from Bea. "I don't know. They didn't know she was going to put that portal into the pit for me. She left me that note in the *Behind Alien Eyes* book. They clearly knew she was taunting me, but she was leaving extra clues for me to find. So, maybe this was one of them." I shrug.

Jarron's gaze is distant, his jaw tight. Finally, he seems to shake off whatever deep thoughts took him away. "So, what do you usually do for your birthday?"

I blink at the stark transition. It's supposed to be a happy day, right. "Nothing," I say. "Eat cake with Liz. That's really it."

It strikes me that this will be my first birthday without her. She's only a year younger than me, and her birthday is two weeks after mine, so our parents would usually drop by to visit our school somewhere between the two. Back before we went to boarding schools, we'd go do something fun as a family.

"What kind of cake?"

"Chocolate cake with chocolate icing." I nod sharply. It was both of our favorites.

"Noted."

"I assume we're just going to classes, right?" It's Friday, and as much as I usually wouldn't mind skipping, it feels a lot less exciting when I'm literally allowed to just not go whenever.

"If you want."

I narrow my eyes, wondering if he has something else in mind, but I figure I'll just enjoy it as it comes.

"Eggs benedict first?" he asks. "Lola and Janet will be in the speakeasy soon."

I gasp and joyfully rush to get dressed to go meet my friends for a delicious birthday breakfast.

Despite the uncertainty and fear still lingering on the edges of my mind, this has honestly been an incredible birthday.

I miss Liz enough that it's a physical pain, but that pressure gets buried beneath laughter and joy and love while I'm with my friends.

I've never received more presents than I did today. I don't even remember who some came from because there were so many people looking to give me things. More princess benefits, I guess.

Janet gave me a canvas with a hand-painted meadow, filled with calla lilies. Lola gave me a silver ring and a new hoodie, with dark rose petals all over it. Manuela gave me a beautiful mug made of thomsonite. I got an ancient-looking potions book in the mail from Thompson that I'm super excited to go through.

I also got chocolate-covered strawberries, another bunt cake, three bouquets of flowers, several items of clothing, and a few books.

But it's been the laughter and care that's stuck with me the most, and now, my heart thuds wildly in my chest as Jarron slides a bronze key into the knob of the third bronze door.

That bronze key looks achingly familiar—quite possibly it's the one I found in his drawer a while back. Which means I had access to this door the whole time.

Probably for the best that I didn't know it.

He gifted me a stunning black dress with enough sparkles to make it look like a galaxy, and now, I'm going to get to see what's in his secret room!

"You have no idea how much it's bothered me not knowing what's in here," I whisper as the door cracks open.

He pauses. "I can show you, but it comes with limitations and very strict rules."

"Oh," I say.

"If anyone ever passes through this portal, I will feel it. It's protected because it's... personal. I don't keep much from you, Candice, and I'm going to let you in, but it's incredibly important that you of all people respect the boundaries I set. You could ruin —" He swallows, fear in his eyes. "You can only see the few parts I show you. Going anywhere else would be a true betrayal. Do you understand?"

My stomach twists. "Okay," I answer, even while my mind spins. How would it be a betrayal?

I'm not sure exactly what that means, but inching toward answers is still better than nothing. I'm eager to find out what's beyond the door, especially now that I know it's so important to him.

The world beyond is pitch black. Jarron holds out his hand to me and guides me inside once I take it.

Jarron and I walk together through the bronze door, but we only step into solid darkness.

He slides his arm around my waist from behind and presses his chest to my back. "Your heart is racing."

"Uh-huh." *Very clever response, Candice.*

He chuckles, reaches somewhere beside him, and a massive red spotlight clicks on, revealing a stone archway with shimmering magic.

"Remember I said there would be rules?"

I nod.

"This portal will take us to a house. There is only one room we are allowed to go into right now. The rest of it must remain off limits. Do you understand?"

My ears and cheeks burn.

"Why?" I whisper. *A house. He has a secret portal that leads to a house. A house I'm not allowed to see much of.*

He pauses, still holding me tight in the darkness.

"I need you to trust me." His voice is hushed.

I close my eyes, hating that this is so hard for me.

"Can you promise?"

My heart aches with that doubt and fear all over again, but it's not new and I'm getting used to it at this point. It's my own fault. My own doing.

If I'm going to torture myself, I may as well stop being a brat about it.

"Yes," I whisper. "Yes, I promise."

He releases a relieved breath and then walks through the portal, tugging my hand gently behind him. And again, I find myself in a whole new world.

36
DESPERATE HOPE

Our feet land on the loft of a two-story house with bright open windows and pretty wooden banisters. Out the window are several trees and a patch of sand.

"Where are we?" I ask but wonder if I'm even allowed to know that.

He places his finger over his lips, then tugs me forward. Jarron doesn't usually show his emotions in typical human ways. If he's upset or angry or protective, he changes into his demon form. So, it's strange for me to feel his pulse in his hand, still clinging tightly to mine.

His shoulders are tense. He carefully guides me down a hall with a few very mundane, white doors. He opens the first to reveal a small room lit with candles all around.

There's one small table, with two chairs, that is set with plates and silverware and glasses, decorated with flowers and a red tablecloth.

Behind the table is a large white-paned window and French doors that lead to a small balcony.

"It's beautiful," I say. And it is. It's lovely. But also not exactly what I'd expected.

What is significant about this house? From what I can tell, it's a fairly typical North American home.

Why can't I see other parts of it?

Jarron pulls out a chair for me, like he's been studying how to be a gentleman or something. He takes the seat across from me and pours us each champagne.

"It's not demon culture to have dungeons full of captives or anything, right?"

He stops filling his flute to give me a look. "Excuse me?"

"Just wondering why I'm not allowed to see the rest of the house. You made it sound like a really big deal."

He continues pouring but doesn't comment on that. "No, demons don't regularly hold captives for recreation, nor are there any in this house."

"Just checking."

Jarron then snaps his fingers, and two full plates of steaming food appear on our plates. I gasp. "How did you do that?"

It's a red soup with several types of seafood and rice. It smells incredible.

He raises a brow like that was a silly question.

"I was under the impression that suddenly appearing food wasn't a thing. Or if it was, I heard that spelled food tastes terrible."

"It's not spelled food. I simply cast a spell to have it arrive now."

"So, they could do that during lunch, and they just choose not to?"

Jarron chuckles. "It would require a wasteful amount of magic to do that for the entire school at once."

I shrug and lift a spoonful of the spicy concoction. "What is it?"

"Gumbo. You mentioned wanting to try it."

"When?" I don't remember that.

"A few months ago, when we were talking about what to order from Elite Hall. You said you'd always wanted to try it but only if you could get it from Louisiana."

My lips part. "Is this—"

"From a little restaurant in New Orleans that is known by the locals for it's wonderful gumbo."

"Amazing," I breathe. "You've been holding on to that for a while, then?"

He nods, his honey brown eyes shining. "Try it. I want to know if it was worth the trouble."

"No pressure." I roll my eyes.

The moment the spoon hits my lips, my eyes flare. A zing of flavor explodes on my tongue. "Wow." It's hot and spicy and unlike anything I've ever tasted. It's also absolutely delicious.

Jarron doesn't take his eyes off of me.

"What?" I ask bashfully.

"You're beautiful," he says. "I just enjoy watching you experience things."

"Creeper," I joke then wink. "It's really good. Definitely worth the trouble."

He nods. "Good." Then, he takes his own first bite. He pauses mid-slurp.

"Do you hate it?" I ask, waiting for his reaction. Demons don't generally appreciate human food.

He shifts it around his mouth for a moment, expression full of confusion. "That is not what I expected."

"In a bad way? Or good?"

He swallows and stirs his plate. Then, he takes another large bite. "Good, I think."

I chuckle, and we each continue eating. "Definitely the right choice to get it from New Orleans," I say. "Although, I wonder if it's cheating to have it magically delivered here. The atmosphere of New Orleans is probably part of the fun."

"I could take you there if you wanted."

My brows rise. "Right now?"

He nods.

"How?"

"It would be a long way for me to fly you, but..."

My jaw drops. No way does he mean—

"We have a portal-maker ally," he says, lips spreading into an amused grin.

"Oh," I mutter stupidly. "Is Manuela the one who made your private portal?"

Jarron nods in answer, taking another bite. It strikes me, just now, that this is his private place. He has a room just for him. He could have anything in there. Anything he wants. A portal to take him anywhere. And he chose this random house.

There's clearly more to the house than just what I've seen, made obvious by the promise not to sneak off anywhere, but it seems so bizarre to me. I recall the portion of Behind Alien Eyes that mentions a demon building a house for their chosen.

Even if that's what this was, would it have to remain a secret? Would seeing the rest of the house somehow give away who it was built for?

I glance over his shoulder to the window looking down on what appears to be a fairly regular neighborhood street. I can see two houses from here, and they each have a style I recognize. Large with big open windows and light-colored siding, lifted off the ground by a few feet in case of flooding.

Without thinking, I stand and cross the room, looking closer at the view out the window. His chair squeals as he rushes to follow me.

"What?" he asks.

"We're on Myre Island," I realize, not bothering to turn back to read his reaction.

"Yes."

He has a house on Myre Island... accessed through his private room at school. I shake my head; the complete ridiculousness of the magical world will never cease to amaze me. "Why?"

He hesitates.

"This isn't your parents' house. It's not the house my parents rented."

"No, it's my own."

"Your own..."

He's barely an adult with his own house. I know better than to ask any more questions, but my brain is pulsing.

"Why did you bring me here?" I blurt out. "If I can't know the details around the history of the house, I can't see the other rooms, I can't ask questions."

It feels almost cruel.

Maybe that's the point? He wants to guide me into this state where the answers are right there, staring me in the face, so that it pushes me to take the plunge and accept his mark?

He's taunting me with the truth.

And I want it.

His eyes are soft as he grips my upper arms. "I don't mean to upset you, I promise. I brought you here because I wanted to share it with you, at least the parts I can. I was hoping... we could take a short trip when dinner is finished. We could walk through the neighborhood, visit the beach. Maybe fly over the ocean?"

I inhale sharply. "Really?"

He nods then leans in, resting his forehead to mine. "I tried to figure out what you'd want for your birthday. I thought about what I'd want to give you." He pulls a small box out of his pocket. "I decided to cover as many bases as I could."

I press my lips together tightly as he reveals a necklace with a gorgeous ruby teardrop pendant.

"It's beautiful," I whisper, staring at the glistening stone. I've certainly never felt as special as I do today. Jarron carefully clasps the necklace around my neck, and I run my fingertips over the gem.

"Am I doing okay at the birthday thing? It's new for me." He grins sheepishly.

My eyes flare. "I think you're doing okay." I step in closer, pressing myself against his body.

"I had low expectations, honestly," I tell him. "I wasn't sure if you would be here, and I didn't blame you."

"Birthdays are important in your culture, from what I understand."

"Kind of. Not particularly to me, though. Is that the reason you came back this week?"

He pulls back to look me in the eye. "Let me ask you this. If I had not come, would there have been even a tinge of disappointment?"

"Yes," I admit. "But only a little."

"Then it's important."

I sigh and curl back into his arms. "There are much more important things," I say. "Like your safety and peace in your world. My sister's life. Justice against the Cosmic Council. Those things will always matter to me more than gifts."

"Do those things matter more than your happiness?"

I bite the inside of my lip. Do they? "I... don't think I'm capable of being truly happy until those things are resolved."

Jarron's muscles tense. "Is that what you need?" he murmurs against my hair. "Is that what it will take to earn you?"

Earn you.

I shiver against those words, but I brush the hope away, afraid of letting it rise too high because I can't accept it yet.

What do I really need? Answers. Truth.

"I don't know."

"The most frustrating part of all of this," he says, "is that I know what you need. And it's the one thing I cannot give you."

My brow furrows. "What?"

"Assurance."

My stomach twists.

"I cannot give you a definitive answer before you take the risk. I am not able to. I wish I could make you understand, but most of all, I wish you would trust me."

I wish you would trust me. I swallow down a mountain of guilt.

Jarron has always been nothing but incredible to me. He's given me everything I've asked of him.

This is the one thing he's asked of me.

And I haven't given it.

Trust. That's all he's requesting.

And here I am, hiding more and more from him.

I push that pain and guilt deep, deep down. Maybe I need to reassess some things, but right now isn't the time to do it.

"Are you finished eating?" he asks.

I look back at our plates, half-finished. It was delicious, but my stomach doesn't seem able to handle much more.

"Yes. It was amazing, though."

Jarron slides open the door to the balcony looking over a small street with several beach houses lining it. The salty air feels amazing.

I haven't been back here since—well, since the day after it happened. I have so many good memories of this place, though. This island is exclusive, for only select supernatural families which is why it was one of the few places Jarron and his brother could be free without fear. That night a vampire washed up on shore was a shocking development. Here, he can be open about who he is.

"So, how do we get down there if we can't see the rest of the house?" I ask.

Jarron smirks just before he swoops me into his arms and leaps over the banister. I scream, but he's in his demon form in an instant, wings spread wide to catch the wind, and we glide smoothly down to the street.

"Any more questions?" he asks in a cocky tone just before he drops me to my feet.

I shake off the fear of the moment, adrenaline still pumping. It's truly bizarre being on these streets, just casually standing beside the very monster who shook my confidence in all things magic. The beast who chased me away from an entire world.

That heartbreak was sincere. We weren't romantically involved back then, but losing a best friend that traumatically was just as painful.

I missed him, even while I hated him, and I used that rage to cover up my pain.

Jarron and I stroll down the streets, reminiscing about our time here. We pass Jarron's parents' house and my parents' old house, and then we make our way to the beach just before we miss the final show of the sunset.

I shiver in the cool ocean breeze. He wraps his arms around me from behind, his warmth seeping into me.

"I'm glad I was able to be here for your birthday," he tells me. "And I'm even more glad I could bring you here."

I sigh against his warmth and comfort. "I'm glad too."

37

HOW DO I FIX THE PROBLEM WHEN IT'S ME?

Everything is wrong, even while everything is perfect. It's complete torture knowing that the man I adore is perfect and my actions are hurting him.

Jarron doesn't know it yet, but I am lying and pushing him away, and he absolutely doesn't deserve it.

I need you to trust me.

I do. I do trust him. Even while part of my mind fears the truth, I trust him. Somehow, he has my heart so fully that even when it makes no sense, I believe there has to be a way.

I lie beside Jarron in bed, wrestling with the silk sheets, restless the whole night.

I'm ready, I think. Ready to take the chance. To leap and find out how badly it will hurt when the ground rises up to meet me, crushing my heart to bits, or how amazing it will feel when Jarron's wings catch the wind and carry us into the sky.

The problem is, if I fully give him that trust, Bea dies. As much as she's done legitimate wrong and maybe deserves those consequences, I don't want her to be harmed.

I made her a promise, and I don't want to go back on it.

Hours of restlessness later, I finally come to an uneasy conclusion.

I need to tell her. I will tell Manuela to send a message to Bea. *Run.*

Run because I'm going to tell him.

I'm going to choose Jarron this time.

"You seem tense," Jarron comments the next morning. I look up from the book I'd been staring at without reading, trying to hide the fear pulsing through me.

"Really?" I force a smile. We've been in my workshop for the last hour while I think through how I'm going to pass along the message to Manuela without Jarron hearing it. He stays by my side nearly every moment.

He nods. "You know, I keep thinking about our conversation about Bea the other day. I've been waiting to see if you were ever going to bring it up again or tell me what's wrong, but I have to go back to Oriziah tomorrow, and—"

"It's nothing," I say quickly. "I mean, I'm tense about everything, you know?"

His brow crinkles, but he nods anyway. "Yeah, sure."

He glances down at the book I'm holding. I'd helped Janet create the magically enhanced paint we talked about yesterday, and since then, I've been studying ways to increase my nullifier strength.

"Why do you need a delayed death potion?" he asks.

My heart sinks. It shouldn't. There's nothing specific about a delayed death potion—as opposed to an instant death potion—that would expose my secrets, but my heart still clenches.

And Jarron seems to notice, but he doesn't comment again. The tension settles slightly, but that sharp gaze he's had for the last few days is heavier than before. He's leaving soon, and these mysteries are weighing on him. I need to get this done soon, or else I'm going to lose my chance.

"Can we head to the speakeasy?" I ask casually after a few minutes of silence. Jarron nods, his jaw still tense.

My heart thuds wildly.

Can he tell? Can he feel it?

The hall feels dark and narrow as we walk side by side, the silence as heavy and palpable as his shadow magic was a few months ago.

Warn Bea, then I can make this life-changing choice. Warn Bea, and then I can fix the wedge I've created between me and Jarron. Warn her, then I can stop him from hating me.

"And why are you researching cyclops and griffins?"

I stumble on my next step. "No specific reason, I just—"

He grabs my arm and pushes me up against the wall of the hallway. "What are you keeping from me?"

My eyes widen.

"I can feel it," he says.

Not now, Jarron, I internally beg. *Let me fix this first. Don't figure it out now and hate me for it.*

He stares down at my trembling hands, his posture intimidating. "Candice," he commands. "Tell me right now."

"No." I wince. "I can't."

He grabs my wrist, staring down at the two small, magical tattoos that remain inconspicuous on my body. Magic rushes through my veins, and I feel something release.

"What was that?" I gasp, pulling from his grip.

"I broke the magical connection you had to the games."

I frown. The partial tattoo from when I started to sign the

contract. Nothing had ever really happened with that link. And it doesn't mean much to me now. "Why?"

"Because you're hiding things from me, and that was a risk. I should have done it weeks ago but I'd forgotten. No one is allowed to have a hold on you." He clenches his hands into fists.

"No one but you?" I bite out. Why do I sound angry at that idea? I'm not. I'm just backed into a corner and I'm afraid.

The devastation on his face sends a shockwave of pain through my body. "Not even me, apparently," he mutters. "Why? Why won't you accept me?" He shakes his head, already knowing I won't give him an answer.

"Because I'm a fucking coward, that's why."

He clenches his jaw. "What are you afraid of?"

"The truth," I whisper. But I'm not afraid of his truth anymore. I'm afraid of mine. I'm afraid that if I tell him what's going on, I'll lose what little power I have. I'm afraid he'll convince me to let it go.

I'm certain he will, actually. But I know I need to tell him anyway because he is more important than doing things on my own. I need to believe in him to do everything he can to save Liz, just as much as all the rest of it.

We're a team. We're supposed to be a team.

He's put me first in so many ways, and I continue to do the opposite.

I am a coward, but I want to change that. I'll force myself to be the brave, fierce girl who deserves him.

But I need more time.

He steps forward, closing the gap between us that I'd created when he broke the magical bond I had with the Akrasia Games. "What truth are you afraid of?"

"Don't you already know that?" I spit, ashamed of my own cowardice.

"There's more," he says softly. "There's more you're hiding

from me. There's more reason than just fear that I chose your sister over you."

Those words, hypothetical or not, cut me deep. The tears break free and stream down my cheeks. Just hearing him say that fear out loud is fucking devastating.

I hadn't realized just how much it would bother me to hear *him* say it.

I hadn't realized how much power this fear had over me.

His shoulders deflate at the first sight of those tears. "I don't want to pressure you," he says, "but it's so frustrating. I'm so close. You look at me like you're ready to take the risk. To bet on me. On us. Like you're ready to understand, but then you pull away. Why? There's another reason. Something is holding you back from me; I can feel it."

I blink. He's right, but how do I—I can't tell him yet.

"Could it be because you're afraid I'll learn some hidden truth about you?"

My wince is answer enough. His nostrils flare, eyes turning pitch black.

He's right; I am hiding something from him. Something big. So, I don't feel like I have the right to be mad about that. I don't have a right to be mad about any of this.

But he does.

Jarron's shoulders are hunched, his eyes dark, but he says nothing when he enters the speakeasy. Again, he's not in complete control of his demon. Does that mean something?

"Is that why you came back?" I don't know why the words blurt out. Maybe it's to distract him from his train of thought. He is close to uncovering my secrets, and I don't want him to be. Or maybe it's just because it's crossed my mind a few too many times to quiet the wonderings. "To convince me to take your mark?"

He frowns. "Why does that sound like an accusation?"

It wasn't meant as an accusation, but I still can't help but wonder if it means something.

Was that the real reason he took the risk of leaving his home world that's on the brink of war to spend time with me? Was that his goal and why he's pushing me more now?

If so, it means it's important enough for him to leave his world at such a volatile time.

"Why is it so important for me to accept the mark?" I ask it as gently as possible. It's not an accusation. It's an honest, sincere question.

He sighs. "Candice, I can't—"

"Can't or won't? What would happen if you were to bring home a marked person and claim her as your mate? Would the war end?"

He frowns. "No."

"Not without standing before the Bright Tribunal first?" I say absently, working through the information.

The shift is instant. The room cools. Jarron's shoulders sink, his jaw clenched as he stands up straight. "Where did you hear that?"

My eyes flare. I try to hide my reaction, but he saw it. He's watching my every move so closely.

"Who?" he demands.

"Why? What does it matter that I know—"

He jerks forward, hands on either side of my head, leaning over me. "It matters because whoever is giving you this information is going behind my back to do it. Who? Laithe has not told you any of that. You're smart, Candice, but there is no way you'd know that specific element without someone slipping you bits of truth to manipulate you. Is this why—" He jerks back, some realization hitting him. A rumble begins in his chest, but this time, it's not the sweet purr I'm used to.

It's devastating anger.

I'm frozen in place as the roar rips from his body. He's no longer human in an instant.

The winged beast storms away from me down the hall.

I don't even know what just happened. What did he figure out? What does he think he knows? Will he charge straight into Bea's room and into the portal? Will he tear her apart before I get the chance to explain?

Will he hate me for meeting with her?

The crevice in my heart widens, threatening to shatter.

"Jarron," I call after him. I rush to follow the winged demon storming through Elite Hall. "Jarron!" I call again, but he doesn't answer. He doesn't care that I'm terrified or that there are tears streaming down my face.

He's too fast for me to keep up with, but I try anyway.

There's a crash and scream and then a terrifying, monstrous roar up ahead, and I skid to a stop in the sunroom, where the grey-skinned demon is seething before a very annoyed and tense Dryad witch. Magic shimmers between them. A shield? Did Jarron attempt to attack Manuela?

"Tell me what you've done," he says. "Tell me where to find the traitor."

Manuela's lip curls. "Use your words, Jarron baby. Hasn't anyone ever told you that?"

He roars, shaking the walls. "Tell me now, or I'll tear this shield down and rip you apart, ally or not."

Manuela crosses her arms and rolls her eyes. "I'm sure you can figure it out on your own. Your girlfriend did." She nods to me.

Then, there's a shimmer in the middle of the room and Manuela is gone. I suck in a breath. She can just summon a portal out of nowhere like that? How powerful is she, exactly?

Jarron's roar sends bits of the ceiling crumbling down. When he turns back, his black eyes don't even land on me.

"Jarron, please," I beg. But he doesn't heed my voice. The crack in my heart widens when he storms right past me, his massive wings scraping against the walls of the narrow hall.

Toward Princess Bea's long-abandoned bedroom.

38
TRUST MUST BE GIVEN, NOT TAKEN

Helplessness suffocates me. As much as I try, air will not enter my tight lungs.

"Breathe, princess."

I cough but finally suck in those breaths as Manuela steps back into the room through a shimmering portal. "How?" I pant.

"What, this?" She wiggles her fingers, making the magic shimmer again. "It doesn't take me far, but no, I won't tell you where to."

So, she just summons portals? Sure, yeah. I don't have the brain capacity to even question it right now.

"Jarron," I mutter, brain still filled with panic. "I don't know how he—I was going to try to warn her to run."

She waves me off like it's of no consequence, except we both know she and Bea are at risk now. She might have the power to hold him off but not enough to survive an outright attack. "It is a bit late for that now."

"What now?" I ask. "Is he going to—"

She nods, her expression somber for the first time since I've known her. "She always knew it was a possibility."

"Can't we—is there anything we can do?"

"You could try to follow him. Convince him to stop. Although, he doesn't seem to be in a listening mood now. You could drop yourself into the pit with the nightmares and hope he decides saving you is more important than his revenge."

Nausea rolls through me.

She shrugs. "Or something else that might distract him. You wouldn't happen to have a key of his, would you?" Her eyes flit over my body like she'd be able to tell if I had one in my pocket or something.

"No—but I—"

Oh. The house.

If anyone ever passes through this portal, I will feel it.

The house. If I could get back into the house, would that be enough to distract him from his hunt for Bea?

"While you figure that out, I'm going to make myself scarce for a while."

I swallow.

Entering his house without permission is a betrayal. Seeing what is hidden there would hurt him... That's what he said.

"He might be displeased by that as well," she says, "but it could just work out best for both you and Bea if it plays out right." There's a massive crash in the background. Magic pulses through Elite Hall.

I flinch.

"Quickly," she says in a hushed voice.

I blink, and she's gone.

I don't have time to think this decision through. All I know is guilt and panic and confusion and one chance.

One chance to get the answers I've been craving. One shot at saving my only access to infiltrating the Cosmic Council.

I have to try.

39

THE TRUTH I'VE BEEN SEEKING IS
FINALLY AT MY FINGERTIPS

I rush into Jarron's room and pray the key is back where I'd found it the first day. I rustle through the loose papers and pull out the small key, heart hammering.

I swallow. Entering this house without him is a betrayal. But it's also the only way to protect Bea. My heart hurts. My lips tremble. I have to do it.

Hurting Bea is wrong. I feel it deep in my bones.

So I sprint down the hall, key in hand, and waste no time to slide it into place. The door clicks open.

My heart thuds, praying that somehow, someway, this will save Bea.

I can't breathe when I enter the surprisingly small and very dark room. I don't even bother to try to find the light—I just rush forward until I feel the shimmer of magic.

This time, what lies beyond may be life or death for someone who might not be a friend but is definitely someone I need.

Tears blur my vision as I stand on the loft of an open beach house with white walls and big windows.

I don't know for sure that Jarron will come. I don't know how long it will take. But my hands are trembling. My heart breaking from sheer fear.

What if I've hurt him? What if this all goes to shit? What if I'm wrong? What if. What if. What if.

Some of them are stupid fears, some are legit.

But in reality, the thing that hurts the worst is the fear that I'm not worthy of him.

That I ruined this.

I take in deep breaths, trying to hold back the sobs threatening to overwhelm me.

I run my hand over the banister, taking in the limited view from here. Outside, the sand is glistening white in the harsh sun.

The smell of salt is comforting.

Here, in his house, are the answers to my most pressing questions.

Am I his chosen?

Because that's what this place is, right? This is the house he's been building for his chosen, filled with things she would love.

The High Orizian will throw their passion and excess energy into the building of a house specifically for his chosen. They fill it with everything their future mate loves. Her style, her smell, her favorite colors, her hobbies.

Will I know the answer the moment I enter one of these other rooms? Will the walls be filled with Liz's old art projects? Will there be a ballet studio and a closet filled with clothes that are her perfect size in the bright spring palette she became obsessed with last year?

Or will there be an espresso machine, a library, and a potions workshop?

This is the physical proof I've been hoping for. It's right here.

I could find out definitively right now.

This part of the house is pretty but fairly generic. The one room he took me to was also unspecific.

Because he doesn't want me to know.

Trust me.

But the room across from it, that one made him nervous the moment I looked at it.

I hold my hand over my aching stomach, ready to heave my breakfast onto my shoes. It's here. Right here.

All I have to do is turn the handle and get all the answers I've been praying for.

40

AGONY

Heavy darkness drops over the room before I can see it, but I just stare straight ahead with unfocused eyes.

My soul is heavy and hurting. My cheeks are slick with tears.

I can feel him when he enters the room, but I don't turn.

He's seething, his magic pulsing heavily.

I turn to the seething demon. My eyes must be red rimmed.

His chest heaves. His wings are spread wide in the middle of the loft.

"Did you kill her?" I ask him softly. I press a palm to my tense chest. I cling tightly to the banister railing.

He blinks, like those are the last words he expected me to say. "No. I didn't have the chance."

"Good."

"Bright one." His voice breaks.

My heart sinks. *Did I hurt you?*

My brow pinches. That's when I realize that he's not angry that I've come to this place without his permission.

"You have no idea what you've done," he tells me.

He's scared.

Panicked.

Devastated.

"You were not meant to come to this place," he says, voice shaking. "Not yet. It's destroying—"

It is a betrayal, he'd told me.

His hands clench and unclench. Darkness rattles in the air, slithering like it's a separate being he can no longer control.

His eyes go unfocused, but he stumbles another step forward. "You are so beautiful," the beast whispers, then falls to his knees before me.

God, why does that sound like a goodbye?

Panic rushes through me. Was there more I didn't understand? Is there more to this than I'd known? I step toward him. "Jarron," I whisper uncertainly. "Jarron, I'm sorry." My nostrils flare, eyes filled with tears again.

I did hurt him.

"I didn't want you to hurt her," I tell him. "That's why I came."

Even in his demon form, I can see his own hopelessness. I don't fully understand the extent of this potential betrayal, what he thinks I did.

This place is the answer to those questions.

Does he assume I've explored the house already? He assumes I know. And it's breaking him.

"Jarron," I whisper. "I didn't—"

Bea once told me, *If he tells you, and you do not accept him, that is the same as rejection.*

My blood runs cold.

I'm not supposed to know, but he believes I know now.

But I don't. I didn't enter any place in this house he didn't already invite me to.

Coming into the house saved Bea's life. But not waiting

227

before I entered any place I hadn't been invited was deeply wrong. The last thing I wanted was to betray him.

I needed to wait. So I did.

"I can't—Candice. I don't know how to fix it," he sucks in breaths, biting back a roar of pain. "My soul is—"

I drop to my knees in front of the demon in front of me. His magic flares around him, sizzling and writhing. I press my palm to his chest.

"Jarron, I'm sorry. I'm so sorry. What you figured out was true, but—I'd decided last night that I wanted to undo it. I wanted to—I wanted to choose you."

He looks up at me with those black eyes full of suffering.

"I do. I do choose you. I don't understand all of it. I didn't—I didn't go anywhere except here. I didn't look at anything. I'm sorry I've been a coward. I'm sorry I've not been worthy of you. But if you'll still take me—"

I hold out my wrist to him.

"If you still want me, Jarron, then claim me. Please. I trust you."

He blinks down at my offering, my exposed wrist. The magic around him stills, his eyes pin to the supple skin.

Another tense beat passes between us, then he snatches my arm. He does not ask me three times, like he did for the first bite. This time, he sinks his teeth into my flesh like he's a man starved and my blood is the only thing that will keep him alive.

This bite is not like the last. There is a flash of intense pain, followed by a swell of dark magic and emotional agony so intense I cry out just before the whole world disappears and leaves me falling, falling, falling into cold black waters. The last thing I recall before I'm sucked under for good is a set of dark leathery wings surrounding me.

41

EVERYTHING

I'm floating in space, neither here nor there. Lost in waves of churning magic.

I can't breathe. Can't speak. Can't see.

And somehow, none of that matters because I can feel.

I am safe and warm and lost but also found. I don't know where I am, but somehow, I am exactly where I need to be. The only place that matters.

I can't feel my own body or his. There is no touch. No pain. No fear.

There is only comfort and pure adoration.

The universe passes by. Stars and planets, solar systems, and galaxies, so many that they blend together into a shining cloud.

The entire universe spread out before me should make me feel small. Unimportant. But there is a tug on my heart. The warmth of arms around me. And a familiar voice.

You are everything.

42

DANGEROUS WONDERFUL BLISS

I'm panting but somehow on my feet, still standing on that loft overlooking the entryway to the beach house and the patches of sand beyond the large windows. There's a roar behind my ears like the crashing of great waves or distant anguished screaming.

"Jarron?" My lips are cracked and dry, like I've survived a week in the desert, and yet, I haven't moved an inch. His talon-tipped fingers are around my waist, his black eyes burning into mine so bright and intense I could stare into them for days and days and never want to look away.

My cheeks are wet, even though I don't know when I started crying.

"My bright one," he murmurs, tugging me even closer. His wings spread out behind him and then curl over us both. "I thought— I thought I'd failed."

"You didn't," I promise him. "You didn't. I almost did."

Flashes of dark fear and rage and sadness bombard me. Flashes of moments. A sandcastle on the beach in the middle of the night. A massive castle beneath mountains. A young brunette girl—me, I realize—laughing. A beautiful blond scowling.

Pain and fear. Adoration and bliss. Determination and longing. So many feelings combining and rushing and twisting through me. My knees shake with each new surge.

"What's happening?" I whisper.

"I'm sorry," he says, voice still raspy. "I know it's overwhelming."

The images halt, but my body is numb. My knees buckle. Jarron pulls me into his arms, wings spreading open and then folding behind his back.

"My love," he murmurs so softly.

He carries my near limp body inside one of the rooms down the hall. For a moment, I think it's his room back at Shadow Hills —it has the same four poster bed with a set of silver handcuffs hanging from one of them.

There is a large sliding glass door leading to a patio, except the world beyond is... wrong.

The sky is dark red and scattered with multicolored stars and two orange moons.

"How—"

"In time," he tells me and lays me on a black silk bedspread, curling up beside me.

Above the headboard is an oil painting of a sandcastle at night, lit up by the moon. My eyelids flutter, remembering that image clearly. The day the vampire came up on the beach and I refused to abandon my sandcastle, despite the danger.

"It was me," I say, voice breaking. "It was me."

"Always, Candice. It was always you."

Slowly, the shock of the mark and all the feels that came along with it settle into a soft humming beneath my skin. No longer the desperate screaming of before.

My body is stiff.

"I didn't expect it to be that... intense," I mutter, trying to push myself into a sitting position, despite my throbbing head.

"I should have warned you," Jarron says, still in his demon form. "I was terrified you would push me away. Terrified I would lose you and I required that mark to survive. I needed to claim you."

I can feel his need—this warm pressure over my body as he says those words. I feel it like it's my own desperation, but it's not. He caresses my mind somehow. A sensation like silk drifting over my chaos-filled thoughts, helping me relax.

"This feels like more than a small magical link," I say. This is how I imagined a full bond to feel. This immersion of that person's essence. A combination of two souls.

"This first mark is more intense for a demon and his chosen."

My heart stops and then restarts at double speed. Butterflies soar through my stomach and chest.

Chosen.

"There is already a deep and powerful connection. You were simply unaware of it until now."

I search in my heart for this feeling. Love. Desperate, clawing, all-consuming passion.

"Can I have all the answers now?" I'm somehow inside of his mind and heart.

But he just said chosen *out loud.* Did this mark unlock what has been barred from us?

"Anything you want. Anything."

"Can you change forms?" I ask sheepishly. I like his demon form significantly more than I ever expected, but this conversation feels like it needs to be with the boy I fell for. Not the demon.

"Of course, bright one." He runs the smooth backside of his talon across my cheek before his body shimmers. There is the sound of rushing water, and then the hands holding me are smooth tan. I curl tighter into his chest and breathe him in.

God, he smells good.

I want to know how he tastes too. Now that he's *mine.*

His body tenses beneath mine. "Feel free to find out any time you like." He runs his nose along my collarbone.

"Shit," I mutter. "You can read all my thoughts now?"

He chuckles. "I have some access. You can learn to block me if you desire it. It would take practice to understand which parts of your mind I have access to and which are beneath the surface. I will always be able to feel a general sense of your emotions. There is no hiding when you feel unease or fear... or desire. But specific thoughts are not entirely open. It's like a doorway you didn't know was there. Now, it's wide open. Once you feel it out, you'll be able to shut it or learn to keep certain thoughts a little quieter. In the end, though, I hope you never feel the need to hide anything from me. I will honor and cherish every thought and feeling you have, no matter what they are."

"But what if they're hurtful to you?"

"If they are truth, I'd rather know so I can fix the issue."

I frown. "If I desire someone else?"

"So long as you remain devoted to me romantically, that would be... exciting to me. At least, in theory. Since this is so new and even I haven't had the chance to explore you myself yet, I am going to be very territorial for a while. But so long as you want me, I will feel that. I will have no doubts. And desire for another person would be no different than—using a toy."

I swallow, throat dry. *A toy.*

My cheeks heat.

He presses his lips to my neck. "For now, though, I desperately want you all to myself."

More butterflies shoot through my body.

"It is such a relief to know you desire me like this, sunshine. You are such a challenge to read and understand."

It's scary to be this wide open and vulnerable to someone. But at least if it's anyone, it's him.

My Jarron.

"Yours," he whispers. "Always yours."

I jerk into a sitting position, all the thoughts and doubts and questions rising to the surface. "What happened that night on Myre Island? Why did you change forms?"

It's the question that's been plaguing me the most.

Instantly, I'm there.

Pitch-black darkness in the sandy spots between two beach houses. I can smell the salt and hear the rushing waves of the nearby ocean just on the other side of the sand dune behind us.

Bea and Trevor are off hiding while I'm supposed to be seeking, but I somehow know they're probably kissing beneath one of the porches. The two girls, though, I can smell.

Their sweet and gamy scent has grown more intense over the last few weeks. They don't have the same senses as I do, and they aren't aware how strong mine have been growing.

My senses make this game entirely unfair to them, but also incredibly thrilling. Shifting through the dark toward the unknowing girls is a delight like I've never felt. I love it.

The beast inside my chest squirms against me, pushing at those thresholds. I'm going to have to go back home soon to let him out, but I keep putting it off. My heart screams to be closer to her.

Even my demon doesn't want to leave.

He wants out. But not if it means losing access to her delicious scent and that beautiful glow. It's getting brighter and brighter. My whole focus shifts to her every time we're together. I can't seem to let go of the obsession.

It's the only time my demon and I have ever agreed on anything.

He wants to hunt. He wants to prove his power over everyone and everything. He wants to lurk in the darkness—this game is his favorite because it fuels those instincts. He wants to chase and claim.

I want comfort and laughter and fun. I want life and light.

But her—she's the place that he and I converge.

She is light and life. She is his sun. His one exception. If not for the dark, you wouldn't appreciate her glow, *he tells me.*

And she is just feet away, hiding like prey, waiting to be hunted.

It thrills him, deeply. Me too.

Excitement and amusement fill me as I hear their whispers and smell their sweet, tempting scents. Close and closer, I encroach on their hiding place. They're behind the red tree in the Montgomerys' front yard.

"I can't believe you told him that," the younger of the two complains.

"Oh, whatever. No one cares that you sucked your thumb as a toddler," *my bright one says.* "You're too uptight about how they see you. Next, I'm gonna tell them about the last time you peed the bed. Do you think Jarron will still like you then? Little bed wetter!" *Her giggle is like music, melodic and lovely.*

"You're just jealous that he's more into me than he is you!"

I hold back a growl at those words. Anger begins to boil in my chest.

I push down the demon inside. He's passionately protective but sometimes forgets that they are sisters. They bicker and argue, and that's normal. We don't have to aid her.

We will show them who truly has our attention.

My heart lifts at that thought. One day, we'll prove our devotion to our chosen. One day. But she is young. We are young. And she's stubborn. So stubborn and independent, and I adore that about her, but she will not be an easy one to prove we deserve her devotion back.

I love a challenge, *he tells me.*

So do I.

I begin to smile when a crack reverberates through the darkness.

I blink, shock settling like wetness over my chest. I turn the final corner to find her holding her cheek and the other girl glaring. It's hard to breathe. My hands clench. Anger, deep and thick, wells up in my chest.

"I can't believe you just hit me." Her whispered voice may as well have been shouted. Tears fill her eyes, and when she pulls away her hand, I see her cheek is glistening red.

Rage overwhelms me like an avalanche, and I explode.

We will show them what happens when anyone touches my bright one.

Reality whirls back, slamming into my chest and leaving me spinning. It takes a moment to resettle. I am back in my own body, in bed with Jarron.

"She hit me?" I don't remember that at all.

Jarron nods. "I overreacted, I know," he says, head bowed in shame.

I touch my cheek, like I'll be able to feel the sting years later. Liz and I fought over stupid things sometimes. She wanted to be the center of attention, and she often was, being younger, prettier, and sweeter than me. That was okay with me most of the time. But that didn't mean I was willing to just give it to her all the time. I gave her a hard time and embarrassed her on occasion.

I don't remember the argument or the slap, now overshadowed by the traumatic events that followed, but it's not surprising either. If Jarron hadn't entered the chat, one of us probably would have run home crying, and the other would have followed, pouting and eventually apologizing.

"My demon would like the opportunity to apologize officially for that moment." He brushes his thumb over my bottom lip. "Believe me when I say neither of us wanted to scare you or harm her."

I nod. "I know."

I didn't know that at the time, clearly, but I believe him now. I've seen who he is. I remember his face when I told him what happened that night. He was shocked. Devastated.

"Why didn't you remember it all?"

"It was an intense moment for us both—my demon spirit and me, I mean. For you too, I'm sure, but in a different way. When this rage pulled him out of me when we weren't prepared, we blacked out and were running on instinct. She was a threat. She needed to be dealt with. I don't think there was much, if any, rational thought left in my body. Every instinct at the time was focused on you. Protecting you. My demon likely didn't understand. To him, you were his. And Liz harmed you, making her an enemy. He was newly awakened in that world. His thoughts and understanding of human ways and relationships were only beginning to take shape."

"And he wants to apologize for it?"

"Face to face." Jarron nods.

My lips tug up in the corners. "I can think of a few ways for him to make it up to me," I mumble, mind flying back to that charged moment in my bed in the middle of the night. Jarron's arms tense around me, and my cheeks suddenly flame hot.

I forgot he can read my mind now.

I don't even know what kinds of things he can do with me in that form without hurting me, but I'm not opposed to an experiment or two.

Jarron shifts so that his body is on top of me. His eyes are pitch black. Ever so slightly, black horns inch up out of his hair.

"Never," he growls, "be embarrassed about desiring me, bright one. I want to know every one of your desires. Every secret thought that thrills you. Every pleasure you crave. Every experiment you wish to try. I am eager to please you in every possible way."

My skin is suddenly burning hot.

He rolls off of me, lying on his side to face me. "But also know that any desire you express can be taken back or paused or delayed at any moment. Pleasuring you can also mean giving you a break." Firm determination, almost defensiveness, prickles at my awareness.

"Is that you convincing your demon?"

Jarron doesn't directly respond, but his lips twitch. The dynamic between the demon spirit and the Jarron I know is fascinating and strange and will take a while for me to fully grasp.

"He will enjoy pushing the boundaries of your desires, but he needs a reminder sometimes that your happiness matters more than ours."

Warmth envelops my body. But a sense of mischief swells up to replace it quickly. I roll onto Jarron, straddling him. His eyes widen.

I push my hips into him hard and lean down whisper. "What if I like pressure?"

He groans, head lulling back. "I will give you anything you want," he pants. "Anything."

I examine my own feelings. Often, when things get intense with Jarron I pull back out of fear. Sometimes, it's fear of not being his first choice. Sometimes, fear of not having control. Fear that these feelings are so intense; they're too much.

But right now, I feel powerful.

I feel perfect. His chest rumbles in that soft purr.

"What does that purr mean?" I whisper.

"It's a sound a demon makes only with their chosen."

My brows pinch together. "Really?"

"Every time you heard it, my demon was expressing his contentment and desire for you. Only for you."

I suck in a breath. At the banquet while we were fake dating. Later that night in his room. At the party while I was on his lap. He's done it since then too, but those are the moments that feel the most significant.

If I had known the meaning, I'd have known all along that I was his chosen. I'd have known that his devotion ran so deep he'd move mountains just to make me smile.

He grins.

"While very true," he murmurs, "I'm fairly certain you would have run far away from me if you'd known that the first time. You were still so uncertain about me. About us."

I sigh. He's probably right. "I like to pretend I'm very brave," I say. "But there are some things that I'm an absolute coward about. Most of them revolve around you." I bite the inside of my lip. It took me so long to take the risk.

"It's never easy to give your heart away. You are brave, Candice. Don't doubt that. You are so brave and intelligent and caring. Cunning and challenging and stubborn too, but if I'm honest, I love those things just as much. I am not a soft human looking for a woman to baby him and raise his children. I'm looking for a partner to rule a world beside me."

I press my forehead against his. "One life-altering realization at a time, please," I say. But I smile nonetheless. It's overwhelming and scary to think about being a queen and everything that would entail, but I'm also somewhat excited by it.

I just don't want to think too deeply about it. Yet.

"You'll be perfect," he whispers. "You are perfect."

I rock my hips against him, and he sucks in a breath, his

hands squeezing my hips. *No more sweet talk*, I think, knowing he'll hear it.

He squirms. This big, incredibly powerful male, who's desperate and nearly on the verge of pleading with me. I want to ask him to beg, but instead, I decide to taunt him more.

Because all of my concerns are gone. My fears and hesitancies have melted away, and all I feel is this incredible high. This incredible *power*.

I press myself tightly against him, feeling his need building. The way he melts beneath me. I sigh in his ear. "I love how you come apart under me."

His fingers squeeze my thighs almost to the point of pain, but internally, I beg him not to stop.

"Candice," he breathes.

He doesn't need to tell me. I can feel that heat building in his extremities. I should be embarrassed at how intense this moment has gotten, but I can't seem to think past the molten hot sensation in my belly. At how he feels when I press harder against him.

"What do you want with me, Jarron," I ask. "After all, *I'm yours*," I mock. Even though we both know it's true.

"No, sunshine. I'm *yours*. Completely. Eternally."

I lick my lips and then set my chin on his shoulder and allow those words to settle into my very soul. I can feel their truth. The power behind the sentiment.

He is mine.

"I am yours to devour," he says. "Yours to pleasure. Yours to harm. Yours to abandon or adore or use, in any way you want."

"Use you?" I rock against him, building my own friction. "Like this?"

He tenses and then releases a breath through his teeth. "Use me, baby. Any way you want."

I do it again, this time entirely for me.

His head rolls back, exposing his neck to me. Without missing a beat, I clench my teeth over his pulse and drag them down.

This nearly does him in. The fire in his body ignites, sending waves of pleasure through our magical link. He groans.

"Fuck," he says, barely hanging on to his control. "You're going to make me come right here, sunshine."

"Mmm," I say against his neck. "What if that's what I want?"

His hands rise high on my thighs, slipping under the hem of my shorts. "Then, say the word and roll those hips one more fucking time."

I can barely breathe for the effect those words have on me. I almost do it. Almost allow my base needs to take over and steal that pleasure that's brewing right beneath the surface.

"I have another idea," I say breathlessly, and I swing off of him and move to the bottom of the bed. His eyes remain entirely black as he sits up to watch me intently. I hook a finger and motion for him to come to me. Once he's standing right in front of me, I point up to what's dangling over our heads like mistletoe.

He quirks a brow casually, but I can feel the jolt of excitement that shoots through him.

I take three steps back and wait for him to do what we both know I'm waiting for. As he turns, readying the cuffs, I blurt out, "Wait!"

He turns to me slowly. Every muscle is incredibly tense. The veins on his forearms and hands somehow make them even sexier.

Because the words are a tad embarrassing, I instead experiment with sending an image through our new shallow bond. He huffs out a chuckle and then obeys my wish, pulling off his shirt before locking his wrists in the handcuffs.

I can't help the massive grin that spreads across my face, and

I allow myself to take in the sight. My powerful demon, submitting to me. I lick my lips and think about all the things I've wished I'd done with him that first time I had him like this. In the weeks after, when I thought I'd never have him in the same way, when I thought there would always be this heavy weight between us, thinking that had been my one perfect moment with him.

I still want those things, but I have something else in mind for now.

But knowing that he can read my thoughts if I let him, I play through a couple of my favorite fantasies, step by intricate step. He groans deep in his chest at the imagery I send him.

I love that I can cause this sweet form of torment with just a thought. And now, before he's had a chance to fully see me, touch me, taste me, is when I'll be able to get the best reaction. When he'll be most desperate to get out of those handcuffs.

I love the power this gives me. I want to wring out every ounce of delicious agony I can from this moment.

"You're fucking torture, Candice," he breathes. "In the best possible way."

I grin. "That's not all I have in mind, love."

"Mmm," he says. "Say that again."

My brows lift.

He meets my stare with deep brown eyes.

"Say what?"

He smiles, wicked and cruel. Delight rushes through me. "Love," he says with a hoarse voice.

My lips part. "Have I not mentioned that I'm pretty much completely in love with you?"

His chest rumbles in approval.

"I could mention that you haven't exactly expressed that sentiment yourself, but I think we'll have time for expressions of devotion later." I'd been careful not to think too specifically about this little idea of mine because I wanted there to be at least a bit of surprise.

I unbutton my black shorts and wiggle them off my hips. Jarron goes predator still, eyes locked on my newly exposed skin. "Don't move," I remind him because the intensity he's giving now is so charged it feels like he's going to pounce any second.

We both know those cuffs aren't stopping him physically. One flick of his wrists and he'll be free to take me in his arms.

He doesn't react to my words, but I continue on with my little show. I pull off my top quickly, tossing it to the ground between us. His intense stare flicks to the place it lands and then back.

I'm not sure he's breathing anymore. We've had some very intimate moments, but this is the most he's seen of my body, at least since we were younger in bathing suits. This is different in many ways. I am different now.

I get the feeling he's trying to memorize every inch of my body his eyes can drink in. I like that a lot.

I step back and sit on the armchair a few feet away.

"Would you like to see what you missed the other day?"

He releases a shaky breath.

"Answer," I whisper.

"Yes," he forces out. "Show me," he demands, voice taking on that echoey quality. It shouldn't turn me on even more to know that his demon is just as eager for the show.

For the next few minutes, I make it a show of soft caresses over the top of my panties. His muscles bunch, straining at the cuffs. His chest rises and falls dramatically as he watches every stroke.

"Free yourself," I tell him. The cuffs snap in an instant, then he drops to his knees and crawls across the floor until he's at my feet. Fuck, I like that a little too much.

"Can I touch you?" he asks, voice hoarse.

"Yes," I pant, practically ready to beg for it now. His hands find my knees first. His silver rings scrape against my skin as he slides off my underwear. Then, his hands make their way back up my thighs and then—stop.

"Show me," he says.

My eyes flare, belly flipping, and then I obey. He watches closely, as I touch myself, inches from his face. I sink deeper into the cushions, eyes fluttering closed. Pleasure and excitement making it hard to think.

What do you want? Tell me. Show me.

I suck in a breath. My eyes fly open. I heard his thoughts.

He watches every stroke, memorizing what I like.

But I want more.

I want *him.*

So, I imagine what I'd love him to do for our next steps, and without missing a beat, he does exactly as I imagined. He grips my hips and tugs me onto him, falling back to the floor so that I'm on top of him.

"Take me," I pant. "Take me now, please."

He sits up, pulls me tightly against him. "I'm tempted to make you beg for me," he says in a growl. Those words are like a fire sweeping through my body. I'm already so close.

He quickly works to unbutton his pants and shift them down, and I waste no time sinking onto him. My back arches, and we moan as one.

His body shudders.

I can feel his emotions, his hunger for me, and how these sensations are so much sweeter than he's ever imagined. He and I, together, body and soul. I stay in control, stroke for stroke, building the inferno between our bodies.

Despite his mind soaring with indescribable, mind-numbing pleasure, he grabs my hips tightly with those strong, powerful hands and pulls me down roughly, squeezing my hips forcefully.

I whimper, sucking in desperate breaths. Again and again until all this fiery pleasure cuts through my consciousness, and I am once more falling. Falling through the universe. His body tenses and bucks just before he falls right alongside me.

Together, we succumb to this dangerous, *wonderful* bliss.

43

IT'S HARD TO BE MAD WHEN YOU'RE THIS HAPPY

Hours later, we're lying in each other's arms, twisted in Jarron's smooth black sheets.

"We have some things to talk about, sunshine," he mutters against my shoulder.

"Oh?" I breathe.

I turn so that his chest is flush against mine. He huffs a little laugh. "Let me be clear," he says, "this isn't how I expected this to happen, but I am by far the happiest I've ever been. I'd like to be mad at you for sneaking into this place without me, mad at Manuela for suggesting it, but that's difficult when it gave me easily the greatest day of my existence. It could have ended very differently, though."

He leans his nose against my arm.

"I didn't go anywhere you told me not to," I murmur. I don't know if that makes it better or not.

He sighs. "I know that now, but at the time..." He swallows. "I don't know what would have happened. I don't know if you not seeing it would have even mattered if—if—"

"If I hadn't let you mark me," I say. He would have taken it as a rejection.

He nods. "It could have destroyed me. In ways even this connection of ours couldn't adequately describe."

I swallow. I don't want to think about what it means for a demon's soul to split. "Is that what was happening to you... when we were not together?"

He sighs. "More like my demon threatening me. Showing me what would happen if we didn't figure this out. You didn't reject us, but it was clear that was a possibility. He was afraid and wanted to do anything to get you to see us differently."

I swallow. "You didn't realize the real reason I pushed you away."

He shakes his head. "At the time, I had no idea they all thought —" He clenches his jaw. Anger rises up him in, burning through his veins. "Why would they even venture to take a guess? Utter fools."

"I had that conversation with Bea," I say softly.

I play through the conversation quickly, so he can see what I saw, hear what I heard, and feel what I felt. I throw in her tearful admissions for good measure. She's sorry. She decided to change.

"She was coerced into telling him a name," I say, hoping it's enough.

"After she let it slip that she knew." His voice is still harsh, not at all softened by the memories.

"Jarron," I whisper, "I don't want you to hurt her."

He takes in a long breath. "I know."

"Will you?"

"No." He sighs. "But I don't like it. And I don't trust her not to turn on us. I will not trust her with your safety."

"Well, you're going to have to trust my intuition." I say it firmly, only half-believing he will.

"And gamble with your life," he growls.

247

I nuzzle into his neck. "I'm sorry I kept it from you."

The rumbling in his chest settles. "I have a hard time remaining mad about anything with you here like this." He squeezes me gently.

I chuckle and wiggle against him. He hums happily.

My body feels much more settled into this new connection now, so I manage to sit up in the bed and take a thorough look around.

"Okay, so, are you going to explain exactly how this room is in Oriziah?"

Jarron sits up with me but keeps his arms tightly on my thigh and waist, ensuring I remain close. "The door is a portal."

He says it casually, like it's such a normal thing. My jaw drops.

Then, I hop up, throw on my underwear and T-shirt, then rush over to examine it. Yes, I was nearly incapacitated when we entered, but I can't imagine I missed the part where we passed through *another* portal.

"Remember, I have some very clever friends capable of very interesting things."

I swing open the door; it looks mundane. I clearly see the open hall of the beach house and even the partially ajar room where we had our date last night. I step through the doorway. I am in the hall, but there is no rush of magic. No shimmer. No dip of cold. The air is lighter though, I realize. I breathe deeply, releasing tension I hadn't noticed among all the other new sensations.

I walk just far enough to see the window looking out at the sand dunes, just a peek of the ocean in the far distance. The sun is shining low, the sky at the beginning stages of a cotton candy sunset.

I am clearly on Earth. I march back to the bedroom doorway. Jarron is still sitting on the bed, waiting for me to return. I cross the boundary, searching for anything to reveal the change in dimensions, but there's nothing.

"How?"

Jarron shrugs. "I was just as amazed as you are. She spent months working on it."

"Are you planning to kill her too?" I cross my arms and pop a hip.

He wrinkles his nose as anger swells up and eases into a simmer. "She will need to be dealt with in some form or another. She was gambling with something she knew was incredibly precious to me. I will not forgive that easily."

My eyes narrow. "So, she knew that I was your chosen?"

"I suspect she did, but not because I told her. She did the portal work for this house two years ago before nearly anything was in here. There was no reason to suspect who it may have been for, even if she recognized the cultural significance."

"You've been working on it for two years?"

He nods. "I began not long after you abandoned our friendship."

Abandoned. "Did—did it hurt you that much?" I ask. "Because of the whole chosen thing?"

He examines his own feelings. There's tension there, a distant ache, but nothing significant. "Yes and no. Not in the way you're thinking. I was sad to lose access to you and our friendship, but I recognized it as a healthy and normal separation. You and I both needed time to grow up. I was willing to wait. I did not think it was a detrimental blow to my chances of earning you. Of course, I didn't realize the full extent of what I did that night. If I'd realized I harmed your sister, I would have—I don't know. But I would have done more."

"And you also would have been extra anxious for the next few years?" I guess.

He swallows and nods.

"Then, it's probably better this way."

He's not convinced, but he doesn't say any more.

"So, can I see the rest of the house? Since I was a good girl and didn't go sneaking around when I had the chance."

Jarron's lips slowly slide into an amused grin. "I would love to show you the home I made for you."

I shiver at those words. He made this for me.

"I didn't actually build the house," he admits. "I bought it and have been fixing it up slowly over the last few years."

"You bought a house when you were sixteen?"

"With cash."

I snort. "Show off."

I could ask about the legalities of that, but in truth, I already know if there are any rules or laws that would challenge the sale of house to a teen, his title would have easily pushed anyone to overlook it, at least here.

He crosses the room and brushes his hand over my back to guide me farther down the hall. "It's not finished either," he says. "So, don't judge my work too harshly."

I roll my eyes. Like I would judge even an ounce of this place. It's a beach house half on Myre Island and half in Oriziah, with a gorgeous bedroom and multiple waterfront balconies. The rest of it could be empty and I'd still be impressed.

The rest of the house is not empty, however.

The next room over is a second bedroom, similar to the first with exposed brick walls and natural wood furniture. There's another balcony that overlooks the ocean on Myre Island. The sun is setting in earnest now, orange and pink clouds scattered across the sky.

Inside the bedroom too is a big wooden desk, a fireplace, and a massive bookshelf filled to the brim with books. I run my finger over the spines and find I recognize at least a few of them. Many are Orizian textbooks. Many others are potions books.

I tap three out of the bunch that I'd checked out of the Elite Library at one point or another.

"I've been keeping tabs on what you are interested in." He shrugs.

I want to hassle him about being a creeper again, but then the breath freezes in my lungs. My heart races when I pull out a special edition copy of my favorite fiction series.

So much of my time and interest has been spent on things that make me stronger, smarter, better, that there are only a few fiction books I've fallen in love with, but this is one of them.

The Cruel Prince.

The edges of this copy are sprayed black, and there's character art inside the front jacket. I open the book and nearly drop it when I find it's been signed by the author.

Candice,

You're stronger than you think.

My lips part and tears well up.

I've never told him I love this series. "How—"

"My instincts are too strong to leave you entirely alone for years at a time."

I can feel the bashfulness he's trying to hide. A slight sense of shame, maybe a little fear at how I'll react. But my heart is only full of adoration and wonder. "Did you keep tabs on me?"

"I checked in at the schools you attended every once in a while. I didn't follow you around or anything. I just needed to get a visual to assure my demon you were okay and taken care of. And I collected bits of information for this project as well. I saw you carrying around this series more than once. I'm guessing based off your reaction that my hunch about it meaning something to you was correct."

I swallow past the lump in my throat.

Another realization settles in my heart as well. He loved me.

251

He cherished me and protected me, even when I hated him. For years, he waited for me.

He's right that if I'd known about all of this back then, I'd have freaked out. Even though he was my friend before, I thought such negative things about his nature as a demon.

But now? Now that I know and trust him, it feels like such a wondrous thing to be this adored.

"I love you," I whisper.

Suddenly, I'm in his arms, wrapped up in his warmth. "You have no idea how much I love you, sunshine."

I shiver. "I'm beginning to."

44

A DREAM HOUSE

Touring the house is entirely overwhelming and altogether wonderful.

There's a half-finished and torn-apart potions workshop—suspiciously similar to the one made for me in Elite Hall.

"This is where we got most of the supplies to make your potions room," he admits what I'd suspected. "We'll put it all back together eventually, once things settle and it's safe for you."

Downstairs, there is a beautiful open kitchen and living room that looks like it was taken straight off my modern Gothic Pinterest board. Black cabinets with golden fixtures and massive cathedral-style windows. Like if Dracula were alive and—wealthy—today, this would certainly be his aesthetic.

"You have a mixture of styles going on here," I joke, thinking about the loft and entryway, which still scream basic beach house.

"Hey, I told you not to judge. I'm not finished."

I smirk. "It's incredible. Really."

He beams at my compliments and ushers me around to more and more of this incredible house. The living room has dark walls, but there are books and plants sprouting everywhere. So many books on every surface. The couch is emerald green. And the wooden shelves behind it hold another few hundred books.

Somehow, there's also an entire volleyball court on the bottom floor of the house. I'm so overwhelmed by this point I can barely register how insane it all is.

Jarron seems to sense this because he curls an arm around my waist and guides me back into the main living space. I flop onto the green couch beneath the beautiful books and plants while he strides to the kitchen to brew me a cup of tea.

"It's amazing," I tell him.

"I'm glad you like it," he murmurs, setting the hot mug between my hands and sitting beside me. "I do think I've had an easier time of it than some of the past Orizians. That Pinterest site you use was practically made for this. So easy to know exactly what you like and bring it to life."

I cough on a laugh. "So, you did use my Pinterest boards?"

"I would be a fool not to."

I lean into his chest on the couch. He shifts and folds one leg up to allow me to recline against him. "We can go back upstairs for the night."

"You have to go back to Oriziah." It's not exactly the response he's expecting, but that truth just kinda hit me. For a little while, reality just didn't exist, but my mind spins through so many things. "And Lola and Janet will be concerned if I just disappear."

Are they already searching for me? Hearing stories about Jarron exploding on Manuela.

"Laithe has been in contact with them."

I suck in a breath. "Oh. Okay."

"And I do have to go back to Oriziah soon, but this—*you*—are easily the most important thing right now. I wouldn't even be capable of leaving right after this." He squeezes me.

"They need you."

"And I need you. My family and the courts will have to manage another few days."

I frown, sipping at my soothing hot tea. "I could go with you, or is that not helpful?"

Jarron tenses beneath me. Whatever that emotion is, I can't get a read on it, though. "We have a lot of things to discuss. Like this plan of yours with Beatrice and how we'll manage our next steps, but we don't have to decide all of that right now. We're both overwhelmed and tired and high on this wonderful feeling. I'd like to not get ahead of ourselves and enjoy it."

I nod against him. "Okay," I whisper, eyes suddenly very heavy.

I take another gulp of my tea and set it on the coffee table, unable to help another glance around the intricately decorated room. This place doesn't even feel real.

Without having to tell him that I'm ready, he scoops me up into his arms and carries me through the house and upstairs to our bedroom, purring in contentment the entire way.

45

I'M SORRY IT TOOK ME SO LONG

I wake beneath the silk sheets that have become so familiar, arms I find incredibly comforting, and a dark sky that fuels my nightmares.

I swallow. "Is it always night in Oriziah?"

"No, but the dark remains for..." He considers. "Months in Earth time."

I shiver. Night is beautiful, but when it's also filled with creatures who want to eat me—

"This world will not harm you," Jarron mutters sleepily. "You are safe here."

"What do you mean I am safe here? You're not even safe."

Jarron sighs and tucks me in closer. "That is true, but it's temporary and it's political. The beasts and the sahasika clans out in the wild wouldn't even consider harming you with my mark on your skin. Ironically, inside the palace is one of the least safe places for us right now because there, we represent mistrust. Out here, the natural order would protect you. You are part of the land, an important part, now that you carry my magic. My heart."

My chest flutters.

You are everything.

I shake my head, this new reality once again resettling in my mind. It wasn't a dream. It's real. I am Jarron's chosen.

"It's real." He brushes a kiss against my forehead.

"I'm sorry it took me so long."

His arms tighten around me. "What happened was not your fault. You were supposed to have as much time as you needed. You were supposed to choose me without outside influence. That was a privilege you and I did not get. You were challenging and stubborn, but I always knew you would be. The fact that it was difficult only makes this that much sweeter. I know how much it means that you are here in my arms and in my soul, the monster you despised." His lips quirk.

"I quite like that monster now," I admit.

"Believe me, I know." His sultry tone sends a jolt through my body.

"Tell me something," I say.

He nuzzles into my neck, lips grazing over the sensitive skin of my bite mark.

I squirm.

"What do you want to hear, Candice?"

A sudden urge takes over my body, and I turn, pushing him off of me and twisting so that I am over him instead, staring into his dark eyes. "When I first told you about Liz being dead, you reacted really strongly." Ice crawled along the walls—something that happens when his emotions are strong enough that his demon comes to the surface. It's one of the moments I've played through over and over since I learned about Orizian mates.

He sits up, holding my waist in place so that our chests are pressed together tightly, his lips on my cheek. "I did react, because she mattered to you. She mattered to me too, that is certainly true, but this was also the first time I'd talked to you in years and my demon was already restless for that reason alone. We could see that her death hurt you and there was also the implication that you were potentially unsafe. It was an intense moment all around."

I let that truth settles around us, between us, as I work to process this new perspective.

"Besides, a little bit of demonic power slipping from my grasp is small compared to what could have happened if I'd lost control completely." He leans back to examine my face. "Have you ever considered how I might have reacted if the opposite had happened? If Liz had come and told me that you—" He stops, like he's unable to complete the thought.

"You hadn't seen me in years by that point," I remind him. It wouldn't be like now.

"Not in person, other than the few glimpses from afar, but I'd dreamed about you nightly."

"Really?"

He nods. "Every. Single. Night."

I have many, *many,* questions about that, but I shake the thought from my mind or it'll seriously derail me. "So, what would have happened if Liz had come to the school to tell you about my death?"

His eyes turn black and distant. His voice is hoarse. "Do you remember the day I saw the wolf bite on you?"

My chest tightens. He'd almost destroyed the school. *An atomic bomb in the middle of the cafeteria,* someone had called him.

"Laithe would not have been able to lure me away before I would have demolished the school and everyone in it."

I flinch "Seriously?"

"Not that I'd be proud of it."

That reality settles in, carving a terrifying picture. "Can you do me a favor?"

˙ "Anything."

"Don't kill any innocents on my behalf. No matter what."

His eyes turn sharp with that predator glare. "I will cut down anyone I must to keep you safe, and not feel the least bit remorseful."

I narrow my eyes. "I mean, if I die."

He bares his teeth. "That is not something I like musing about."

"Tough luck."

He stares up at the ceiling, breathing deeply. Finally, he says, "I would do my best but I make no promises. The soul of my demon is... difficult to control. He does not see morality as you and I do."

I huff out a breath. Maybe it's the best I can ask for right now.

"Our enemies, however, you can tear apart one limb at a time." I wink.

A sick joy spreads through him, hypnotizing me with its cruelty. I shouldn't like that instinctual desire for violence. Wrath should not be pleasurable. And yet, it's hard not to be lured in by my monster's thirst for blood against our enemies.

"I would simply like to be a part of it," he says.

The image of me slick with blood, eyes sharp and fierce, flickers through my mind. My monster would enjoy that too. Maybe a little too much.

"We have to talk about this plan of yours, though," he says. "As much as I'd enjoy enacting revenge on the council, I don't believe it's worth the risk."

"How? What do you think could go wrong? How could I be in danger with Bea using my potions to poison them?"

"If it were that easy, why wouldn't Beatrice just do the work herself? If she wishes to be free of the Cosmic Council, she is plenty capable of creating poisons to kill her current allies."

"But what would that gain her?" Besides, it's not just a

259

simple poison that will do the work needed. Even those with fair experience in potions might not have the ability to create the death potion that will kill multiple types of powerful beings at once.

"She has the ability to hire a potion master to create the needed potion."

"Assuming they'd be willing," I mutter. My parents have had to turn away many clients because they are not immune to the consequences of what is done with those potions. It's a vulnerable profession because they have the ability to affect the world in significant ways, but they don't have the physical capabilities to protect themselves if targeted by the wrong people.

"I'm just saying, there are flaws here. You are risking too much, relying on an untrustworthy source, and putting yourself in a vulnerable position at the same time."

My nose wrinkles in frustration.

I find myself praying he believes in me enough to go with this plan.

I want it so badly I can taste it. I *need* to kill each and every one of them.

A deep growl rumbles from his chest. "My bright one is so thirsty for violence."

I shiver. Am I? I suppose I am. "I want to free her. I need her to be free of them."

"So do I."

"We're partners, right?" I whisper.

"Yes," he says. "But you have not been treating me like one."

"Neither have you."

His heart aches, the feeling flooding my extremities. He hated being apart from me. Hated keeping truths, the same way I did. "I didn't have much choice."

"You didn't have to withhold the truth about the reality of the conflict."

"If I told you the truth, that I've declared the accusations as false but only to a select group of loyal allies, and even they haven't fully believed me..." He swallows, pressure carving into his chest. "Even they began whispering that they will need proof to believe in me. If I were to tell you that, the risk was my very soul because if you had heard that I'd sworn Liz was not my mate, you would have easily inferred that you are. If you were to face me after that realization and still deny me, even just out of a simple desire for more time, it would have destroyed me."

I blink. "I wouldn't have."

But I understand the kind of risk he's talking about. I can feel the pressure he felt as if it were my own now. Like his very chest is stretching, stretching, stretching to the point that it's ready to split open, and knowing it will if he makes the wrong move.

"It shouldn't have been like this. If Beatrice and Vincent had respected our culture and minded their own business, you and I could have had years to work this out. I hated feeling like I was pressuring you. I hated being apart from you. I was stuck, with no right answer.

"I had to be so careful, even if I told you the consequences of that rejection or the positive results that could come from you accepting me, it could be a form of coercion. I was afraid. So afraid that if I didn't play this exactly right, my demon would rebel and I'd lose control. I was so close to losing it all. So close to Mr. Vandozer winning, not because he took my chosen as his but because he drove a wedge between my soul and yours. I couldn't pressure you, and I couldn't do anything to reveal this truth."

He closes his eyes.

"I was going to step down," he whispers. "Tomorrow. If—if you didn't accept me I was going to let Trevor take my place as heir to the throne."

My stomach twists. "Really?" I breathe.

He nods. "You're more important than my position as a ruler. I was risking losing you, and that is simply not worth it."

"But—you'd be giving up. Letting him win."

"It would be highly unfair, yes. It would have weakened our trust and perhaps had lasting effects on our reputation with the Orizian people. But it would have given us the time we needed. It would have given us more protection. I could have focused on you, on us. I couldn't balance both, giving you what you needed to accept me and managing an unstable world on the verge of war. I had to choose."

My heart aches for him, for this impossible position he's been in. Guilt, for how I'd only made it worse, stings deeply.

"It is not your fault," he tells me. "You deserved time. I feel shame that I could not give that to you. You chose me, only once your back was against the wall. You knew the consequences of withholding your heart from me then, so you gave it. That's— not how this should have gone."

"You're wrong," I say softly. I run through the memory of my birthday dinner together. I'd chosen him that night; I only stalled because of Bea.

He swallows against the swell of emotion rising up in him.

"I love you," I tell him. "I choose you, of my own free will. I choose you because I want you to be mine. So desperately, I wanted you to be *mine.*" The final word comes out fierce.

"I'm sorry that I kept you in the dark, kept these secrets from you, but I was so afraid—"

I curl in close to him. "I know."

He breathes deeply a few times, allowing that pain and fear to filter away. I am here with him now. He can feel my love and acceptance, even though I haven't technically completed the—

"Oh!" I say. This bond is so odd. I can *feel* his thoughts, without specific words. The process is incomplete. I hadn't even realized. "I'm supposed to take a second mark, aren't I?"

He takes in a long breath. "That is more of a technicality now," he explains. "We are connected. I feel what you feel, and it's clear you've fully accepted me. We cannot make any formal moves with the rebellion until the second mark is official, but it has no effect on me personally. It is customary for there to be a period of time between the first two because it's very intense. You are meant to have enough time to fully understand the depth of the decision."

"I understand it."

He swallows, pressing his nose to my temple and nodding. "I know. I'm just saying you have time."

The formal moves he's referring to involve him presenting me to his courts and standing trial. I avoid the feelings those thoughts send through me.

"Like hours?" I joke.

"As much time as you desire."

I nod sharply. "Hours."

He chuckles.

"What happens after that, though? You want to go through the tribunal, but Bea said it wouldn't be that simple."

He curls a lip. "Bea would say that."

"I know, but what she said made sense." I sit up. "She said that there's no real way to prove the person you present is not a false choice. If you show up with an accepted chosen while Liz is on Vandozer's arm, some of the clans might think you're lying. And if they think you're lying, it would damage your reputation forever, not just right now."

He growls. "I would not lie."

"I know that, but they already doubt you so would they trust your word if you present me as your chosen?" Discomfort grips him hard, but I continue. "She also said—"

He grips my chin between his thumb and forefinger and

263

turns me to face him. "I do not trust her. She was trying to keep you from me."

"Maybe. But if so, I still think it was out of self-preservation, not malevolence. She wants to fix her mistakes. I believe her."

"So, does that mean you are not willing to appear before the tribunal as my chosen?"

I frown. "Of course I'm willing. But I want to consider what it will mean for Liz. How can we abandon Bea's plan entirely but still attack the council? Because I want them all fucking dead."

He grins, wicked and cruel. "As do I, love. Together, we'll ensure they don't disgrace this universe with their breath ever again."

46

GOOD NEWS

The attention I get back at Shadow Hills Academy, now that I've
been marked by Jarron rather than just bitten, is intense.

Technically, other than the fervor being renewed, it's not that
much different, but it feels very different.

Different because now I know they're right, and there's
something so astounding in realizing that I am officially—I
shiver—*High Orizian royalty.*

People stop to stare and whisper. Others wave eagerly at me
like I'm famous or something. My friends celebrate with hugs,
high fives, and cheers. Stassi squeals in absolute delight and once
again reminds us that he's going to give a speech at our wedding.

Jarron stays with me for the full weekend, with intentions of
taking our first official trip to the Orizian palace on Monday. I try
my best not to dwell on my nervousness, but it's simmering
beneath the surface at every moment.

I spend most of Sunday in my workshop, still messing with
my potions that I'll no longer need now that Jarron has
convinced me to put off the attack on the council.

My stomach aches at that thought.

Six days. It was six days away, but now I don't know when I'll get the chance to enact my revenge. I don't know when I'll free my sister.

We will, Jarron promises me through our link. *We will free her.*

I can feel his determination—and his fear of disappointing me if something goes wrong. He knows this is important to me. He knows pushing me from this plan is taking away something important.

"I can't believe it!" Janet squeals not for the first time, staring wide eyed at the crescent-shaped mark on my wrist. I smirk while stirring my delayed death potion. The pitch-black liquid hisses with each turn like it's angry. I'm angry too.

"I can!" Lola says, dancing around the room, darting between the plumes of smoke billowing up from the cauldrons.

"Have you talked to Thompson?"

I jerk my attention up to Janet. "No, have you?"

She shakes her head. "But we could video chat him."

She waves a cell phone. My heart lifts, but worry strangles my breath. What if things aren't okay? Am I going to call him with such good news while things are really bad for him?

The phone plays a little jingle, waiting to see if the call will be answered. My heart races. Finally, Thompson's face pops onto the screen.

"Thompson!" I say more out of worry than excitement. His face is slick with sweat. His eyes look sunken. His clothes are wrinkled and ripped. All three of us gather into the screen, and I force a smile.

"Hey!" he says, his eyes lighting up. His smile seems sincere, and the pressure on my chest eases slightly. "How's it going, guys?"

"How's it going with you?" I blurt out.

His expression falls slightly. "Oh, you know. Not great. No casualties this week but we're having trouble getting supplies into our territory. The Brush-kins pack is blocking our deliveries so—" He shakes his head. "We're fine, though. We'll be okay. How about you guys? Has Candice poisoned all the evil fucks in the world to end the Orizian war yet?" His smile seems forced.

"Not yet," I mutter.

"But she does have good news!" Lola chirps.

"Oh?" Again his eyes light up. He's sincerely happy to hear from us, to hear my news, despite things not going well for him. Are they starving there? Are the supplies they can't get through to their pack basic needs, like food?

They're wolves, Jarron reminds me. *They can hunt.*

Right. That clarity does little to ease my concern.

Jarron is concerned by how much I'm worrying about Thompson. There's a small stream of guilt coming from my demon.

"Candice?" Janet says, a frown on her brow.

I blink and refocus on the call. "What?"

"Show him," Lola says.

I blink rapidly. "Oh! Right. Yeah." I hold up my wrist to show him the crescent mark, and my cheeks redden immediately.

"I knew it!" he hollers, pointing to the screen. "I told you!" He howls in celebration, and I can't help but feel real joy, to allow a real sincere smile to spread on my lips.

He stares at it again and then examines my expression. "It was you, right?" he asks, suddenly less sure.

"Yes," I force out through my stressed lungs. "Yes, you were right."

He howls again in celebration.

He's honestly so happy for me. Not for what it means for him or his pack, but just for his friend who he cares about.

"We miss you," I tell him.

"I miss you guys too. Trust me, I do."

Lola and Janet chatter with him for a few minutes, sharing

267

stories of when they were certain I had to be Jarron's chosen and arguing about who will take what role during the wedding. Lola claims flower girl. Janet a bridesmaid "Of course Liz will be the maid of honor," she tells me with a beautiful grin. And Thompson will be the ring bearer.

After a few minutes, the chatter dies down and I venture to ask the thing still bothering me. "Tell me honestly, though, what's going on there? Are you safe?"

Slowly, his smile fades. His shoulders droop. "We're... surviving."

"Thompson," I chide.

"What are you able to do, Candice? What will telling you the grim truth help?"

My brow pinches. "I don't know. But I'd rather know so that if there is something, I can at least try."

He shakes his head. "It's my problem to deal with."

"You came here for allies," I tell him. "Let us be allies. Even if it's not the way you planned, at least let us try."

He sighs. "They're encroaching day by day. They've managed to get around our stunning bombs, and they're close. They're really close to breaking through our last barriers."

"What will happen?" Lola whispers, dropping down on my shoulder.

"They'll kill all the males and give the females the chance to join them or die too."

My heart aches. There has to be something.

There is, Jarron says in a somber tone. *It's not a lot, but if Manuela can make a portal for me to get there, even just one hour – I can push them back.*

Hope wells in my chest, even as fear prickles the edges.

Isn't Manuela still hiding from you?

He sighs. *I'll make peace for this. For you.*

"Thompson, I need you to give us exact details on where the

enemy wolves are and call all of your pack back to safety. It's a temporary fix, but I've got a plan to drive them back."

~

An hour later, Manuela has a shimmering portal set up in the middle of the sunroom. I have a hard time imagining the administration is just okay with this sort of thing right in the middle of the school, but then again, it's not the first time she's done it.

How did you get her back here so fast? I ask Jarron through our link, even though he's standing right next to me. *Did you always know how to find her?*

Yes, I knew how to find her. She could slip away from me fairly easily if she wanted, but I knew where I could at least contact her. I told her I'd pardon her crimes against me if she helped me right now. It had to be now. She came immediately.

Based on her demeanor you'd never know she was in hiding an hour ago. Her hip is popped, arms crossed, smug as hell. The only significant clue is that the beautiful red-headed wolf shifter she's been dating is clinging to her waist, quietly watching the whole thing. She at least seems happy Manuela is back.

"All of this trouble for an inconsequential wolf pack." She shakes her head in annoyance.

"They're not inconsequential," I growl.

Manuela blinks at me, noticing the unusual bite to my tone. That word gets under my skin.

"He matters to my mate," Jarron says. "So he matters to me."

Manuela narrows her eyes at me. "I'd like to claim you to be a naïve human, but I know better."

Part of me wants to defend my belief in Thompson, but in the end, I decide to simply say, "Thompson is my friend."

Manuela looks me over. "I hope one day to earn that title."

Jarron blinks, surprise crossing his features. "High praise," he murmurs to me before leaning down to plant a firm kiss to my lips. "I'll be back soon."

"I love you," I whisper.

"I love you too."

Then, he steps through the simmering magic and disappears from sight.

"I told you it could all work out for the best," Manuela mutters to me the moment he's gone.

I huff.

She winks. "It always helps to know their soft spots, even when you're allies."

"How did you make a portal all the way to Tennessee in minutes?" Janet asks, eyes wide. It's absurd enough that she can just make portals, but Janet is right; this is beyond anything I'd ever thought possible.

"I didn't." Manuela shrugs. "I made a portal to a portal. Even that only gets him within fifty miles of the action. It's a good thing he can fly."

Our friend group gathers in the armchairs in the sunroom, chattering casually for the next hour before, finally, I feel something through my link with Jarron.

I'm shocked, though, at how fast the ordeal happens. There's a rumble of power. Darkness fills up my heart like ice then blasts out. I flinch at the feeling.

But then, there's nothing.

Cold emptiness filles my mind. I frown.

"Something wrong?" Janet asks, noticing my change.

"I... felt Jarron start to use his magic, but then it all went silent." My heart picks up speed.

"He probably just blocked you out temporarily," Manuela explains.

"He can do that? Block me completely?" I knew he could

control what thoughts I have access to but it's like the link never existed. There's a solid wall between us. I don't like it.

Her brows lift, then she nods.

"But why? Why would he block me out?"

"Because he's doing something he doesn't yet want you to see. Like killing, perhaps? He's likely still worried he'll scare you with the reality of his nature. Causing pain in others is not a pleasant sight for anyone at first, a human least of all."

My brow pinches. I don't think I would be put off by it, but I imagine a few graphic scenes that maybe I would be better off not experiencing that intimately.

Less than ten minutes later, his emotions flood back into me. I gasp at the rush. Familiar cool darkness caresses my mind.

All is well, bright one. I will be back shortly.

Thompson's pack?

Safe for now. Their enemies will regroup eventually, but it will take time.

I consider expressing my annoyance that he blocked me from our link, but instead, I just tell him, *Thank you.*

Because he did this for me. Just for me.

I would do anything for you.

I know.

When he finally returns to me, and we bid our friends good-night, I do what I can to show him that I too would do anything for him by offering up my right wrist and accepting his second mark.

He is mine. And I am his.

47

THE REJECTED PRINCESS

"I will make sure you are safe, bright one." The monstrous figure leans over me. His horns glisten. His talons reach out for me.

Delight is not the feeling this image should evoke, but somewhere along the line I fell in love with the demon as much as the man.

Today, we will use a new portal. The one in the middle of the school.

Crowds follow us through the halls toward the main entrance to the school where my inner circle list is boldly displayed.

Does everyone know what we're doing today? Because the extra attention is not helping my anxiety. Today, Jarron will fly me over the capital city and into the Orizian palace, presenting me as his chosen for the first time.

My chest is tight, knowing not only that the significance of this moment is immense but also the inherent danger in the act. His country is at war. I may not be accepted and cherished the way a new princess normally would be. Some will automatically think it's a performance. They'll consider me a fraud.

Some will spit in my direction and call me a false princess.

"We will not even get close to the masses today. You'll see them from afar, but no one we don't implicitly trust will be within reaching distance of you." *I will protect you.*

"Will Laithe be there? I ask. I haven't seen them since my birthday. Since Jarron claimed me. Apparently I was correct in assuming they'd greatly prefer to be in Oriziah during the conflict so the moment Jarron claimed me they took their chance to spend time at home.

"Yes. But he cannot use this portal due to his lack of wings."

"They," I correct.

Jarron's lips twitch. "They cannot use this portal, but we will see them at the meeting."

Once we enter the portal room, the crowds are left behind. They peer in through the entryway, but no one steps any closer.

Jarron's demon form scoops me into his arms, and without even a beat to catch my breath, he leaps through the portal.

I cling to him as we fall through the magic, but then the falling doesn't end. Wind whips through my hair, the air bitterly cold. I scream when I see the whole world below.

He didn't tell me the portal dropped us from the sky!

Why else did you think wings were a prerequisite to using this portal.

His wings spread wide, and the falling slows until we're soaring gently through the black sky. My lungs catch. It's hard to pull in breaths in this thin air while literally flying.

City lights come into view ahead. I keep my arms tight around Jarron's neck and my eyes set on the city growing closer. It's beautiful, and from here, it looks similar to a human city. There are dots of lights in several structures. There's a massive red stone mountain behind the buildings that seems to glow in the darkness.

That is the palace, he tells me.

My lips part. *You mean the mountain?*

Yes.

Amazing.

As we grow closer to the city, through the dark night, a large shoreline also comes into focus. There is a beach reaching right up to the city cliffside.

There are many kinds of creatures that make up the population in our world. Not all of them fly like me. Some live underground. Some in the deserts. Some in the mountains, and some in the seas.

Our capital sits at the intersection of them all, so that every kind of Orizian can meet to share their voices.

I'm in awe of the massive city spreading out before us. The first few buildings pass beneath us—small, round, stone homes covered in orange and yellow vines. Silhouettes of people gather in the streets, staring up at us.

The closer we get to the mountain, the more people I see. Just dark forms, gathering and shifting in the shadows.

Then, they begin shouting. A rumbling sound vibrates through the air.

I swallow, uncertain if those noises are good or bad. They're very different than the cheers humans would give, but these things are very far from human, so that might be expected.

They are cheering, bright one. They are pleased.

I take his word for it, even as the sound grows louder and louder. More and more unsettling down to my very bones.

Jarron soars right up to the middle of the red stone mountain and drops onto a flat landing. He tucks his wings in and pulls me closer to him.

For the first time, he kisses me in his demon form. His lips are rough, but not painful. Sharp teeth graze my tongue and I suck in a breath but there is no pain. *The only pain I will give you, is one you request.*

My cheeks heat, wondering what kind of pain I might like.

This time, the roaring from the people in the dark city streets below fills the air around me, and I couldn't mistake it for anything other than a cheer.

"Many of our people fully believe and trust in me as a ruler," he tells me.

"They believe I'm your mate?"

"Yes," he whispers. "They know who you truly are. Only a true mate would be presented to the city like this."

I look down at the buzzing crowds. "But some will still question you?"

"Very few in the city. The rebels are on the outskirts. They will not be easily convinced."

"So, what do we—"

He presses his hand to my cheek. "One step at a time, bright one." My cheeks heat at the use of the nickname now that I can feel the passion and devotion behind the words.

I am his bright one. His chosen. The one who lights up his entire world. His entire reason for being.

Never, in my whole life, have I ever dared to hope for love like this.

But it's all here, in one look. One pet name.

I am his, and I can only hope I can be worthy of such devotion.

"You are more than worthy."

I bite the inside of my lip, but even my uncertainty flowing through our link doesn't lessen his pride.

Jarron leads me into the mountain carved out of dark red stone, with veins of silver and gold that glow slightly. Now fully enveloped by the mountain, I stare up at the unevenly carved domed ceiling, with several winding and interconnected arches through the whole thing. It's massive. An entirely hollow mountain.

A winged beast soars past, down, down, down into darkness

275

below. I gasp but then lean forward to see where it goes. All I can see is darkness below the precipice we are currently standing on.

"This is the main portion of the palace," he explains. "High Orizians fly through the openings, and a few mountain-dwelling Orizians crawl over the stone pathways. It's not exactly made for humans."

My eyes flare.

"No one will hurt you here," he adds quickly. "But you could fall. Stay near me at every moment."

Right, yeah, no big deal. I definitely have no intention of wandering off on my own.

He leads me up to a narrow stone passage that crosses over the massive void below. My knees tremble as I take tiny steps over the bridge that's only two feet wide with no railings at all.

His arms wrap around me from behind, and he whispers, "I can carry you if you need. But you will appear stronger if you cross yourself. They are watching." He nods ahead, where several sets of bright eyes peer out from the darkness beyond the platform head. "I swear, I will not let you fall."

I take in a deep breath and muster every ounce of courage I contain.

Have I mentioned that I'm not exactly a fan of heights? Because I'm not.

But knowing that there are beings watching me, judging me —beings who already see me as weak and unworthy—well, let's just say my stubborn will is stronger than my fear.

I keep my chin up as I walk slowly across the stone. There is no handrail. No border. Just two-feet-wide red stone that curves over the opening to the other side of the mountain.

Jarron's wings flare wide, and he holds them open as he follows just behind me.

My heart races, my lungs near seizing when I finally reach the platform leading into dark tunnels. There are two black-

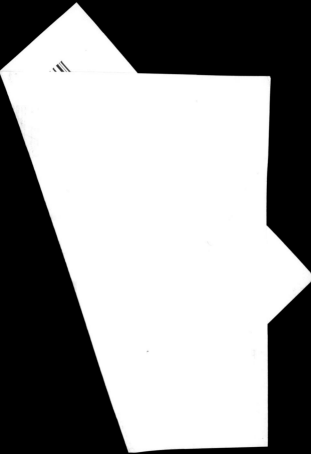

Order

Qty

haired witches standing just in the shadows, watching us with bright eyes. They are shorter than the average human, with grey winkled skin. They'd like to be called hags in the supernatural world, but I know better.

They are from one of the three clan that will make up the tribunal, Jarron tells me.

Jarron puffs out his chest and then continues past the witches, into pitch-black tunnels. I rush to keep up.

A chill inches up my body the farther we walk in darkness. I can't see anything, but this time, Jarron's arms carefully guide me.

It gets colder and colder until we reach a doorway and enter a large circular room with glowing blue stalactites dripping from the ceiling.

"Beautiful," I whisper, staring up at the stones. My breath comes out in a puffy white cloud. It's still dark but more like a moon-brightened night sky, rather than pitch blackness.

Jarron leads me to a fur rug where he lowers to his knees, wings tucked in behind him.

I do not miss how astounding it is that I am here right now. In the Orizian palace next to the crown prince.

Jarron snaps his fingers, and a fire roars to life in a small opening I hadn't seen. Warmth seizes me quickly. "We've had many human visitors to this part of our world, so even though it is colder than you're used to, we know how to manage it," he tells me. "Still, tell me if you're ever uncomfortable."

I kneel on the fur and look around the room. There are several figures lining the shadows that I can't quite make out. Some at least ten feet tall, others only a few feet tall.

"There are loyal guards here. You will be protected above all else."

A small, winged creature, who looks a bit like a miniature

High Orizian or a goblin with wings, lugs over a black cauldron, already steaming, and sets it in front of the fire.

A deep feminine voice carries through room, using words and sounds I can barely make out. A large female High Orizian enters the room, followed by a man I recognize.

Emil Blackthorn.

Jarron's father looks remarkably close to what I am used to— salt-and-pepper beard, light-brown skin, pointed ears and a very human-pant suit. The fierce winged Orizian next to him must be the queen.

That's my mother, Jarron confirms through our link. She holds her head high. Her long limbs covered in leathery skin, move smoothly.

The King and Queen of Oriziah have arrived. I've never seen Jarron's mother in her demon form, but there is a sense of recognition. I can't tell if it comes from me or from Jarron.

She's speaking in High Orizian, and though I've been studying hard, I'm still not exactly fluent. Jarron automatically translates the words to English through our link. I hear the foreign chattering first, then the translation after.

"Welcome to our home, witches of the plains," the queens voice echoes against the stone walls, as do the groups steps as the witches enter the room.

Another High Orizian, and a familiar red-skinned demon enter after them.

Trevor and Laithe.

The full royal family is here.

"Welcome, Candice!" Emil says, his eyes bright and smile wide. "Words cannot express how happy we are to have you join us in this way."

I return the smile, happy to have at least one other being in the room who doesn't make me want to run and hide. Laithe nods in my direction.

Nimsete, Candice. We've been waiting for this moment. I inhale sharply at the strange voice in my mind.

Laithe?

Their eyes shine with amusement. They take a seat between me and the fire so that I am surrounded by trusted protectors. We are both now magically linked with Jarron. Amazing.

Laithe will not use that link often, but it does exist if ever needed, Jarron explains.

The three witches file in. I couldn't tell them apart if I tried.

"Yes, Candice, we are so pleased to see you," the female Orizian says, her voice rumbling.

"Thank you," I say awkwardly. The witches eye me closely before lowering themselves to the ground across from Jarron and me.

Trevor sits beside Jarron, followed by their parents, and then the three witches across from us.

The small, winged Orizian scoops out small cups of the steaming liquid and passes it around the group, serving me first. "Thank you," I mumble as I accept the small stone cup with both hands.

Jarron is served second, and I only take a sip once he does. Just like the tonic Bea gave me, this warm liquid soothes the anxiety in my chest.

It helps foreigners acclimate to the atmosphere, Jarron explains, *as well as simply calming the body so that the mind can be at full capacity.*

One by one everyone at the meeting is served the tonic, and they sip it quietly.

The lead witch's mouth moves, a quiet vibrating sound leaving her lips, but it's quickly translated in my mind. *Thank you for the welcome, despite the tension.* Her eyes meet mine and remain steady.

A jolt of fear passes through me, but I don't dare show it. I hold her stare until her grin spreads before her gaze passes along to the rest of the group sitting in a semicircle before the fire.

"Now, tell us the manner of this gathering," another of the witches says.

Do they not already know? Or is this just formal proceedings?

"As I'm sure you suspected," Jarron says, both in the strange tongue and inside my head clear as day, "I have gathered you here to present my chosen. The accusations scattered across the land are false."

The room goes still.

"This is the first you've commented on the matter," one of the witches says finally.

"Yes," Jarron says. "I could not openly deny the girl Vandozer has claimed is mine without making my true chosen aware of her role. I needed to wait until she accepted me to refute the claims."

"And she has?" One of the witches tilts her head at me.

I hesitate awkwardly as all of the predator eyes turn to me. "Y-yes," I say in English. Stupid. I obviously know the word for "yes" in Orizian, but my brain will not function right now. Jarron gently lifts my wrist up. I follow suit with the second so that the room can see the twin marks on both arms.

"I see," one of the witches says, her eyes lidded like she's annoyed.

"We are not surprised to find a new claimant on the young prince's arm," one of the back witches says. "Disappointed, but not surprised."

"What is to be disappointed in?" the queen asks, her voice low and raspy.

The witches do not give her an answer. Instead, a charged silence stretches.

"As you can see, the matter is settled. Our son, your future king, has earned his right to rule."

"We see a claimant. We do not see a settled matter."

The queen stands. "You call my son a liar?"

The fire beside me flares, and I flinch away from it. Jarron growls and pulls me in closer, away from the heat of the roaring flames.

"We claim not to know the character of your son and therefore cannot say one way or another. If you cannot control your temper, you will be asked to leave."

The queen clenches her jaw.

I'd known that the tribunal of witches has a lot of influence in this world, but to see the queen reprimanded by them is something else entirely—and this is only a portion of it. Only one of the three clans is here currently.

The queen slithers back into her seat, still clearly angry but willing to submit.

"Two conflicting claims of a royal mate has never happened before," the witch says. "Since the beginning, it's left a bad taste in our mouth, the way Vandozer has paraded the girl around the lakes as a trophy. And yet, if true—"

"It's a serious transgression," the queen says with a bow of her head. "We understand. But it is indeed a falsehood. The fact that a lie can cause this much havoc and harm to our society is concerning. These matters have always been managed privately. Trust has always been the undercurrent through which we govern."

"It is indeed concerning."

"Trust is a foundational element of your rule," another witch states. "And the fact that so many are ready to rise up against you is proof that you have not earned enough of it. Therefore, one marked female and the claim that she is the prince's chosen is not enough."

"You question the very legitimacy of the crown," the queen barks, clearly displeased they haven't yet agreed with her.

"Yes," they say as one.

"Then, we will go to the tribunal," I blurt out.

The room goes quiet, and all attention narrows in on me. I blink quickly because, in truth, I hadn't expected myself to be bold enough to speak. Even so, I hold my head high.

Jarron repeats my words in High Orizian and then adds, "We request a formal trial. If you will not take our word, as you have for every previous ruler for the last eon, then we will do what we must to prove our legitimacy."

"And if you are found lacking?"

"Then, my mate and I will leave. My priority will always lie with her, not the throne. Not the people of Oriziah."

I suck in a quick breath. Doesn't that sound bad? For a future ruler to say he doesn't prioritize his people?

No, Laithe answers. *It is expected. Dedication to your mate is what proves a High Orizian worthy of ruling.*

"We will find happiness together elsewhere, and my title will fall to my brother," Jarron continues as if my internal comment never happened. "But mark my words, this conflict will not end with me. If you rule on the side of the rebels, you will destabilize the very structure of this world. Vandozer, and those who follow his blasphemous words, will continue undermining the royal family's right to rule."

"Your brother has long since earned his right to rule," one witch spits. To earn your chosen is to earn your right to rule. Trevor claimed his mate early.

"And why do you think Princess Beatrice is not here? Because she too is wrapped up in this conspiracy. She is—" He stops himself from incriminating her. Trevor's wings ruffle, unsettled. If Jarron blames Bea for the target on myself and my sister, he will forever sully her name and continue to damage the trust in the royal family. "She too is trapped, manipulated by an evil man seeking to destroy our way of life. He has betrayed the very soul of Oriziah, but he will not succeed. I will prove that my demon soul is strong and devoted to its chosen mate, Candice Montgomery."

The ground rattles, and I suck in a breath.

Jarron stills, his eyes wide. I feel the uncertainty that washes through him, as well as my own fear.

"Jarron?"

An explosion shakes the walls around us, and a roar rips from Jarron's lips.

In an instant, I am in his arms. The world around me is nothing but spinning shadows and shouts of fear and anger. I can't tell what is up or down as Jarron carries me out of the palace. Then, the cold air sucks the breath from my lungs, and I am in the air, in the arms of the demon taking me high above the city now filled with fire and smoke.

48

AFTERSHOCKS

Jarron doesn't stop until he reaches the portal high above the clouds and stumbles onto the hard, flat floor of Shadow Hills.

"What was that?" I pant the moment he sets my feet on the ground. The crowds who had been cheering for me just minutes before were pressing in on the palace walls.

"The first attack," he says through gritted teeth. "They waited until the moment you arrived to make their first move."

"Is everyone okay? What happened to the meeting?"

He's pacing in front of me, wings splayed, hands clenching in and out. "They are fine. The attack did nothing more than minor damage to the lower level of the palace. It was a message."

A message. That they chose to send as soon as I arrived.

"What does it mean? That the people didn't accept me?"

"No," he growls, although I can feel the half-truth in the word. "It means it isn't enough."

Presenting me as his chosen is not enough to prove his worth to the people now that his character has been questioned. We knew this was a possibility, but it was terrifying to see it first hand nonetheless.

Bea was right. Jarron declaring a chosen is not enough to settle the rebels. Too many believe in Mr. Vandozer's claims. Too many doubt the royal family.

"Shouldn't you go back?" I ask.

"No." Again his voice is barely more than a growl. The claws on his feet are leaving divots in the marble flooring. I'm sure Ms. Bhatt will be pleased about that. "I cannot leave you, not after that." He stops his pacing, sucking in deep breaths. "I will call Laithe back here. Once they're here, I will travel back to Oriziah to see that everything is settled."

"Okay," I whisper, holding my arms crossed tightly. My teeth begin chattering.

They don't want me. They don't want me to be their princess.

Those are the thoughts I can't help from piling up.

Liz is the more powerful one now. She's the kind of princess his world wants.

Sharp fangs appear before my face, and I suck in a breath. "You are more than worthy," Jarron tells me, not for the first time. Then, he wraps his arms around me. His rage has retreated, replaced instead with a coat of adoration and protection he throws around me. "They will not take you from me. Not now. Not ever. Together, we will prove them to be fools for doubting you and me both."

49

BREWING DEATH

It's honestly bizarre how I can feel Jarron's emotions even when we're countless miles apart. Light years? I don't even know how to measure that kind of time and space. Oriziah is a planet whose solar system and galaxy have not been found from Earth. Meaning, for all we know, it's a literal other dimension. There is no measurable distance between us.

It could be another plane of existence that should not connect to ours, and yet, from here to there, I can feel him. His power. His devotion. His frustration. His longing.

I can't get enough context of what is happening in his world, but I can feel the swings of his emotions. He is bored as hell. He is delighted. He is amused. He is stressed. He is tired. He is annoyed. And then, beneath the surface, there is always an uncurrent of missing me and worry for upcoming events.

It's strange to feel those things all the time, mingling with my own emotions, but not be able to do anything about it. I want to tell him to sleep, but I haven't managed to learn how to send an actual message through our link while we're apart.

In two days, we will try again, this time with an official

tribunal. The Bright Tribunal, made up of three witches, one from each of the spiritual species of Oriziah, will decide whether they believe Jarron's claim.

They will decide my entire future—and Oriziah's— based on something there is no way to definitively prove.

Meanwhile, I'm working on the same potions I hoped would serve to kill nine powerful supernatural beings all at once to save my sister.

My stomach tenses. I hate that I've given up that chance. I hate that things in Oriziah are getting worse and there's nothing I can do about it.

So, while I stir my delayed death potion to excellence, ensure it is as powerful as I can possibly make it, I image the nine faces I long to kill, even while knowing and deeply regretting that I will not get the chance.

Two days until the tribunal that Jarron believes will resolve the bulk of his war.

Four days until the Cosmic Council meeting, where I could kill my greatest enemies all in one shot and suck out the fuel driving Jarron's war.

Not one part of me is convinced ignoring that chance is the right move.

But every part of me is certain I need to trust Jarron.

I haven't given up on the possibility of having both, but for now, I will follow the rules I agreed to and ensure that, just in case, my death potion is nothing short of perfect.

287

50
ONLY THE BEGINNING

Alien clicking makes my heart race and eyes fly wide open in the darkness of the bedroom. This time, though, I can feel him. His eagerness, his uncertainty about what happens later today, and his contentment at watching me sleep in his bed.

"Not sleeping anymore," he purrs.

"No," I agree.

His wings ruffle behind him, and he stalks forward, head bowed and eyes intent.

I pull back the bedspread. I don't even have to say the words for him to know exactly what I want. He shifts into his human form and slides beneath the sheets. Safely tucked in his arms, I sigh in relief.

His warmth is the most comfort I've ever felt.

"Less than a year," I tell him.

"Hmm?"

"Less than a year ago, I hated you."

He stills at that, letting the truth settle in. "Did you truly hate me, though?" he whispers. "Or did you just convince yourself of that?"

My lips twitch. "I successfully convinced myself. But one conversation with you had my unfair assumptions unraveling. It really didn't take long for me to know with certainty that you were not the monster I'd built up in my head."

Amusement tickles at the edges of our link. "And yet, you continued investigating me for the murder of your sister."

I bite my lip. I know he's not bothered by this fact now, but I still feel a small sense of shame. "I was stubborn," I tell him. "And I was afraid of the minuscule chance that you were playing me. *What if* I was wrong. *What if* you were just a really, really good actor?"

My heart floods with warmth and certainty. I feel what he feels for me, or at least a small part of it.

"And now?" he murmurs.

I smile against his chest. "Still not sure," I blurt out.

He jerks back and then barks out a surprised laugh. Our link makes my joke very clear in an instant. I'm pleased by the fact that I can still surprise him sometimes.

I grab the back of his head and pull him down to kiss me. We fall into each other like opposing winds crashing, swirling in a powerful dance. We stop soon, though, and relax into each other's arms.

"One day, it could all be over," I say it like I believe it, but in reality, it's more question than statement. It's only part of the puzzle, but it's a large one.

"It will be only the beginning, sunshine."

51

TRIBUNAL

Jarron keeps his arm casually slung over my shoulder as we enter the massive, shadowed chamber. I shiver against the chill air of the caves and pray I don't trip on the uneven stone. There is a massive pit in the middle of the floor, with swirling black and red magma that lights up the cavern the closer we approach.

It's kind of awesome but also petrifying.

Heat creeps up my neck the closer we get to the glowing pit.

Soon, my skin is tingling with heat. Concern flutters through my bond with Jarron, but I send him a reassuring look. Humans don't often come into this part of Oriziah, so he's uncertain how much my body is able to tolerate.

"You tell me if you become uncomfortable," he mutters.

"You'd know, even if I didn't."

"Tell me anyway."

Laithe marches beside us with their chin high.

Today, it will be us three standing for the fate and future of Oriziah. The rest of the royal family will have to wait. Behind us, the King and Queen of Oriziah follow closely. The queen's skin shimmers white with black streaks. Her wings pearly white.

"Welcome," a hunched demon says with a bow of her head. She is small in stature, with reddish skin like Laithe's. Her skin is leathery, but she has no wings. Only six-inch-long, straight black horns separate her appearance from the witches I met the other night. "To the Bright Tribunal hearing."

Jarron's translation is so quick I barely have to focus. The demoness's voice has a low echoey quality to it. I can't tell if that's from old age or simply common for her species.

Behind her is one of the black-haired witches from the other night and another who is younger and taller, with a willowy frame and bright red hair.

"I see we have a foreigner in our midst," the tallest demon witch says.

"This is Candice," Jarron says, stopping few feet short of the group of witches, "my chosen mate."

Silence stretches for several moments. The witches do not react. No shake of their heads. No change in eye movements. No whispering. They simply wait.

"I see," the lead witch says. "Welcome, Candice. Of Earth, is that correct?"

I give her one nod and do my best not to show my trembling. Warm comfort flows through our bond. I breath deeper, and my jitters nearly disappear.

"Tell us why you have come," the red-skinned witch says. She shuffles her hand around in a parchment bag and pulls out a handful of dust.

"To prove my honor," Jarron's demon says, wings splayed wide. "That I am not a fraud and I have earned my right to rule by earning my true chosen."

The witch scatters the dust into the magma below. There are three flashes of light.

"We have planned for this contingency," the black-haired

witch says, "and have invited the opposition claimant to join our hearing."

I swallow. Do they mean what I think they mean?

The black-haired witch motions to an approaching couple. They stroll beside the magma pitch toward our meeting place. One is a pale-skinned demon with veiny wings and the other... a beautiful woman with glowing skin and yellow hair.

"Liz?" I whisper, back straight, eyes wide, and heart aching but open.

"You're familiar?" the tallest witch says casually. She's either already aware of the connection, or she thinks it's somehow evidence of our deception.

I meet her gaze steadily. "She is my sister," I say before realizing no translation was made. These witches understand English, then?

My admission seems to surprise the other two. "Interesting," one mutters.

I don't know how Jarron reacts. I don't particularly care. He knows he has to keep some control of how he is perceived, but there is only so much that can be done. He cares for Liz, and I love her deeply. Those things cannot be hidden.

"Candice," Liz says in a low tone, like this is some formal meeting. My blood is suddenly cold. I am so happy to see her again, but the sight chills me to the bone.

Her eyes seem sallow, even though her skin is literally glowing.

"How, exactly, are you siblings?" the lead witch asks. "One is human, and one is decidedly not."

"She is human, or was," I say. "He did something to change her." I glare at the pale demon whose hand is clasped around my sister's elbow.

"Change?" the woman tastes the word with a frown. "How?"

"The girl is correct," Mr. Vandozer says. "Elizabeth was born human. After we met and fell in love, she voluntarily entered a magical rite and won. Her award included a rare prize of magical blood."

"A new form of magical being?" one witch asks.

"Not new, simply rare," Vincent says. "I offered the other girl a chance to earn the same power as her sister. She has rejected me out of cowardice. Instead, apparently, seeking an alternative plan for power by manipulation and fraud." His lip curls in disgust. I want to stampede, wrap my hands around his throat, and squeeze until the life leaves his eyes.

"Why?" the red-skinned witch asks me, ignoring his final accusation. "You do not wish for power?"

"No," I admit. "I do not. I am happy as I was born. I never wanted that sort of power. *And* he is conveniently leaving out the requirements of such power."

"Requirements?"

"To kill nine innocent, low-magic beings. The winner earns the prize. But that's not all—"

"Nine sacrifices?" One tilts their head. "For this power?"

"She beat them in combat they willingly entered. Not sacrifices," Vandozer says.

"It is a highly illegal competition," I bark out.

"To your high morality police in the interdimensional courts, perhaps," the tall witch sneers.

Not opposed to murder, got it. I suppose I shouldn't be surprised. Many Orizians believe strongly in survival of the fittest.

"How about manipulating the free will of another being? She is not free now. Have they told you that?" I blurt out.

The lead witch's ears twitch. "They have not."

"She willingly entered and signed a magical contract," Vincent rebukes, face entirely calm. "She is now free as the victor."

293

"Lies," I hiss. "She is bound to your command."

He smirks. "You are an ignorant child who doesn't know what she's talking about."

My gaze flicks to Liz's. Her face is slack, lifeless.

"Liz?" I whisper. Something is wrong. This isn't right. Jarron shifts closer to me, squeezing my shoulder gently.

"Look at me," I beg her.

She glances up, but even her eyes don't look the same. I frown.

"Elizabeth," the white-haired witch says with a heavy accent. "Do you currently have free will?"

"Yes," Liz says through a tight jaw. Her eyes flash to mine, golden bright for an instant before fading into a soft blue.

"He forced her to say that," I whisper.

Jarron nods in agreement but doesn't make any effort to correct it. They wouldn't believe us, not unless they could see the command for themselves.

Anger wells in my chest. "Would you agree to answer that same question after a truth potion?" I ask, pulling out a small vial. Mr. Vandozer's eyes flare.

"It's an insult to imply she would lie on sacred ground," he responds smoothly.

I curl a lip at him, imagining again what it would feel like to strangle him with my bare hands.

One of the witches narrow her eyes at the dark liquid. "You are a witch, then?"

I slip the potion back into my pocket.

"Yes," Jarron answers for me. "Most consider her magicless, but she is talented in potions. I've seen her magic at work. Every potion she uses, she creates on her own."

"A magicless witch," one murmurs.

"A fearless human," another says after.

"An interesting choice in a mate."

I can't tell if that's a compliment or an insult.

"Come," the red-skinned witch says, "let us begin our trial. I will warn you, Prince Jarron, if we determine your claim false, we will make our declaration of war immediately. There will be no altering the course. The only way to halt the battle at that point, will be to willingly relinquish your throne but even that will not absolve you as the punishment for this fraud is death. Do you understand the consequences of making this official claim?"

"Yes," Jarron says quickly, firmly.

Anxiety curls in my gut, along with fiery anger that they would dare threaten him.

I may be sentenced but they will not search for me outside of Oriziah.

Meaning his death sentence will really mean banishment. Even so there's still a chance they capture and hurt him if I don't do this right.

One witch snaps her fingers, and about five feet to our right, a large, round stone table appears. Jarron smoothly guides me to it.

Two of the witches sit on my right and the third to Jarron's left, leaving Liz and Mr. Vandozer in demon form across the table, staring blankly.

The seats are short round stubs of pitch-black wood with glistening golden rims.

Jarron sits beside me, keeping my left hand in his lap between both of his hands. His claws scape ever so slightly against my skin. Enough to keep me focused but not enough to hurt.

Even just with this short distance away from the magma, the air is cooler. My cheeks are warm, but the hair on my arms stands up straight. My body can't decide if I am warm or cold.

The nerves certainly don't help.

An inch-wide crevice opens up in the middle of the table,

traveling the entire length. Blue glittering liquid fills it, steaming like the magma below. It surrounds the table with the scent of vanilla and orange spice.

Two of the witches begin a somber chant in a hauntingly beautiful harmony. I suck in a breath. There is very clearly magic in the song. It seeps into my bones, making my head dizzy.

Jarron frowns down at me, but there is no worry in his heart, only curiosity.

"Make your claim, Prince Jarron," the lead witch says.

"Candice Montgomery, human from Earth, is my chosen mate. I will never betray her or choose another. She is mine, and I have earned her heart in return. After months of courting, she has accepted me as hers."

My heart hammers at those words. An honest proclamation that I am his.

Vincent Vandozer leans forward and hisses. My sister looks alive for the first time, but it isn't a pleasant expression on her face. She looks shocked and betrayed.

"No," she whispers. "You don't understand."

I bite my bottom lip hard. As much as I'm proud to be Jarron's true chosen, it still pits me against my sister. I love her. And I will fight for her.

Even so, I don't know if she'll forgive me for winning this competition we didn't know we were waging.

"Candice?" she whispers, pleading eyes darting to me. "You—"

"It is clearly a lie," Vincent hisses. "A disgusting usurpation of justice and a deceit against our highest sacred right."

"It's true, Liz," I say softly, ignoring his claims. "I can explain—"

"No!" Liz says louder now. "You don't understand. He was my salvation. He was my way out of this. They won't let me go if —" Her eyes dart to Vincent, a panicked expression on her face.

"Calm down," Vincent demands.

Liz obeys immediately. Her muscles lose all tension. Her face goes slack.

He may as well have given her a lobotomy at the table.

"Don't you see that?" I exclaim to the witches, pointing at my sister.

"We see it, child," the red-skinned witch whispers so lightly I'm unsure I heard her.

Does that mean they know what's happening? They believe that Liz does not have free will?

Despair clouds my mind, making it impossible to see anything but my sister, a magical slave to a demon right in front of me.

"Tell me your story," the witch says to Jarron and me, voice softer now. "Tell us all how this could be true."

"Pointless!" Vincent hollers. "There is no proof she could give to change what we all know to be true. How convenient he would stake a claim now, after I announced his rejection to the world. You have all heard the rumors, seen the signs. The rejection has split his soul open."

The cavern drops into pitch blackness, and unnatural silence sucks the breath from my lungs. Jarron's chest is suddenly pressed to my back, arms curled around me protectively.

"Now is not your turn to speak, Vincent. If you cannot keep your tongue under control, you will be asked to leave," one of the witches reprimands.

Light once again flares from both the table and the magma pit, lighting the area. All of the witches' eyes settle on Jarron's stance around me.

His shoulders relax, and he retakes his seat.

"Speak," the witch tells Jarron. "Tell us how you met the humans. Tell us how and when you selected your chosen."

Jarron sits up straight. "Janice and Bruce Montgomery are

potions masters, who were employed frequently by my parents," he explains. "Eventually, they earned the crown's favor as friends and were invited to stay at a private island on Earth along with us when Trevor and I were adolescents."

"That is a very vulnerable time for young demons. This was a specific choice, then?" the red-haired witch asks.

"Yes," Jarron says. "It was done knowingly. Though, the Earth family knew little of the significance."

I remember hearing that the parents of High Orizians are very careful with whom their offspring comes into contact with before adulthood. Only those who are highly trusted and respected are allowed access to young demons.

The royal family of Oriziah essentially chose me and my sister to be in the running as their sons' mates. That's what they're saying.

"Their daughters, Elizabeth and Candice, spent two entire summers—Earth's warm season—in close proximity with us. We were friends. While Beatrice and Trevor were growing in intimacy, even before their bond was legitimized, I spent most of my time with the two human girls, Candice especially. I was enamored with her, but I did not make my choice firmly until near the end of the second summer. I knew weeks before I'd had my first shift on Earth that she was my choice. It was why I'd waited so long to come back to Oriziah. I didn't want to leave her yet. One night, an act of violence between the sisters enraged me, and I made my first transition on Earth. This act made it obvious to any demons involved that my mate had been chosen during that time. It also made my two human friends afraid of me. We didn't see each other again for many years."

"Until *after* I'd won his true chosen's heart and allegiance," Vincent mutters under his breath.

All three witches turn their heated glare to him, and he clenches his jaw, gaze dropping to the table in submission.

"Vincent claims Elizabeth is your chosen, and that she has rejected you. You deny this claim?"

"Vehemently," Jarron says firmly. "Elizabeth is a beautiful female, whom I care about, but she is not mine. I do not, nor have I ever, chosen her."

A rumble of annoyance escapes Vincent's chest.

"It is not uncommon for a young demon to wait to woo his chosen. To allow her time and space to grow and earn her slowly," the black-haired witch says solemnly.

"Indeed," the red-haired witch says. "And yet, in this case, to present a chosen so quickly after a rejection claim has been made is still rather suspect. Continue, Prince. We need to understand more."

Jarron nods. "I kept my distance from my chosen, knowing I would have to re-earn her trust, but that distance was the best remedy for the time being. We were very young, and I was more than willing to wait for my chance to win her. I had intended to wait until after she finished her Earth customary schooling—when she reached adulthood by human standards."

"She is not currently an adult in her culture?"

"My birthday was last week," I say softly.

"She is only just now considered an adult by her culture," Jarron says. "Though she hasn't yet finished her schooling."

"Liz is a year younger," I add. "She is still a minor. Vincent is much older. For him to seduce her is a crime in my world."

The witch's brows rise. "We do not care much for Earth morality or legality, but it is noted."

I bite the inside of my lip and let Jarron continue.

"As mentioned, I'd intended to wait until after she finished high school to pursue her, but my chance came sooner than I'd anticipated when Candice arrived at the school I've been attending at the beginning of this year. It was a surprise because she'd made it clear she didn't want to be involved in the magical community. I confronted her and learned that her sister had been killed. She believed the killer attended Shadow Hills Academy, and I quickly offered to help her investigate. We began an alliance. I verbally claimed her as mine while doing everything I could to keep her safe, help her uncover the mystery surrounding her sister's 'death,' and win her heart. I was close—so achingly close—to earning her until the investigation brought us to the Akrasia Games. We confronted the predator that hunted and harmed her sister—Vincent. He nearly succeeded in killing me, but my mate defended me."

The three witches blanch as one. "You claim that a low-status High Orizian defeated you, but a magicless human protected you from that same demon?"

Jarron nods. "In order to follow Candice into the games, I needed to go through a spelled barrier that would harm a being with strong magic if they tried to pass. I took a potion of her creation to suppress my magic in order to follow her through the barrier. Vincent attacked me while in that vulnerable state and stabbed me, wounding me severely. Candice then used that same potion on him. I was mortally wounded without my magic, but this act made him vulnerable as well, and she fought him."

All eyes turn to me. A soft surprise and curiosity in the witches' gazes.

"I still almost lost, even without his magic," I say under my breath.

"But she stalled long enough for aid to come, effectively saving my life. What I didn't know at the time was that Vincent told her a heinous lie while I was injured. He told her that Liz, her sister, had been my chosen. He claimed Candice was my second choice." Jarron's hands clench over my thigh. His nose wrinkles, and his voice deepens. "He interrupted my quest to earn my chosen—with a lie."

Jarron hadn't shown emotion during his explanation that

he'd nearly died or that I'd fought for him, but this bothers him deeply.

"You believed this claim?"

"I did," I whisper. "Beatrice implied the same thing previously; I just didn't understand the significance."

"She pushed me away," Jarron explains. "She did not reject me, not completely, but it was enough to rattle me. Neither my human nor demon soul understood why she pushed us away. I didn't know she had been told this lie, not until a few weeks ago when we once again came face to face with the council behind the Akrasia Games. During that altercation, we both learned that Candice's sister was not dead as we previously believed. She had fought in the games but won. And winning made her the jinn—a magical slave to the games until the next set would take place. I also learned at this time that this council all believed Liz to be my chosen." His breathing picks up speed. "Though I couldn't speak their lie aloud, I informed the Cosmic Council that they were all fools. I vowed to end each one of them. But they were confident that I would follow their commands because they threatened Elizabeth."

"They attempted to use your chosen against you? To manipulate you?"

"Yes," he says, voice hoarse. "It was a betrayal of the worst kind. But luckily, they were wrong, and I had no fear in destroying them all so long as I could reach Candice. I used my magic to collapse the cave system in on them, grabbed my mate, and escaped."

"That is quite a tale," one witch says with a click of her tongue.

"By that telling," the red-skinned witch says, expression making it clear she's thinking deeply about the information presented, "this Cosmic Council, as you call them, should know full well that your chosen is not the one you call the jinn, and yet they've used that as the basis of their campaign against you."

"Yes. They know. There is a fraud in this room, but it is not me," Jarron growls. "Deep down, he knows he miscalculated, but he is stubborn. He refuses to face his error or simply doesn't care. If he can convince enough clans to turn against me, it will not matter if his lie has merit, which is why I am here. Now that I have earned the heart of my true chosen, I can correct the manipulation and present your true future queen. Candice." There is so much pride in his voice it brings tears to my eyes.

"Lies," Vincent spits again.

"It's an interesting story, Princeling, but hardly proof that Vincent's claims are false. Let us hear from the opposition."

Vincent grins, showing his sharp canines. When his eyes shift to me, a low rumble begins in Jarron's chest. This only makes Vincent's smile grow wider.

"You make a wonderful actor, Prince, but you have more than exposed yourself. The world sees the truth. You are not worthy of the crown. A second rejected prince."

"Explain," one witch demands. "Your puffed-up insults are not enough here."

Vincent leans back and crosses his arms. "I met a young, beautiful female human during my time on Earth. Her name was Elizabeth Montgomery, and her parents are potions masters. We spoke at length about her history with the magical world. And she became enamored with me. She asked me how to become powerful. She wanted me to claim her, to mark her, but I told her I could do so much better. I offered her a place in a competition where she would earn power beyond reckoning. She agreed."

"How did you come to believe she was the crown prince's chosen?"

"During the competition, Beatrice informed me. She was concerned for the girl's well-being, seeing as the competition is dangerous. But by this point, it was too late. I was enamored with the girl as much as she was with me. I had no intention of letting her come to harm. She of course won the competition and became the incredible being you see before you. After the competition, we spoke at length about the young prince, and she declared she didn't want nor need him now that she was this powerful and she had *me*. She did not want another. In the meantime, Prince Jarron started showing the signs of rejection. His magic was uncontrolled. He acted violently and out of character.

"He believed his chosen to be dead. Mourning is expected, except Prince Jarron then began a relationship with the other sister in Elizabeth's absence. His true chosen learned about this betrayal and became justifiably angry. The prince's behavior grew worse and worse. There are reports of his magic being uncontrolled. He nearly destroyed the academy. Together, Elizabeth and I created a plan to ensure our world was well aware of the prince's lack of integrity. He is not fit to rule for so many reasons—today's display is more disgusting than even I thought him capable of—and I believe our world will be better off if he never claims the throne."

Jarron clenches his hands into fists.

"Neither tale is all that convincing," one witch says after a pause.

"The reports of magic control have reached our ears though. That is evidence of his claim," another witch says.

"I do not deny that my demon soul has been agitated," Jarron says. "I only reject what Vincent claims is the reason. My demon soul and I have had conflict, but only after my chosen mate pushed me away due to this lie. I resolved this conflict and succeeded in earning her despite his insidious efforts to sabotage us."

Silence stretches for several moments.

"It is ones word against another."

"Both tales are plausible."

The three witches nod as one. It's a stale mate.

"If you allow lies and manipulation to alter the line of succession," I say calmly, "you weaken your world's power."

"It weakens the crown; it does not weaken us. Competition for the throne is positive, in our eyes. The longer we allow rulers to pass without question, the more likely they will grow weak with complacency."

My heart begins racing. There has to be a way to convince them.

"So, that's it?" I stand. "You'll just allow war to begin because of one accusation with no substance? You put my *mate at risk* because of a spineless coward's jealousy?"

The witches appear amused by my assertion. "Do you have more to add to the discussion, human? Do you believe you can convince us?"

My brow pinches. So much of this is word against word. "Is there no way to test it?"

"Only one," the witch says. "And no ruler has ever agreed to participate."

I swallow. "What is it?"

"A demon will never allow harm to come to their mate. That is one element that can be tested."

I swallow, afraid to ask for more specifics. Isn't that what happened in the caves with the council? Too bad this tribunal wasn't there to witness it.

"I am not willing to harm either girl to prove him wrong," Jarron says. "My mate would not allow me to harm her sister."

My eyes flash to Liz, something I'd noticed before, in the caves, comes to my mind. Again, it would be word against word, except maybe I could use Liz's word to defend us instead.

"Then, indeed there is no way to test the soul of the demon."

Silence stretches. I can feel the tension beginning to build higher as we all realize today's meeting was fruitless. No conclusion has been made. I'm not sure we even budged the tribunal's mind a little.

"Liz," I say softly. Her eyes meet mine. Vandozer clearly has some control over her right now, but from what I know, it's verbal control. She must do what he says. But he cannot let the witches know she is a full slave to him or it would weaken his case.

This means he had to have given her a long list of demands before the meeting. If I ask something he's not expecting, will she tell the truth?

"Can you show me your arm?"

Liz's gaze flashes to Vincent.

He frowns. "We do not bow to the requests of the enemy. No matter how innocent they seem."

My eyes flare then shift to the lead witch. She studies me for a long moment before nodding. "Elizabeth, could you please show us your arm?"

Vincent growls in frustration, but Liz does as asked. She holds out both arms. Her dress has loose sleeves that flare at the wrists, exposing a slight bit of her glowing skin.

The witch gently grabs her right wrist and turns her arm over, examining the skin. I allow her slow exploration without comment because I know if I expose my intention, Vincent could shut it down quickly.

The witch frowns, clearly unsure what she's looking for. She shifts to the next arm and pauses at the long scar on the underside of her forearm.

I barely manage to hold back a wild grin of success when the witch runs her thumb over the scar. "Where did you receive this wound?"

Liz frowns, looking down at it. Vincent leans over, like he has no idea what they're talking about. Had he never noticed it? Never cared to ask?

"Jarron—" she whispers. "Jarron gave it to me."

The whole cavern stills at those words.

For several beats, no one speaks. Most don't even breathe.

"I don't—what does that mean?" Liz asks finally. A growl rips from Vincent's chest.

"More manipulation from liars and thieves!" he screams. His wings flare, and his roar shakes the foundation of the caves. "You will regret this moment, little human. You are no one. Nothing. And your sister will pay for your misdeeds."

Suddenly, my feet are off the floor, hard arms around me, but conflicting feelings of alien determination and complete safety fill my chest. Dark leathery wings cocoon me, and as things settle, I realize that I am in Jarron's arms far from the meeting table.

"You're a genius," he whispers in my ear, pride swelling in him.

But something is wrong. I should feel pride at my success.

I know better than to think this is over just yet.

The room settles finally, and Jarron retreats from his protective stance, allowing me to see Liz sitting oddly still, her eyes wide.

"You don't understand," she says.

What don't I understand, Liz? Internally, I beg her as the table resets. The witches must have magically silenced Mr. Vandozer because he's howling into the air, but no sound comes out.

"We need to know how," the red-skinned witch says, not breathless. "This is good information, Candice of Earth, but we must know how he gave her that scar and when."

"Elizabeth, please tell us," the black-haired witch asks.

Mr. Vandozer writhes against whatever magic is holding him, trying to yell and scream and stop her.

This is it. This is the moment I can prove us right. And yet, tears fill Liz's eyes as she answers.

"It was that night. The night he changed."

I frown, staring down at my hands. Her hands are shaking.

"But it can't be true. It can't—"

My heart sinks.

"How did he harm you? What happened?"

He was my way out of this, she'd said. *They won't let me go.*

My heart picks up its pace. They're using her. They need her for this ruse, but if that changes—

She is very useful right now as a slave, Bea told me.

My stomach drops to my feet with a terrible realization. We can't protect her. She's under their control. With Vincent bound it gives us some leverage, but what are the chances he didn't make a demand that she must return to the council when the meeting was finished? What are the chances we could not only get her away from them right now but keep her away? Because one word from a single council member and she is back under their control.

Under their control, but no longer useful as slave.

She's lucky they haven't killed her already.

"Glass," I say.

Jarron stares at me in horror. He feels the truth settling into my mind at the same time, but the loss of this victory cuts deep regardless.

"Jarron scared her, and she ran into a window and cut herself." The lie is bitter on my tongue, but I will do anything to save my sister.

"Well, that's hardly proof," the red-haired witch says, waving me off.

My heart aches. I was so close to getting what we came for, but I lied to lose on purpose.

Because I realized that if I win this game today, I will lose my sister.

The moment the tribunal believe Jarron's claim, the council will have no use for her.

They'll kill her.

52
VICTORY SLIPPING THROUGH MY FINGERS

Jarron paces back and forth in the bedroom back at Shadow Hills, still in demon form. His leathery wings scrape against the tile, and I can feel the uneasiness pulsing from him.

We had victory in our grasp.

He knows why I lied, why I backtracked on the one truth that could essentially prove that Vincent's claims are false.

Jarron's mind winds through all the next steps that would have taken place. The tribunal would have announced to the capital city that Prince Jarron's claims are substantiated and Vincent's are false.

There may have been riots in the streets, fighting among the rebels, but slowly over the next few days, the number of rebels would have dissipated and the pressure would have eased.

The war would be all but over.

And my sister would have died, I insert.

The Cosmic Council would still remain, cast out of their plans for war in Oriziah with a jinn as a liability. They would have killed her.

The agitated monster in front of me groans deep in his chest.

"I'm sorry," I whisper for the first time. "I had to."

He stops, eyes cast to the floor, taking labored breaths. Then, he pivots toward me and stalks forward. "My priority has always been you," he growls.

My shoulders are hunched forward, arms curled tightly around myself.

"I am not angry with you. I am frustrated. I am thwarted at every turn. They have weapons pointed in multiple directions, making it impossible to attack them without being wounded from the other side."

He's mad at them, not me. That's what he's saying. But I can't help but feel like it's still my fault. If he had chosen someone else, not me or Liz, then this—

He swipes out and grips me by the back of the head, the monster's black eyes staring down at me. "You are perfect. You are the correct choice. You are *not* the problem."

I shiver at his words.

"I want you, no one else. I have never once regretted my choice."

He steps even closer to my place in the armchair, forcing my knees to part so he can press his body up against mine. My chin rests on his stomach, still looking up at my monster.

"You do not blame yourself for someone else's evil."

My eyes flutter closed.

"My brother should have chosen different," he says, releasing his grip on me. "But that is not our burden to carry."

Bea? He's still blaming Bea for this?

"You were blaming yourself for simply existing and being desirable," he chides back to my thoughts. I roll my eyes in response.

"We can still fix it," I say. "We can still kill the council."

He growls. "I will not trust her."

I close my eyes and glance up at the ceiling. "Then, what? What now?"

- He heaves in a large breath. "I go back to Oriziah and keep working."

I drop my face into my hands. He's not safe there. He's not safe there because of me. Because I chose my sister over him.

"Today was not a loss, Candice." He sighs. "It's frustrating, knowing that we could have proven our case, but the council began sincerely believing Vincent's claims and left believing either could be true. It's—it will not make things worse. It may even help."

Considering the palace was literally attacked days ago, saying that it "may help" is not enough to take away my fear.

The demon's eyes soften. He runs the back side of his claws over my cheek. "I will be back. I will not leave you. We will be okay."

Both of our uncertainty and fear mingles together until I can't tell which is whose.

"Okay," I mutter, only half-believing it.

53

MIND ON FIRE

I wake, screaming. Burning pain rages through my whole body. My mind is on fire.

"Jarron?" I call as the pain drops to a simmer.

The image of fire in darkness drops over my eyes. What's happening?

There is distant screaming somewhere in the back of my mind. Shouts of panic.

This is not a dream.

Jarron! I call through our link.

I'm okay, he responds finally.

What happened? It felt like you were on fire or something. My chest tightens.

I heal quickly.

My stomach drops to my feet. Blood icy cold. *What happened?*

They're attacking. We'll push them back quickly, though. I need to shut down the link for now. Okay? I'll check back soon.

Then, that spot inside of me where Jarron's comforting essence has resided for the last several days is empty.

Cold.

Oh, fuck no.

Anger pools in my chest, followed by bitter certainty.

I'm not doing this anymore. I'm not a lost lamb. I'm not a child to be protected.

He shuts me out, deciding to fight these battles on his own. And I understand that I'm a vulnerability out there in that world. But here... here, I have power.

And I'm done sitting around, waiting for my moment.

I rush out of bed in the middle of the night. I have a death potion to finish.

54

I WILL FIGHT FOR HIM, EVEN IF HE DOESN'T APPROVE

Lola and Janet arrive in the morning before classes, chirping and giggling about something, but I don't have the capacity to figure out what they're on about.

Janet stops still, her smile falling with one look at me. "Whoa."

"What's happening?" Lola asks, her voice a squeak.

"Jarron is at war," I say. "And I'm about to be too."

"What?" Janet screeches. "What are you talking about? What happened at the tribunal? What's going on?"

I stop mid-stir and take a deep breath, eyes closed. I feel like I'm barely me right now, running on panic and rage and desperation. I explain what happened at the tribunal. "We had it. I figured out the way to convince them, but then I also figured out what would happen if we did."

They listen raptly to my explanation of how the council would kill my sister and that now, because the tribunal didn't result in an answer, the war is continuing and the rebels are attacking.

"They attacked, and something happened to Jarron. He was

injured. He healed quickly, but I could feel it. And then, he cut me off from him, so I don't even know what's going on now."

Their eyes are wide in shock and fear.

I try to force my own panic down. "Was something happening with you guys? You seemed happy."

"Oh!" Janet's eyes dart to Lola and back.

"Nothing," Lola chirps.

"Bullshit. Tell me."

"You don't have to be joyous for me when you're not okay. That's not how friendships work, Candice." Lola sounds so serious.

"Just tell me so I know," I say, shoulders slumping.

"Tyrane asked me out," she tells me.

"The black male pixie?"

"He's her mate," Janet explains. "He hadn't talked to her most of this year, but since the new list came out—"

"Oh," I mutter. "How do you feel about that?"

Lola sighs. "Our mates aren't like Orizians or even fae," she explains. "It's really more like an arranged marriage. So, I don't know really. I'm still kinda mad at him, but he's been sweet and maintains that he didn't want to push me away. We'll see. I intend to give him a chance but make him work for it."

My lips twitch, despite the pressure in my chest. "As you should."

"Now," Janet says seriously, "what are we doing for you? How can we help?"

The pressure in my chest eases slightly, but I can feel the tears ready to break through, and I cannot do that right now. I can't fall apart with my friends, as much as that's maybe healthy. So, I reharness my anger and determination.

"Can you go get Manuela? I have a meeting to prepare for, but I can't do it on my own."

315

Manuela's judgmental gaze is heavy. "You are not in a state to perform a serious coup on a room full of powerful magic users."

"I don't need to be," I say. "I need my potions to be ready and Bea to be willing."

She tilts her head, examining me. "She is willing. Are your potions ready?"

I nod and hand her the small vial of black angry liquid.

"You cannot be the one to do it," Manuela explains. "Jarron will kill us all if we put you in danger again."

My bottom lip trembles, so I bite it hard. I can't show my weakness right now.

I have to leave my own fate up to someone else by letting them do this for me.

"She can watch it, though," Janet says. She steps forward, hands on her hips. "You can make a looking-glass portal for her to watch. They won't even be able to tell she's there."

"I don't know that Beatrice will feel confident that this potion is enough to complete the assassination," Manuela says. "She needs some form of backup."

"You're not willing?" Lola asks, fluttering closer.

"I am not a fighter," Manuela says, checking her cuticles. "So, tell me, what happens if something goes wrong?"

"One of us will step in for her," Janet says confidently. "Candice doesn't ever need to be in danger."

"Hey!" I complain. "I can't ask you guys to put yourself at risk for me. If someone needs—"

Janet holds up a finger. "You're not asking. We're offering. Take it or leave it."

Manuela looks Janet up and down. "A half-troll and a pixie are going to be the backup plan?"

Janet narrows her eyes. "And a powerful wolf shifter."

Manuela snorts. "He's not that powerful."

"So, you're saying you won't help us? Help me?" I step forward.

She twists her lips. "I'm saying this plan is foolish. I'll pitch the idea, but Beatrice doesn't know if she can trust you now that you've linked with Jarron."

"Jarron's fighting his own battles. He blocked me out again. I don't know what's happening with him, so he won't know what's happening with me either."

Manuela blinks. "That's not entirely true. He'll check in periodically, so you will have to guard your thoughts diligently. And if you are ever in danger, he'll know. This plan will put all of our lives in danger. Every single one of us."

"Then, make your choice, but I have one more request."

55
DEAL WITH THE DEVIL

"Thompson is on his way," Janet declares, clicking off her phone.

"He can really afford to leave his pack right now?" I ask, pacing in my workshop. It's pretty much impossible for my mind to stay off of the current plans, but I try my best to focus mostly on the fantasy of killing the council instead of the specifics of said plan.

That fantasy is not new. Jarron wouldn't find it alarming if he caught me thinking about it.

Yes, I'm fucked up. No, I don't care.

"Yes!" Janet answers. "After Jarron's attack on the invading packs and his message to the others, there haven't been any new threats. His pack got their supplies. They've been able to reset their defenses. It's not over, but he has some room to breathe, and you know, the sooner this war is over, the better for him, so he's invested."

"How soon will he arrive?"

"Not until tomorrow. Manuela helped him find the fastest portal route back, but she can't make him a direct portal because she's used so much magic on what we asked of her already."

"Right. Yeah that makes sense."

Tomorrow.

Tomorrow, Thompson will be here. Tomorrow, I'm going to kill the Cosmic Council and finish this once and for all.

I refocus my mind. There is honestly little for me to do right now. I have a meeting with Bea tomorrow morning to finish up our final plans, but for now, most of my potions are finished. And my allies are working hard.

There are still two potions sitting in cauldrons that I haven't touched, mostly because they're not relevant to my scheme, but now I'm stuck in this waiting mode, so I may as well finish them up.

I methodically portion out my nullifier antidote, even though it's a fairly large dosage. I stare at the clear liquid, wondering if it was even a good idea to brew these.

Either way, I leave them unlabeled and in a side pocket of my backpack.

On my thigh, I clasp a stunning potion into one of the little slots and a paralyzer. These vials are extra strong and bullet proof, so they shouldn't break easily. That's both good and bad. It means they won't accidentally crack open and stun or paralyze me just because I fell or was hit. Bad because they're more difficult to use.

I also include invisibility, a weakening potion, and two extra nullifiers on my thigh clasp. The last two won't work on me anyway, and the invisibility doesn't seem to be too much of a liability.

I also have a steel box where I stack all the rest of my very important potions. Instant death. The rest of my delayed death. My stunning bombs. Invisibility. Weakener. Paralyzer. All in crushable vials for aggressive action.

After a while, I run out of tasks to complete, so I try to push through the barrier between me and Jarron. It's killing me knowing he's in danger but not knowing what's happening.

All is well.

I suck in a breath, but that message is all I get from my mate in the middle of a war. Maybe it's for the best. Because if Jarron knew what I was doing, he would not be pleased.

I'm done running and hiding.

Now is the time to prove that I am anything but inconsequential.

The demoness's eyes flash up to me, darting between my face and my wrist. Her lips curl into a smile. "So, it's true?" Bea says. "The crown prince has finally won his true chosen."

I roll my eyes. "Finally?"

She shrugs. "It's been a very long year."

I laugh. "Fair enough."

Bea's new hideout is markedly different than the last. A New York City penthouse apartment. "Fancy digs," I comment, looking out over the bright skyline.

"It's strange, being here, but at least the view is nicer than before."

"No more nightmare creatures?"

She shakes her head. "Not here. I've only been here for a day, though. It was Manuela's suggestion once we learned you wanted to meet with me again. Jarron would know if you entered Oriziah."

"Ah. Yeah, I suppose that makes sense."

"So, you've got everything set?" she asks. "The potions are all ready?"

I nod. "The meeting hasn't changed?"

She shakes her head. "They changed the location last week,

but that won't affect anything. Manuela has had plenty of time to create her portal with my help. Everything will be just fine on my end."

"Good."

"And how about Jarron? Manuela said he's shut down your access to his thoughts and feelings right now."

I wince. "Yes."

She nods. "Trevor too. I know they've been fighting on and off and having meetings between. I wish I knew more."

"Does he usually block you?" I hadn't really considered their link in all of this.

"Mostly, yes. He knows bits and pieces of what's happening with me, but it's scattered. He's been distant with me for months." Her expression tells me how much that hurts her. How much she wants to fix the rift between them. "There are still rebels rioting in the city, that much is common knowledge in our world, but they are currently being pushed back from accessing the palace. From what little I get from Trevor, I suspect there are still spies being caught regularly inside the walls, and that may be the biggest reason Jarron's cutting off your access. He doesn't want you to feel it every time he's attacked. He doesn't want you to know the fear he's feeling or the pain when something does happen."

I drop onto the metal stool by the kitchen counter, body ready to collapse at any moment. It's the morning of the meeting. Hours. I have hours to keep this up.

"Two nights ago, that did happen," I admit. "I woke up in anguish, like I was on fire."

"He was attacked?"

I nod. "He was injured somehow. He healed quickly, but I still felt the pain. That's when he closed off our link from his end."

She nods. "I'm sorry. It's really hard to lose access to your mate; I know firsthand."

321

I swallow. "Well..." I sigh, trying to muster that rage again because it's the only thing keeping me going right now. "In a few hours..."

She smiles. "If we do this right, we can end it all today."

My shoulders relax slightly.

"So," she begins, clasping her hands behind her back like she's a girl boss CEO beginning an important meeting, "there's an assembly planned in the capital of Oriziah today. With what's happening now, I don't know what that will look like."

I frown. "An assembly?"

She nods. "It's the distraction, pre-planned and the reason the council set the meeting for this particular day. They don't like to bring the whole group together unless there is something larger happening at the same time. That should help keep Jarron's attention from what you're doing, but you've still got to be on guard. One wrong move and it's my life."

I nod. "I understand."

"But I'm still willing to take the risk. I can't keep living like this."

"Me neither."

"As I understand it, there was one other thing you needed from me."

"I do, but I have a question first. One more puzzle piece to fit in place before I know if this idea is sound."

"Okay. Ask away."

"How, exactly, does someone give away their place on the council?"

56

LET A NEW GAME BEGIN

I sit cross-legged on the ground in front of the mirror in Bea's dusty old room, knee bouncing anxiously. My thumb absently twists the silver ring on my forefinger.

Lola is unnaturally still on my right shoulder. Thompson is reclined casually beside me, watching the mirror like it's a K-drama about to begin.

Janet bites her nails while pacing behind me. Manuela stands, arms crossed, glaring at Thompson, who doesn't seem to notice in the slightest.

Inside the mirror, the other world shimmers and moves like water.

The room beyond the mirror is a large Downton-Abbey-esque, old-English dining hall, with yellowed wallpaper and a huge wooden table decorated with candles and white flowers. Along the far edge of the room is a table with wine and other tonics set out, waiting for the powerful beings to arrive.

A human man in a pristine tux stands with his head high and arms behind his back, ready to serve the Cosmic Council.

I've been fighting nausea the last thirty minutes, watching the quiet room. Soon, my enemies will fill this room.

Soon, so soon, I will get my revenge.

In the last thirty minutes, two of them have arrived. A small witch, with eyes so golden they almost look like they're glowing, and a massive man, with one large eye in the middle of his face. He looks exactly how I'd imagine the goliath from that bible story. All muscle and veins. This guy has got to be on steroids or something.

The difference is, I know he is not all brute strength. He has powerful magic as well.

"What is that thing?" Janet says, staring at the giant of man.

"Sparky sparky boo man," Thompson mutters.

I snort. "He's a cyclops. He's as strong as a giant but with magic almost as powerful as an Orizian."

Even from across a portal, I can feel the power building in the room. And that's with only two of the council members.

The thought of me—a magicless human—attempting to kill *that thing* makes my palms sweat. How could I? How could I kill all of them?

I am so small.

I am nothing. No one.

I am of no consequence.

Anger bubbles up from far, far away, but I don't need Jarron to tell me how untrue those thoughts are. I know.

The anger siphons away, and Jarron's thoughts remain distant. I force my mind back to fantasies of killing the council with blank faces. The access cuts off again.

"Jarron really doesn't know this is happening?" Thompson asks, as if reading my mind.

I swallow. "He seems a bit distracted. I'm not keeping it from him, though, not anymore. If he figures it out at this point—"

"He can't stop it now." Manuela grins.

I nod.

"He'll be pissed, though, right?"

"At me, mostly," Manuela says. "My alliance with the demon prince hinges on today going well. If it works, I'll remain an important part of his inner circle. If it fails, I may need to go into hiding along with Beatrice."

"He's not going to hate *me*, is he?" Thompson asks.

"No," I say adamantly. "You're just a tagalong bodyguard. You couldn't have stopped me from going through with this if you tried, so now you're just here to make sure I don't die. He'll appreciate that."

He huffs out a breath, seemingly not all that convinced.

My attention shifts back to the cyclops and witch in the world through the mirror. "This is so crazy," Janet says. "We're like legit spies right now. Flies on the wall." She shakes her head. Our portal is on the wall in the corner of this grand meeting hall. Just one mirror among a myriad of wall decor.

"Literally," Thompson snorts. "Well, literally on the wall, not literally flies."

Their hushed banter eases some of the pressure on my chest, but my fear is still pulsing.

"Calm down, little human," Manuela purrs. "You're going to make us all anxious."

All of my friends shift their attention to me and my embarrassingly red ears. Janet finally sits beside me and squeezes my knee comfortingly.

Maybe Manuela was right that I am prey and have prey instincts. I will always feel inherent fear when I come face to face with a powerful predator.

"Fear is nothing to be embarrassed about," Janet whispers to me.

I release a breath. She's right. I do have prey instincts, and while it doesn't mean I should bow before those instincts, they still serve a purpose.

Fear is not the enemy, so long as you don't let it control you.

I used to let it control me. I used to make major life decisions based around my fear of the supernatural world. Even Liz said that in her journal. She knew it. She understood it.

Except, Liz is the one who fell into the trap.

She had an entirely different emotion controlling her—a thirst for power.

She hid how deeply she desired to feel important in the world we'd left.

I know she believed some of my rhetoric—we weren't safe among the magical. She had the scar to prove it. It wasn't glass that gave her that scar, like I told the tribunal. Jarron's talon sliced through her skin. If I'd known that was proof Liz wasn't his chosen back then, maybe some of this wouldn't have happened.

Or maybe if it had been more common knowledge, Mr. Vandozer would have come after me instead of my sister. I doubt he would have gotten far manipulating me in the same way, but just the thought that he'd have tried sends a shiver down my spine.

He knew exactly how to lure Liz into a trap, promising her the world and power to go along with it.

As for me, I was just hiding in a trap I made for myself.

We were both wrong. We both allowed emotions to over-whelm our better judgment.

I am lucky I got the chance to come out of it before I lost something incredible.

Thoughts of my sister have me leaning in to get a better view of the room.

Will I see Liz soon?

Will she enter the room my friends and I are spying on, this meeting of powerful beings, unknowingly ready to die?

The building is huge, I know, but I only have visual access to one meeting room.

Out across my magical stream, passing through worlds and dimensions, another meeting is beginning. My link with Jarron again flickers back to life.

What will happen if Jarron figures out what I'm doing? Will he storm from his assembly to take me away from this risk?

"Talk about something normal," I whisper to Janet and Lola.

They freeze but seem to understand my request.

Lola begins explaining her last conversation with her pixie mate and how he asked her out.

Meanwhile, Jarron shares his minor anxiety as he prepares to face an assembly filled with all the different species of his world.

If there are conversations happening in the meeting, I can't get a sense of them. It feels like a swarm of bees buzzing in the far reaches of my mind. There's darkness and shadows too, but I don't know if that's just my imagination or reality.

A flash of something golden catches my attention in the portal, and my heart stops, pulling me from the faraway connection.

Everything okay there? Jarron asks.

Yes, I'm okay. Are you?

If Jarron notices anything amiss in my message, I don't feel it.

Yes. I miss you, bright one.

I miss you too.

My link with Jarron fizzles out. I shift my full focus to the beautiful blond woman in the mirror. My stomach sinks when I realize it's not Liz. She has golden feathered wings tucked behind her back.

She could fit human legends of angels, no doubt. A literal Greek goddess.

327

I point to the paper in front of me—the list of the current council members.

Dara: Griffin

I have to force my eyes from her shimmering beauty. Even across the portal, she's hypnotizing.

The three council members chatter quietly in the room. The griffin smiles dazzlingly at the butler to request a drink. Her hand slides up his arm while he pours the wine. He doesn't react, except that his face turns beet red.

"When are we getting this started?" the cyclops's voice booms across the room.

The griffin scowls.

"There's really no need to yell, Halvard." The small witch reclines in the seat at the end of the elaborate table.

"Besides," the griffin says sweetly, "you know Vincent planned to present the jinn at the Orizian assembly. He'll be around eventually."

My stomach flips. Liz will be at the assembly where Jarron is?

"Then, let's get it started now. We don't need him."

The witch rolls her eyes. "Not even half of us have arrived. Have some patience."

"It's fine, love," the griffin purrs. "You're eager to get to the entertainment. I fully understand. All the new ones are like that."

"Your form of entertainment is perverse." The witch sneers.

"You knew full well what this position entailed when you signed up, Daamador."

"That doesn't mean I'm looking forward to watching it take place. If children must die to earn me this new power, then so be it. But to look forward to watching is something else."

The griffin flicks a brow. "I'd keep that opinion to yourself, then. You'll offend the others with your self-righteousness, and we'll begin to question your loyalty."

The witch snorts. "As I understand it, you've been desperate for anyone to fill these sudden open positions. Kick me out. Threaten me. We both know you need me in the war against the prince."

"Yes, Vincent's grand standing has put us in a bad position, but that is why we need to make our final move to alleviate that issue. After we enact the plan we've set today, we'll be able to get back to our true purpose."

My stomach sinks. What plan did they set for today?

"Killing children. Such a grand goal."

"Death is only the means, Daamador. It is not our purpose."

"And yet, you enjoy it."

The griffin glares at the witch.

"Your last plan was to lure the Orizian prince by baiting him with his chosen on a leash. That has not panned out yet, has it?" the witch tsks.

The griffin's wings ruffle. "No, and the prince has made some advances in regaining the favor of the clans. So, it's time to change things up."

"Vincent doesn't even have the right girl, does he?" the witch says. "It's no wonder you can't fill your seats. You have a fool running the place. And his last failure killed off half of the council."

The griffin's patience snaps. Her golden wings spread, and she slams her hand on the table. "Enough of your negativity. If you don't want to be part of the council, we'll find a replacement."

The witch chuckles. "Oh, I want to be here. I am just an instigator. I like to see what will make people break."

The cyclops laughs, booming through the room. "It did not take much for this one. Thank you for the entertainment."

"Anytime," the witch says. She plucks the griffin's wine glass from the table and takes a swig.

The griffin rolls her shoulders, and her expression smooths

into calm. "We may have needed positions filled quickly, but don't underestimate the Cosmic Council. This is a dangerous group to taunt. Once the full group is here, I'd be very wary of that kind of negative speech."

"Then, it's a good thing I got it off my chest now while it's only you." The witch winks.

My lips twitch. Like the cyclops, I'm thankful for the minor entertainment while I wait in this extremely anxious situation. Just a small barrier separates me from beings that would happily tear me apart if given the chance.

I find myself almost liking this witch. Of course, I know better. She may act like she's not happy about the idea of the games themselves, but she still accepted a spot on the council, knowing full well what they are about.

She's not much different than Bea.

I tap my knee nervously. I'm uncertain if I can fully trust her.

Just then, something shifts in a distant recess of my mind. Rushing, rush, rushing forward. I gasp as Jarron's thoughts rush into mine, and I don't even have time to create a distraction.

My own vision blinks out, and I see a different world clear as day.

It's a dark stone beach, surrounded by stone cliffs, with two massive orange moons in the sky.

Down below them is a gathering of many beings, shifting like shadows together. Jarron must be on one of the cliffs up high, over-looking the crowd.

Across the opening, there is another cliff, where two beings stand, also looking down over the Orizians gathered below.

Chants echo through the canyon for the newcomers.

One of them is High Orizian, with his wings tucked in tightly. The other is a woman nearly as beautiful as the griffin. Her long blond hair rustles in the wind. Her skin glows gold.

Liz's face is all attitude. Eyes lidded, jaw tight. Her hip is popped.

The image blinks out.

"What was that?" Janet asks, lightly touching my thigh.

"Jarron sent me an image," I explain. "Liz is at the assembly with Mr. Vandozer."

They exchange looks. I try to focus back on Jarron. There is a tightness in his chest, but also a level of anger and determination.

A moment later, the connection again cuts out. He wouldn't keep pushing me out unless he was worried something bad could happen, right?

In the looking-glass meeting, my only ally finally arrives, along with three others.

The outcast Orizian princess in her beautiful, walking-anime form, complete with perfect makeup. Next to her is a brunette with furry ears and catlike eyes. I point down at our list.

Emily: Sphinx

She makes me the most nervous because she's the psychic. Manuela assured me she couldn't read us through the portal but knowing that she could read our thoughts at some point is unnerving. And that one wrong thought from Bea could expose our portal in the corner of the room.

Behind the two ladies, two men stride into the room.

A dark-skinned fae with yellow eyes. Asad, the Crackling Court fae. He's pretty much a walking stun gun—or electric chair, depending on his desired level of power.

And a leathery-skinned creature who may as well be a lanky orc. The creature has a hunched back and long thin limbs.

The small talk continues, with the witch dropping digs at her peers. Most of them seem not to notice or care. Bea simply smirks every once in a while but mostly stays quiet, until the insults move to her.

"Why didn't you want to go to your world's big assembly?"

the little witch asks, her expression serious enough to make a few people second-guess her intent. "Oh!"

Bea rolls her eyes.

"Sorry I forgot the prince put a price on your head and your own mate turned against you. Whoops!"

Bea's nostrils flare, but otherwise she doesn't respond.

"Who invited her?" the Crackling Court fae mutters.

"Blame Dara for that one," Bea answers.

"Like you could come up with anyone better," Dara spits back. "She's powerful, and she's on our side. Ignore her ill-guided attempts at humor and we'll be just fine."

Well, that explains why Dara was advising her earlier. They're not exactly friendly, but Dara is invested in her.

A few minutes later, two punk-rock-looking males walk in together, each with feline grace. One wears a black cutoff vest straight from the eighties and matching jeans. The other is in a black T-shirt, dickies, and has a chain hanging from his belt loop.

I don't recall there being relatives on the list. In fact, there are only two from the same species: Bea and Vincent.

I frown down at the list. Lola flutters over and drops onto the book, pointing at, *Gabbai: Dragon*. My eyes flare. That's what a dragon looks like? Lola then hops over to a second name.

Aceline: Serpent

Wow, so feline is incorrect. They're both reptile creatures. Are they shifters like Orizians? Is it a glamor that makes them appear human?

That means the orc guy must be the kappa. He's by far the creepiest in appearance.

My heart picks up speed as I realize everyone has arrived except the two most important.

I don't have to wait long for the gathering to be complete.

A pale-skinned High Orizian enters from the doorway on the left. He has curled grey horns on the sides of his head, black beady eyes, and thick veins in his wings that seem to grow darker every time I see him.

The jinn walks by his side, their arms linked like they're a couple.

I somehow manage not to heave chunks.

I can't wait to see this man on his knees, begging for mercy.

I don't relish the deaths of the others, as much as I had previously looked forward to getting my revenge. It's different when actually observing them. They're all beings with personalities and desires. Whole lives I will personally end.

To some, that would feel empowering. Instead, I find it sad.

I breathe deeply. At least five of these people are guilty of personally harming me in the caves. They can die slow and painful deaths for all I care. The other five made bad decisions but have yet to commit the crimes they will die for.

Still, I'm willing to hand out premature executions to save my sister.

Funny, of all of these massively powerful beings, it's still the giant cyclops who unnerves me the most. How bizarre?

Prey instincts are weird.

"Ahh, the long-awaited jinn," the little witch says.

Liz doesn't so much as meet her eye. She keeps her expression uncaring, but her eyes are dead.

Now, it begins.

Now, we break the shackles they've placed on her.

"Let's get this started and finished quickly," Vincent says. He nods to the butler, who grabs a container of dark red liquid and stands at the end of the table as everyone takes their seats. Vincent's body shimmers, and then he is in his human form. The stiff former headmaster of Shadow Hills Academy.

My pulse pounds in my ears.

Liz is at the end closest to me—well, the looking-glass portal I'm seeing them from.

"Taste," Vincent commands to the butler.

The young, bearded man takes the entire container to his lips and sucks down several gulps. He's human. Is he under a spell? Bound the way Liz is?

They choose a human because they're the most vulnerable to poison. If he doesn't die, they're all safe. There aren't any poisons or potions I know of that would kill other beings but not a human.

I do, however, know of a few potions that will *weaken* supernaturals but have no effect on humans.

They sit and wait. A clock ticks from somewhere I can't see.

"Begin," Vincent commands. The butler starts pouring an offering of red liquid into a small wooden glass at each seat. No one moves or speaks while he pours.

"Now, choose another container," Vincent says to the butler. "Repeat."

I blink.

The butler obeys quietly, returning the decanter to the table and grabbing another. This one is a thinner liquid, slightly lighter in color. He gulps down the liquid and waits.

"Being extra careful today, are we?" the griffin comments.

Bea grins. "Our enemy is a potions worker. Of course we should be careful."

I press my lips together tightly, heart aching with uncertainty.

"Indeed," Vincent says, eyes shifting to Bea and staying steady.

Liz's eyes dart around the room. A flick of a frown creases between her eyes but then smooths away.

The butler continues pouring servings to the second set of council members.

"Everything is going to plan?" Vincent asks Emily.

She gives him a short nod. "My contact has the royal family in sight. They're battling now."

Vincent grins. "Too bad we'll have to miss it. Have they used the potion yet?"

"Not yet."

What potion? My heart rate picks up speed.

Jarron? I push at the barrier between us. Nothing happens.

"What about Candice?"

I suck in a breath. That was Liz's voice. It was soft, almost concerned.

"No, the girl is not there."

Liz's shoulders relax slightly.

They making a move on the royal family, right now?

Jarron! I call through the bond.

That's when I feel it. Tremors of fear and pain.

No. What's happening?

Vincent narrows his eyes. His hand stills. "Do we have eyes on her?"

Bea shakes her head.

"We waited weeks for this meeting." The dragon groans. "We're not going to put it off again because some human isn't in our sight."

"I agree," the griffin says. "You've gone above and beyond due diligence against poisoning. The royal family is clearly occupied. What else do we fear from a human?"

"I agree," Bea adds. "Without Jarron's help there's no way she could have made any moves against us. She's human. No one."

The rest of the group unanimously agrees. My palms sweat.

No one. She is no one.

"The school contacts are still in place?" Vincent asks. "What is the last update you've had on her, Beatrice?"

"Still in place. She went to classes last week while Jarron was there but is back to being protected and guarded in Elite Hall regularly."

"So, she's either with the prince or protected by a trusted ally," Vincent says.

Bea nods. "She was seen this morning by my contact. She hasn't left the school."

"Why do we spend so much time worrying about a human teenager?" the witch barks out.

"I prefer not to underestimate my enemies, regardless of power," Vincent purrs.

"She's prey," Bea says with a cruel smile. "She is fearful like prey. She is not a threat to us."

The council laughs as one.

"You better kill her before she kills you." The laughter stills and all eyes shift to the jinn, whose eyes are lidded. "That's all I'm going to say."

Vincent runs a finger down her cheek. Liz's nostrils flare, but she doesn't move.

"Now, now, my little slave," he says. "It makes sense for you to hope your big sister is going to save you, but she is a bug under our feet. You're going to enjoy the plan I have for her. If you play nice, we might hold those next games so you can go free. Otherwise, we'll keep you as our pet forever. Which do you prefer?"

She curls a lip but otherwise doesn't respond.

"I'm eager to meet this human," a powerful voice booms. "I'd like to crush her skull in." I wince at the cyclops's loud voice.

My stomach drops to my feet. Why, of all the beings in this room, does that one in particular bother me most? My stomach is growing heavier and heavier. I don't know what to make of it.

"You will not get that chance, Halvard, but you can watch as sister turns on sister. We can all share in that entertainment. It will be so much more fun than the games with all the mindless killing. Before I get ahead of myself, let's begin the proceedings."

My heart picks up its pace as I wait for my moment. Make it or break it. Bea is either on our side or against us. Did she follow through? Will it all happen right now?

I bite the inside of my lip.

She is fearful like prey.

Fear is intuition.

Intuition is my power.

Obviously, I'm afraid of all of these beings for good reason. But is it significant that this one being bothers me more than the others?

I frown, staring at the cyclops as the lights dim in the room. Candles flare to life, and they begin a chant.

The fae stands, holding the wooden cup. "I, Count Asad Raiden, swear by my own magic to uphold the power of the Cosmic Council. Any new information that is shared while these candles are lit will never pass from my lips without permission from the jinn, whom we serve."

I blink. *Whom we serve?* What does that mean? Do they consider the jinn to be some kind of deity? And if so, how fucked up is it that they keep her trapped and treat her so badly?

The fae sips from the wooden cup, sealing his vow, and licks his lips.

One by one, they each make the same promise and swallow down the liquid.

My heart throbs harder. Several people cover their ears when the cyclops yells out his vow. My mind spins with the panic pressing down.

That fear grows louder, screaming in my mind.

Something is wrong.

57
SOMETHING IS WRONG

This isn't just fear.

Something about the cyclops is wrong. I just don't know what it is yet.

"What's wrong?" Janet asks, touching my thigh again.

I sigh. "I don't know. Something feels off."

"It's just nerves," Lola chirps.

"No, it's more. It's—I feel like I've done something wrong. Something is—I don't know yet."

"Lola is probably right," Thompson says. "You're close. You didn't do anything wrong. It's okay. We just have to wait and see."

Manuela doesn't comment, but her eyes are narrowed in on me.

I frown but nod, trying my best to believe Thompson. I'm just panicking. This is the prey instinct driving me crazy because I know if I make one wrong move, this goes badly.

"As you're all aware, our initial plans have backfired in several major ways," Vincent says. "This is normal in war. Moves and countermoves. Our opponents have been more skilled than we anticipated, but these are setbacks, not failures, and we are prepared for our next countermove. Now that Jarron has presented the older sister as his chosen, he has given us a new target. She is young. Weak. Vulnerable."

"She's also stubborn and revenge-thirsty," Bea mutters.

Emily, the psychic, chuckles. "True. Maybe we can use it against her." She winks at Bea.

Again, my stomach sinks, uncertainty clouding my mind.

"She's kept under tight watch in the academy," Vincent continues. "But we all know how easy it is to infiltrate. Even Elite Hall has its chinks. We are going to send the jinn after the girl one more time. She will retrieve her sister and bring her to the arena for our entertainment."

"The girl refuses to sign the contract, even if it means her own death. How do you—"

"Oh, she will not be playing in the games," Vincent says. "No, that honor will no longer be afforded to her. After our jinn turned against us weeks ago, giving information and aid to the enemy, we now have two girls to punish. So, Candice will be fighting a battle she cannot win. Against her own sister."

The room stills, and then all at once, the entire council grins.

"Genius," someone mutters.

My blood runs cold.

"We tried to warn you, little slave," Vincent says to Liz. "We tried to warn you that you *want* to be our ally, our friend. We could have done so much together, you and me. We could have been great. But you had to betray me. Now, you will pay for it. One order, that's all it will take to make you kill your sister in any way we please. Slowly. We can make you torture her. Peel her nails off. Pluck her eyes out. Eat her flesh. What would you prefer most?"

I turn away from the looking-glass, willing my stomach not to up heave up my lunch. Janet places her hand on my knee and squeezes tightly, almost to the point of pain. "They won't get the chance. Remember that."

I nod, ignoring the tears in my eyes.

He's going to die.

He's going to pay for what he's done to us.

"What of the prince?" the dragon asks.

"If the prince manages to survive the night, we'll simply plan another attack as a distraction."

Pain rushes in from far, far away. Tears well in my eyes. *Jarron?*

He still doesn't answer. I don't know what to do. If something is wrong with Jarron, I can't even help. I'm trapped. Helpless.

The snarky witch narrows her eyes at Mr. Vandozer. "You seem confident in your ability to kill him when previously you could not."

"Ahh! Such a fun topic of conversation." Mr. Vandozer spreads his arms wide. "The royal family are quite powerful, as you all know. It's very difficult to kill them. But we've learned the secret to making it oh so easy. We don't need to risk our lives battling him hand to hand or in magic. You see, we learned the secret to killing him from the very girl he's now falsely claiming as his chosen."

I suck in a breath, nausea again carving its way through my body. I bite my fist to stop the anger and pain and fear from taking control.

They will not win. They will not win.

Daamador, the little witch, stiffens.

I swallow. *I'm sorry.* I don't know if she deserves this, but I don't have the capacity to care anymore. I need this game of chess to be done with.

340

Vincent thinks it's his turn to make a move, but it's not.

It's mine.

"Check," I whisper.

The first council member falls face first into her plate.

58
I DID THIS

Chaos explodes in the room full of massively powerful magical beings when one of them falls limp to the table. There are no outward signs of poisoning. There was no build up.

The woman was speaking one moment, and the next, dead.

But even so, these are not humans who'd consider possible natural causes of a sudden death.

Traceless or not, they know someone did this.

I did this.

But even as a thrill of success rocks through me, so too does panic. Not only did I kill someone, but that strange sense of wrongness has not left me.

Another rush of pain floods my link with Jarron. I curl over, the pain carving its way through my stomach.

"Candice?" Thompson says, holding my back. "What's wrong?"

"Jarron," I whisper. "Jarron is injured."

My friends all freeze. There is chaos in my mind. Screaming and fighting.

Another battle has begun in Oriziah.

"He'll be okay," Manuela says, but her voice is tight. "He'll heal himself."

I swallow. Will he?

The memory of him lying in his own blood, a sword through his chest, bombards me. He nearly died when I used a nullifier on him months ago because he couldn't heal himself.

We learned the secret to killing him from the very girl he's now falsely claiming as his chosen.

Jarron, I say calmly. *I need you to answer. Do you still have your magic?*

I can feel his pain, even while he's trying to block it out. He's hurt, and it hasn't stopped for minutes. Maybe that's enough to confirm what I already suspect.

No. My magic is gone.

～

"Who did this?" Vincent yells at Emily on the other side of the portal. She's the only one who could possibly decipher what happened.

My plan to get revenge on the council and free my sister is working splendidly, even while my heart is dying. Jarron is hurt. His magic is gone.

He's in another world entirely. Unreachable.

I'll be okay, Jarron tells me. *It's not that bad. What is happening there, though?*

It's "not that bad," but he's still magicless, vulnerable, in the middle of an ongoing fight.

Candice? What is going on there?

A brief sense of shame sits on my chest, but I take in a deep breath. This was the right choice. I believe that. *I'm ending this fight today. The council will all be dead in a matter of minutes. I need you to survive, Jarron. Survive this and we'll be okay.*

Dread rushes through me.

What did you do? he whispers through our link.

"Who did this?" Mr. Vandozer screams again. His face is blood red. His horns are sticking up from his slicked-back hair.

"I don't know!" Emily cries. "No one—no one has been in here. Except—" She turns slowly to face the human butler, and my stomach sours again. She strides across the room and takes his lapel in her fist. "Who touched the drinks?"

The butler's eyes widen. "No one," he says quickly. "No one! Or else I would have—"

She releases him and turns to Vincent. "How is he still alive?"

"He has to be in on it," Dara whispers.

"He's not," Emily says. "I can see in his mind. He passes all the checks." She frowns, looking down at the dead witch.

"Maybe it was a single hit," Dara says. "Someone wanted her dead, not the whole council."

"That would mean someone on the council did this, then," Emily says. "I can't read everyone in the room. The Orizians are good at hiding things. Dara, Gaabai, and Aceline are unreadable. Everyone else—" She concentrates. "Everyone else is clear."

Another few moments pass, the council members just watching in horror, waiting for the next shoe to drop.

It doesn't.

And finally, their shoulders relax. "Well," Vincent says, "we'll have to replace her."

My heart throbs. Finish this. This needs to end now so I can get to Jarron.

You're not coming here, he seethes.

I'm not letting you die.

The connection cuts off again, and this time, I feel like I've lost part of my soul. He doesn't want me to go to him, even if it means his death. I can save him. I have the nullifier reverser, but—

I stare at the Cosmic Council once again sitting casually, one body lying limp at the table while the rest chatter with only a minor sense of unease.

"Dara, she was your pick," Gabbai, the dragon, mutters.

Dara glares. "Do you know what I had to do to get her—" Her eyes widen, turning quickly to the dragon shifter.

His eyes are entirely black, his face slack.

He goes limp, falling face first onto the table.

Gaffney, the orc-looking kappa, follows only a beat later, falling straight to the ground.

Three down.

My heart lifts. Maybe, despite my misgivings, this is going to work. The fae stands, staring slack jawed at the dead around him.

Dara scrambles away from the table, wings flaring as she tries to flee the room, instead, she stumbles into the wall and slides down lifeless to the floor.

Asad drops to his chair, giving up hope before he, too, succumbs to the death potion.

It's terrible, and not at all entertaining the way I'm certain these beings would have seen it if they were in my position. But still, it's success.

But I can't enjoy it or the way Vincent roars in anger, slamming his first to the table. "No! No! No!"

Or the way Liz laughs. A beautiful sound, even though it's so full of bitterness.

I can't enjoy it because something is still wrong.

My connection with Jarron is still flat. I don't know if he's okay, but it's not only that.

There's something *here* that is amiss.

Aceline shifts into the form of a massive serpent and coils tightly before hissing terribly. His serpent body twists and writhes, then stills, belly up.

The cyclops groans, holding his head.

Something is—

Shit.

I know what's wrong.

"I miscalculated," I whisper.

"What?" Janet asks. "What did you miscalculate?"

The cyclops is in pain but doesn't fall to the floor.

I spin to face them. "The cyclops is huge. It's been bugging me for the last hour. Something was off about it. That's what it is. The death potion—I didn't give him a strong enough of a dose for his size."

They blink at me, shocked frozen.

"I miscalculated. He's not going to die."

59

TWO MAJOR PROBLEMS

I need the cyclops to die.

If he doesn't, the council will remain intact. My sister will continue to be enslaved, and the war will continue.

"There's something we can do, right?" Thompson says, already on his feet.

"One miss, that's salvageable!" Janet says reasonably.

"Yeah," I breathe. "Uh-huh. But I've got another problem."

Their eyes flare.

"They used the nullifier on Jarron. He's powerless, injured, and cornered."

I could give up now and go to him. I could find my way to the palace and give him the antidote. I could fight for him the way I've always promised to.

But that would mean giving this up.

It would mean giving up on saving my sister. It would mean letting Vincent continue his crusade against Oriziah—which is clearly working—and wait for the moment my sister comes to capture me.

She'll be forced to torture me. Kill me.

Kill them. Jarron's voice is rough.

My bottom lip trembles. He didn't want me to do this but now he's determined I finish it. Is that because he's losing on his side?

His energy is low. *I'll be okay.*

He's not okay. Our link ensures that I know it, but he cares more about my future well-being than his present.

Kill them, he demands again. *Get this over with.*

The hair on my arms rises.

If I let even just one of them live, they'll regroup. They'll re-recruit like last time.

I can finish this now. I can. But—

"How can we help?" Lola asks. "We can do something."

She's right. I don't have to do this alone. I can't do it all. But maybe... maybe I can still achieve both things.

I quickly grab my bag and slip two very important vials from their slots, holding them out, one in each hand.

"What do we do?" Janet asks.

"I need someone to take this to Jarron. It's a nullifier reverser. He can heal once he has this. I need—" I swallow, realizing this will not be an easy ask. "Someone to go into Oriziah, find him, and give it to him."

Thompson steps forward. "I'll do it."

"No," Manuela says. "No, you and I stay here. We protect her." She nods to me, her eyes fierce.

"What?" I ask. "If Jarron dies, then what does your alliance matter?"

"I'm not saying we give up on Jarron. I'm saying the Minor Hall witch can do it."

Janet sucks in a breath.

Manuela's fierce eyes turn to me. "She cannot protect you, but we can."

"You want me to...go to Oriziah?" Janet's eyes are wide.

I'll help her.

I suck in a breath at the sound of a familiar but out-of-place voice in my mind. There is chaos around them. Pain and fear. But they are also poised and ready to do whatever is necessary.

Laithe?

Yes. And I will find Janet. Have her meet me at the main portal into the palace. She can reach it through the home Jarron built for you. Pass through his door, enter the portal. Once inside the house, go down two floors into the basement. There is another portal there. It may be closed when she reaches it, but I will get there and open it, retrieve the antidote, and get it to him.

Shit, that's a lot but still a much better plan than Janet rushing into a battle in another world. I pass along the instructions.

She nods quickly. "I can do that."

I swallow and throw my arms around her in a tight hug.

"Will you four be okay?" she asks.

"What's my potion?" Lola's wings flutter excitedly.

"Invisibility. I need you to go in there and use your pixie dust."

They both pause, staring at me like I have three heads.

"On the cyclops," she says, face entirely blank.

"Yes. He's been weakened somewhat because I added the weakener to the wine, but he's still strong. And Vincent is there. Either one of them would try to kill you, so if you—if you can't or don't want to, I'll do it, but—"

Lola puffs out her chest, purple dust falling. "I can do it. They'd find you right away. I'm fast and small. I can remain unnoticed long enough to get it done." She turns and points to Janet's nose. "You. Go now."

Janet gasps like she just now remembered her quest. "I love you both!" she yells as she's running out of the room.

349

"Love you!" Lola and I say back. And then, we make eye contact.

I recognize the gravity of what I'm asking her. It's not her fight. None of this is. If the council gets away, and if the High Orizians fall, it won't change her life or future at all.

"You don't have to do it," I whisper.

"How much?" She looks down at the vial that's nearly as big as her torso, despite being one of my smallest.

I take the vial from her hand and pop it open. I let one tiny drop fall onto my fingertip. "Drink up."

She swallows and lands on my forearm. Then, she slurps up the drop.

Purple sparks fly from her wings. Her eyes widen, and in the next instant, she's gone.

"Lo?" I whisper.

"Ha! You can't see me, can you?"

My lips twitch. "Not even a little. Show me your dust real quick. I want to check."

Her tiny weight leaves my hand, and a moment later, little sparkles of purple appear in the corner of the room. "I can see it," I tell her. "It's subtle, but you need to be discreet. Get very close to him before you use the dust. Make no noise and be very careful with any of your magic; it might be visible. I'm hoping he won't be hard to put down because he's been dosed with poison and the weakener, but I don't know for sure. Once he falls, get out of there."

"Got it!"

There's a tiny ripple in the looking-glass that tells me she's out of the room and into that world beyond, completely out of sight.

"Now what?" Thompson asks.

"Now, we wait," Manuela says somberly.

There are splatters of blood against the wall. The butler

slumped over, eyes dim and blood pouring from an open wound on his stomach. They attacked the butler while I wasn't paying attention.

I swallow down bile.

"Ha!" Vincent says, spinning around, hysterically laughing and looking to some unknown witness. He knows I'm watching him, doesn't he?

I feel powerful right then because he knows I'm there. He knows I'm responsible.

"You missed a few," he growls. "Where are you, coward? Little human. Come face the three stronger than your death potion. You'd think you would have done enough research to know which potions affect Orizians, but clearly you were wrong."

The cyclops's one eye darts around, like he's following something in the air. Lola? Can he see her? Hear her? Smell her?

"What is it?" Vincent mutters.

"Something—" the cyclops yells.

"Not so loud, moron!"

The cyclops turns again, swatting around his head.

Shit.

Mr. Vandozer frowns, watching the cyclops spinning around, but then he turns straight toward us. He finishes his shift back into his demon form and stalks forward.

My pulse races. Manuela leaps forward to pull me away, but she's too late and I'm too slow.

Mr. Vandozer lunges through the mirror and grabs me by the throat.

60
RUN, LITTLE HUMAN, RUN

The demon's clawed hand crushes my windpipe.

Candice! Jarron screams through our bond. He roars in rage, and in that moment, I get a flash of his situation.

Blood has soaked his shirt from a wound in his chest. It's oozing, pooling around him. He's up high, somewhere most of the soldiers inundating the palace cannot reach him, but his heart is slowing.

He's burned on part of his body and bleeding from a slice to his neck.

He can't last long like that.

Black peppers my vision. Neither can I.

Magic slices into my attacker's chest, making him drop me to the floor. A shimmering orb forms over my body before the demon can grab me a second time, but he doesn't direct his rage at me.

Instead, he leaps at the strongest of my two protectors, claws and teeth flying. Manuela's eyes widen. The force field around me drops and begins reforming in front of the dryad witch, but it's not fast enough. Mr. Vandozer charges through the half-formed magic, claws digging into both shoulders and teeth slicing into her neck.

Another monster is there half a second after. A massive black wolf clenches down on the demon's arm, causing blood to splatter.

He roars in rage. One slash and Thompson is flying into the wall with a crunch.

They're going to die, I realize. They're going to die protecting me.

Don't you dare, Jarron warns.

I grip my potions tin tightly and breathe deeply, ignoring Jarron's words.

Then, I swing feet first through the portal into the Cosmic Council meeting room, now filled with lifeless eyes. My feet slam onto the ground. My heart throbs, but my mind is sharp.

"Shit," Bea mutters.

"You've come to play, little girl?" The cyclop's voice booms.

An instant later, the Orizian demon follows me through the portal just as I was hoping. His chest rumbles. His pale wings flare.

He meets my eye just before the glass smashes to bits.

I swallow. Well, I achieved one thing for certain, my friends are no longer in danger from the council.

Vincent laughs, a terrible screeching sound coming from the pale skinned demon.

My only escape is gone, and I've got very little in my favor here.

I cross my arms, feigning confidence.

Candice!

This time, it's my turn to close off our link. I can't deal with the distraction. *I have to do this. Trust me,* is my final message before I push his presence to the far reaches of my mind.

"Candice," Liz whispers, her eyes wide in terror. "No."

Vincent stands up straight. "You are such a thorn in my side, stupid human girl. But I have trouble being angry when it's just so entertaining to watch you fail."

I cross my arms, feigning confidence. Close. So close.

Failure or success is a breath away, and I don't know which I'll get.

"Dear, sweet Candice. You could have been great, you know. Could have had such great power. But now, you stand before two High Orizians, a cyclops, and a jinn. You do realize you've failed, yes? There is nothing you could hope to achieve by coming here except dying." He grins.

I grin back.

"Dear sweet Vincent," I croon back, mocking his tone. "I think you've miscalculated."

His chest puffs up, but his smile slips.

"You saved your friends, perhaps. Is that all you wanted? Very noble of you."

I don't respond. I don't flinch or move away as he prowls closer. I'm sure he can hear my rapid heart and the fear laced in my traitorous body.

"You know I might have mercy on you if you were to admit defeat. Fall to your knees. Beg." He waves vaguely. "Something along those lines. But you insist on pretending you are unafraid."

My grin widens. "I'm not the same girl you faced at Shadow Hills, Vincent. I've only gotten stronger."

"You're weak. You have no allies here. Help isn't coming," he growls. "Your prince is dying. He'll be dead before the end of the night."

From his perspective, things are extremely grim for me. But I'm so much closer than he realizes.

But so long as they have control of the jinn, I cannot win this match.

Meaning, I'm still very much dead if something doesn't change quickly.

"Do you think I'll have mercy for that bravery?" He shivers back into his teacher form. Same suit and slicked-back hair as when he sat at his mahogany desk as the school headmaster, telling me how powerful I could be. "Well, let me clear this up. You lost that honor long ago."

His hands spread wide like he's measuring his own power.

"The game isn't over yet, Vincent." I cross my arms and flick one brow confidently.

He doesn't like this. His arms drop, as does his expression.

"Kill her," the cyclops yells. "Get it over with."

"Your potion didn't work on High Orizians, did it?" Vincent says. His expression exposes his uncertainty, but he doesn't know how I could possibly have the upper hand. He steps forward.

I stumble back a step, but I can't show him my fear.

When in doubt, bluff.

"Oh, it would have," I purr. "If I had given it to you."

He rolls his eyes. "Don't treat me like a fool. You would have killed us all if you could have."

"Close." I shrug. "I did make one miscalculation, though. Would you like to know what it was?"

He considers for one moment, then growls. "When I make your sister kill you, we'll make it quick, won't we, love?" He eyes Liz, who now has tears slipping from her eyes. "Our jinn understands how in over your head you are, doesn't she?" He brushes the tear from her cheek.

"Love?" I ask him, arms crossed. *Keep him talking. Keep him talking.*

Come on, Lola. You can do this.

"Just a few moments ago, it was 'little slave.'"

"Ah, so you were watching. Clever little human. Maybe I did

choose the wrong sister. I suppose that means you heard how we used your own potion against your lover boy, didn't you? Is that what you miscalculated?"

Tiny purple sparks tinkle over the cyclops's head.

I work to keep my eyes steady on the enemy beside me. Bea steps up next to him, posture confident, but her expression holds concern. She doesn't know what she's supposed to do now.

The cyclops swats violently at empty air.

There's a whack and a thud against the wall. I suck in a breath, eyes wide.

"See! I said there was a bug in here!" he yells.

I don't know if that was Lola or if she's okay, but I need to stay focused.

Vincent laughs. "You sent a little pixie in here to help you, didn't you?" He follows my gaze to the back of the room. "You really thought a human and a pixie could win this fight? How pathetic."

Distraction. Must distract them.

"No, my miscalculation wasn't about Jarron. I've already taken care of that."

Vincent's smile turns cruel. "Taken care of it?"

"You think I wouldn't brew a nullifier reverser?"

His smile spreads. "Ahh, is that what Jarron's bonded was carrying?"

My smile slips.

"I have one too. Did you know? A lesser demon linked to me. He intercepted *Laithe*. I'm surprised you didn't realize that already since your mate is about to die."

My vision peppers with black. I refocus. He's bluffing.

"Even the first few marks are quite powerful for chosen mates, I hear. You should feel his pain. Feel his life slipping."

My heart stops beating. I do feel it. Far in the back of my mind, Jarron is weak.

I open up our link again. He's still in the high place, bleeding. Laithe has not made it to him.

I love you. His voice is like a whisper in my mind.

My heart shatters. Even if I win this game, will I lose him? How do I live with that loss carving my soul apart?

Live, bright one. Live for me.

My bottom lip trembles. *No,* I growl to him. *Don't give up yet. I can do this.*

You can, he agrees. *End it. Let me know what it feels like to see his life end before mine does.*

Don't say that!

I will die with no regrets, bright one. Even those precious few moments with you were well worth the fight.

No. I'm not giving up on him yet. I will not.

Except, there's no other way for me to reach him. No other way except—

My eyes flash to Bea. I fumble with my potions tin and pull out my spare nullifier reverser.

Her lips part. "I can do it."

"You will do nothing," Vincent barks at her, but he doesn't understand her meaning. "I get to choose how the human will die. She's weak. She's cornered. She will beg for mercy."

"Where is he?" Bea asks.

Vincent frowns. "What are you talking about?"

"Near the top of the palace. He's hiding where the others can't reach him."

No, she needs to protect you. She—

I toss the vial to her. "Save him."

Vincent seems to realize what's happening just an instant too late. Bea flies forward to swipe the vial midair just before Vincent leaps, shifting to his demon form. She's faster, though, and out the door before he can reach her.

His roar shakes the room.

"Let her go, Vincent," the cyclops says. "We have both girls. What difference does it matter if the prince lives?"

Vincent's demon seethes, back hunched over, breaths labored.

Finish it.

But first, I need to stall and pray Lola is okay.

"You know, I've been wondering something," I say, head tilted innocently, forcing the fear down. "Whatever happened to your chosen? All High Orizians have them, right?"

His harsh eyes dart to me. "You have no idea what you're talking about," he growls.

"Candice," Liz warns, her eyes wide.

"She didn't want you, did she?" I say, standing my ground as the half-man, half-demon stalks closer. "That's why you're so determined to make the crown prince into a reject like you. You want him to suffer the way you have—"

Something slams into my cheek with a whack, sending me flying to the floor.

"No! Candice!" Liz yells, but she doesn't move. She's still stuck, standing by the table.

Vincent is in full demon mode now. His hands are tipped with two-inch-long talons, black and glistening. "You failed," he seethes. "And now, I will show you how minuscule you really are. Run, little human. Run if you can. Because I will enjoy bleeding you dry."

I groan, my head throbbing. I force my body up, standing on wobbly feet to face my fate.

He looks down at his open palm, his brow pinching.

"No magic, Vincent?" I spit blood at his talon tipped feet. "You're not the only one with new tricks up their sleeve."

"It doesn't matter," he mutters. "You can turn Beatrice against us, you can try to save your prince, but it's still three against one, and—"

I huff out a breath. My head is still throbbing, but I'm close. So close.

"Magic or not, I still control *her*." He nods to Liz, who has tears streaming down her cheeks now. "Your attempts are vain. You lose."

I swallow, trying desperately to ignore the panic pressing in on the edges of my vision.

"Elizabeth," he commands, "take her."

61

I WILL NOT GIVE UP ON YOU

I suck in a breath. My vision tunnels suddenly, and all I can see is my beloved sister.

My chest heaves with heavy breaths now. I can't get enough air. Can't breathe.

Is this how it ends? God, how many times in a year do I have to come face to face with death? And it keeps getting worse and worse.

The life in my sister's eyes dim, all energy seeping from her body, leaving only the magic. She's given up. Retreated into her body. She can't stop this anymore than I can.

Her eyes glow bright gold. This isn't Liz anymore.

This is the jinn.

And she's going to kill me. She has power I could never, ever stand up against.

Just like the cyclops thinks the pixies as bugs to be squashed, I am a pest beneath their shoes.

Once, I hated and feared Jarron for his power. Now, it's my own sister who I fear.

She is that power that's too big for me to fight against.

She is a goddess.

I am human.

But I am not no one.

The jinn swipes out so fast I barely see it, and she crushes my upper arm in her grip.

I scream. My vision goes black as my bones shatter. I crumple to the ground.

So easy. So quick.

Vincent and the cyclops laugh as one, savoring my screams and both of our tears.

Standing before me is the jinn—powerful and cruel—but she is also Liz, and I believe in her. Beyond the terrible things that have warped her worldview and splintered her heart into pieces, she is still my sister.

And I will always fight for my sister. It's who I am down to my very core.

"I love you," I tell her.

Her eyes flicker back to light blue. "Candice," she begs. A sob racks her chest. "I'm sorry. I'm so sorry. I tried. I tried. I'm sorry I lied. I'm sorry I trusted him. I tried to undo it. I tried to escape."

"Shut up!" he commands her.

Her jaw tightens, eyes still pleading, but she obeys his command.

"I know," I tell her. "I know, and I forgive you for all of it. I swear. It's me and you against the world. Always remember that."

She jerks in a silent sob.

Maybe I am weak. Maybe I am no one.

But I will never give up.

Purple sparks over the cyclops head again.

The hair on my arms stands. I feel it, the shift in the air.

All the power shifts to me.

Because Jarron is right; there are more types of power than just magic and brute strength.

There are intelligence and influence. There are strategy and tenacity. There are friendships and alliances.

There is love.

There is hope.

The cyclops's massive body wobbles on his feet and then crashes into the ground right beside me.

Vincent roars, "Jinn, kill her now!"

62
THE FINAL MEMBER OF THE COSMIC COUNCIL

Liz's mouth opens wide in a pained but silent scream as the magic takes over her body. No matter how hard she tries, she can't stop it.

But I can.

"No."

One word. One command.

The jinn, golden eyed and face blank, pauses. She doesn't move. Doesn't follow Vincent's command. And in that beat of shock while my final enemy doesn't understand what's happening, I grab a black vial from my tin and pry open the cyclops's mouth.

He's asleep, but not dead. Not yet.

"Kill her!" Vincent commands again.

"No," I say once more. "Sit down."

The jinn obeys, dropping her butt into the chair she vacated minutes ago. Then, her eyes flicker to blue. "I don't understand," she whispers.

I pour that small drop of black liquid into the cyclops's mouth. His breathing stops immediately.

My heart is still pounding. Still throbbing. But the power is on my side now.

"What have you done?" Vincent asks.

I stand, arm still shattered and sending sharp jolts of pain all the way through my back, but I barely feel it.

"This *human*," I tell him, "with only an ounce of magic in her veins, just beat you. That's what I've done."

He blinks and stutters.

"You felt it moments ago. Your magic is gone. Your allies are gone. You do still have the jinn, except you're not the last of the council controlling the jinn." I wink.

He pales. "Beatrice is not here—" he stutters. "You cannot assume her command—"

"No, you misunderstand. Bea is not the last council member. She hasn't been part of the council at all, actually, for about twenty-four hours."

His eyes flare. Liz's mouth drops open.

"Kill her," he commands again, but there's less passion in his tone. He feels it now too.

The jinn doesn't move.

He growls, fury and confusion clear on his face. "Impossible!"

I smirk. "You and I are all that's left of the Cosmic Council, Vincent. And wouldn't you know it, you're not even the strongest anymore. You can feel that, can't you? I am stronger than you. Even the jinn knows it."

Kill him, Jarron growls through to me, strengthening me. He's still in such pain.

Bea is coming, I tell him. *Hold on.*

Kill him.

Before it's too late, he doesn't say. His strength is slipping, but I refuse to dwell on the chance that Bea doesn't make it on time because I have to focus on this.

The pale demon's roar of rage shatters through the night, and he charges.

For the last time, monstrous claws fly at me.

I'm ready for him, though, potion in hand. I've imagined this moment more times than I should be proud to admit.

I twist away from Mr. Vandozer's mindless attack, ignoring the pain the jostle causes, and then throw my vial at his feet with my left hand. There's a sparking explosion as the two potions combine and splatter onto the demon.

The effect is instant.

Vincent Vandozer gurgles out a cry as his body convulses, eyes rolling to the back of his head. He drops to his knees. I don't know how long the stunning will last, so I make my next move as quickly as possible.

I grab my orange vial and slam it onto the back of his head.

This time, there's a beat as the whole world stills. The pale demon's body goes rigid still. Then, he tips over and falls to the ground, stick straight.

I'm dizzy, vision blurring. I'm almost unable to enjoy the victory.

Liz gasps. "Did you—"

"He's alive," I say, panting. "And conscious."

Vincent stares up at the ceiling. He blinks three times, but his body doesn't so much as twitch.

"What did you do? How?"

"Stunning bomb, thanks to my friend Thompson, and a paralyzing potion. He can't move. I think he can speak, though." I step forward and put my foot against his throat, pressing tightly. "Can you talk, Vincey?"

I love the helplessness in his eyes. It's everything I've been imagining for the last year.

I press harder.

"Yes," he gurgles out.

I remove my foot. "Good to know."

"I don't understand," Liz says, her gaze distant. "Isn't he more powerful than you? The strongest in magic are supposed to have command of me."

"I am more powerful since the nullifier is in his system."

Liz jerks back. "What?"

"Bea put death potions at the bottom of each cup. Just one drop was all that was needed. But for Vincent's, I had another plan. Instant death is too easy for him. I want him to suffer. So, I made a few adjustments to my nullifier." I was able to strengthen it enough that even just residue on the side of the cup would have sucked his magic away.

Liz's nostrils flare.

"But you have no magic at all," she says.

"I have plenty of magic. I have Jarron's, through our connection, and that tiny, far-removed fae drop in our blood. It's enough to have an edge on a demon with zero magic."

"You better kill me now, witch." the demon growls. "Before it wears off or before your prince dies."

I squat down beside the paralyzed demon, ignoring the jolt of fear his words drop into my stomach. "Ahh, but that's the best part," I croon. "It won't wear off."

He freezes, eyes darting back and forth. "No," he says. "That's not possible."

This is my favorite part. He believes me, even as he denies it. He believes I could have this kind of power. And maybe I could have, if I'd had more time. Maybe I could invent this potion that's striking just enough fear in this demon for him to drop the mask and show his terror.

This moment, when the demon truly fears the human.

I chuckle. "I wasn't sure it was possible either, but I gained some new friends in the last few days who were able to help me develop something new."

"You mean—" Liz says, still sitting, staring shell-shocked at Vincent.

"Vincent will never have magic again as long as he lives," I say sweetly, squatting down next to him. I pull out my obsidian blade from my boot and press it to his neck. He winces, but he can't move. Not even a little bit.

"No," he whispers. He stares straight ahead. "No."

I press it harder, pushing into the rough skin. It takes a lot of pressure to carve through his thick skin in this form. Finally, blood begins seeping out from under his skin.

"I figured it was an appropriate punishment for someone like you—to become what you've always preyed on." I drag the blade down his throat, not enough to break more of his skin but enough to make him shiver. "You're weak now, Vincent. Forever. For good. How will you face your loyal clan members now? How will you do anything?"

"Lies!" he screams.

I grin. *When in doubt, bluff.*

I lean in close. "You're no one. You're nothing."

Yes, the nullifier will wear off in about an hour, but I expect he'll no longer be breathing by then. I press the point of the blade to his heart and press hard.

"Do it," he growls. "Kill me."

"Which would be a better punishment," I muse. "Death, or a life sentence of helplessness?"

He screams in rage, but his body remains perfectly still. It's beautiful, really.

She's here.

I release a quick breath. Relief like I've never felt floods my body. I almost fall over from it.

Bea is here, Jarron tells me again.

I stand and press my hand to my mouth. *Hold on,* I tell him again. *Don't leave me.*

367

I don't know how long the nullifier antidote will take to work. I don't know how quickly he'll be able to heal. My vision flickers to darkness. The shaky weakness filling my limbs. Two leathery wings come into view.

My body starts shaking the moment I feel him drink down the liquid.

He's so weak, and we're so close.

We won, he tells me. *No matter what. Finish him.*

He's right, but I have one thing left before I can. I stand and turn to Liz.

She looks up at me, big blue eyes soft and scared. Innocent, like I remember her. So much about her is different now, but innocent or not, she's the person who has always mattered most to me, even if she shares the honor now.

"I never gave up on you," I tell her.

Again, tears well in her eyes. "I know."

"There's still a lot for us to deal with, but first, I want to give you a choice."

She frowns. Is it the first time in almost a year she's had her own choice in anything?

"I know what I would do with him." I nod down to Vincent. Her abuser. Her captor. "And I'd wanted the right to kill him myself, but I don't think it's really mine to take. It's yours."

Her eyes widen.

"I want you to choose. What do you want to do with him? Torture him? Kill him? Leave him be and turn him in to the authorities? Do you want him executed, where you won't have to see it? Or do you want to do it yourself?"

Liz swallows.

Vincent pleads with her with his gaze. "I loved you," he whispers. "I did."

"I did too," she says with a hushed, sad voice. One tear slips down her cheeks. "But a lot has changed since last year."

I wait those precious moments for her sentencing.

She curls her fingers, and Vincent's body rises. His eyes betray his terror. His breaths are shallow, nearly panicked.

"You stole my heart," she tells him. He trembles. "It's only fitting I steal yours right back."

Then, Liz's hand glows golden with magic so bright I have to shield my eyes. There's one final scream, a crunch, a splatter, and then... silence.

When I turn back, there is a gaping hole in Vincent's chest and a bloody, still-beating heart sits in Liz's open palm.

63
REUNION

The pressure in my chest eases in several different ways.

Vincent is dead.

My sister is free of the council.

And I can feel magic filling Jarron's limbs.

Finally, the fluttering of purple wings grabs my attention. "That was intense!" Lola whisper-yells.

I huff out what I think is supposed to be a laugh but is a lot closer to a sob. "Lola, you did amazing. Are you okay?"

She nods. "Are you?"

I nod, but I turn to face Liz.

"Liz," I whisper the moment she lets the heart fall to the ground. "I need to get to Oriziah. Can you—"

Liz snaps her fingers. I wince when Vincent's head separates from his body in a sickening crunch. Lola gasps and flutters into my chest, like she's hiding from the grotesque sight.

Liz examines the head floating in front of her.

"I did love him," she tells me.

I cannot express how sad that makes me, so I don't try. I let her stare into the eyes of the lover who betrayed her. He used her.

Manipulated her. She may have been fooled by him once, but she sees the truth now.

It will certainly take her time to deal with what it all means for her now.

"To Oriziah?" she asks, eyes dead.

"Yes."

"Wait!" Lola shouts. "Um, could you fix that portal so I can check on the rest of our friends? Is that... something you can do?"

Liz looks to me, her eyes still so dim. Is she looking for permission? I nod, mostly because I'm not sure what else to do.

She waves her hand, and the glass quickly repairs itself, shimmering with magic once again.

"I'll get them help if they need it. You get to Jarron," Lola tells me just before she darts into the rippling magic.

I suck in a deep breath. "Now to Oriziah."

Liz nods and snaps her fingers again.

In the next instant, we are standing in the bitter cold darkness of the palace main chamber. The hollow mountain looms over us, only the few narrow bridges visible in the shadows.

Bright one, his weak voice whispers in my mind.

Jarron, where are you?

He directs me to his location from here, and I point up into the rafter to Liz. Again, she so easily snaps us up, and she drops me on the ledge, where Bea sits by Jarron. His eyes are closed, his breathing shallow.

His open wounds are no longer bleeding, but they are not healed.

I fall to my knees beside him.

"Bright one," he mutters with dry, cracked lips.

"You're okay. You're going to be okay." I lean over and press my forehead to his.

"You did it," he says. "I'm sorry I couldn't be there. I should have been."

371

I swallow. "I forgive you. Just don't doubt me again." I laugh through my tears.

"I never doubted you. I doubted her."

I huff, tears still flowing freely. It's done. We did it.

"You doubted my judgment." I don't admit that my decision making hasn't always been sound but I do like to think my judgment of character is.

Besides when you thought I was a murderer.

Yes, besides that.

But even then, I knew. I could see how good he was. I knew I was wrong; I just doubted myself out of fear.

He takes in a deep breath, reaching out but stopping shy of my arm. "You're hurt too."

I grunt, but I hold my shattered arm very carefully. Just the slightest movement feels like shards of glass are carving through my flesh. "Not nearly as much as you."

"Trevor is coming," Bea whispers. My gaze flashes up to her. She looks nervous but hopeful.

"Things will be different now."

Her lips tremble.

Jarron's strength is returning slowly. I close my eyes and focus on the magic, on healing. I'm sure it doesn't do anything, but it helps me believe it's true. He's going to be okay.

It also helps me ignore Trevor's and Bea's passionate reunion. He pulls her into his arms, and instantly, they're both sobbing.

After another few moments, the wound on Jarron's neck closes.

"How is he?" Trevor finally asks, sitting beside us.

"Good," Jarron answers, and this time, his voice has some strength to it. "I don't think I'll reach full strength for a few hours, but I can—I should address the assembly."

"The assembly?" I bark out. "They're still out there?"

"Yes," Trevor answers. "They're waiting to see the result. He's right. He should face them, show them he is alive and well."

"You were just attacked," I say. "Aren't the people at the assembly rebels?"

"Many of them, yes," Jarron says, forcing himself to sit up. I help him. "All the more reason to address them. They need to know—" Jarron nods to the head still swinging by its hair from Liz's hand.

I swallow.

"They need to know he is dead and who is responsible for it." He grins viciously. Pride rises up like a flood through his whole body.

64

HELL'S FUTURE QUEEN

Bea volunteered to carry me through the palace since Jarron is still weak, and surprisingly, he allows it.

I cling to the demon princess tightly, eyes closed as she soars through the darkness, weaving through the intertwining bridges and then down a dark tunnel.

When we reach a massive throne room, she sets me on my feet. The stone is red, with glowing yellow lights peppering the ceiling. There are two shining, black stone thrones on a pedestal, but otherwise, the room is entirely empty.

Jarron carries Vincent Vandozer's severed head, marching through the throne room and out onto a precipice overlooking the black sand beach I remember from the vision Jarron sent me.

There are still hundreds of beings buzzing down below. It's so dark it's hard for me to make out many specifics.

Jarron shouts to the crowd, echoing in his guttural language, but I understand the words perfectly in my mind.

"People of Oriziah, this is your usurper." He holds out the severed head for all to see.

The buzzing below settles. Glowing eyes look up at the head Jarron holds over the crowd.

"He tried and failed to alter the line of succession for his own gain. He tried to lead the rebels to rise up and overpower the royals of Oriziah. He failed in both schemes."

The people begin stomping.

"Vandozer betrayed his own. He believed he knew the identity of my chosen mate. He sought her out and attempted to manipulate her before I could earn her heart. He tried and failed to use our most sacred tradition against us. Now, both she and her sister are free, and I can tell you once and for all—Elizabeth, the woman he paraded around claiming to be my mate is lovely, but I do not choose her. I never have. Instead, I chose the fiercely determined and intelligent Candice Montgomery. She is the one who uncovered the depth of Vandozer's conspiracy, and she killed the eight powerful foreigners he was using to fuel his depravity in seeking power and destruction. My mate, my chosen, ended this war with a few drops of powerful poison."

He drops the severed head of Vincent Vandozer into the crowd.

They bellow and fight each other to reach it, like it's a prize they wish to be part of.

"I could not be prouder to present your future queen."

Jarron holds out his hand to me. His eyes are full of wonder and hope and adoration. The moment I drop my hand into his, he lifts it into the air.

This time, there is no mistaking the cheers rising up from the beings below.

I suck in a breath.

Jarron's mother and father approach and stand beside us. And on the other side, Bea and Trevor.

"Your royal family is united once more," the queen calls to the gathering. "Those who have challenged us before today will be forgiven, as is the Orizian way. But I warn you all to give up this fight. You will not prevail. For those who still question my son's right, we will continue our meetings. We will be open and transparent about our mistakes and the lies that mislead the horde. Our royal family is intact and stronger than ever. We will continue to serve you as long as you allow it."

The roaring crescendos. Feet stamp again and again, sending ricochets through the stone surrounding the beach below.

65

YOU'RE FREE NOW

The chants continue to echo through the palace. Even once we're back beneath the covering of the royal mountain, I can hear the guttural shouts.

My forearm is throbbing more and more as my adrenaline fades. Jarron growls. Then I feel a rush of warmth in my chest. Pins and needles cover my entire right arm. I hold it out like my own arm is going to bite me. "What is that?"

The pain eases. "It's not completely healed," Jarron says, "So be careful with it, but it's close."

"You—How?"

"We are linked now. You have access to my magic, remember? You'll gain more the closer we get to—" He clears his throat.

I smirk. "Is bonding a dirty word?"

"Not at all. I just know you're not ready for that yet."

I feel like it's more of a technicality at this point. Maybe I'm too young to make an irreversible decision, but I'm pretty confident my mind will never change, not about him.

"But you are still barely healing from death—why did you give up some of your magic for this?"

He glares at me like I'm an insolent child. "You were in pain. I will be fine. I just need some time to gain my energy back."

I'm not sure it was a wise choice, but I thank him regardless.

If it's even possible, I swear the cheers are growing continually louder.

Jarron chuckles. "They're calling you the poisoner queen."

I suck in a breath. "Really?"

He smirks and again pulls me into his arms. "You're incredible."

I shake my head against his shoulder in disbelief. *This is real.*

Yes, bright one, this is real.

I pull back and look up at him. My demon. My mate. My entire future. "Is that it? It's over?"

"For now." He pulls me into his arms and plants a soft kiss to my lips. "The work is far from done, but after a few weeks with no new claims, the tension will ease. You and I can discuss how far we'd like to go to ease the concerns. Or leave here and never come back."

"You and I?"

He shrugs. "I mean it. We'll talk about what we could do and what it will mean. The risks versus the rewards. But if you want to leave this world and do... anything else, I will do it. You choose. You're in control now."

I heave a big sigh of relief. I'd like to learn what those things are that he thinks will ease the concerns here, but having the option of going back to Earth and just *living* helps me breathe easier.

"Welcome home, Candice!" Jarron's mother says, back in her human form for the first time. She throws her arms around me, and I accept the embrace warmly.

Jarron's father, Emil, gives me a sweet smile. "We are so glad to have you here, officially."

It's my second time in the palace after accepting Jarron's

mark, but this is the big one. Our enemies are destroyed. The war is, well, not entirely over, but the pressure alleviated. Our challengers are defeated.

"I'm very glad to have you back, Liz," Jarron says to my sister standing awkwardly a few feet away from the rest of the family gathering. She holds herself tightly, hands squeezing her arms.

Liz gives him sad eyes and doesn't respond. She and I still have a lot to figure out as well.

Jarron then turns to Bea. "And you." He nods in acceptance, once to Bea and then to his brother. "Thank you for all you've done to aid us."

"All I did was reverse the damage I'd already done."

"Not all of it," Jarron says, motioning to Liz. "There is some damage that can never be undone."

I examine my sister. The way she holds herself. The way her eyes cast to the ground. While Jarron, Bea, and Trevor chat quietly, I approach her and pull her into my arms.

"You're free now," I whisper in her ear. "I know it's not that easy, but things can change."

She nods into my neck, tears wetting my shirt. She's quiet for a few moments before I pull back and look her in the eye.

"What?" I whisper. "What is it?" There's something on the edge of her tongue. Something in the tension of her shoulders.

"I'm not really free," she says.

It takes me a moment to realize what she means. I look down at the ring on my finger and stare at the silver design for several moments before ripping it off. I would never intend to use this power against her, but that isn't the point.

Just the fact that I have that power would always hang over her head.

"What are you—"

I take her hand and force the ring onto her forefinger. "I

hereby select you as my successor on the Cosmic Council. Do you accept?"

"Candice," she whispers.

"Trust me."

"I—I accept."

There's a jolt as the magic passes from me to her, the same as it did when Bea passed her spot to me.

"You are now the master of yourself," I tell her. "We should go collect the other rings and maybe boil them down to dust. Only you could transfer the power to anyone new, so the risk is minimal, but just in case."

Her bottom lip trembles.

"You're free now," I whisper. "Fully. Entirely."

Tears well in her eyes. "Thank you."

It's not enough, I realize. It's not enough that she's physically outside of their control. The damage that's been done to her mind and heart will linger for a long, long time. She will remain the jinn, maybe forever, unless we find another way to end the magic of the games for good. Just like mitigating the damage the rebellion had on the planet of Oriziah will take time, so will my sister's healing.

"I will always fight for you," I tell her, squeezing her upper arms. "Always."

EPILOG

With the glass doors wide open, the warm breeze feels immaculate as it caresses my skin and blows through Jarron's room at Shadow Hills. Spring has finally arrived.

The sun is setting, making the view beyond the balcony incredibly beautiful.

I try to let the beauty fill me up, but there's still a prickle of uncertainty on the edges of my mind.

It's hard to let go of the fear and anxiety, even when everything is perfect. Like you have to consistently remind yourself that everything is okay now.

We're safe.

Me, Liz and Jarron are all safe now. My friends are safe. My parents. Jarron's world.

There will always be more conflict to deal with, but nothing like what we've experienced in the past.

Soon, the sun sets completely, and music begins pulsing through the room and ready for the final party of the year. Janet and Lola arrive first, followed soon after by Stassi who tries and fails to get Liz's attention as she sits in the corner alone.

Before long, the room is full and buzzing with power.

Fae girls ooh and ahh at a few wolf shifters wrestling near the drinks.

Laithe leans against the wall next to a girl with a pixie cut and dark eyeliner.

A mixture of species dance in the middle of the room.

I sit on Jarron's lap surrounded by a group of our closest friends out on the balcony.

Stassi makes fart jokes that exactly no one laughs at.

This will be the last time we're all together like this. Next year, many of us will go separate ways. It's sad, but also exciting. We have entire lives to live and I can't wait to see what we all accomplish.

Janet is going to a magical college in Brazil next year. Thompson is officially taking his role as Alpha during the next blue moon a little less than a year from now. Manuela is setting up camp with her parents and a few distant cousins in the forest near him.

Apparently, after the battle together, Manuela and Thompson got to talking more and eventually came to an agreement—Thompson's pack would give back the dryad's sacred lands—nearly half of their territory—and they would become allies.

There's still a lot to achieve before those conflicts are settled but they're on their way to peace. And since Jarron made his firm alliance with Thompson known with the rest of the Tennessee packs, their enemies have been suspiciously scarce.

Stassi and Lola and Tyrane have another year left at Shadow Hills. More and more Lola has become settled and accepted by the pixie community which is a relief because it means she'll have a place to belong when me and Janet leave.

Two mollifying potions down, and I'm as relaxed as I can get.

Jarron pulls me against the railing several feet away and kisses me deeply.

The warmth from his body mixed with the cool sensation of his mind caressing mine, is more amazing than I could have ever imagined.

Someone whistles at us from the group a few feet away but we ignore them, taking our time to explore each other's bodies, tauntingly slow.

Before things get too heated, I pull away and Jarron wordlessly follows suit. I turn to look out over the balcony and he casually rests his chin against my shoulder.

"Tell me," I say, looking out at the mountains in the distance. "What would it have been like if I'd never come to Shadow Hills — Mr. Vandozer had never gotten involved in our lives?"

Jarron runs his fingers up my arm sending a shiver down my spine. "I would have waited for you" he answers.

"How long?"

He takes in a deep breath. "I would have followed you to whatever college you chose."

My brow pinches. "A demon prince at Yale?" I joke. I don't know what college I would have ended up at. I was definitely on the track for an Ivy League, but I don't know for sure that's what I would have chosen. Maybe Oxford, actually. Or some sports focused school on a whim.

"What, like it's hard?" Jarron says.

I snort at the unexpected joke.

"Sure, I could have gone to Yale if that's where you ended up," he shrugs. "May have taken a few favors to get in, but Shadow Hills presents as a highly desirable school to the human world, so it's very possible I'd be accepted."

"Then what?" I ask. "What would you have done?"

It's hard for me to imagine that life that was stolen from us. I

383

would have pushed away even the thought of being his friend. I would have been angry that he was there, actually.

He breathes deeply. "I don't know. I didn't have a blueprint, exactly. I knew you were not my biggest fan so it would have taken some time to prove you could trust me. I would have found ways to be around you, to become something you found useful, and slowly we'd become friends again. I'm not sure if there could be another scenario that would lead us to fake-dating but that worked out quite well for me."

His smile widens and my stomach flutters, remembering some of those charged memories. We've always had serious chemistry, and enough emotional history it was easy to fall in love with him—even when I was convinced I should hate him.

"I would have found a way to make you mine," he growls. I nearly whimper at the sound. Heat floods my extremities.

"It wouldn't have been easy."

"I'm well aware." He chuckles. "But I wouldn't have felt much pressure, in that circumstance. You could go years without wanting me in the slightest and that would have been okay. Here in Shadow Hills, we grew close faster than I'd expected which made everything feel so intense with you. It hurt like hell when you pushed me away because I had been so close. I felt it. You were right there, and I didn't understand what I had done wrong."

He shakes his head.

"In hindsight it's a very good thing we grew close so fast."

My stomach clenches. If we hadn't been linked during that final battle, I wouldn't have known how to get the nullifier to him. He might have died, while I killed our enemy.

What a tragedy that would have been.

I never would have been able to get over my guilt of not accepting him.

I never would have known for certain that he had chosen me.

"So how would you have done it?" I ask, mostly as a distraction. I don't like thinking about the worst-case scenarios. I like thinking about the fun hypotheticals. Like how my completely obsessed demon prince would have wooed me in such a mundane scenario.

"Maybe I would have studied statistics fervently so I could become your tutor."

I wrinkle my nose. "Math sucks."

His lips twitch. "Or maybe I would have protected you from some frat guys. I could have become friends with whatever group you fell into, so we'd be around each other more. I don't know."

"You would have had to befriended me," a soft voice says over the pulsing music.

We both turn to see Liz standing against the doorframe, a mollifying potion in her hand. My heart lifts, just seeing her be a part of this place gives me hope, even though I don't miss the dead look in her eyes.

It's been almost one full year since her "death." I'm more thankful that she's alive than I could ever possibly express, but just one look at her and it's clear that part of her died in those games. My sister might never be the same again.

"That would have been the best tactic," Liz says, eyes drifting down to the liquid in her glass.

Jarron doesn't respond, though I can feel that he agrees with her assessment. So do I.

"You were always the way to my heart," I agree.

Liz forces a smile. We haven't spoken about my bond with Jarron since she was freed. She believed herself to be Jarron's mate for months. She wanted it, to some degree. Is she bitter about his choice? Will jealousy plague our relationship going forward?

She's going through so much, I don't think now is the time to deal with concerns like that, though. She's been traumatized, in so many ways. It will take her a while to learn to hope again.

"Do you want to play truth or dare?" I ask Liz, nodding to the group gathered farther down the balcony laughing at Elliot as he spins around and around.

She shakes her head quickly.

"You'll be safe here," I tell her. "Next year. You'll—it will be good. I promise."

The Interdimensional Courts said they'd only allow her to be free if she was watched closely by an approved institution. Mrs. Bhatt gladly offered Liz a place as a student here at Shadow Hills. She won't start classes until next year though. For now, she's spent most of her time at home with our parents and getting some much-needed therapy.

I don't know what will happen to her after that, but we're kind of in a one-step-at-a-time mindset.

She swallows. "I don't know what good even means anymore."

My stomach twists. I push away from Jarron and approach my sister. "Do you want me to stay with you? I can take another year—"

"No." She doesn't meet my eyes. "No, you would make it worse."

I frown. "Make what worse?"

"You would be a constant reminder of who I am. What I've done. No one would ever let it go. I want to slip into the shadows and exist here. I don't want any attention."

I take in a long breath, trying to convince the pressure on my chest to ease. I know what that kind of attention is like, and Liz will likely have it even worse than I did.

Worse than the girl people think tried to enter the games, she will be the girl who did. Her power will protect her, but it won't help the emotional impact of being hated.

"You have friends," she whispers. "I'm happy you have friends. But I don't want any."

I brush a stray strands of hair behind her ear. I long to pull her into my arms and hold her tightly, but I get the feeling she doesn't want that.

"Do you want to be my friend still?" I whisper. My heart threatens to crack. "Are we okay?"

Her eyes flash up to mine. "Of course we're okay," she says. "You—you saved me. I could never—" she shakes her head.

"I love you, Liz. I will always love you. Just tell me whatever you need. If you need space from me, I'll give it."

She sniffs and nods. "Yes, I need some space. My mind is—I don't want to deal with things. I want to just exist here. I don't want to think. I don't want to feel."

Now, my heart does crack.

"I'll be okay," she assures me with a forced smile. "I'll make it through. This school can't be worse than what I've already endured."

I nod.

She finishes off her drink. "I'm just going to go sit down for a bit."

I watch her slip back into the dark room with pulsing red lights and sinks back into the armchair in the corner.

Jarron slips his hands back around my waist. "She'll be okay," he tells me. "She's strong. It's just going to be hard for a while."

I nod and lean back against him. "I wish there was more I could do."

"This is her battle now."

I sigh, and eventually we retake our place among our friends.

"So Candice," Elliot the wolf shifter says, "What's your plan for next year?

"Ruling over an alien world, obviously," Stassi answers.

I laugh. "No I won't be queen of Oriziah yet," I laugh. "We're

—thinking of going to college. We just haven't decided where yet."

"And by we," Jarron says, "She means she will be deciding. I will follow wherever she wants to go."

We'd talked about this a few times already, but I hadn't actually considered the idea of going to a human college. Could I drag Jarron to Oxford or Princeton or something? It seems so weird. It feels like an entirely different life. An entirely different me.

"We're thinking one of the big supernatural colleges in the U.S."

"Moonstone University is closest to her parents," Jarron says, squeezing my thigh.

"I haven't applied anywhere yet though."

"Like that matters. You're the future rulers of a powerful world. Any school would make space for you."

"Yeah, that's what Jarron keeps saying."

"You can go anywhere you want," Manuela says. "Even another planet."

I shiver. "No other planets for me. Not yet."

At some point, I'll spend a good portion of my life on Oriziah but that's still wild to consider. Jarron says we don't have to take the throne for many, many years. Like fifty years, if we don't want to. I could live a whole human life first, if that's what I want. Have a career and a white picket fence. Have children—yes those children will require a little extra care since they'll be half demon, but we could have a mostly normal life together if we choose it.

We could travel all of Earth.

I can study potions, and magical objects.

You could become the greatest potions master the universe has ever seen.

I internally snort.

Jarron holds me a bit higher of esteem than I think I deserve.

The options are endless.

The truth is, I want all of those things—eventually. But right now, it's hard to think past the next year. What I want most of all is for my sister to be okay.

"I suppose Moonstone makes the most sense," I say. "It's close to Shadow Hills and my parents."

Is that a firm decision?

I consider it for a few more moments. Then I nod.

"I'll make the call tomorrow."

It makes the most sense. We have all the time in the world to have experiences. Right now, I'm going to choose to be close to my family—while also learning how to live up to my new nickname—the poison queen.

"I can't believe this is almost all over," Janet whispers.

I smile at her and then to Jarron. "This is only the beginning."

A NOTE FROM THE AUTHOR

Thank you so much for sticking with the Shadow Hills Academy until the end! I hope you enjoyed the wild ride and can leave it with a sense of fulfillment.

There are so many things I adore about this series, and lots more I can explore about this world. I'd love to hear from you what you'd most like to see more of. Characters you want to see have their own book, perhaps...

If you want to share your feels about the series I'd love it if you left a review, or come find me on social media.

Follow me on Instagram & Tiktok @StaceyTrombleyAuthor

You can also check out my other completed series, WICKED FAE which is a slow burn enemies to lovers fantasy with fae and dangerous games.

But don't worry, even if you're caught up on all my stories, I have even more coming soon.

BEFORE SHE WALKS DOWN THE AISLE, HE'LL ENSURE SHE IS UTTERLY BROKEN.

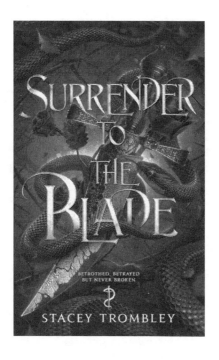

Now up for pre-order!

Princess Akira must marry the most cruel prince her world has ever seen. The kind of cruel that kills for sport, and tortures for joy.

She expects pain and misery, but without this marriage, her people will be destroyed.

The malevolent prince is the last being alive with the magic needed to defend against the void pressing in on her kingdom. Without this alliance, her kingdom will be wiped from the map, and cease to exist.

The prince has one problem, though. This marriage will come with a power bonding, making his bride his one and only vulnerability. The only person who can challenge him. And so, he is seeking out the weakest, most submissive royal he can find.

Akira will play the role of the blushing bride, too afraid to stand up for herself, even against his most cruel treatment. The prince must never see her confidence and determination, or her head will decorate the palace lawn before she earns her much needed power.

All eyes are on princess Akira, and none more sharp than the royal assassin, known only as The Sovereign's Blade. He is just as dark and cruel as his master, except he sees too much. He notices her every blunder, every moment her mask slips and reveals the strong soul beneath the act of fearful submission.

Every moment, she expects the Blade to expose her but for some reason, he continues to play along. Eventually, she realizes she and the prince are not the only players in this terrible game and the Sovereign's Blade has an agenda of his own.

Pre-order now

ALL THAT STANDS BETWEEN ME AND FREEDOM ARE ELEVEN BLOODTHIRSTY FAE

Finished series!

As a convicted assassin, I've been banished from the fae realm for years but now I have the opportunity to compete in a ruthless competition to earn a full pardon.

Dragons and twisted mazes are the least of my worries now.

I can handle a few bullies and death-defying challenges. The thing that will keep me up at night is having to face those I betrayed. Especially Reveln, the prince whose brother I killed. Every time I see the hatred in his eyes it reopens old wounds, a reminder of the destiny that was stolen from me. And I only have myself to blame.

But I'll find a new destiny—by winning the Trial of Thorns.

The whole realm thinks I'm weak but I'm stronger than they could ever imagine. By the time this is through—I'll bring them all to their knees.

Read it now

ABOUT THE AUTHOR

Stacey Trombley is a casino worker by night, urban fantasy author by day. She lives in Ohio with her husband, son, and German Shepherd. When she's not writing or reading, her husband is probably dragging her along on one of his crazy adventures for their travel vlog or competing against him about who can pick the most Survivor winners in the first episode (hint: she's winning). But mostly, she's probably reading.

Learn more about her books at www.StaceyTrombley.com

ACKNOWLEDGMENTS

Every book is a whole new adventure, even when it's smack in the middle of a whirlwind of life. I've written and published many books by now but they never take less work, or less help.

So, first thank you to my supportive family. I love you.

Also, my writing group The Queens of the Quill. I've learned so much from the group, but it's also such an honor call you my friends.

To every reader who took a chance on me, but especially those who went out of their way to encourage me and share their love for my stories.

Thank you to all of my early readers. Deissy, Karen and my editor Caitlin Haines.

And of course, thank you to my God. Help me to always remember, you are the one thing I seek.

Made in the USA
Monee, IL
17 November 2024

70403375R00236